THE THREE PRIVILEGES

A.V. DAVINA

For all the privileged that believe everything is possible.
There are more of us than you think.

CHAPTER 1

He had been tracking that scent for four hundred and fifty-eight days, around the world. The man hoped by dawn, the hunt would be over.

He straightened and sniffed the air, all his senses told him the boy was here, in some corner of this remote region.

A layer of ice covered the forest. The cold of winter made his mission harder. That night, the trees, leafless and twisted by the strong winds, appeared dark and sinister.

"He has hidden you well," the man murmured to himself.

With each passing day, he felt more pressured. If he didn't find the boy soon, he ran the risk of losing him forever. The burst of *cym*, the enzyme which made it possible to track the boy, lasted only for a brief period of time during adolescence, and the window of opportunity was closing.

A low howl sounded in the forest, piercing the silence. It could have been taken for the cry of a wounded animal if it weren't for the fierce purpose of the cry. Another long howl rang out to join the first. And so it went on, from the shadows, the wolves called out and answered one another.

And thus, the animals' pursuit began.

Nahuel Blest awoke with a start just a few kilometers away. The boy felt someone calling for him. He immediately grabbed the nearest ski pole to defend himself. His room was in darkness, but the teen could sense everything with unusual clarity. He was breathing heavily and sweating. He touched his forehead and felt feverish. This wasn't the first time he suffered an episode like this one. But this time, something felt wrong. Some strange, defensive instinct had been set off in him, but why? Was it because of a dream? Or something else?

He immediately looked for signs of danger.

He heard the steady breathing of his grandfather and mother in the adjacent rooms, but he couldn't shake the strange feeling that something wasn't right.

Outside, far away, in the forest and at sea, a change was underway.

The ice caves in the mountains came alive. The bats awoke from hibernation, increased their heart rates, and raised their body temperature. A black gust soon shot forth, headed straight towards the valley.

The small rocky island with the white and red lighthouse was left deserted. The sea lions slipped their huge bodies through the frozen waters, encircling the bay. The sea lions were corralling the small city, ready to halt any escape by sea.

One command alone governed the region and all the animal species felt the need to abide it. The boy had no chance to escape.

Uneasy, Nahuel tried to go back to sleep but every time he closed his eyes, he was overcome by a sense of alarm. He heard voices calling him, the urge to get out of his room and run away was powerful.

A purely instinctive feeling had taken hold of him. It was an irrational fear, almost primitive, an emotion that had awoken in some corner of his mind and taken control of his body.

The first light of dawn appeared in the east. The small town would soon be awake.

The bats had surrounded the valley, like a shadow. They were to enter the houses, stream through the chimneys and use their sonar to find their prey.But most of the houses were tightly shut against the cold and no intruders could gain access.

In the forest, the howls of hunting arose on all sides. A pack of silhouettes ran down the mountain and drew close to the city. The wolves' fur was dense and thick and their gray coats hid them in the morning fog.

They moved through the trees, kicking up snow and frost. Their breath froze in the air and their snouts were covered in ice crystals.

Nahuel began dressing, frenetically. His body demanded he stay alert. He checked his watch. It was 6:30 in the morning. Where could he go?

He was putting on his shoes. He stared at his huge backpack, he could run away. He froze for a moment and forced himself to think, to clear up the confusion he felt. What he was feeling could only be the result of a dream. Maybe the void had filled with paranoia. But why couldn't he shake the feeling someone was coming for him?

The wolves arrived at the town just a few minutes later. The alpha wolf raised his snout, sniffing the air anxiously, his tail tense. On his command, the other wolves spread out and cautiously entered the town, hiding in the bits of remaining darkness.

The foxes came forth as well, from the brush, to join the hunt. All their senses aroused. They were stealthy, stalking, listening and sniffing with each step.

Even the domesticated dogs were overcome with the same urge to find what all the others were searching for.

The man remained hidden in the forest but his drive to find the boy had spread to all the animals, for whom the hunt had now become irresistible.

This is my last chance, I won't let him hide you again, the man thought. Walter had taken too much trouble to hide his grandson, but, why?

This time, the tracker was really close and wouldn't let them escape. The Council of Privileges expected the mission to be a success.

Nahuel was downstairs, where his two Siberian dogs waited for him anxiously. He stood there, fighting with the incoherent need to leave the house. He could wake up his grandfather. But with what excuse? He was losing his mind. Adrenaline stimulated his instincts and he could sense every footstep, every pant of breath outside.

One kilometer to the northeast, a white-coated wolf was roaming about, head bent sniffing some shrubs. Suddenly he stopped. He had smelt it. That scent they were all tracking had made its way to him, like a faint perfume of leather and audacity.

He turned around and changed his path, running toward the scent. It led him to the west of the small town. He stopped in front of a solitary house, surrounded by a stone wall.

Nahuel paced between the living room and the dining room, not knowing what to do. He felt awkward, what was that smell?

Suddenly, his Siberians shot toward the front door. Nahuel followed, opened the door and peered outside.

In the shadows he could make out a pair of yellow eyes glowing like embers. Nahuel held the wolf's gaze, while his heart beat uncontrollably. The wolf stretched out its savage body deliberately with an air of triumph.

Nahuel knew that with one jump the beast could overpower him. Nevertheless, he kept staring, completely horrified and fascinated at the same time.

The wolf let out a formidable howl. The sound slid under the boy's skin and broke him from his spell. He closed the door and locked it.

Wolves never came so near the town.

Nahuel crossed the kitchen. He looked through the window toward the forest and squinted. Up until that moment, he had always thought he was lucky to have the forest as his backyard.

Something was moving quickly and with increasing urgency among the trees. Behind some pines, two wolves appeared, bearing their fangs.

Nahuel heard the crunching of frozen ground and leaves as they were tread upon and could smell the greasy scent of fur. More wolves were surrounding the house.

He locked the kitchen door and closed the curtains. He had nowhere to go.

Outside the house, a pack of wolves had gathered. A muscular, dark-skinned man was approaching behind them, victorious.

He was the best tracker in the world, which is exactly why he had been chosen for this mission.

CHAPTER 2

"What the hell is going on?", Nahuel muttered to himself.

He walked away from the kitchen door and ran into something.

"Grandpa!" the boy said, as he turned, and mumbled: "There are wolves in the backyard."

"Speak up, Nahuel."

"Wolves, in the yard," he enunciated, still out of breath.

The expression on Walter Blest's face suddenly changed. He drew back the curtain and looked outside.

"Over there," Nahuel said, standing beside his grandfather and pointing to the pines.

His gaze searched all over the yard, up and down, right and left. He strained to see even further, to where the yard gave way to the forest, but he couldn't see anything but trees.

There was no sign of the wolves.

"They were there. I swear."

He could still feel the last traces of adrenaline running through his body. But now it all seemed like a scene from a horror movie.

"Go up to your room," his grandfather said.

"Why?"

Just then, someone knocked the front door, swiftly and precisely.

The muscles in Nahuel's neck tightened.

"Just do as I say," Walter said, leaving no room for argument. "I'll take care of this."

Nahuel opened his mouth to argue, but his grandfather said: "Trust me. Go upstairs."

Nahuel made his way up to his room, with Apollo and Atila, the two Siberians, by his side. Something in his grandfather's tone of voice told him there was no room to negotiate.

5

He went into his room but left the door open so he could hear what was happening below.

He could smell the scent of wolves around the entrance to the house, but he knew very well that they would never have called the front door.

He heard the squeak of the hinges and footsteps entering the house, but then nothing. Only a persistent and annoying buzzing.

Walter Blest opened the door.

"Ankona," he said and gestured for the man to enter.

The dark-skinned man bowed his head a bit and extended his hand. He had a powerful jaw, thick lips, and deep eyes.

"Can I offer you something to drink?", the old man asked. "I guess you've been up all night."

"A cup of coffee would be fine."

The old man left him in the living room and went to the kitchen. He didn't need Ankona to tell him why he was there. But he didn't know if he would just accept Ankona taking his grandson.

"If I wasn't so upset that you found us, I would feel proud about your tracking abilities," Walter said as he placed the tray on the coffee table.

"It took me longer than it should have," Ankona replied.

"But not as long as I would have liked."

"You went through a lot of trouble to hide him," Ankona added.

"I thought Ushuaia would have been cold and remote enough to hide us away forever."

When his son had disappeared, Walter took his grandson and daughter-in-law to live at the edge of the world, in a small town in Patagonia, Argentina. Ushuaia was located in the extreme south of the continent and was north of nowhere. It was known as "el fin del mundo," the "end of the world". It was a singular place of astonishing beauty, where landscapes of sea, forests and mountains collided. For years it had been the source of inspiration for myths and legends.

"I wouldn't have found you if it hadn't been for Nahuel. His *cym* enzyme is so intense it has led me even to this remote place."

The old man nodded his head in a gesture of acceptance.

"He felt me coming from miles away," Ankona added.

Walter cast a glance upwards towards his grandson's room. He knew he couldn't keep Nahuel in the dark for much longer. The boy's body was beginning to reveal what he himself had not had the courage to explain. Nahuel was not only a CymAnis, but he also had the potential to become the strongest member of the family.

"You can stop interfering with the forest's rhythms," the old man said with just a pinch of disgust, which didn't go unnoticed.

Outside, nature's balance had been completely upset, its usual harmony deeply disturbed. Walter could sense that the forest's frequencies had been altered to suit Ankona's purpose. Ankona was even stronger than Walter had remembered.

"I'm doing what I need to do. You know I can't leave empty-handed," the man replied.

"Are you afraid I'll resist? That I'll resort to force?" Walter said, in a more threatening way than he had intended.

"I know you're considering it," Ankona noted. "However, my mission won't end until I hand the boy over to the Council."

It wasn't exactly a threat, Walter knew it. He even trusted Ankona. But he couldn't control the feeling of impotence growing inside him. He should be the one to decide when the time was right to let go of his grandson.

"These days the Council is your best bet," Ankona added. "The Ignobles have crossed the line. They've gone from being a threat to being a real danger."

"I've heard the rumors," Blest replied.

"Then you know they're getting closer and closer to finding *The Foundations*. We can't let them, and we can't let them have Nahuel."

The old man grimaced. If even Ankona acknowledged the possibility that the Ignobles could reach *The Foundations*, then the rumors he had been hearing in recent months must be true. Ankona wasn't known to exaggerate. The fears Walter had been burying since moving to Ushuaia now came to the surface all at once.

"If I have found you, you know they will too, eventually," Ankona forewarned.

Walter pressed his fingers against his eyes, feeling waves of fear, anger and frustration. The windows suddenly darkened as thousands of insects climbed up the walls at an unusual speed, scratching at the curtains. He knew he wouldn't be able to protect his grandson.

The living room was in shadows, barely lit by the fire burning in the hearth. A shudder of apprehension lodged in the old man's heart like an icy serpent.

Ankona turned toward the windows. They were now completely blacked out. He scowled, looking perturbed and said: "You can't control your *privilege*."

The corners of Walter's mouth turned slightly upwards, in the briefest of smiles, but he said nothing.

His eyes wandered downwards, toward the basement. He was weak. He had sacrificed his energies and now they were gone.

"The boy will be safer with the organization," Ankona said.

Walter opened his mouth to reply, but restrained himself. Reality had slapped him in the face. The events of that very morning had proven to him that with the passing of time and the loss of energy he was no longer able to protect his grandson from the Ignobles.

"Klaus has assured me you may both return," Ankona added.

"I have unfinished business here," Walter mumbled. "Maybe later."

Ankona nodded.

"Nahuel's identity must be kept secret," the old man added.

The incoherent buzzing suddenly ceased and Nahuel enjoyed the silence. He couldn't hear voices nor movements from down below. He dared to leave his room and make his way toward the stairs.

"Come here Nahuel," his grandfather said, much to his surprise.

The boy went down cautiously, flanked by his dogs.

He was a medium sized boy for his age - a thin and wiry 13-year-old. His face was sharp, his jaw square. Thick eyebrows framed his hazel eyes which danced between green and gold. His hair was chestnut with unruly waves.

Nahuel's nostrils dilated as he entered the living room. He immediately recognized the smell of wolves coming from the dark-skinned man standing by the sofa. *Who is he? And what the hell is he doing inside my house?*

"Nahuel, you have a visitor," his grandfather said. The expression on his face was unusual. It looked like defeat.

"My name is Kudzai Ankona," the stranger said.

For a few seconds, they looked one another in the eyes with curious intensity. Then, Ankona held out his hand firmly. He was wearing short, thin gloves and hadn't removed them despite the heat from the fire.

"I have come on behalf of the United Nations to offer you a scholarship," Ankona explained.

Nahuel wasn't sure what he had been expecting to hear from the man, but it wasn't that.

"What? Me?" he asked frowning, and gazed toward his grandfather, who simply nodded.

"Yes," Ankona said. "It will last for one year, with the possibility to carry on for two more years, at our headquarters in New York. There will be young people like yourself from all over the world."

"So... you're from the United Nations?" Nahuel questioned.

"That's right," Ankona agreed. "The program starts next Monday, but orientation day is this Friday, which is why we must leave tonight."

"Tonight..." Nahuel repeated. He weighed for a moment the idea of travelling far away from there and it didn't displease him, but his instincts told him that the man was hiding something. "There must be some mistake."

"No, there is no margin for error," Ankona replied sternly.

"But, why did you choose me? I haven't applied for any scholarship."

"I did it for you" assured his grandfather taking a step forward. "As you know I lived in New York for several years and still know some people there."

Nahuel's throat was dry, "why didn't you tell me before?"

"I wasn't sure when it would happen."

"So, that's why you told me a few months ago to always have my backpack ready?"

"Exactly," the old man answered. He hated lying to his grandson, but he believed that it was best to inspire him with confidence and security to face the journey that lay ahead. Also, Nahuel had to learn to protect himself when he was no longer able to.

"And if I refuse to go?"

"Why would you do that?", his grandfather asked, examining him with his eyes.

"I don't know," Nahuel said without thinking, shifting his gaze to his dogs: "Who would look after Apollo and Atila?"

"I would, of course."

"I have your letter of acceptance right here. Take a look," said the envoy from the United Nations.

Nahuel opened the letter, breaking apart the waxen seal. It was written on soft paper, with the water mark of the United Nations, signed by Director Z. Klaus next to the organization's emblem.

The whole thing looked very official. However, the mistrust he felt did not completely fade away.

"Grandpa?" he asked. His grandfather had always taken care of him and was the one who knew him best.

"It's an opportunity you can't refuse, Nahuel," the old man stated.

CHAPTER 3

As soon as Nahuel Blest set foot in New York, the sea horse resting in Klaus's office woke up. The Director had just received information that would change the course of a silent and unseen conflict. He was confident that now the balance would shift away from those who sought to generate chaos.

Nahuel hurried behind Ankona and through the automatic doors at the airport. He noticed the humidity, warm and sticky, and quickly confirmed he was not used to heat. In Ushuaia, temperatures barely rose above 15 celsius, even in the summer.

He left Ushuaia so quickly that he didn't get to say goodbye to anyone. Although, thinking about it, Nahuel didn't have anyone to bid farewell to.

The trip had seemed crazy to him. They had left Ushuaia, in southern Argentina, thirty-six hours ago. The trip had meant more than four connecting flights, plus wait times spent rambling through carpeted hallways. But it was the usual route for someone who travels between the extremities of the world's longest continent.

To top it all off, every time they landed, the weather worsened. It seemed crazy, but the runways were covered with fog while hurricane force winds blew all around them. This meant that every single flight was delayed. Nahuel had more than enough time to come to realize how much he hated feeling locked up.

It was only later that he came to understand that the trip had always been part of his destiny.

"Get in," Ankona said, pointing at the first black taxi in line. "We're going to Mrs. Penington's house. That is where you'll live while you're in New York."

Nahuel was startled, it was only the second time the man had spoken to him since they had left Ushuaia. The first time had been when he told him which seat was his during the first flight. For the other flights, he had simply pointed at the seats. He had also managed to answer Nahuel's questions with a series of monosyllables, which in Nahuel's opinion didn't count because Ankona was only replying.

All in all, Nahuel wasn't bothered by the lack of conversation. On one hand, he himself wasn't very outgoing or talkative and on the other, he still couldn't help but mistrust this man who had shown up at his house, "out of nowhere", smelling like wolves.

Nahuel was sure the man hadn't slept for at least three days. His face was tense, like a hawk. He hadn't once relaxed his gaze nor taken off his gloves, not even to eat.

They drove into the city as the sun set behind the outlines of the skyline. New York's lit streets gave off a boundless energy. That night, the Empire State building was lit up red and gold, everything was wrapped in a perfect haze. Except for that bustle, Nahuel didn't know how he would get used to the sounds of a busy and vibrant city like that one.

The realization hit hard, he had indeed left behind his remote city with his wooden buildings and the forest that surrounded it.

He thought of his bitter goodbye in Ushuaia. His mother hadn't even tried to make an excuse for her absence. Only his grandfather had gone with him to the airport. Leaving was painful, because Nahuel felt as if this would not only be the first, but also the last time he bid his grandfather farewell.

Nahuel had lived with his mother and paternal grandfather since he was six years old.

On the morning of his sixth birthday, his father had performed the same ritual he did every year. He painted a picture and hanged it on Nahuel's bedroom walls. Then, without warning, his father disappeared. Nahuel didn't know anything about that tragic day. He only knew that it marked the end of his relationship with his mother and that it was the reason they decided to move to Ushuaia, leaving Buenos Aires behind forever. His grandfather had stepped in to fill the void and had been his unconditional protector and champion ever since.

Before long, the taxi was making its way out of the city, leaving the hustle and bustle behind. It moved through a residential area and came to a stop mid-block on a street lined with leafy Norwegian maples.

The foundation of Mrs. Penington's home had been laid several decades ago. It was a small, four story building. The traditional architecture had been recently renovated, in keeping with the homes around it. It's white siding gave it an immaculate look and its huge picture windows allowed more than a peak inside.

Ankona helped Nahuel get his backpack from the taxi's trunk. The boy slung it over one shoulder, and as he went up the front steps, he tried to comb down his unruly hair in order to make a good first impression.

The impressive oak door opened, revealing a plump woman wearing a Christmas apron.

Mrs. Pennington was petite and had her deep chocolate brown hair cut short like a man's.

"Good evening, Ophelia," Ankona greeted her. "This is Nahuel Blest."

"Oh, my goodness! Nahuel, how wonderful! What a pleasure it is to have you here at last!" Mrs. Pennington gushed, more effusively than Nahuel would have expected.

"I trust you knew we were coming," Ankona added.

"Yes, yes. They told me about twenty minutes ago," she replied, smiling and patting Nahuel's back in a motherly way.

"This is where I say goodbye," Ankona said.

"What a pity you can't stay," Mrs. Penington replied quickly. "There's enough food for both of you."

"Next time," Ankona promised. He extended his hand to Nahuel and made his way down to the street.

Ophelia Penington invited Nahuel into the house.

Nahuel followed Mrs. Penington across the unvarnished wood floors. If it weren't for the smell of meatloaf floating out from the kitchen, Nahuel might have noticed the funny stride of the lady of the house.

They made their way down a long hallway covered with paintings. At the end were two staircases. One went upstairs, towards the bedrooms and upper floors and the other, small and tightly closed, led to the basement.

Before leaving the hallway, Nahuel passed by a series of paintings which illustrated the construction and expansion of the house. It was somehow the same and different. The most notable difference was that the house had been surrounded by columns.

"The other kids had dinner at seven. Some have gone up to their rooms, but others are still in the dining room," explained Mrs. Penington.

They passed through the living room, it was large, and it had an English style window. A coat of arms hung above the fireplace, it represented old New York City.

"Emre darling, how nice you're still here," Mrs. Penington said as they entered the dining room. "I'd like you to meet Nahuel Blest. He will be your roommate."

"That's good. I was starting to feel lonely," Emre answered, winking at the girl next to him.

Emre Soydas had arrived three days earlier. He had a wide, good-natured face and his skin was kissed by the Turkish sun. His eyebrows were heavy and his eyes were small.

"Have a seat, Nahuel," Mrs. Penington said kindly. Lowering her voice, she added, "I'll bring you one of my specialties. You let me know if you like it or not. If you don't, I'll prepare you something else. I'll only give you that option today because it's your first day here and you're the last one to arrive. Imagine if I let each of the 24 students here ask for whatever they had a craving for at each meal! I'd end up bonkers like my dear friend Suzzane."

"Whatever you bring will be fine," Nahuel assured her when she paused for breath. He was sure that if the food tasted as good as it smelled, he would be more than satisfied. Besides, he suspected that it would be rude to ask for something he hadn't been offered.

Nahuel waited quietly, a bit intimidated by that large rectangular table full of people. The truth was that he had never been in such a situation before in his life. There have always been three of them, first, his mother, his father and him and, then, his mother, his grandfather and him. That's why he had learnt to enjoy the company of nature and his dogs.

The mood in the room was lively.

At the other end of the table, a tall boy with a thin face and long neck was taking bets on who would be the first to go home and drop the scholarship.

"I bet it'll be you, Eric. I've seen that pillow you brought from home. I bet it's filled with all of mommy's love for you."

Eric turned as red as a tomato and hunched down in his chair.

"You're so mean, Tristan," a girl wearing bright pink lipstick blurted out, between giggles.

"He who tells the truth, never betrays," Tristan quipped with a nasty smile.

He had dark eyes and an arrogant mouth, almost cruel. He wore his hair slicked over to one side, making his ears even more noticeable.

"What a dog," Emre murmured, clicking his tongue.

Nahuel's lips turned into a fine line. He gathered he wouldn't be on friendly terms with Tristan, but his thoughts were interrupted by the delicious meatloaf Mrs. Penington had just brought him. He grabbed his fork eagerly and scooped up an enormous bite.

As he ate and his hunger faded, Nahuel turned his attention back toward the conversation around him.

A girl seemed obsessed with finding out more information on the nature of the scholarship, she sounded French.

"Do you all know why you were chosen?" she asked, seeming to want to evaluate her competition.

"I don't know. It just happened," Emre responded as he took a huge bite from the piece of apple pie he had grabbed from the kitchen as soon as Mrs. Penington's back was turned.

"*Pardon?* How was that?" she insisted.

"One day I was at school and the princi….pal asked me to go get my parents. We lived just…. acr...oss the street," he explained with his mouth full. "My father immediately started with the usual, 'when are you going to grow up and act like a man. Your sisters never put me through this. You're making me age faster than the speed of light' you know - blah, blah, blah…"

"But why did he say these things?" the French girl asked.

"No idea," Emre said, shrugging his shoulders. "I hadn't even had a chance to put the rat in the girl's bathroom yet." Emre paused and took a gulp of water.

"And what happened when you returned with your parents?" the girl asked impatiently, tucking her bangs behind her ear.

"The principal introduced us to a man who came on behalf of the United Nations. He explained that I had won a scholarship. Of course, my dad couldn't believe it, least of all that the whole thing was paid for. 'Your son possesses qualities the United Nations is seeking in younger generations'," Emre quoted, imitating the stranger's voice "Emre Soydas's IQ demonstrates the desired characteristics."

"IQ?!" Emre continued in a deeper voice, pretending to be his father. "But what are you talking about, man! Clearly you don't know the boy. He has the IQ of a chicken!"

"Ssshh, darling. Emre is an exceptional boy. He never fails to surprise us. You say chicken, but I would say goat, and a goat with a long beard at that." Emre's impersonation of his mother's high-pitched and whiny voice was remarkable and everyone at the table burst into laughter.

Nahuel thought the way he ended up in this situation was also weird. Ankona turned up out of the blue at the door and his grandfather, who was the most reserved person that Nahuel knew, had let him go with a stranger. He hadn't even had time to think whether or not he wanted to go to New York. And now, whether he wanted it or not, he was there.

"Time for bed ladies and gentlemen. Tomorrow is a big day," interjected Mrs. Penington, popping in from the kitchen. "You need to be down for breakfast by 7. At 8 Benjamin will take you to the UN."

They made their way to the staircase at the end of the hallway. Nahuel grabbed his backpack, waiting for him in the corner. The boys' rooms were on the second floor.

Nahuel opened the door of his new room. Emre's suitcase was lying open just beyond the door. Nahuel had to skirt past it to get in. Inside his roommate's suitcase, the clothes were a wrinkled jumble, making it impossible to distinguish shirts from pants from underwear. A few stray socks and a thick overcoat were strewn across Nahuel's bed.

"Wait," Emre said, coming in behind him. "I'll clean everything up right now."

He crossed over to Nahuel's bed and with one swipe, pushed the heavy coat and all the socks to the floor.

"All done," he declared calmly.

The room had only two beds separated by a long nightstand. There were no paintings, nor color. Just a small desk squeezed into the corner. The room seemed to be waiting for the occupants to decorate it.

Nahuel set his backpack down in the only empty spot in the room. He opened it and tugged his pajamas out from under his precious chess set. As he put on his checkered pajamas he thought how lucky he was that he had been assigned a roommate as friendly as Emre.

Maybe it was because he had been sick so often, or maybe it was due to what had happened that time with his only childhood friend, but whatever the reason, the kids his age in Ushuaia had never been very comfortable around him.

Or perhaps it was his unconventional family. His grandfather who looked after him, did the shopping and tied on an apron to cook every day, while his mother acted like some kind of sullen and resentful teenager.

In that provincial city, it was damaging to your popularity to have a family that was anything but normal. It was also public knowledge, thanks to the gossiping postman, that Nahuel's family never received any mail from family or friends. They didn't have a phone in their house either and the Internet could only be accessed after signing in with several passwords. "They're hiding something," everyone said.

Above all else, it was Nahuel's illness that set him apart. Ever since he could remember, he had suffered from *episodes*.

They always started the same way. He woke up, with his senses sharpened. He could make out the eyes of a spider crossing his ceiling and the victims caught in its web. He could smell the salty sea air, miles from his house and the fresh baked bread of Mrs. Makowski.

But what bothered him the most were the sounds. He could hear the footsteps of the priest making his way up the belltower, the irritating drip of the neighbor's faucet, and waves breaking out on the coast. His Siberians were the only ones who cooperated. They knew that on those days they mustn't bark.

And then, just as suddenly as it came, it went away. His senses clouded over and he lay prostrate in his bed, carried away by feverish dreams.

This could last for weeks, preventing him from leaving his house. The fever brought on chills, sweat and increased his heart rate. When the episodes were at their strongest, he lost consciousness and became delirious.

In spite of all that, they never took him to the hospital. His grandfather gave him medicine each time it happened and recited poetry to help him fall asleep. The verses were impossible to understand, spoken in an unrecognizable language.

When the episodes ended, it was like nothing had ever happened. Nahuel was healthy as an ox.

As Nahuel grew, the episodes became more regular and harder to overcome.

The last relapse was the strongest ever. It had happened only three months ago. It had started like the other times, but it quickly turned into the most dangerous yet.

His grandfather, who always seemed so calm and steady in those situations, hadn't been able to hide his concern. Nahuel was unconscious for more than 4 days and delirious for weeks.

Then, one day, they received a visitor. Nahuel gazed at them as if from the other side of a river whose turbulent waters were dragging him toward his subconscious.

His grandfather was standing near a man. Was he a doctor? He wasn't dressed like one.

"This will help him get better," the stranger assured. *"It was a good thing you called me. This is an unusual case."*

"What did the analysis show?" asked his grandfather.

"That his CYMMANCINA is the strongest I've ever seen -even stronger than Martin's. The levels build up in his blood until his body erupts and starts to attack it. That's the reason for the high fevers. But now, with what I've given him, his body will have the tools to absorb it."

"This is our secret, understood?" his grandfather stated.

"Of course. I was waiting for the day I could repay you."

Nahuel watched Emre's failing battle with his bedside lamp for a while. It seemed that his roommate had dropped it that morning and the base broke when it hit the floor. Now, he was trying to fix it with some glue he had taken from a drawer in the kitchen.

Seconds before falling asleep, Nahuel asked himself again, *what am I doing here?* The question had been following him since leaving Ushuaia. Even if they told him why he was there, at that moment, he wouldn't have believed them.

CHAPTER 4

It was Friday morning and Nahuel had just grabbed one of the first window seats in the van that would take the students to the United Nations.

Emre was in the seat behind him, next to a girl from Japan and another girl who was wearing a dark blue veil.

"This is just no way to hold a conversation," Emre confided in a whisper to his roommate.

The problem was one of the girls was very shy and the other one could only understand half of what Emre said, and she needed a dictionary to answer any of his questions. In that regard, Nahuel was lucky. His grandfather had dedicated many of his afternoons to teaching him English.

"Hurry up, everyone, we should get going, it's 8 already," said a tall and good-looking young man who was making his way up to the van.

Benjamin was just a few years older than the kids and had been living in Mrs. Penington's house for the last three years.

"Twenty...four, yes, that's it, you are the last one," Benjamin said when a short and chubby boy stepped into the van, and, in a loud voice, he added "we can leave now," so the driver could hear him.

The vehicle was set in motion and Nahuel observed through the window how a flock of pigeons that were standing on the tree started to fly.

"Well, guys, are you ready for your first day? I hope you have all you need," Benjamin said, turning toward the students.

Nahuel was so close to him that he could see, under his black vest, a necklace with a reddish ball pendant swinging near his chest.

"Were we supposed to bring something?" asked a girl wearing pink lipstick.

"Your courage, of course, as you should expect a very interesting day...and year," Benjamin replied winking an eye. "But, let's not get ahead of ourselves. Today is orientation day. Professor Sebastian Kendrick will give you a tour of the UN and then you will discuss the contents of the Educational Program, which will begin on Monday."

"Have you also done the Educational Program at the UN?" asked Emre.

"Yes, I've completed the three years and, now, I've been chosen to continue working there."

Nahuel saw the proud smile on Benjamin's face when saying it and asked himself again what he was doing there. The truth was that he has never been an outstanding student; he was all about the woods and nature. The only subject he was good at was sports, but he didn't know how that would help him at the UN.

They were greeted by a swarm of flags as they arrived at the United Nations headquarters, located on 1st Avenue, the east side of Manhattan. Beyond the flags, they could easily make out two buildings: one was tall and impressive with a crystal facade and to the left, another huge structure, but made of grey cement and rectangular.

The entrance to the UN was bustling with people. The students gathered around Benjamin.

"The building in front of you is the General Secretary of the UN," Benjamin explained as he ran his hands through his golden hair. "Mr. Meyno will welcome us at the entrance. You will be given your ID cards there."

All twenty-four teens followed Benjamin to the security station, where a uniformed guard checked the authenticity of their documents. Then he handed them each the ID that would allow them to enter and circulate throughout the headquarters. Nahuel hung the blue cord with the plastic card showing his photograph and name, around his neck.

The group moved past the guard, leaving the public area behind.

"Over here, Benjamin," waved a man with dark brown hair, parted down the middle.

He was standing in the main hall of the glass building.

"They are all yours," replied Benjamin as soon as the group reached the man.

"Good job, as always. Remember to pick them up at 1 pm sharp."

Benjamin nodded and greeted: "See you later, guys."

"Good morning, ladies and gentlemen. My name is Sebastian and my surname is Kendrick. But due to the nature of our relationship, you may call me by my first name," the man said, now talking directly to the kids.

He wore dress slacks, a white shirt and a black vest with silver edging, just as Benjamin's. A black leather briefcase hung from his shoulder and in his other arm he held a pile of folders which apparently didn't fit in his bag.

"It is my great pleasure to meet you. I hope you are quite well," he continued, ceremoniously.

At that moment, he shook Nahuel's hand vigorously. Of all the students, he was the closest. Nahuel felt a bit uncomfortable because his palms were sweaty. Then he realized that the professor wouldn't even have noticed since he was wearing black gloves.

"Before we begin our tour of the headquarters, I will tell you the most important thing," Sebastian announced, puffing up his chest.

"The United Nations is an international organization founded in 1945 as a gathering of world leaders. Since its beginning, it has included among its members very high-ranking diplomats, important state officials, and experts in all areas, regardless of their background or nationality. Now I will show you where the magic happens," Sebastian laughed at his own joke and began walking.

They crossed the ground floors of the Secretary building until they reached the cement structure to its left, where Sebastian would show them the Security Council and the main hall of the General Assembly.

"The territory we are on, the land we are walking over, is declared an international zone," Sebastian explained. "The US government cannot make decisions regarding these buildings or the area they are built on. This place belongs to all of us, to each of the member states.

"Many of the world's most influential men walk these halls, above and below us," he added and his blue eyes sparkled. "You should consider yourselves lucky. This is the place everyone would like to be."

It was clear to Nahuel that Sebastian was a fervent supporter and defender of the United Nations. He spoke of the UN as if it were unique and amazing. Nahuel had only ever heard of the UN on TV, but he couldn't even remember exactly what it was.

The tour continued until the main hall of the headquarters, the General Assembly.

Sebastian's blue eyes locked with a man passing by, wearing an identical, silver-edged vest. Without looking at Sebastian, the man secretly slipped a deer's tail into his hand, which Sebastian quickly hid in his pocket.

Sebastian carried on, as if nothing had happened and as they entered the next hallway, he pointed out with his left hand:

"This is the Security Council. Leaders from nations and organizations around the world must be ready at any time to meet here whenever there is a threat to world peace."

A girl in their group opened the door Sebastian was pointing at without asking permission. To everyone's surprise, the room wasn't empty and dozens of faces turned to look at the girl with incredulous and reprimanding stares. Her name was Emma. She was from Los Angeles and wore her pink sunglasses on the top of her head.

"What a snooper," murmured the French girl that Nahuel had met the night before.

Sebastian hurried back and shut the door. The movement was so quick and rough that before he could grab them, some of the folders he was holding, full of papers, fell to the floor.

"We cannot go in now. They are in session," he grumbled, clearly agitated as Emma stared at her feet and giggled.

The French girl who was standing beside him helped Sebastian gather up the papers, organized them the best she could and handed them back to him.

"Here you are, sir."

A few seconds later, Nahuel narrowed his gaze and noticed something bright shining out from below a door near the Security Council. But before he could figure out what it was, Tristan bent down and grabbed it.

It was an ivory-colored card, and once Tristan touched it, it changed into a deep red color.

"I think it's Sebastian's," Nahuel said to Tristan when he joined him. They were both some steps behind the rest of the group.

"Are you sure?" Tristan said sarcastically while he put the card in the back pocket of his pants.

"Give it back."

"Mind your own business," Tristan replied with a half-smile as he quickened his pace and left Nahuel behind.

Nahuel felt a tingling in his fingertips, as if something wanted to come out of him. He tightened his fists, trying to control his instincts.

"Asshole," he murmured.

When the tour finished, Sebastian led them to a large auditorium in the Secretary General building. He asked them to wait there a few moments until the Director arrived to speak to them.

Nahuel sat in the center of the auditorium next to the French girl. Most of the kids avoided the first rows.

The space was located on the ground floor. To the back there were large picture windows which showed a narrow back garden which ran along the edge of the river.

The chairs were arranged in a semicircle in front of a podium where Sebastian and a middle-aged woman were speaking. She sat with her back straight and chin up. The woman had ash blonde hair cut in a short bob and wore light camel-colored gloves.

When Nahuel observed her, he saw the woman's brow was furrowed and her hair was being blown by some invisible wind. By sharpening his sight, he thought: *what's that?*

Emre slapped him on the back as he entered the auditorium, brought his attention back and took the other seat next to the French girl.

The teens chatted in low voices, trying not to make too much noise.

"We have been here for eleven minutes," the French girl observed. Her hair was black, straight and cut just above her shoulders. Her oval face had delicate features and her skin was paper-white.

Nahuel rolled up his sleeves and checked the time on his wrist-watch.

"These watches are no longer made," she said pointing at Nahuel's watch.

It was an old wind-up watch with scratched up glass.

"It's my grandfather's," Nahuel explained. He had given it to him right before he left Ushuaia.

"Oh, great taste. I can identify a relic when I see it. One of my uncles has an antiquary shop in the center of Paris where all the movie stars go."

"Cool", Nahuel said, not knowing what else to say.

Before long, he learned that her name was Isaline Fleury and that behind that flippant and vain attitude, a very loyal and fair person was hiding.

Just then, an older man wearing an elegant gray Marengo suit, white shirt and loud orange tie walked with an elegant gait into the auditorium. He was a man with fair skin and an extravagant air. The only hair he had left, which was gray with age, was his goatee and moustache. Otherwise, he was completely bald.

Sebastian and the woman stopped talking, the students copied them and turned to look at the new arrival.

"Good morning, Mrs. Sparling, Sebastian," he greeted them with a slight bow, he sounded German.

"Director," they responded, with a nod of the head.

A silver chain with a platinum sphere hung around his neck. He crossed the room with his majestic stride and took his place behind the podium.

"Welcome everyone," he said, addressing the students. "My name is Klaus and it is a great honor for me that you are all gathered here. This will be a very meaningful day in your lives."

He paused and let his sky-blue eyes connect with his crowd, landing on Nahuel for a few moments, for no visible reason. He continued:

"I must admit that we have gathered you here under false pretenses. We have brought you here to receive an education different from the one we promised. Each of you has been specially selected by us. Your singular qualities and the effort of the trackers have brought you here."

Trackers? Nahuel thought. *What does he mean?*

Klaus adjusted the knot on his tie. Nahuel noticed he was also wearing gloves. With a more animated voice he continued:

"In a few moments, you are going to hear what I am sure is one of the most exciting pieces of information to ever be revealed to a group your age."

CHAPTER 5

Klaus paused, purely for dramatic effect and the result was spectacular. The group fell silent and leaned in closer.

"You will learn that the world you live in is not the world you think it is. History is nothing like you have been taught," he continued.

"As far back as we know, history has been manipulated, tampered with. The world is not exactly organized the way the average person imagines. It is true there are countries and religions, but there is also something more underpinning all of these institutions which has stood the test of time."

Klaus continued with his speech, as he paced back and forth on the stage, gesturing with his hands and posturing as if he were rehearsing a part in a play.

"There is another society, the Privileged, and another organization, the Council of Privileges, both have been in existence from the very beginning. This society is comprised of us and of course, you. You had no idea –that's obvious. However, we have selected you in order to teach you OUR history, YOUR history. The true history of mankind."

Silence ruled the auditorium.

"Everyone here - we all have something in common," the Director said, sure of each word he spoke.

Beep…Beep...Beep…Beep.

The ill-timed sound interrupted his monologue. The Director took a pocket watch hanging from a golden chain from his pocket. He silenced it and continued gazing at his audience as if nothing had happened.

"I can tell that many of you are asking yourselves why you have been selected by the United Nations. You are wondering why we have chosen you in particular. Why have we made you travel so far?"

Exactly, Nahuel thought. He wanted to know where he was and what was going on.

"Many of you are trying to guess the real reason you are here."

Klaus took a step forward, enjoying the suspense he was stirring up.

Everyone's eyes were glued to him. No one even blinked. Nahuel noticed that Isaline's legs were shaking nervously. Klaus walked to the edge of the stage and said:

"As you must already suspect, you are DIFFERENT. You are special."

Tristan looked at Klaus with a sickening smile, like someone who is a little too proud of himself. Nahuel found him really irritating.

Klaus, relishing the group's anxiety, continued with a soothing and captivating tone of voice:

"You have privileges."

"*Pri*...what?" was the collective response.

Klaus smiled excitedly, as if he had just revealed the deepest of secrets. The group shot confused looks at each other, in every direction, checking to see if anyone had understood the speech. Most were puzzled.

Isaline was now strangling her seat cushion. She had gone from being nervous to being hysterical. And she wasn't alone.

"The Privileged Society is made up of the CYMMENS, CYMTERS and CYMANIS," Klaus continued. "Each of you possesses only one of these privileges. For those of you who are looking at me strangely, what I am telling you is that you all enjoy certain special abilities which only very few of us are blessed with...That's right, you have heard correctly —you are the privileged ones."

Nothing Klaus was saying made any logical sense to Nahuel, but, at the same time, his instincts said the opposite.

The group continued to exchange confused and worried looks. Klaus's soliloquy swung between genius and madness.

"Enough of those skeptical looks. Everyone raises one hand."

Some raised their hands timidly but when they noticed that the others did not raise their hands, they quickly put them down.

"Let's go ladies and gentlemen... One hand up. Everyone does it," the Director ordered.

Nahuel raised his arm firmly and highly in the air. Klaus wasn't fooling around and he wanted to know what the Director was trying to get at.

Before long, twenty-three hands rose up beside Nahuel's.

"That's better," Klaus went on, smiling. "Now, put your hand down if you have never suffered from a bout of presumed illness which involved a heightening of your senses followed by fever. These bouts end as quickly as they begin and neither your family members nor your doctors have ever been able to make sense of them."

To Nahuel's surprise, all the hands remained in the air.

"What? You too?" Isaline asked him, slightly bewildered.

Nahuel nodded. He also found it hard to believe that other kids had grown up suffering from a similar sickness.

"So you see, I told you we all had something in common," Klaus said jovially. He explained: "All the members of the privileged society have suffered these bouts of illness, some stronger than others. These apparently unexplainable attacks actually do have an explanation. They happen when the *Cym* enzyme, any of the three types which exist, spread through your body and take it over in a way, activating the privileges within us. And that is why the trackers are able to find us."

Cym? Nahuel vaguely remembered his grandfather's conversation.

If his grandfather had applied to this scholarship for him, what did it mean? Did he really know what this Program was about or has he been deceived?

"So, we're not sick, and we actually have powers? Are the privileges powers?" Nahuel heard Emre asking Isaline, who appeared not to have heard the question.

"The privileges are energy that runs through our veins, but not without its limitations," Klaus said. "Mrs. Sparling, would you be so kind as to open the windows? I wouldn't want to break the glass," he suddenly asked, without even turning to look at the woman sitting next to Sebastian.

Nahuel heard a bang come from behind. It was sudden and loud. Instinctively, the group turned to see where it had come from.

The windows which looked onto the river were wide open, letting in a breeze.

Nahuel turned back toward the stage. Mrs. Sparling was still there, her face unchanged. There was no way she could have opened all the windows at the same time, so quickly and by herself.

They could hear the river running and the birds singing.

Then in it came, through the back, like a green tsunami filtering through the windows. But it wasn't water.

A twisting mass of leaves and branches broke into the auditorium, invading it with incredible speed and strength. It was like a bomb had exploded in the river and the shock wave had blasted them with bits and pieces.

A branch grazed his head and Nahuel's instincts activated immediately. He threw himself on the floor and grabbed Isaline who was nearest to him.

"We're under attack!" Tristan shouted randomly.

And then everyone else threw themselves on the floor, most trying to hide under their seats. A storm of dirt churned above them, blocking out the light from outside.

Emre was flat on his stomach like someone trying to escape a round of bullets. Everyone exchanged frightened glances.

Nahuel hated to admit how scared he was.

"What the hell is going on?" he wanted to know.

"We're in a goddamned videogame!" Emre replied.

Nahuel could see all his classmates on the ground, lying down or crouched in the same position he was. Across the room, Tristan seemed to be paralyzed.

Nahuel looked up. With each passing second more and more branches flew into the room. Or were they the same ones, just getting bigger? Whatever they were doing, it was at an unnatural rate. He could hear buzzing in his ears. The auditorium was filling up with leaves and bark.

There were branches of all shapes and sizes. The thickness and speed of some of them was truly threatening. They brushed past the seats, just missing them with such precision that they seemed to have a mind of their own.

Two branches in particular caught his attention. They zig-zagged over his seat and Nahuel couldn't understand how they managed to balance a bird nest between them.

And then suddenly, out of the blue, it all stopped.

No one spoke. A deep silence followed the surprise attack.

Nahuel looked at Isaline. Her eyebrows were lifted nearly to her hairline.

"What was that?" she murmured.

Nahuel shrugged his shoulders and shook his head. He was overcome with curiosity but also confusion.

The moment that it seemed that everything had stopped and the branches were still, Nahuel dared to stand up, but he couldn't tell if he was being brave or just stupid. Tristan didn't want to be left behind, so he quickly stood up too.

Nahuel stood there with his mouth open, as if he was worried he might be hallucinating.

Through the windows, he could see that the trees along the river's edge had grown in a matter of seconds. It took his mind a minute to process the scene. The tree trunks and branches had stretched in impossible ways, coming through the rear garden directly into the auditorium. They were so thick and long and numerous that almost no light could make its way in through the windows.

Nahuel felt the ridiculous urge to reach up and touch the branches. Then he turned toward the stage. Only Klaus, Tristan and himself were on their feet. The Director was looking at them with pure...satisfaction? Behind him, Mrs. Sparling and Sebastian remained seated, without the slightest expression of wonder nor fear on their faces.

Just above Klaus's head, the branches formed a symbol. It was three circles, entwined vertically. The circles were perfect and the branches forming them were thick and full of white flowers.

Before long, Emre got to his feet and stood by his side, followed by Isaline and then the others.

Klaus then raised his hands in a conciliatory gesture.

"I didn't mean to frighten you," he said. "The Council of Privileges of the United Nations has brought you here to begin your training in these special skills," Klaus announced in a deep voice.

As the mood calmed, the branches began withdrawing to where they had come from, retreating slowly above the students' heads.

"These are definitely super powers," Emre whispered again, looking up.

Nahuel felt a gentle breeze blow from the stage toward the river, lifting the dirt and leaves that had blown in, leaving the auditorium as clean as it had been before.

"This is impossible," blurted one of the students.

"Actually, it's not. Simply unimaginable," Klaus replied.

Everyone returned to their seats and the windows banged shut.

"You all possess a certain sensitivity which others do not," the Director confirmed. "The matter is quite complex, but I will summarize it for you so you stop looking at me like that and can start getting excited once and for all. We, the Privileged, have the ability to affect other living beings and that is a truly magnificent gift. If I asked you what other living organisms there are on the planet beside the human being, I imagine your first reply would be all the animals and plants... Right," he nodded despite the fact no one had answered the question.

"One type of Privilege gives you the ability to affect animals. These are the CymAnis. The second type has the ability to affect everything that comes from the earth. These are the CymTers. And the third type, a bit more complicated, has the ability to affect change in microorganisms, those living beings which are so minute we cannot see them nor feel them. These are the CymMens."

Klaus gave them a moment to take in everything he was saying. No one said a word, but Nahuel knew everyone must be remembering some unexplainable moment in their lives, just as he was. This information made sense out of those moments in the most extraordinary way.

"Perhaps you didn't pay attention to it," Klaus said a few seconds later. "You were most likely taught that it must be impossible, and therefore didn't look closely at that which you believed could not possibly happen."

Beep...Beep...Beep. The alarm went off once more. Klaus silenced it in his pocket and took out a small silver package. He scooped something out of the envelope that looked to Nahuel like a piece of wet seaweed. And he unexpectedly placed it in his mouth.

Klaus continued:

"You each form part of a group of young people who will receive an exclusive education at the United Nations. We host a new group of teens every three years to take part in this program here, in our own installations. There is no question that the most well-equipped place to host you is the Council of Privileges and by being here, you take your place as protagonists in our story. How can I explain this? You now become part of the most influential private club on earth," Klaus stated.

"Your professors will teach you everything you need to know to handle the difficulties that may arise during this year of learning. Rest assured you are in the hands of experts. I know it will be hard. Initiation is always the most difficult part. I know it was for me," Klaus made an attempt at false modesty, "Even though some people don't believe me. But you must be patient. Don't give in to despair, which is not a good friend. This training will require strength and practice. You must be avid apprentices, especially considering that times have changed and we now find ourselves in an era of contingencies."

Sebastian made a point to clear his throat on purpose but Klaus carried on, unflinching:

"I have no doubt that at some point your participation will be inevitable. The day will come in which we must resist. A certain storm is approaching, and unfortunately, it will be here sooner than I would like."

Sebastian looked at Mrs. Sparling nervously, but she remained rigid, unmoved.

Isaline whispered to Nahuel, "It can't be true, but it seems they need us for a new crusade."

"You're right," he murmured back to her.

"But, let's leave that for later. You needn't concern yourselves with that yet," Klaus continued, returning to his warm, welcoming voice. "We are gathered here for other reasons right now."

Klaus's eyes glowed with excitement and he recited:

Our allies are three.
They hold our virtues high.
They unite our gifts and shield us from swords.
The mind lights the CymMens.
The earth supplies the CymTers.
The animals guard the CymAnis.

An image from Nahuel's past flashed across his mind. He tried as hard as he could to keep hold of the memory and add voices to it, but it was soon gone, back to the dark.

Klaus moved elegantly to the door, confident in the clarity of his speech. Before exiting, he asked, "Did I forget anything, Sebastian?"

"Actually Sir, to tell you the truth, yes," he replied, standing up dramatically.

Klaus checked his pocket watch again and added:

"Well then, I'll leave them in your hands, Sebastian. Have nice day Mrs. Sparling. Ladies and gentlemen, it's been a pleasure."

And with that, he was gone.

Nahuel turned to look at Sebastian and Mrs. Sparling. She looked impatient. She was seated with her arms and legs crossed constantly checking her watch. She suddenly stood up and with a frown said, "Sebastian, it's time to show them where the Educational Program for the Acquirement and Proper Use of Privileges will be."

Sebastian quickly checked his list of key points from the presentation.

"You're right, Mrs. Sparling. It's time." Turning back toward the group he said, "Follow us, please."

The students jumped to their feet. Isaline rushed clumsily toward the door. Nahuel tried to keep up with her the best he could, but Tristan pushed him aside. They all bunched up in the door, eager to find out more.

Nahuel wondered where they would take them next. He assumed it would be outside of the United Nations building. As Sebastian had explained it was such an important and recognizable building, on a global scale, and always so full of people, it seemed impossible that an entire organization could be hidden within it.

They followed the professors to the glass building of the Secretariat. There, they made their way to the big elevator.

Nahuel had an annoying buzz in his brain. He spent the next few minutes consumed by a whirlwind of questions. How did the privileges work? What privilege did he have? Who were these people? Where were they being taken now? He wished he could read minds, to see what was going on inside Mrs. Sparling's. Isaline incessantly shifted her weight from one foot to the other, a ball of nerves.

Once the last girl had squeezed between Emre and Emma, the doors automatically shut. Mrs. Sparling turned her back to them, took off her gloves, opened a large brown leather organizer and took out an ivory-colored card. Nahuel saw that as her skin touched the card, it turned from ivory to blue.

There was no doubt about it, the color changed, but the card was the same as the one Tristan had grabbed from the ground near the Security Council.

Once she laid the card against the elevator buttons, they began to descend without stopping until they reached the sub-4th floor.

Isaline's eyes opened as wide as saucers and she nudged Nahuel.

"Incredible! I was sure there were only three underground floors at the United Nations."

CHAPTER 6

When the elevator doors slid open, one could say this place was not governed by the laws of nature.

The room they stepped into was clear and luminous, fine rays of sunlight streaming in from above, which was impossible since they were extremely deep underground.

Nahuel had already figured this was going to be strange, what he hadn't imagined was that it could be wonderful.

The room was wide and its oval ceilings were covered with a fine shiny film, as were the walls. If he hadn't known better, he would have thought they were liquid diamonds painted on the walls.

To the right there was an office of dark glass and in the back there was a meeting room featuring a large library.

The entire chamber was a crystalline structure where light chased out all shadow. When Nahuel looked up, he came face to face with his own dazzling silhouette, which left him dumbstruck. The outline of everyone present followed the group with each step, on display above their heads.

Sebastian announced that he would catch up later.

Mrs. Sparling stopped at a counter a few feet from the elevator. This was the reception.

"Has my classroom been prepared for the procedure?" It was a question, but it sounded like a warning.

"Of course, Mrs. Sparling. It was done as soon as you requested," the secretary assured her.

Katya was a tall and muscular woman, with skin as fair, or maybe even fairer than Klaus's, and dark hair that hung to her waist.

"If you have a second, could you sign the Steinhauser Operation report so I can archive it, please?"

Mrs. Sparling took the pen from her leather organizer and signed where the secretary indicated. Then, she walked on without turning around down the hall, with the students following behind her. She walked past the office and before reaching the back, she stopped in front of a door.

Unfortunately, she had lost the group a few feet behind.

The students were stopped in their tracks staring at an enormous climbing plant covering a lattice. They were absorbed by the amazing way the plant grew and shrank to its liking. Nahuel followed one of its vines as it made its way zig-zagging through the rest. As it approached to the edge of the wall, Nahuel saw that it had written three words using its leaves and flowers.

Council of Privileges

They could certainly expect the unexpected down there.

The most remarkable thing about the plant was its color. Its flowers bloomed in multiple shades depending on the person standing near it. When all the students stood in front of it, it bloomed in all the colors Nahuel could imagine, there were blue, orange, purple and some were even silver and gold. In the spot he was standing, the flowers were a deep shade of red.

Mrs. Sparling opened the door and waited until finally the students filed past her into the room.

"Hurry up, Miss Pierwiet," she ordered.

The girl gave the plant one last look and then ran to join the group. The small yellow flowers dotting the plant quickly closed up and disappeared.

Martha Sparling led them all through a labyrinth-like space which wound and unwound and seemed to never end.

They were making their way deeper into the clandestine organization within the United Nations, a secret realm that at one time was only open to the first privileged ones.

The sub-4th floor proved to be really old, but it was mostly maintained by being constantly remodeled to be on the cutting edge of design and to mask the undercover operations of the Council of Privileges.

They made their way through rooms of all kinds and sizes. There was one large room which Nahuel thought was really old. It reminded him of a great hall from medieval times where large parties and balls would be held, although he suspected no one ever danced there. It was a round room and the mosaic floor featured floral patterns.

At one point on the tour, Mrs. Sparling used her ivory pass card again.

They came upon a corridor completely surrounded by a glass wall. Behind it, Nahuel could see dozens of screens hanging from the roof with images of worldwide news. Below them, there were desks and people working.

Mrs. Sparling suddenly stopped, turned towards the News Room and, with an unflappable expression, opened the glass door.

Even though Nahuel was not able to listen to what Mrs. Sparling was saying, it seemed she was calling the shots here and there. Three men had stood up when she stepped in. Then, another woman was standing by her side nodding and taking a phone. Mrs. Sparling had that authority in her eyes that everyone was willing to obey.

At that moment, all the screens in the room changed and synchronized the same Belgian channel, which showed a flooding in the middle of the city caused by the overflow of a canal.

When Mrs. Sparling stepped out of the News Room and left the corridor, they stepped into a hallway flanked by a marble statue of a cherub. Just beyond it there was a door on one side and voices leaked from behind it.

"I've told you that the intensity must be reduced! You'll never pass as a bat with the vibration in that frequency!" exclaimed a male voice from behind the door.

"And I've told you a thousand times that I will never achieve the same reaction as a bat doing it the way you tell me. You sound like a hoarse whale," replied an impatient female voice.

The sign in the center of the door read:

Sound Wave Laboratory

"Stay close to me. I will not come back to look for stragglers," Mrs. Sparling growled in a threatening way. "And be quiet. There are people working here."

Nahuel ran to catch up to the group. The last thing he wanted was to have a problem with Mrs. Sparling. They continued walking through the sub-4th floor, the unadmired underground hideaway.

They made so many right and then left-hand turns that Nahuel would bet that the sub-4th floor covered the entire property of the United Nations.

Nahuel saw Isaline at the front of the group, close on the heels of Mrs. Sparling.

Finally, what seemed like a never-ending tour came to an end and Mrs. Sparling invited them all to pass into the next room.

Once they were inside, she shut the door firmly. In this room, everything was pristinely white. The walls were white, the ceiling was white and even the floor was immaculately white.

"What are you waiting for? One desk per student," she said as she faced them.

Nahuel went toward one of the white desks. Underneath it there was a red cushion on the floor, but no chair.

Mrs. Sparling walked toward her desk, at the front of the room. As she passed by them, the cushions began to rise into the air. One by one they became suspended a few feet off the ground.

"Take your seats," their professor ordered.

Automatically, Nahuel stepped forward, overcome with curiosity. Just as he was about to sit down, he noticed that Isaline had her eyes glued to him, waiting for Nahuel to make the first move.

Nahuel, conscious of her gaze, sat down slowly on the cushion. It remained in place, supporting his weight. He was relieved the cushion hadn't let him fall. That would have been an embarrassing mess.

He watched the other cushions from the corner of his eye, as his classmates sat down. If this trick was due to some special ability of Mrs. Sparling's, it didn't seem to be demanding any of her energy.

Just a few seconds later, Sebastian arrived. The students remained still, not daring to turn around for fear of falling off their seats with the slightest movement.

As Sebastian came into his line of sight, Nahuel swallowed. Isaline clapped her hand over her mouth and Emre started shaking on his cushion.

This was one crazy day. Sebastian wasn't alone.

A dark-skinned man with a beaded necklace walked beside him. It was Ankona. But that wasn't everything. A clouded leopard strode in next to him. It was a powerful and gorgeous wild cat, and Ankona looked pretty comfortable next to him.

Its fur, covered with large irregular spots, outlined by black and brown on the inside was mesmerizing. In its own habitat the spots provided the perfect camouflage. It moved silently down the rows, between the desks, placing one paw in front of the other rhythmically.

Mrs. Sparling opened a cupboard and took out more red cushions.

"If I may have your attention, I will continue Klaus's eloquent explanation," Sebastian offered seriously.

"Go ahead," Mrs. Sparling replied.

Sebastian cleared his throat before speaking.

"As the Director explained, the world, as you currently know it, is not really what you think it is. There is another society, ours, which lives mixed in with common people. This society, although secret, influences the way things happen in the world. It determines…"

Sebastian stopped mid-sentence. He turned to look at the way the leopard climbed effortlessly and silently onto the cushion Mrs. Sparling had set out for him. His body was supple and muscular. He sat still and tall next to Ankona.

"As I was saying," Sebastian resumed, somewhat offended by the cheek of the leopard and the permissiveness of his colleague. "Our society is organized by an international organization of immense power. The Council of Privileges is our governing body and is the seventh body of the United Nations. It oversees the regulation and control of the privileges."

Even though Nahuel knew Sebastian was answering many of his questions, his attention was divided. He couldn't take his eyes off the leopard. It looked so majestic and vigilant. What was it doing there?

Sebastian took a few steps forward and placed himself in the center of the room. He said, "Regarding the program, we choose a new group of young people every three years to educate and train in the use of the Privileges. The program will last three years. Each year, your skills will be put to the test and you must increase your knowledge. You will compete against each other and against yourselves in order to advance, first within the Educational Program and then within the Council of Privileges.

"This first year, you will have some classes all together and some separately depending on your privilege. In each class you will learn about your particular privilege and about your classmates'. We will teach you to recognize your potential and also your limits. That's why you also need to know our history," Sebastian stated and took a deep breath.

"And what are they waiting for to tell us each our privilege?" Isaline murmured to Nahuel, unable to contain her anxiety.

He turned to look at her, but Sebastian went on before she could say more.

"You must understand that of all the young people possessing privileges in the world, the trackers have chosen those who they perceive to be the best – you are the best. They have searched the entire planet and gone to a great deal of trouble to bring you here. You represent a vital part of the privileged society."

"Are there others like us?" Tristan asked loudly.

"Of course. There are many who possess privileges and don't know it," Sebastian replied. "And there are also those who were born into a family of Privilege and have been using their skills for as long as they can remember. Some of them will join our group and the Educational Program next year."

This society was larger than Nahuel had imagined at first. The fact it was housed at the United Nations was proof. All the same, he couldn't stop wondering how the trackers managed to find someone in the farthest corners of the globe.

Nahuel watched Ankona closely. His eyes were as dark as his skin. He didn't smile, but he didn't seem angry or bored. His expression was discreet and reserved.

According to what Sebastian was explaining, Ankona had tracked him down to Ushuaia, "the end of the world" Did that mean that his grandfather hadn't actually applied for him? Nahuel felt a stab in the stomach.

"I should tell you," Mrs. Sparling interrupted, standing up. "We sincerely hope you are all up to the challenges we will present you with. The Council of Privileges is the most powerful and complex in the world. You must make an extreme effort to meet our minimum levels of expectations in order to continue on to advanced study in the next phase."

She pursed her lips into a thin line and said, "You need to know that our time is limited. We will not tolerate short-lived success nor continued failure."

"That will be all. Ankona, you may begin the procedure," Sebastian said.

"With your permission, Mrs. Sparling," Ankona asked.

"If there's no other way," she replied and stepped back from her desk.

"Karma," he said, looking at the leopard.

The feline crouched, low on the cushion and then pounced onto Mrs. Sparling's desk, using its powerful back legs to spring and its tail to balance. It landed gracefully in the middle of the desk.

"Make a line in front of the desk," Ankona said.

The students looked at each other nervously. The leopard was now looking down on them. It's presence was powerful and its claws sharp and intimidating.

"Let's go, we don't have all day," Mrs. Sparling pressured.

"There is nothing painful about the procedure," Sebastian stated, giving them the nudge they needed.

Slowly, the students got down from their floating cushions and formed a line in front of the desk, facing the leopard. Tristan was the first, then two girls Nahuel didn't know and then it would be his turn. What was this procedure about? And why did they need a leopard?...His questions would soon be answered.

Sebastian spoke, "I can't stress enough how important it is that this all remain a secret. It is a matter of safety for everyone. It is vital that you understand that everything we speak of today must remain confidential.

"All of us who work for the Council of Privileges or its partners organizations share a core value of extreme and unwavering privacy and loyalty and we expect the same from you."

Everyone in the sub-4th floor of the United Nations knew the importance of keeping their secret hidden from the rest of humanity, as well as the need to prevent any type of leaks which could give away what was really going on in that mysterious basement of the UN.

Ankona showed Tristan how to stand and once he was turned to the side, he told them all, "There is a kind of tick known as the icymea which only lives on the backs of clouded leopards and which only this kind of leopards can control. Karma will give the order and then these ticks will attach to your skin. This will let us know if any of you ever reveal the existence of the Council of Privileges."

It was almost unnoticeable, but Nahuel knew it had happened when he saw Tristan wince in pain.

It was only when the girl in front of him was in position that Nahuel could see the tick. It was a tiny insect, no bigger than a freckle. It jumped from Karma's back and attached to the skin behind her ear.

As soon as it was in place, the tick changed color, turning slightly yellow. No one would ever notice it was there if they hadn't been told beforehand.

"This type of tick can detect the *cym* enzyme in your blood," Ankona explained. "That is why they change color according to the privilege each person possesses. Blue is for the CymMens, red for the CymAnis, and yellow for the CymTers."

It was Nahuel's turn. His pulse began racing against his will. The leopard was just inches from his face. His whiskers were long and white and he could see the black spots got smaller the closer they got to his nose.

Before turning to the side, Nahuel felt the urge to stroke the leopard and he raised his hand, without thinking. Then, to everyone's surprise, Karma raised up and placed its front paws on his shoulders. He could feel the weight of the claws pressing on his skin. Then, suddenly the leopard started licking his brown wavy hair, as it would have with another large cat. Nahuel felt the rough tongue slide from his neck upward.

He was petrified. He didn't dare to move, let alone push the cat off him.

"Easy, Karma," Ankona said and Karma returned to her seat and her previous poise.

Nahuel composed himself. That was stupid. It could have turned out very differently, with Karma's enormous fangs on his skin.

He turned to the side, his heart beating a thousand miles an hour.

He waited.

He felt a pinch behind his right ear, like a wasp had stung him. The pain lasted only a second. He realized the icymea tick served the same purpose as a microchip under his skin.

"It is *rouge*," Isaline murmured behind him.

Nahuel could have guessed as much.

Next it was her turn, then Emre's.

"Again, I can't stress enough the confidentiality of the information that has been shared with you," Sebastian emphasized, pacing from side to side. "The Council of Privileges goes to great pains to maintain its secrecy, even going to the trouble of mass plans of disinformation to alter public knowledge.

"This is why I must reiterate the importance and necessity of this procedure."

Once the procedure was finished and all the students were once again seated at their desks, Ankona notified them, "Don't try to tear out the tick. It's impossible. If you talk too much, the tick will secrete a toxin which will immediately show on you."

"That is all for today. Now Mrs. Sparling will hand out your timetables and the supplies you will need. We will begin on Monday morning," Sebastian concluded, wrapping things up.

Mrs. Sparling opened her cupboard again and took out a stack of papers and laid them on her desk. In the blink of an eye, the stack disappeared from her desk and Nahuel had his timetable before him on his desk. The entire movement of papers around the room had been imperceptible.

"Hey."

Nahuel turned and looked upwards.

"Let's change places," a girl standing by his seat said.

They were in the van going back to Mrs. Penington's house.

The atmosphere was lively and loud. Most of the students were in a state of exaltation. They wondered what the classes would be like and what they would be capable of doing. Several hypotheses about their new abilities were being shared.

"Benjamin, which privilege are you?" Tristan wanted to know.

"I'm CymMens," the seventeen-year-old boy answered while he combed his golden hair with his hand.

"Then, maybe you can tell us if it is true."

"What are you taking about?"

"That the CymMens can fly."

"On a broomstick, for sure" Benjamin answered with an impish smile.

"Can we, the CymAnis, transform ourselves into animals?" an Israeli boy asked.

"Only when there's full moon."

"You are teasing us," Isaline said while rolling up her eyes.

"Don't be mad, darling" Benjamin said while taking the phone from his pocket and raising it to his ear. "You will have to wait till Monday for the professors to answer all your questions."

Nahuel never thought he would want a weekend to end so quickly.

All his life he had been sure that certain things that had happened to him had just been coincidences, but the information he had received that day transformed all those moments into proof. He had privileges and this news changed everything.

CHAPTER 7

That night, just as the humid heat became unbearable, rain began pouring down. The storm grew more violent near dawn and water beat against the huge picture windows in the living room at the students' residence.

Nahuel awoke upset. He'd had a troubling dream. His grandfather was trapped in the basement and he wasn't there to help him out. They needed to have a conversation. He turned over in bed, but couldn't get back to sleep. He would call his grandfather as soon as he could find the right moment. He glanced at the clock on his desk and realized it would be morning soon. He decided to go downstairs to the kitchen to get some water, and try to clear his head.

The Japanese masks on the wall in the dining room were spooky in the dim light. He turned on the kitchen lights. He poured himself a tall glass of ice-cold water and gulped it down. He went to the window to watch the sky rumbling, and the lightening lit up Mrs. Penington's garden.

He turned off the kitchen lights and went back toward the dining room. But he stopped in his tracks just before crossing the threshold, turned halfway back toward the kitchen, he shook his head and headed for the stairs. He convinced himself he would not get carried away by Mrs Penington's rapidly growing vegetables in the garden. If he did, he would never get back to sleep.

He got back to his room. No matter how hard he tried, he couldn't get back to sleep. Since he arrived to New York, he had been having a hard time to get to sleep. The hustle and bustle of a big city felt amplified in his ears.

He looked at the desk. The two paper bags they had given him and Emre the day before were there, with the supplies for the Educational Program inside. He grabbed the one with his name on it and took it back to his bed. It was starting to get light outside and his roommate was sleeping like a log.

He dumped the bag on his bedspread and some packets wrapped in clear paper spilled out. The largest fell on his knee and by the weight of it, he guessed it must be the books. He stuck his hand in the bag to see if anything was left and found a piece of paper.

NAHUEL BLEST

The Council of Privileges of the United Nations has provided you with the following supplies to be used in the Educational Program for the Learning and Proper Use of the Privileges.

-*Calendula, Ten Thousand-Year Bookstore*: introductory texts for beginning CymAnis.

-*Rubirio and Brothers, Exclusive Clothiers*: a tailor-made caterpillar skin vest.

-*The Bowl Path:* A Tibetan singing bowl and seven strikers, a magnifying glass, a pair of tweezers, a pair of gloves.

-*The Store of Beasts:* A steel a-bula, a jar of termites, a first rate talesmas pouch.

Hedge Garden
65 Transverse Street
Entrance on The Carousel
Central Park
New York, NY 10023
United States

What the hell?! He could never have imagined a list of school supplies like the one he had just read.

He was eager to learn what an a-bula was and to see if the termites were alive or not. He opened one of the packages. Inside was a black vest with gold edging like the one Sebastian had been wearing the day before. He pushed aside the heaviest package and opened the next, which was more like a box.

Inside there was a jar, a small habitat for live termites...They looked a little too lively. As he raised the jar to his eyes, he watched as two of them attacked a smaller one. In the wrapping, he found instructions for how to feed them. They had to be given a piece of wet wood every day. In the box was a small bag with the bits of wood.

He unscrewed the lid and dropped a piece of wood inside. The termites jumped on the food, leaving their victim in peace.

He also found something that looked like a necklace. It was a thick, gray metal chain, with a hollow ball hanging from it, that could be opened up and things stored inside it - like a round locket. The last thing he found in the box was a pouch with small objects which ranged from a small, dried up insect to an arrowhead.

Wait a minute, something's missing.

The package that should have had the Tibetan singing bowl, the gloves, the magnifying glass and the tweezers wasn't there.

"Dammit," he muttered, remembering how he had set the bag down in the empty seat next to him on the van on the way home from the United Nations yesterday afternoon. Then, two of his classmates that were looking for seats together asked him to change seats, so he got up and sat next to Emre. In the process, he dropped his bag, dumping everything on the floor of the van.

That last package must have got left behind. Just my luck for being a gentleman.

He pushed everything aside on his bed and went to the desk to see what was in Emre's bag. He had four packages. Without a doubt, Nahuel was missing one.

He had to figure out what to do now. He couldn't start classes with only half of the supplies, and he didn't dare tell Mrs. Sparling. That would be like sentencing himself to utter failure before the program had even started.

Just as his stomach grumbled loudly and he concluded it was a reasonable time to get out of bed, he decided to go downstairs for breakfast. Their hostess had told them they could open the cupboards when they liked and help themselves to what looked good.

Downstairs, he ran into Mrs. Penington, sporting orange rubber gloves as she washed up some dishes from the night before. His French classmate was sitting alone at the table. Isaline had woken up very early, the result of her own anxiety and her infallible alarm clock.

"Another early rise," Mrs. Penington said. "Nerves not letting you sleep, Nahuel? You'll soon get used to the privileges." She turned and addressed both of them. "Have you two met?" And before they could reply to any of her questions, she had introduced them.

Nahuel sat down across from Isaline and for a moment, he felt like her dark eyes were scanning him. He knew that his hair was always a mess in the morning.

"Are you going to have breakfast? I haven't had a chance to make the honey cakes you like so much, Nahuel, but I can heat up some water for tea or coffee and there are chocolate cookies and fruit. Don't forget that there are always dried fruits on the counter."

And she headed into the kitchen to get everything.

Nahuel realized that Mrs. Penington was the kind of person who asked questions without needing to hear the answers. And he had no idea on earth why she thought honey cakes were his favorite.

"Before I forget, Isaline," Mrs. Penington said, as she came back from the kitchen with two tea cups and a teapot, "I don't think I can do anything about your request. I know you had been promised a single room, but in the end, we have more students than expected. I must plan for more residents, although I don't think your roommate will eat much. Have you seen how tiny she is?"

"Yes, it's good. Don't worry," Isaline replied quickly, pouring herself some tea. She had planned on getting Mrs. Penington on her own to talk to her in private about her roommate situation.

Mrs. Penington smiled at her and then grabbed a large green umbrella that was hanging on the kitchen wall. She opened the glass door that led to the garden and went out. A gust of fresh air rushed into the dining room and the sound of the rain grew louder for a moment. Nahuel watched her as she pulled some herbs from the garden.

When she came back in, she asked:

"Have you thought of going to see some of the city, Nahuel? I've already explained to Isaline how to get to some of the best places to visit on a rainy day."

"Yes, I had thought of going out today," Nahuel replied as soon as Mrs. Penington paused for breath. Then he took a chocolate cookie from the tray. These were in fact his favorite and their hostess made delicious ones.

"If you would go together, I would feel so relieved, you know? Isaline has been to New York before and has all the subway stops marked on her map," Mrs. Penington explained.

"Maybe later," Nahuel said, knowing deep in his guts that he preferred to go alone. It wasn't that he disliked Isaline or anything like that, it was just that he was used to being alone and he knew how to be on his own.

"I was thinking of going now," Isaline said.

The more he thought about it, Nahuel realized he needed Isaline's map. He had no idea how to get to Central Park. He would go with her. It would also be a good chance to be friendly. After all, that was one of the few things his grandfather had asked him to do before he left.

Nahuel figured he better end his breakfast as he ate one more chocolate cookie and felt they would soon come popping out of his eyes, he had eaten so many.

"OK, Isaline, lead the way."

Isaline, who had finished breakfast several minutes ago, stood up and grabbed her blue raincoat and her beige leather bag.

"You won't bring a coat?" she asked. "It is colder with the rain."

"I only feel cold when the temperature drops below 40 degrees," he replied simply.

"Very well. So, let's go," Isaline said, saying goodbye to Mrs. Penington before leaving.

"See you when you get back!" she said.

Nahuel had to buy an umbrella from a street vendor for a dollar. The entrance to the subway was muddy after the downpour and he had to watch his step. Inside, the musty smell was sharp. It reminded Nahuel of the strong smell wafting from his tennis shoes the day before. He didn't even want to think about what they would smell like tonight.

The subway was almost deserted. There was open space everywhere - something pretty uncommon on NYC public transportation.

"We can be at the Museum of Natural History in only 18 minutes," Isaline told him, as she had calculated with precision the exact time and way to arrive at their destination. Her map was marked with pencil lines showing the routes they could take.

"Actually, I'd rather go to Central Park," Nahuel told her.

"On a rainy day? No, no, no. Not a good idea," Isaline objected.

"You don't understand. I need to go there. Will you show me how to get there?"

"Why? Why do you *need* to go there?" Isaline wanted to know.

"Because there is a store there…that I have to go to."

"What store?"

Nahuel debated with himself whether or not to tell her that he had lost some of his school supplies. But she probably wouldn't help him get there unless he answered her questions.

"*The Bowl Path*," he replied, hoping that would appease her.

"One of the stores where they bought our materials?" Isaline asked, quite surprised.

"Yes," he replied, hoping the questions would end.

"And why do you want to go there?"

She wouldn't stop until he told her.

"Because I lost one of the packages of supplies they gave us. I need all the things from that store," he replied quietly.

"You lost them *already*?" she asked, unable to believe it.

"Yes," Nahuel stammered, avoiding the disapproving look of the girl and fixing his eyes instead on a man who had just got on the subway. He had a violin on his shoulder and a beret that he used to gather a few coins after he played.

"Alright, I'll go with you," Isaline decided.

Nahuel hadn't expected her to say that.

"I need a new book and there is a book store there," she explained. "And also, I am very curious to see where they get the supplies they have given us."

"Maybe the termites came from a vet," Nahuel guessed.

"What? Termites? I was not given termites. Do you think I should buy some?" Isaline asked, starting to worry.

"Did your list say, "a jar of termites"?" Nahuel asked.

"Of course it did not."

"Then I don't think you need any," he replied. "Don't forget, we are in different groups based on our privileges."

"True," she agreed. "What I can't figure out is what the singing bowl is for."

"I just hope they don't make us eat out of it," Nahuel said.

"Of course not. Tibetans use it to balance the frequency of the human body, for example to deal with stress," Isaline told him. She had clearly been thinking about it for a while.

"Ah," Nahuel responded mutely, handing her the paper with the store's address on it.

Isaline tucked a strand of dark hair behind her ear and traced a new line with her pencil on the map. They had to change trains a few stops later and in fifteen minutes they arrived at their stop. The rest of the way they would walk.

They hadn't walked more than a hundred yards when a gust of wind turned Nahuel's umbrella inside out. He couldn't expect more from something so cheap. He imagined he must look pretty ridiculous trying to stay dry under the broken umbrella because Isaline pointed out every garbage can they passed as soon as she saw him, hoping he would make the wise decision to throw it away.

They made their way into Central Park. They walked by a pretty stone bridge, stretching across a pond. Nahuel heard the cooing of pigeons, looked up and saw a flock of black pigeons, brave enough to fly with this weather. They followed Isaline's directions until they reached 65th street, which cut through the width of the park.

"I don't understand," she blurted out as she stopped.

"What is it?" Nahuel asked.

"It should be here."

But where Isaline was pointing there was nothing more than the entrance to the classic park Carousel. There were no shops and no Hedge Garden.

The Carousel was a round structure that looked like a circus tent, except that it was made of bricks and cement. A plaque explained that it was built in 1871.

"Let me read the paper I gave you," Nahuel asked. He reread the address and said, "It must be here, somewhere. I'm going to see what's behind the Carousel."

But on the other side, there was no shop, just well-cut grass. Nahuel was getting worried. If the address on the paper was wrong, he would never find the Hedge Garden and he would have no choice but to show up on Monday with no supplies.

"The Carousel is open. Let's try inside." Isaline suggested as Nahuel came back around to the front.

"Ok," he said and followed her.

Inside, the Carousel was stopped. It was early morning and there were no parents and kids who wanted a ride. The wooden and metal horses were well taken care of. The paint was bright and bold.

Nahuel could see a clown statue standing against the painted brick walls. He had never liked circuses or clowns.

"There is the operator. We should ask him," Isaline said.

He was a rough looking guy, with a shaved head and grumpy face. Nahuel imagined he couldn't be good for business, as the kids might be afraid of him.

"Maybe you can help us," Isaline said to him. "We are looking for the Hedge Garden."

"Who are you?" he asked.

"We are with the United Nations,"

"We have this," Nahuel added, handing him the paper showing the address.

The man looked at it and looked at Nahuel.

"Is this your name?" he asked, pointing at the top of the paper.

"Yes, it is," Nahuel replied.

The man stepped back a bit, and turned to each side, like he was looking for something, or checking to make sure no one was there. Then he said, "Follow me."

They followed him toward the back of the building. There was a door that said, "Do Not Enter". The operator took a key from his pocket and used it to open the door. It appeared to be a small storage closet for cleaning supplies. Just big enough for some brooms and buckets.

Nahuel and Isaline looked at each other. Nahuel thought the man must be looking for an umbrella before taking them to the Hedge Garden.

Instead, the man flicked a light switch and the floor, which had appeared to be cement, revealed its true identity. It was opaque crystal. There was a whistling sound and it opened, revealing a crystal staircase. It was a high-tech entrance to an underground tunnel.

Nahuel saw words etched into the first step: *Hedge Garden – 900 feet.*

He should have known. The Hedge Garden, like the sub-4th floor of the United Nations, was underground. All the same, he thought this wasn't the main entrance, but rather the one for maintenance. Either way, as long as it got him to *The Bowl Path*, they would take it.

The operator invited them to enter with a slight nod of his head. Nahuel took the first step, but Isaline looked unsure and stayed glued to the door frame.

The man waited a few seconds and then said roughly, "Are you staying or going?"

"We're going," Nahuel said, taking Isaline by the arm.

They descended a few steps.

"Just go all straight," the man said.

Then they heard the whistling sound and the crystal floor closed above their heads, sealing them inside.

"If we get to the end and don't find what we're looking for, we come back this same way," Nahuel said. "I saw a switch at the foot of the stairs which must be the way to open the floor."

The temperature was comfortable and the tunnel was glowed with a blue sheen. The floors were polished and the lights stretching before them were reflected in it. The ceiling was held up by some type of postmodern column that reminded Nahuel of the bottom of the ocean.

They walked on in silence, entertained by the advertisements projected onto the walls around them. Isaline was especially interested in one that showed the Hedge Garden in Beijing. It was a set of buildings built entirely out of bamboo and when Nahuel took a closer look, a digital panda poked its head through the stalks, inviting him to visit.

"The Hedge Garden is an international chain of shopping centers," Isaline commented, pleased with the information.

When, halfway, they saw on the right some deep stairs, they understood the directions that the man had given to them.

They continued straight, until they came to the end of the tunnel. A set of hermetically sealed stainless-steel doors separated them from the Hedge Garden. On each door there was a sensor, where the visitor had to place their hand to be allowed to enter.

"Is this the normal level of security for a shopping center?" Nahuel asked, since he had only ever visited one in his whole life.

"Not really, no," Isaline replied. "I think it is clear that this place is only for the privilege people," she noted.

Nahuel took a step forward.

As he placed his right hand on the left door, Isaline placed hers on the right side. Both doors lit up. Nahuel's door was bright red and Isaline's, a deep blue. Nahuel's stomach turned, red usually meant access denied. But then he remembered that his tick had turned red the moment it touched his skin.

Both doors announced that they should not remove their hands until notified. Three seconds later, Nahuel had a red circle stamped on his hand and Isaline had the same, but hers was blue.

Really cool, Nahuel thought.

With a slight hum, both doors opened, letting them pass.

As soon as they were inside, Isaline looked up and shook her head in disbelief.

"Definitely not what I expected," she said.

CHAPTER 8

Nahuel strained his eyes to take it all in. He wasn't quite sure what he was seeing, but was certain he had never seen anything like it before.

The most amazing thing about the Hedge Garden was that it was built under the lake in Central Park. It felt like you were outside, because the ceiling was bright blue and the light from above came through the water.

Nahuel was sure the ceiling of the garden must be made of some translucent crystal separating it from the lake, but no matter how hard he tried, he couldn't see a reflection, or sheen, or anything that revealed the boundary between the lake and the space they moved in. It looked like just the water was floating above their heads.

He could even see raindrops beating against the surface of the still lake. He also noticed the orange webbed feet of a duck enjoying a swim in the rain.

A delicate stream of water fell straight from the lake into an impressive marble fountain in the center of the Hedge Garden. It was a round white fountain, with this single stream of water.

The Hedge Garden lived up to its name. It was a large, green, beautiful garden. Incredibly realistic topiary surrounded the fountain, there were images of apparently very important people and large exotic animals.

All around them were different kinds of shops. Nahuel found what he was looking for, *The Bowl Path*, on the other side of a leafy saber tooth tiger.

Nahuel was just as shocked as he was impressed.

"How is it possible that no one in the park notices this is down here?"

"The only thing I know is that I want the architects who built this to build my future house," Isaline said, unable to take her eyes off the water ceiling.

Nahuel looked at Isaline, in disbelief.

"Look, there is *Calendula*," she exclaimed, pointing to a shop on her left. Without a word, she walked off toward it.

Nahuel would have preferred to go directly to *The Bowl Path* but he followed her anyway. She had already followed him this far.

On the way to *Calendula,* they passed by a cafe. There were two men sitting outside at a table having breakfast. The smell of the exquisite plate stirred Nahuel's memory, and even though he couldn't place what he was remembering, he felt moved.

When they were in the door, Nahuel read the enormous sign that said: *Calendula, Ten Thousand-Year Bookstore.* It was decorated with orange flowers on both sides.

Once they entered the store, they were enveloped in its smell. Nahuel thought the name was very appropriate as it seemed the store hadn't been aired out in ten thousand years.

No one greeted them. There were no windows and the only light in the room was from some lamps on side tables. Thousands of books were piled everywhere. The ceiling was high and the walls were completely covered with books. There were books piled on the floor, others on chairs, there were books on the front counter and even books inside an empty cage.

"Ah-choo!" Isaline sneezed.

A cat with a brown tail had jumped from a shelf, brushed against Isaline's blouse and settled itself on the only chair without books on it. From its perch, it looked at them with disdain.

"This smell?" Isaline asked, covering her nose with her sleeve. "It is so horrible."

Nahuel went toward the front counter. His only goal was to get out of there as fast as possible. The smell was driving him crazy. On the counter there was a vase full of wilted calendula which added to the rank smell in the room. A slightly rusty bell hung from a lamp. Nahuel rang it and it clanged feebly and strangely.

"What are you looking for?" A small man with a crooked beard asked in an annoyed voice, appearing from out of nowhere behind the counter.

"Oh! Hello!" Nahuel said.

"I was looking for…," Isaline started to say.

"It's that way," the man interrupted her and pointed down the row to his right. His hand was covered with grease.

"But, I have not told you what I am looking for…"

"It's that way," the man insisted, his eyes fixed on the blue circle Isaline had stamped on her hand.

"I want a novel…" Isaline tried again.

"Young CymMen woman, it's that way," he pointed again to the right and disappeared again behind the counter. Then they heard the sounds of a hammer hitting metal.

"Hmph, what does that have anything to do with it?" she grumbled and stomped down the row to the right.

Nahuel watched as Isaline started to get frustrated, took a book off the shelf titled "Historical Novels," took a deep breath and approached the counter again.

"Do you have some novel similar to this one?" Isaline asked, showing him the book in her hand.

"The books you see are the books I have, so look for yourself," the man muttered, barely poking his head over the counter.

Isaline sighed, read the back of the book again and decided that even though she didn't like the shopkeeper, it was worth it to take the book.

The man wiped his hands on his overalls, put the book in a bag and took the money Isaline handed him.

"That's it," the man stated, taking a last look at Isaline's right hand. The blue circle was still showing. Turning toward Nahuel he added, "you're young and don't' know this yet, but the CymMens are greedy and back-stabbing people."

Nahuel stuttered.

Isaline shot a look of disgust at the man, his overalls, his dirty hair and his crooked beard.

"You are a cretin! And throw those flowers in the garbage once and for all," she blurted out, at a loss for words for the insult she could feel but not fully understand.

"I think we should go," Nahuel said, pushing Isaline out the door.

But once they were outside, he realized she wasn't going to forget about it that quickly.

"What's that guy's problem?!" she yelled indignantly.

"I don't know. All I do know is that we can't ever go back to that place," Nahuel replied.

"I don't know, it seems like he liked you very much," she retorted. "You think he heard me criticize his bookstore while he was behind the counter?"

"I don't know why you are worrying about it now. When you had him in front of you, you made sure he knew exactly how you felt," Nahuel said, trying to put an end to the conversation. He tried to distract her and added, "Let's go the *The Bowl Path* now."

"Fine," she accepted reluctantly.

They walked in front of shops of all kinds. Isaline dawdled in a shop full of globes, with maps covering the walls. There were maps of all sizes and of every country. They saw globes of only the oceans and their islands; from far away they appeared to be simple blue balls. But as you got closer, you could see how the ocean currents moved and even hear the sound of waves.

They walked past a refined and much more well cared for shop than *Calendula*. It was called *Rubirio and Brothers, Exclusive Clothiers*. Their speciality were vests.

Nahuel and Isaline stopped in front of the store window to watch how one of the mannequins undressed itself. It took off a vest made of red fox fur and put on another made of sea-green silk.

Nahuel wondered which privilege would make the mannequins move that way.

A few feet away was *The Bowl Path*. There was a sign over the door showing a chubby, smiling woman standing next to a man with thick glasses pointing the way into the store. Above their heads was written *"With you in adventure since 14853".*

Inside, the shop was paneled with wood and you could buy all the gear for any expedition according to the climate and ecosystem. On one wall there were lightweight backpacks, shovels, climbing ropes, sleeping bags, and waterproof tents.

There were display cases throughout the shop showing artifacts from famous expeditions. There were antlers, medals, antique compasses, relics, fossilized animal tracks and specimens in amber. There were also explorer's journals on display and yellowing newspaper clippings of the most amazing stories.

A cat with gills caught Nahuel's attention. As he got closer, he read it was in a section dedicated to the lost city of Atlantis. Nahuel had always liked the story of Atlantis. In the same section there were maps and drawings and a well-preserved column from Poseidon's temple.

Discovered by Z. Klaus, 14958

"Do you think that Z. Klaus is the same Klaus that we know? The Director of the Council of Privileges," Isaline asked.

Nahuel shrugged his shoulders, and, instead, he said "Have you noticed the dates? In the sign at the entrance and the one here," he said pointing to the registration.

"Yes, it seems as if they use their own calendar and it's really old."

The woman tending the shop was showing a man some protective glasses that blocked out both the sun and sandstorms. The man, a scientist, had won a research grant to study how CymAnis adapt to extreme climates in order to develop the formula for a hydrating serum.

"How can I help you?" She asked them as soon as she finished with the scientist. She was wearing ruby red gloves. They matched her lipstick perfectly, but her lips didn't offer the smile featured on the sign outside the store.

Nahuel and Isaline made their way to the counter.

"I need these supplies," Nahuel said, showing her the paper from the United Nations.

"I didn't think we had forgotten any packages. Wait here. I'll fix one now," she said walking to the back of the shop. She moved behind a wood and glass wall.

"I don't have a reflection in this mirror," Nahuel noted, as he leaned in close to a mirror on display on the counter. The strange thing was that it reflected all the things that were behind him.

"Don't mess with me. My blood is blue," Isaline replied.

Nahuel looked at her strangely.

Isaline rolled her eyes and told him, "Everyone knows that vampires have no reflection and they drink blood…. *red* blood."

Nahuel was starting to like Isaline. She was endearingly odd.

"Here are your things," the woman's voice interrupted. She placed a box on the counter, opened it and showed them what was inside. "Here is the singing bowl and the seven strikers."

The bowl was bronze colored and made from seven different metals: gold, silver, mercury, copper, iron, tin and lead. The strikers were made from wood of trees that had died of natural causes.

"And here are your gloves, the tweezers, and the magnifying glass," the woman said, showing him the contents of a black suede pouch. The name *"Frederick Schliemann"* was embroidered on the front. "He was a very important archaeologist," she explained.

Nahuel tried on one of the thin leather gloves and it felt like it molded perfectly onto his skin. After a few seconds he couldn't even tell he was wearing it.

"That's everything. I'll charge it to the United Nations account," said the woman, returning to the back of the shop.

Nahuel felt a bit embarrassed, but at the same time relieved. He wasn't sure if the money he had would have covered the cost of everything.

Once outside *The Bowl Path*, they saw rays of light streaming through the lake water, the sky above the park having cleared momentarily.

Nahuel thought he saw a flash of red. He went to the fountain in the center of the garden and took a close look at the stream of water falling from the lake. He noticed that the fountain was home to some small fish and that every once in a while, one of them slipped through the hole in the ceiling.

They left by way of the same door they had entered through. As soon as they were on the other side of the hermetic doors, the circles on their hands disappeared. Nahuel had been right, there was a switch next to the stairs that let them back up to the surface.

Once they were outside the carrousel, they decided to return to the student residence for lunch and leave the visit to the Natural Science Museum for another day. When they crossed over the lake on the stone bridge, Nahuel peered over the edge. He wanted to see if he could make out any sign of the Hedge Garden hidden below. But all he could see was the solitary duck swimming by.

A few steps later, they ran into Benjamin. He was standing over a flower pot full of water. Only one sad, half-drowned daisy poked out, her sisters having been buried in the rain water.

The rain had finally stopped for a while.

"Mrs. Pennington would help you," Benjamin told the daisies, his hands in his pockets.

Nahuel stopped by his side to take a look at the victims and the sole survivor.

"Looks a little too late for help," he said.

"I wouldn't be so sure. Mrs. Penington is full of surprises, one of the best CymTers I've ever met" Benjamin replied. His teeth glowed in the frame of his perfect smile, against his tan skin.

He turned to look at Isaline and said, "Have you had a nice day, love?"

"My name is Isaline," she huffed, offended.

"It really doesn't matter. Most likely I will forget it shortly," he replied.

He took one hand from his pocket. Nahuel saw he was wearing black gloves. He raised a hand toward Isaline's hair. She stepped back instinctively.

"Don't' be scared, love. You have something in your hair."

He got closer and one by one, picked some leaves from her hair. When he finished, he looked at Nahuel and said, "You shouldn't let her roll around out there."

Nahuel saw Isaline blush, clench her teeth and try to mutter something.

"What are you doing here?" Benjamin asked. "It's not the best day for a romantic walk in the park."

"It's nothing like that," Isaline said, with a furrowed brow while Nahuel shook his head until it almost fell off his neck.

"I had to go to the Hedge Garden," Nahuel explained.

"And I have gone with him to go to the bookstore," Isaline added.

"Gone where?"

"To the Hedge Garden, under the lake," Nahuel repeated, glancing at the pool of water.

Benjamin looked at them with surprise and ran his fingers through his silky hair.

"Ok guys, I'll see you back at the residence for lunch," he said, taking his leave as he ripped the last leaf he had taken from Isaline's hair into tiny pieces.

"Aren't you coming with us on the subway?" Nahuel asked, checking his watch.

"Actually…I prefer to walk. I could use a bit of…fresh air now that it's stopped raining," he said.

They watched him walk away calmly.

"I can't believe I had something stuck in my hair and you didn't tell me!" Isaline scolded as soon as she was sure Benjamin was out of earshot.

"I just hadn't noticed," Nahuel responded, shrugging his shoulders.

During the short walk to the subway, Isaline continued griping about how arrogant and full of himself Benjamin was, but Nahuel wasn't paying much attention to what she was saying. He was busy putting on and taking off one of his new gloves.

At the bottom of the subway stairs, they came across one of their classmates sitting alone in front of a large subway map. Even though she was staring hard at it, her mind seemed to be elsewhere. On her rain-spattered lap was a paper bag full of sunflower seeds that she picked at now and then.

Her name was Aremi and she was Isaline's roommate.

"It's amazing what humans can build underground. Don't you think?" she asked, as they got close to her.

"Um...yes," Nahuel hesitated.

Up close, he could see tiny freckles on her cheeks, blending in with her skin. She had long blonde wavy hair that turned reddish in the sun.

Aremi was pretty, in a girl-next-door way.

"Are you waiting for someone?" Nahuel asked, looking around.

"Just the train, to go back to the residence," Aremi replied.

"Do you even know which one to take?" Isaline asked.

"Not really, no." Aremi replied simply.

She didn't seem at all worried about being lost in a large, unknown city.

"Where are you from?" Nahuel asked.

"From Helapad. In Australia."

"Ahh," he doubted.

"Don't worry. No one's ever heard of it," she added. "It's in the desert. A tiny town in the west. It's so small, I can ride through the whole town on my bike and the only way to get there is on the small plane that brings the mail once a month."

Nahuel thought New York must be the exact opposite of her town. And like him, who also came from a small town, Aremi must feel a bit lost.

"You can come with us, if you want," Nahuel offered.

The three sat together, but didn't talk much. Isaline let them know when it was time to get off and change trains, while Aremi offered to share her seeds with them. No one accepted.

The first thing Nahuel saw when he walked into the residence was the basement door opened and Benjamin finishing his lunch. There were only crumbs and a leaf of lettuce on his plate. He was sitting in the dining room with a girl with olive skin. She wore her hair in a ponytail.

"Would you like me to fix some coffee," the girl asked, standing and heading into the kitchen.

"What I would like is to be on my way to Dublin. It's really annoying knowing that I'm going to miss all the action. How do they expect the interns to learn if they never let us join the fun?"

"All I know is that acting like a victim doesn't suit you."

Benjamin bestowed one of his already famous smiles on her and said, "A bit of coffee would be fine."

The girl moved easily through the house, like Benjamin, leading Nahuel to think she wasn't new there either.

"You're late for the broccoli quiche," Benjamin said as soon as he noticed they had arrived.

Nahuel saw that the quiche dish was indeed empty and the bread bowl was almost bare. The spinach quiche was half-gone and the corn one had only three pieces left. Benjamin had torn through lunch like a hurricane.

"How did you do it?" Isaline asked, squinting her eyes.

"How did I do what?" he fired back.

"How did you do to arrive before us?" she insisted.

"Walking…" he replied coolly.

"Impossible."

Nahuel wasn't so sure either. Central Park was several miles away from the residence and it was crazy to think someone could walk there so fast.

"Some people are faster than others," he said insolently.

"I'm not going to argue with you, it would be a waste of time," Isaline stated firmly and headed to her room without looking back.

Nahuel went up behind her. He wanted to leave his package from *The Bowl Path* in his room before anyone noticed it.

He entered the room. There was no sign of Emre. He opened his backpack and before putting the package away, took out a postcard his grandfather had given him with the watch he now wore around his wrist.

The picture was of a small rocky island with a white and red lighthouse. Behind it, tall snow-covered mountains rose up. It was a typical Ushuaia scene. He turned it over and read the message written in his grandfather's tidy and elegant handwriting:

So you don't forget where you came from and what makes you feel good.
When your instincts want to control you, master them.
Keep in mind that in your life, nothing is random.
You have the power to choose your way.

With much love,
Your grandfather.

Ps: Apollo and Atila will be a little sad that you're leaving, but I will give them extra food to cheer them up.

Nahuel thought of his two Siberian huskies standing guard by his room, waiting to go for a walk, like they did every Saturday. He put the postcard in the drawer of his bedside table, next to his passport and plane ticket. He would call his grandfather soon; he needed some answers.

And for a moment he believed it might be true that his life had direction and order.

CHAPTER 9

Even if Edgard had known at that moment that they had already found him, he wouldn't have cared. He couldn't take his eyes off the scene. It was like he was hypnotized, reliving the horror stories he had relished as a child. At the same time, his mind was seeking a rational explanation for what his eyes had revealed.

Edgard peaked out from his hiding spot and saw that the wild dogs had stopped. He had been following them since he first discovered them, running on the Sandymount beach in Dublin. They were a mix of wolf and hyena. The heavy fog and dim light of early morning made him wonder if his eyes were playing tricks on him. He thought maybe he had seen something like them once in a documentary, dragging down a boar, but how could they have arrived here from Africa?

He was watching them now from a gap between two streets. There was no doubt about it, this bordered on supernatural.

The wild dogs had stopped next to the Grand Canal in the heart of the city. Someone was waiting for them. They were human, but their hair was matching silver white, as if they were ghosts, and they dressed entirely in black. They were led by a couple. The penetrating eyes of the woman shone with a demonic force, but it didn't make her any less beautiful. The man had a shaved head, and a nasty scar spread across his scalp.

They started to move.

Edgard could make out the white heads through the dim light and fog. The minions spread out along the side of the Canal with the dogs swerving in and out among them, almost as if overseeing things.

What the hell are they doing?

The minions crouched down and placed their hands on the cold, rough ground. And then, suddenly and without warning, the ground beneath Edgard's feet began to shake.

He had never seen anything like it in his life. Edgard looked around. Nothing else seemed to be shaking. He looked back toward the Canal and the white-haired group of people.

It was gradual. At first, the vibrating ground made the loose rocks on the sidewalk knock into each other. Then, the still water in the Canal started to move, spreading out in expanding rings across the surface.

Edgard watched it all in amazement.

But then the earthquake increased to a frightening intensity and the earth growled.

I shouldn't be here. But there was no turning back.

One of the Grand Canal's walls broke. Edgard jumped out of his hiding place. He had to. The water rushed out of the Canal, wiping out everything in its path, except the perpetrators, who remained untouched by any water, except perhaps their own sweat.

"Take care of him," the woman shouted, her voice ringing out over the sound of the water.

One look from the leader to the Alpha dog was all it took.

The pack moved toward Edgard, turning their heads in perfect unison with their leader. They all fixed their threatening eyes on him. Edgard pointed at them, unthinking, as if his mind, betraying him, needed to point out the horror surrounding him.

Edgard turned around. He knew he had to run or die.

The Alpha got to him first, jumping over his shoulder, going straight for the throat. Amid a frenzy of fangs, another body was devoured.

"Hurry up. Those morons from the Council will be here any minute," the leader shouted at the minions.

The section of the Grand Canal the group was gathered around had emptied and at the bottom, they found what they were looking for. The bottom was made of tightly packed chiseled rocks. In the middle, one of them poked up a few inches higher than the others and around the edge, there was a symbol of three intertwined circles carved in the side, covered with algae and time.

"We've found the entrance," the woman said, pointing to the carved rock which led the way into a system of tunnels below.

With a slight wave of her hand, she made the stone rise in the air, and then flung it suddenly against the Canal wall, where it burst into pieces.

"Go down," the leader commanded the five men who had caused the earthquake. "Search every part of the tunnel until you find them. If you come out with your hands empty, you'll be sorry."

The men, with matching white hair, hurried into the hole that had been covered just seconds before by the large stone. Unfortunately, they returned just moments later, with their hands empty.

CHAPTER 10

When Nahuel went down to the dining room for breakfast on Monday morning, he found all his classmates were already there. Mrs. Penington, who was wearing her usual Christmas apron and smelled of fresh-baked bread, told them they shouldn't go to the UN on their own today.

As soon as he sat down, Nahuel grabbed his fork and began shoveling in some scrambled eggs.

"Look at this! Apples, come to me, come to me," Emre commanded, extending his arm and shutting his eyes tightly.

He was sitting far away from the fruit basket, at the other end of the table. After a few tries, he opened one eye, to see if his powers had worked. Then he shut them again and kept calling out, this time with even more emphasis.

When Isaline got tired of hearing his fuss, she pushed the fruit basket toward him.

When he opened his eyes, Emre shouted triumphantly, "It worked, they're closer! I'm sure of it!"

Everyone started laughing while Emre waited for the cheers and congratulations.

"As if it were so easy," Isaline chirped.

Nahuel took one look at Emre's shocked expression and nearly choked on his bacon.

Before Emre could demonstrate his "powers" again, Benjamin's friend, the girl with olive skin, walked in.

"Hi kids, my name is Victoria. Today Benjamin and I will take you to the United Nations."

Isaline whispered to Nahuel, "Kids?! *Seriously?* She is just a few years older than us."

Behind Victoria, Benjamin entered, wearing a vest just like the girl's - black with dark blue trim.

"I've been living here for more than three years and Mrs. Penington still manages to surprise me with her delicacies," Benjamin declared affectionately, biting into a warm biscuit he had grabbed, reaching over the Japanese girl's head.

As usual, he had prepared a compliment for their host. She blushed and then went into the kitchen smiling, to get more peach jam.

"Good morning, guys!" Benjamin said brightly, as he adjusted his vest. "In five minutes, we will meet at the foot of the stairs."

"And kids, don't forget to bring the supplies and tools that you were given," Victoria suggested.

Isaline left her cup of steaming coffee on the table, leaned close to Nahuel and whispered, "Obviously! Duh. *Don't forget your supplies.*"

It seemed to Nahuel that Victoria's reminder was in fact useful for some of them. With the excuse that he needed to get his vest, he quickly ran upstairs.

The boy from Israel, Damian, was crawling along the hallway looking for his necklace.

"I saw it this morning when I woke up, but I can't remember what I did with it."

"Check in the bathroom," Nahuel suggested.

"Yes, I will."

Nahuel had less than a minute to get his things together. He went into his room, dodged a pair of sneakers and grabbed his backpack. He opened it and stuffed all the packages inside.

At the foot of the stairs, he rejoined the group, but Benjamin didn't lead them out the front door. Instead, he opened the door that led to the basement. Nahuel thought that was strange, but strange things seemed to be more and more normal to him every day. He had never seen anyone enter or exit from that door.

They entered the basement. Nahuel thought it might look like any other basement, but he couldn't be sure. The basement back home was his grandfather's lair and he was rarely allowed to get in. His grandfather, who wasn't a doctor nor anything similar, had spent several sleepless nights over there trying to help Nahuel with his episodes, or at least that's what he told him. He spent hours and hours studying books that had the covers that were so worn-out that the titles couldn't even be read.

Mrs. Penington had a few boxes piled in the corner of the basement, there was a boiler and small wine cellar. Benjamin went toward the wine, lifted a bottle labeled Toscana 1908, and placed his hand in the space under the bottle.

Just then, the wall that had seemed to be solid brick turned to glass, and just like at the Carousel, the wall slid open with a whistling sound, letting them through.

It smelled like moisture, old stone, and clay. One by one, they went down worn steps, carved into stone. The staircase was narrow and steep and scary looking.

Nahuel's ears were plugged. They were much deeper than the subway.

Finally, they came to the end of the staircase.

"What is this place?" Emre wanted to know, looking around.

Nahuel's heart skipped a beat. Aremi couldn't have been more right when she said it was amazing what humans were capable of building underground.

Nahuel observed the fascinating tunnel stretching out before him. The end of it was out of sight, far ahead of them. Unlike the narrow passage they had just come down, this tunnel seems like a spacious route.

A long line of small glass carts stretched out before them.

"This place is magical!" Aremi smiled, her green eyes sparkling.

Nahuel looked up and to the sides. Small lights floated near the walls and ceiling of the chamber. They were a type of bioluminescent organism. They didn't go near the students or the carts, like they were stuck inside an invisible force field.

"That's impossible," Isaline stated.

Nahuel never could have imagined that such a place existed deep underneath New York. He would have thought that only rats and other critters could live so far underground.

But those lights were fireflies.

"These tunnels were made of Nicca stone. It is thought that they were built in the 14th century, before the arrival of Europeans in these lands," Benjamin began explaining, as a guide.

No one paid any attention to him. Nahuel, Emre and Aremi were gathered around one of the walls, which was crawling with the glowing bugs.

"There's no artificial light, just them," Aremi told them, pointing at one of the little glowing bodies which circled above them.

Nahuel looked down the tunnel. The low light that reached into the distance was coming from the fireflies. He wondered how they had got there. He hadn't seen one for years.

Benjamin raised his voice to be heard above the students chatter and the buzz of the millions of fireflies. It took him a few minutes to gather them all together and get their attention.

"The carts lead to the sub-4th floor of the United Nations. Straight to the Council of Privileges. Three people to a cart, maximum four," he stated.

But the students were slow to respond.

"What are you waiting for? Get in or you'll be late," Benjamin ordered, losing his patience a bit.

Nahuel opened the door of the last cart carefully. He was afraid it would shatter in his hand, but the glass was stronger than it looked. He got in slowly with Isaline and Aremi behind. In a few moments, all the students were seated and Victoria and Benjamin made sure their doors were tightly shut. There was a screen in each cart with symbols on it, and after pressing the corresponding button, the glass doors closed themselves and sealed hermetically.

"Now, you finally know," Benjamin said, pulling strongly on the emergency brake.

Nahuel looked up toward him and Isaline gave him a confused shrug.

"I know I kept you awake at night...Well, not me exactly, but not knowing how I got home faster than you the other day," Benjamin said.

"I just don't like to be tricked, that's all," Isaline blurted out.

"No one's tricking you, love. It's just that there are things I'm hiding from you." And without another word, he walked away, tossing his messy-on-purpose hair just slightly.

Nahuel watched as Isaline fidgeted in her seat, shook her head several times and crossed her arms.

The three students watched Benjamin walk away and their eyes followed him as he got into the first cart in line.

"He seems to be taking this task pretty well, though, I don't think he had much choice," Aremi commented from the back seat of the cart.

"What do you mean?" Nahuel wanted to know.

"To get his job, he had to accept to be our warden, just as Victoria. It was a direct request from Mrs. Sparling."

"What job?" Nahuel asked.

"His internship on the Security Committee."

Isaline didn't turn around, but Nahuel could tell she was hanging on every word.

"*Committee?*" Nahuel turned around to ask.

"Yes, from what I can tell, there are several committees within the Council of Privileges," Aremi replied.

"And what does the Security one do?"

"They protect the privileges, I guess. Today we'll have Botanicals class with Professor Greenwood. Her husband is also on that committee."

"And how did you find this out?" Nahuel was curious.

"Mrs. Penington let it all slip while I was helping her gather veggies from the garden for dinner," Aremi replied.

Just then, Benjamin stood up in the first cart heading toward the United Nations and explained, "...so remember that each cart is separate from the rest and you must use the code to get to the destination."

Nahuel entered the code on the digital screen. The screen showed the route they would take in green and with a hum, the cart began moving.

He looked down, the glass was so clear, he could see everything beneath his sneakers. The cart seemed to glide along an invisible track, not even touching the ground. Nahuel would have bet that some type of magnetic track made the levitation possible.

The tunnel was serpentine. As they advanced, the temperature dropped and Nahuel saw that Aremi's knees were shaking. He took his jacket out of his bag and offered it to her. She accepted with a sincere smile.

"I suggest you duck," they heard Benjamin's warning come through the speaker they had in the cart.

Bit by bit, the terrain began slanting downward and their bodies were involuntarily flung forward. Nahuel grabbed the front edge of the cart. The tunnel was so close over their heads now it felt like they were almost touching it.

"Girls, watch your hair! The fireflies will take no pity on your hairdos," Benjamin's voice made Aremi laugh, but Isaline just rolled her eyes.

Still they covered their heads, following his advice. Aremi wrapped her long blonde, wavy hair up in Nahuel's jacket, and Isaline's two hands were enough to protect her shoulder-length bob.

They couldn't see Benjamin from where they were, far behind the rest of the group. They could only see the cart in front of them, which held Tristan, Emma - the girl who had walked in on the Security Council at the United Nations during their first tour - and a boy, whose name Nahuel couldn't remember.

"As we make our way to our destination, I will shed some light on a few urban myths," Benjamin went on through the speaker. "When these tunnels were renovated, the Council found the den of a large family of albino crocodiles. So, you can see that the legend of New York's sewer system, is more than just myth." He paused for dramatic effect. "Please ladies, don't get scared. They have already been relocated."

"He's inventing this story," Isaline huffed. "It's impossible."

"Just like everything else around here," Nahuel replied.

The tunnel widened and Tristan's cart slipped toward one side. Ahead there was a split in the path and it seemed like Tristan's cart would take the left. But they continued on the same path and the route marked on the screen indicated they would take the right.

The map didn't look like any they had ever seen before. There was an infinite number of tunnels, with codes and names, all impossible to understand if you were using common sense. The end of the route was not labeled with any name they could recognize.

"Left or right? Which way?" Aremi asked, moving her head from side to side. "Place your bets now."

"It's important to turn correctly. We don't know where the other routes go," Isaline pointed out. "Did you enter the code correctly, Nahuel?"

"I thought I did," he said.

The cart that Tristan and Emma were in was seconds away from taking the opposite route as theirs.

"Tristan! Tristan!" he shouted at the top of his lungs.

"What do you want?!" asked the other, turning around in his cart.

"What was the code for the United Nations?!"

After a pause which frustrated Isaline to no end, Tristan shouted: "8573!"

In just seconds, they saw the split in the path coming up. Nahuel punched in the code on the screen.

"The Code Does Not Exist," announced the screen in purple letters.

"Try it again. You put your fingers wrong," Isaline insisted.

Nahuel entered the code again, this time more carefully.

"The Code Does Not Exist"

He felt a rush of heat up his spine. At that time, the lights of fireflies went out for a moment, as if there had been a power outage. When they were back on again, Tristan had already disappeared in the split path.

"He tricked us!" raged Isaline as Nahuel spewed all kinds of adjectives toward him. "Try another number."

"It could be anything. There are thousands of combinations," Nahuel replied.

"Quick! Put anything! We must not turn," she insisted.

Nahuel put in another number - his birthdate -but the cart continued on the same path. Isaline bumped heads with Nahuel and put in another combination, similar to the one Tristan had shouted at them. But nothing happened. Nahuel tried another - his grandfather's birthday - and another route appeared on the screen, but it was also taking the right turn.

Isaline and Nahuel were fixated on the screen when Aremi, seated behind them, calmly stated, "You might like to know that we've already gone right."

They both looked up at the same time. Isaline looked at Aremi and then forward.

"What do we do now?"

Her question hung in the air.

The cart turned right again and then continued in a straight line. It soon began picking up speed and they had to hold tightly onto the sides to keep their balance.

It got darker as they went on. Among the fireflies, they could see the rock walls around them. They were entering an area of tunnels that appeared seldom used and that hadn't been renovated yet.

Nahuel saw that a few feet in front of them, old rusty tracks, like from an abandoned mine, rose out of the ground. He braced for the impact. Their glass cart that was levitating above the track wouldn't be able to keep going.

"Hold on!" he warned his friends.

But there was a screech, the cart shook and four wheels emerged from below.

"We need to get out of here," Isaline said, looking around.

They had slowed down and were almost in the dark, but they could just make out a large hole ahead, that reminded them of the burrow of some animal.

Nahuel leaned toward the screen and put in another number, his postal code.

"The Code Does Not Exist"

"Try 2828," Aremi said, from the backseat.

"The Code Does Not Exist"

"Shoot, that was my lucky number," she said.

"Put in the date the United Nations was founded," Isaline said.

Nahuel stared at her blankly.

"1945," she clarified. "Did you learn anything on orientation day?"

"The Code Does Not Exist"

A longer message appeared on the screen and a feminine voice came through the speaker:

"You have surpassed the limit of failed entries. Vehicle 177 will stop in 3...2...1"

Everything fell quiet.

"So, are we sure they relocated the albino crocodiles?" Aremi asked in a small voice.

"I wouldn't believe a word he says," Isaline said, denying Benjamin's stories. "But I don't like this place either."

Aremi got up from her seat and crawled into the front. She squeezed in between Nahuel and Isaline. The three fit snugly only because Aremi was so tiny.

She pointed at the letter E shining in red on the screen.

"This looks like an emergency symbol," she said.

"It must be," Isaline agreed, and touched it. "We have to hurry or we will be late."

"When Benjamin sees it, he will come to get us," Aremi added.

Isaline groaned. She didn't want to imagine Benjamin saving her.

Nahuel couldn't get over how mad he was. His mouth was clamped shut with anger. What had he ever done to make that jerk lie to him? There was no doubt about it, Tristan was a complete asshole.

Holding still was the most annoying part of the whole thing. All they could do was wait, for the cart to restart or for Benjamin to arrive. It was the first day of the program and they were already lost and they would definitely be late for their first class.

Nahuel knew how to get out of there, he had memorized the route from the residence. But they would have to walk, and it would take them hours just to get back to their starting point.

Aremi tried to break the tension, and wondered out loud where their wrong turn led, and why they hadn't updated this tunnel, but as hard as she tried, her classmates stayed stuck in their bad moods.

After what seemed like an eternity, they heard the screech of wheels against the metal tracks. A cart approached them out of the shadows. It was Benjamin, by himself and with a smile on his face.

"I see I can't leave you alone", he joked as he came close to them.

He jumped out of his cart and added, "I'm going to ask you to please make some room for me."

The door slid open and Isaline stood up and got out of the cart first and then Aremi and Nahuel did the same.

Benjamin climbed in easily.

"Well, Nahuel. It appears we can't give you a driver's license just yet for this kind of vehicle," he laughed, but Nahuel didn't find it funny. "It's true the codes can seem confusing at first, so you might want to write them down. 7385 is the Council of Privileges and 0420 is Mrs. Penington's house."

Nahuel noticed how Isaline slyly grabbed her notebook and quickly wrote both codes down on the edge of it, turning her back on Benjamin for a moment.

"If you hadn't pressed the Emergency button, I would have had to ask Ankona to track you down. This part of the tunnel is...complicated," he added as he accessed the cart's navigation system.

"What makes it complicated?" Aremi asked.

"It's one of the oldest lines and it's not even in use nowadays. It's never been completely explored and I'm not even sure where it goes. But when someone presses the Emergency button, I activate the rescue program and my cart brings me directly to the cart in distress," Benjamin explained.

"And how do the trackers track?" Nahuel suddenly wanted to know.

Benjamin looked at him from the corner of his eye. He was restarting the navigation system.

"By smell. It's something only the CymAnis can do, which is why I don't know exactly what it entails. If you want to know more, you should talk to Ankona. He's the head of the trackers."

"Yeah, I know him. I have class with him today," Nahuel said.

"A word of advice - be careful how you ask him," Benjamin added. "I've heard the way he became a tracker wasn't very pleasant and he can get...sensitive if you try to find out too much about it."

"But...then do you know how he became a tracker?" Nahuel asked.

"It's' a long story," Benjamin started to say, getting out of the cart so they could climb in again.

"I think you should give the briefest version possible," Isaline said impatiently. "We are already late."

"Alright then," Benjamin said, entering the correct code. "Ankona started working undercover in South African intelligence, you know - fighting against dictators with privileges who were working hard to tear Africa to pieces. They say one of them kidnapped his pregnant wife and he turned into a tracker to find her. I don't know how the story ends. No one will talk about it. All I know is that since then Ankona can't stomach the smell of human blood."

After hearing that, Nahuel stopped asking questions. That story truly inspired respect.

For the second time that day, Benjamin made sure the door was tightly shut, got into his cart and shouted, "Let's go!"

Both vehicles started moving.

Benjamin turned around repeatedly to make sure they were still behind him.

CHAPTER 11

The tunnel led them directly to a cozy room with hanging chairs, just in front of the classrooms.

Only a few of their classmates were still there.

"Why were you late?" Damian asked, swinging in one of the chairs.

"A problem with numbers," Aremi replied.

"Where are the others," Isaline asked, visibly worried.

"The CymMens went that way," Damian replied, pointing at the room with floating cushions. "With Sparling. Luckily, I'm not in that group."

"Tell Tristan that I will make him pay for this," Isaline swore before leaving.

But now was not the time. Her classmates had already started the lesson *Transportation and Movement*, taught by Mrs. Sparling.

She walked to the door, grabbed the door handle and stood up tall, filling her lungs with air, steeling herself with courage and then entered the room.

"Ok, good then. One less." Damian said. "What privilege are you, Aremi?"

"CymTers," she smiled, letting him see the book she was carrying, *The Complete Guide to Botany*.

"Ok, that way then. They went with a red-headed woman," Damian pointed the way toward another room.

"Ok, see you later! Thanks for the ride Nahuel," Aremi said walking away like a dancer.

Then Nahuel spotted him. Tristan was leaning against a wall with his arms crossed. He would soon wipe that smug expression off his face.

"You gave me the wrong code," Nahuel got in his face.

"7385," Tristan replied.

"That's not what you said."

"Seven, three, eight, five. Do you need me to spell it?" Tristan challenged.

Nahuel came to Tristan, as the power in his blood was raised in response.

He felt a strong urge running through his veins.

Master your instincts, Nahuel.

His grandfather's words echoed in his mind. Nahuel clenched his fists and used all his self-control to turn back.

He went and planted himself down in one of the swinging chairs. He rummaged through his backpack with more strength than necessary, looking for his timetable, and trying to focus his mind on another thing. He found the remains of one of Mrs. Penington's chocolate cookies, squished under his books, and a sock that had stowed away that morning in the hurry to pack everything up.

The piece of paper with the timetable was wrinkled up beneath the Tibetan singing bowl. After smoothing it out, he read his schedule for the day.

8.00 Animal Communication and Behavior
Professor Kudzai Ankona.

10.00 Zoology
Professor Héctor Reyes.

13.00 Limits
Professor Salim Swarup.

15.00 International Security
Professor Sebastian Kendrick

It seemed that Ankona was running late.

They heard loud steps. Their professor approached, putting on a vest as he took an ivory-colored card from the pocket. He walked in front of them and went on down the hall, past Mrs. Sparling's classroom.

"Should we follow him?" Damian asked from the chair across from Nahuel's.

"Yes," he replied. Even though he didn't know him well, Nahuel remembered Ankona was a man of few words.

They hurried behind the professor who moved with the swift pace of an athlete.

Nahuel would have to find the right moment to talk to Ankona. Could all the CymAnis become trackers? What skills would they need? After his father disappearance, he had fantasized about becoming a detective. He had even asked his mother to hire one, in one of those moments in which they still had a mother and son relationship…

Ankona stopped in front of a door, turned the handle and said, "Go in. There are some desks at the front of the warehouse to make things easier."

Nahuel and his classmates felt small when they entered. The space was huge and rough and desks seemed recently put together. Nahuel sat down at one and left his backpack on the ground. A classmate who wore her curly hair in a long braid took the desk to his right and Damian sat on his other side.

The door closed and Ankona started to explain. "Nothing stays still. Everything moves, everything vibrates. Each particle in the universe, every organism, every plant, every animal vibrates at a certain frequency.

"People with privileges, we can perceive the frequencies that microorganisms, plants and animals nearby us emit. And we can change them. That is, we can manipulate these vibrations."

Nahuel listened closely, eager to hear explanations. Ankona was precise as a teacher, and Nahuel liked it. Ankona didn't seek to decorate what he was saying with cute examples but rather used logic to help them understand.

"CymMens can influence microorganisms," he continued. "These unicellular organisms are everywhere and in immeasurable numbers. By manipulating them, a CymMens can make them move objects, create wind and even move water, among other things."

"The CymTers can harness the vibration of the earth and what grows in the soil. They can influence dirt and plants by manipulating their frequency."

"We are CymAnis. We work with the frequency of animals. Most people cannot feel it or understand it. The ordinary human ear is poorly developed, like their sense of smell and their vision. Our senses, however, are different."

Of all three privileges, CymAnis, the one Nahuel possessed, was the one he would have chosen, if given the choice.

In Animal Communication and Behavior, I will teach you how to connect with animals. You will harness the sounds and vibrations they give off. And later on, you will be able to acquire their skills.

Ankona spoke clearly, showing his vast knowledge of the privileges. He wore a necklace of dark red and moss green beads that poked through his shirt and shone against his dark skin.

"Now, I want you to take out the termites," he said.

The students crouched down and took the identical jars of termites they had been given from their backpacks. Nahuel raised his to his eyes. They were on their backs and bunched against one edge of the glass. He immediately remembered he hadn't fed them the day before.

"Professor, should we leave them in the jar?" The girl with the curly hair asked, looking at the others suspiciously.

"For now, yes," Ankona answered. "First I will teach you to communicate with small invertebrates," he announced, walking among the desks. Nahuel covered his jar with his hand slyly as Ankona walked by. "Then you will learn how to manipulate them, that is, make them do as you ask."

"Professor," another girl put her hand up.

She had big, almond shaped eyes, behind glasses which made them seem twice as big. Ankona nodded and the girl went on, "Will we be able to communicate with elephants? I read that they communicate using their feet to make and capture sounds that are too low for humans to hear."

"That's right. The CymAnis can feel and hear all the sounds the animals make because we have the ability to situate ourselves on the same frequency," he responded.

Nahuel stared at him, gaping. He had never even seen an elephant and now, all of a sudden, he would be able to communicate with them?

"But it will be a long time before you can communicate with mammals of that size and complexity," Ankona continued. "It takes a lot of energy to connect with them and it will take you a lot of practice to learn to channel that amount of energy."

Nahuel finally understood why tigers in circuses didn't bite the head off their trainers - they must be CymAnis.

"Can we turn into animals," a boy asked nervously.

"Like werewolves?" Damian wondered.

"No," Ankona replied, but his eyes shone brightly. "But it is possible to gain the skills of some animals. The strength of some, the vision of others, their agility...And only some of you, with a lot of practice and talent, will be able to connect so much with the animals that you will feel what they feel. And then one day you will be one, you and the animal."

And the thought of this possibility amazed Nahuel.

"Today we will start practicing with small insects, since they are the easiest to manipulate. Find a partner," Ankona asked.

Nahuel looked at Damian who was already turning toward him.

"As soon as you have your a-bula on, place the winged beatle inside it," Ankona instructed.

"Do the boys have to wear it too? I mean...it's a necklace...." Tristan asked, holding the steel chain from one end and swinging the hollow metal ball.

"These are not necklaces. The a-bulas are tools people with privileges use to transport our talesmas," Ankona replied, showing them his own. He had it tucked under his vest. It was made from a different material than the ones of the kids. Ankona's a-bula was just like Klaus's. He added, "Everyone must use it. Only those who have their privileges extremely developed can go without it sometimes, or in emergencies.

"The talesmas are used to channel and enhance the energy and quality your privilege is using at a certain time. The talesma represents the strength of the thing you want to invoke," Ankona explained. "The winged beetle, for example, represents the height of the strengths of nature and humans. It has been used since ancient Egypt to increase communicative abilities."

Nahuel had taken his small wooden box from his backpack and took out his winged beetle. The insect was dried, dark blue and its transparent wings were spread. He picked it up carefully and placed it on his desk.

"The talesma simply intensifies the qualities we each possess which is why you will only need it until you master that skill. In this case, communication with invertebrates," Ankona explained.

Nahuel wondered how long it would be before he could communicate with Apollo and Atila. On the other hand, for some reason, he had the feeling he was already able to do it.

"Don't underestimate the power of insects," Ankona said. "Keep in mind that for every person, there are a hundred million of them. And many of them possess qualities that would surprise you."

Nahuel knew that what Ankona said was true. He had read that a cricket could jump over obstacles five hundred times its height. That would be like a human jumping over the Empire State Building.

He took out his a-bula and hung it around his neck. He grabbed the gray chain around his neck, opened the ball in the middle, and put the insect inside.

"The termites we have given you were workers in their colony," Ankona continued. "Because they have lost the link with their queen, it will be much easier to sense their frequency and since they are free from her commands, it will be easier to manipulate them.

"This is a team project. I want each of you at the same time to focus on achieving the goal you set for your termite. Concentrate on what you want it to do and try to communicate it. It's easier to do if you do it together. A double command is always more effective."

Nahuel took a termite from his jar. He tried to choose the most active looking one, placed it on his desk and waited.

But the termite just fell flat.

He decided to try with another one. The second one he took out had a crushed antenna and couldn't hold itself up.

"What did you do to them?" Damian asked. "Did you starve them to death?"

Nahuel gave a slight nod with his head to let Damian know he had guessed right on his first try.

"Let's try with mine then," Damian proposed.

"You have to get on the same wavelength as your termite," Ankona said, facing the class. "It is key to have a clear mind. You must wipe your mind clean of all other thoughts except the command you want to transmit."

The door opened and a monkey with a black face and blue testicles entered the room. It looked like it was wearing gloves. Its hand and feet were black like its face and stood out against its cinnamon-colored fur.

"Americus," the professor greeted it.

The monkey went up to Ankona and stood at his feet, pleased he had completed whatever task Ankona had given him.

Nahuel noticed that Ankona grimaced and then looked worried, shaking his head and nodding several times. Were they talking? The monkey swung his tail back and forth like a pendulum until it seemed like the conversation had ended and Americus walked away on two feet, somewhat slowly.

Nahuel turned to see where he was going. At the back of the room there was a woven hammock suspended in the air between two stakes. He hadn't even noticed it until now.

"Don't let it get away," Damian said, blocking the way for the termite.

Nahuel snapped his focus back to the desk. He looked closer. At least this one moved all over the place.

The boys started to concentrate again on their task. Damian furrowed his forehead and stared hard at the termite. No matter how hard he tried, Damian couldn't clear his head.

But Nahuel had a lot of practice on it. From an early age, his grandfather had challenged him to focus on one activity at a time. He had spent long hours playing chess until he could calm his mind down and master his attention.

"Are you deaf or what, Hugo? The professor said we have to both give the same order," they could hear Tristan as Ankona gave instructions to another group and was beyond earshot. "If I'm telling it to hold still and you come along and tell it to turn, is that the same order? I don't think so."

"Could we both give it the order to turn?" Hugo suggested.

Tristan looked Hugo in the eyes. "The termite will follow the strongest order," he said.

A complete and utter asshole, Nahuel thought. Tristan was the kind of person who tried to expose others and make them look bad in order to make himself look good. Nahuel couldn't stand that kind of person.

By the end of class, Nahuel and Damian had been able to persuade their termite to turn a full 360 degrees to the right. Tristan had only managed to get his to hold still for two seconds, while the group of girls were unable to make theirs walk in a straight line like they had intended.

"That is all for today," Ankona announced after the second hour of class. "Practice at the residence. And do the work on page 28 of *Animal Communication: a zoosemiotic approach.*"

Nahuel ran into Isaline sitting next to Emma in one of the hanging chairs. He went over and sat with them.

"No, that's not what Mrs. Sparling said," Isaline was saying. "To move objects, we must first manipulate the microorganisms."

"Ugh, but it's impossible for a microbe to lift a car!" Emma replied, pushing her pink sunglasses onto her head like a headband.

Nahuel saw Isaline rolling her eyes.

"Of course it is impossible for one alone to do it, but millions of them can do it. It's the first thing she told us, the size and weight of the object will determine the number of microorganisms that must be manipulated," Isaline said, emphasizing each word. "You must clear your mind, feel the organisms around us, feel yourself on the same frequency and then connect with them."

"Right, sure," Emma said already tuning her out. Emma's attention was now on the CymAnis, who had just got out of class. She put on bright pink lipstick and hopped from her chair. Nahuel saw her head straight toward the group Tristan was with. Emma was starting to rub him the wrong way.

"So, how was your class?" Nahuel asked Isaline.

"The task for today was to move a piece of string and thread it through a button," she replied, showing him. "We used the talesma for the movement, an ostrich feather from Shu, that invokes lightness and movement."

"Wow," Nahuel said, truly impressed by everything they were learning. "Can I see it?" he asked.

"No, not now."

"Come on. Show me how you do it," he insisted.

"No."

"Why not?" Nahuel asked.

"Because I can't do it," Isaline said, looking at her feet. She quickly added, "But Mrs. Sparling says it requires much practice."

Soon, they were joined by the CymTers. Aremi, coming over with Emre, joined them.

"Hey guys! We just had the best class," she gushed.

"What did you do?" Nahuel asked, sitting up a bit to see her better.

"We made the roots of a bean grow," she said, her freckles dancing on her flushed cheeks.

"That's great," Nahuel replied.

"It was a complete disaster," Emre joined in. "I swear man, my root actually got smaller. The more I concentrated, the more it shrunk."

"Could you do it?" Isaline asked Aremi, unable to hold back.

"Mine grew almost an inch!" Aremi responded, smiling.

"I have to hurry," Isaline stood up quickly. "I'll be late to the next class."

The last class of the day was International Security. It was taught by Sebastian and all three privileges had it together.

Sebastian explained to them that over the years, different people or groups have tried to use their privileges for their own gain, threatening international safety. To keep these people in check, secret peace keeping missions were carried out across the globe. Their professor gave them several examples.

"One of the last operations was carried out in sub-saharan Africa. The international community accused a government of using bioterrorism, but we knew that particular dictator was using his privileges," Sebastian assured them.

"He used his powers to gather millions of insects which laid waste to the crops of the region in less than a week. That way, the government was the only source of food for the people, and therefore he could force them to do whatever he wanted."

It was the first time Nahuel had realized that the privileges could be used to cause harm.

"As you are surely learning," Sebastian said, offering another example,

"The CymMens, with their ability to manipulate microorganisms, such as bacterias, can create illness or spread it. Which is why, when you hear of an ebola outbreak, there is most likely a CymMens behind it.

"Throughout history, people with privileges have used their skills to generate plagues in cities or destroy crops in a way that most people assume is natural.

"You must train your eye to detect when the privileges will be used to generate disaster."

CHAPTER 12

"Hang on, your grandfather's coming," Nahuel's mother said.

As soon as he arrived back at the residence, Nahuel settled in the living room, left his backpack by the couch and called Ushuaia.

His grandfather had waited for him to go to New York to buy a phone. Nahuel had lived almost all his life without one. He never felt the need to call anyone, but what he didn't quite understand was why neither his grandfather nor his mother wanted a phone.

The phone rang three times before his mother picked up. For a few seconds, she seemed surprised and excited to hear his voice. But then she realized that the man calling her was only her son.

It was hard for him to understand that after so many years, his mother was still hoping that one day, by some act of magic, his father would appear. His grandfather had explained that his deep voice sounded exactly like his father's and even confused him sometimes.

His grandfather had told him one night after he had woken crying from a terrible nightmare. He still remembered the pain he felt that morning. His mother neither let him get in bed with her, nor did she comfort him.

"I can't remember his voice, grandpa."

"Don't worry, my boy. All you have to do is listen to yourself."

"But I can't remember what he looked like either."

"This will help you."

That night, Nahuel had realized that his grandfather was growing older, just like the yellowing photograph he had been given. His sad eyes longed for the past that was gone, just as the present overtook them without permission.

"Nahuel, I couldn't wait to hear from you," his grandfather's voice brought him back to the present moment. "I'm so happy to hear your voice."

But that joy was not reflected in his voice. His grandfather sounded worried.

"Are you OK, grandpa?"

"Yes, yes, sure. I just got back from the store. Mrs. Makowski was asking about you, she still remembers when you used to go to the shop to buy bread on your red bicycle."

Nahuel smiled slightly, remembering Mrs. Makowski. She was one of the few people in that city who had cared about his family. She always said Nahuel was like a grandson for her. But he suspected it wasn't just because she was fond of him, but was secretly fonder of his grandfather.

"Here, things continue their course," the old man added. "But let's not talk about me. Tell me about you."

"Today it was the first day of school and I just got to the residency."

"But, how are you? How are you *feeling*?"

"Everything is alright…"

Walter Blest sighed with relief.

"Have you made new friends?"

"Mm…"

"Nahuel, remember what you promised."

"I know, I know. But it's a little bit too soon, grandpa."

He couldn't expect him to make new friends in three days. He had spent more than eight years in Ushuaia without making any friends, except for that one exception…

"Maybe you still haven't had time to figure it out on your own, but friends not only make good days even better, but their power lies in making bad days tolerable."

"Sure…"

"You don't know this about me, but, in my youth, I had great friends. They were the cornerstone that supported me on my dark days."

"Don't worry about me, grandpa. My roommate is really funny, and I have met a French girl that is…a little bit weird, but determined."

"I think I would like that girl. I like motivated people."

There was a silence in the room. Nahuel couldn't continue getting round the subject; however, he asked:

"How are Apollo and Atila?"

"Your dogs are definitely missing you. They seem a little lost. I'm doing everything I can so they don't notice you're gone, but the house just isn't the same without you."

Nahuel understood that this was his grandfather's way of expressing just how much he was missing him. When he had left for New York, they both knew his grandfather would be alone. His mother wasn't company for anyone.

After his father's disappearance, his grandfather had moved without a second thought to Ushuaia, leaving everything behind to look after him and his mother. He had moved to that tiny hidden corner of the planet without ever going back to his old home. And until then, he had lived there, in isolation, surrounded by natural beauty.

Nahuel was sitting in the living room, in front of the large bay window that looked onto the stormy afternoon. When Tristan walked in with Emma, Nahuel groaned a little, got off the couch and went upstairs to his room.

When he was alone in his room, he dared to say:

"Grandpa, there's something I want to ask you."

"Shoot."

"Your acquaintances of New York…"

"What about them?"

"You… How well do you know these people?" Nahuel wanted to know, he wanted to ask him if he had applied for the scholarship and if he really knew what it was about. But he reached behind his ear. The tick was still there, stuck to his skin, hidden under his brown hair.

"I haven't seen them for a while, as you may imagine…it's been almost a decade, but I used to know them quite well. There are good people among them."

"So…Did you know?" Nahuel couldn't ask directly, as there was a risk that the tick would alert the Council. He didn't know exactly what would happen if he revealed the existence of the Council of Privileges, but he didn't want to find out now. It was too soon to be expelled. Sebastian had made it very clear that this was all a secret and it shouldn't be shared. And Nahuel wasn't completely sure if his grandfather was part of the secret.

"If I knew what, Nahuel?"

"About the Educational Program…"

There was silence, followed by a long breath.

"This is a conversation that we'll have some other time, face to face."

Nahuel could perceive that his grandfather was uncomfortable, and, sad? Before he could answer, Walter added:

"You are always on my mind, Nahuel."

The boy was afraid to keep on insisting, and he realized that little it had to do with the Council or the tick. He was afraid that his grandfather had lied to him on purpose, that he had hidden the truth about his powers. His grandfather was the only person he could trust.

"OK" he said. He would give him the benefit of the doubt, his grandfather deserved it. He already had too much to think about regarding the Program and the privileges, anyway.

"Nahuel, remember that a quiet spirit…"

"…masters his instincts," completed the boy. "Yes, grandpa, I know."

He had that phrase etched in his memory. It seemed as if his grandfather loved to repeat it each time he had a chance.

"Very well, son. It's important for you to find your balance in spite of change and uncertainty," Walter said and added forcefully "Find a chess partner."

"I don't think chess is very popular these days," Nahuel said with a smile on his face.

"Nahuel…"

His grandfather said it with concern. He had always encouraged him to play chess, but never with such an urge.

"What do you say, grandpa. Meanwhile, how about we play chess long distance?" Nahuel suggested.

"I'd love to," he admitted. And without hesitating, he added, "White knight to 3C."

By the next day, the wind had blown away the dark clouds and the storm had ceased, as quickly as it had begun. The sun burned brightly and suddenly, but not as intensely as before.

When the glass cart left them on the sub-4th floor, Nahuel entered the room of the hanging chairs followed by Isaline. That day, his first class would be with Ankona again.

"See you later," Isaline said and went away to her Structure and Transfiguration class.

Nahuel saw how the girl passed in front of a man who was wearing, through and through, a grey overall and, with his privilege, he made the hanging chairs fly, as he seemed to be cleaning.

When Nahuel continued through the next hallway, he run into a woman who was wearing the same grey overall, but, with her CymAnis privilege, she was leading a group of tiny insects through every corner of the hallway. He couldn't find an explanation to that.

Nahuel use his Tibetan singing bowl in the next class of Serums, that Tuesday morning.

Their Serums teacher, Professor Patricia Greenwood had spent the first hour of class trying to memorize the names of the 24 students. She held the list of names, read each of them out loud and tried to guess who the owner of each name was. She had three chances, according to her own rules. Everything was fun until she confused Isaline for Emma. Isaline screwed up her face into such a look of disgust, which everyone could see, that the teacher decided to stop the game and turned her attention instead to giving them examples of serums.

With these complicated mixtures, the privileged ones could gain the skills of microorganisms, animals or plants and use them for their own benefit.

The serum that Nahuel was most impressed by was the one for eagle vision. You had to mix the second feather from the white ruff of a young condor, the talon of a dead golden eagle, the eye of a Saker falcon and more ingredients he had already forgotten about.

With this fluid, any person with privileges, not just a CymAnis, could grant themselves extremely sharp eyesight. It allowed them to see any object from great distances and gave them two focal points in their eyes - one to see forward with and one to look to the sides. This came in very handy during battle situations, their professor commented.

"Nahuel, pay attention. You must cut the leaves in bigger pieces, like this," Isaline corrected him, holding up some large piece of polar algae.

In this, their second hour of class, the assignment was to make a natural camouflage that allowed them to hide from even the most dangerous predators.

Nahuel reluctantly got up to look for more polar algae at the back of the lab. As he walked by Emre's station, he noticed his roommate had pulverized his polar algae into a sticky red goo. Aremi, who was working beside him, seemed to have lifted her own algae perfectly from the book's illustration.

A fishtank took up the entire wall of the back of the lab. Nahuel took a fishing net by the handle, but when he lifted it up, he noticed the end was chewed up. He chose another one. He stared at the water, a bit hypnotized. Five baby sharks tussled over the remains of what had been their food. He cautiously dipped his net in the water and snagged some algae from between the coral, before the sharks noticed him.

"I am thinking it is better if I cut them and you mix them," Isaline spoke up, as he reached for the knife.

Nahuel crouched down, opened up his backpack and took out the Tibetan bowl and the strikers. He liked this class. Professor Greenwood let the teams work alone and talk amongst themselves.

"Did you write down how many times to mix the serum in the first phase?" he asked.

Their teacher had explained that the bowls produced sounds and vibrations when they mixed the ingredients for serums in them. This meant people with privileges could change the frequencies of the ingredients and cause different reactions.

Isaline was silent.

Nahuel looked at her. She didn't blink and her eyes were fixed on one spot on the table.

Raising his voice, Nahuel repeated, "Isaline."

She looked up.

"What are you doing?" he asked her.

"I am practicing."

"What are you practicing?"

"Displacement. I'm trying to move a piece of algae. But..." her faced expressed her efforts had been in vain.

Isaline was one of those people who practiced stubbornly, even if they had only a little skill.

"The instructions are written on the board," she replied impatiently without taking her eyes off the algae.

Nahuel said nothing and looked at the board, reading:

"Phase one:

1) Cut the polar algae as demonstrated in the book (3cm. X 1cm.) Serums and Essences from Around the World, page 23.

2) Mash 5g. of yellow polar moss.

3) Add ½ liter of pale octopus ink.

4) Rub the bowl on the outside with the cedar striker, 5 times at 360 degrees to the right, 2 times at 90 degrees to the left and 10 times around at 360 degrees once more to the right.

Nahuel took his bowl and dumped the octopus ink in. It was dark and runny. He reached out toward the moss.

"Hold still," Isaline ordered.

Nahuel withdrew his arm and wondered what he had done wrong.

Isaline turned her wrist, so her palm was facing upwards. A red slimy piece of algae began levitating a few inches off the table. Nahuel noticed that the girl's face was so tense it looked carved in stone. Uneasily, the algae began rising higher, until it came to rest in Isaline's open palm. She shut her hand tightly, stood up and began hopping up and down.

"I did it! I did it! I did it!" she sang a bit wildly.

She had a special gleam in her eyes Nahuel had never seen before.

After her private party, Isaline sat down, opened her hand and let the algae fall into the bowl. She wiped her hand off and exclaimed, "What's this?" she held her open hand just inches from her eyes.

"What is it?" Nahuel asked.

"Look!" she replied, sticking her hand in his face.

The first time Nahuel saw them, he thought he was imagining it. It looked like a rash. It wasn't until he saw it on Isaline's hand that he knew it was real.

"It wasn't there before and it won't go away," she said, trying to rub it off, unsuccessfully.

Isaline had the mark of a circle in the corner of her hand. It was slightly darker than her pale skin, like a faded tattoo.

"So I'm not the only one," Nahuel stated.

"What do you mean?"

"I had one too. They must be normal," he explained.

"Show me," she asked.

"I don't have it anymore. When I saw it, I was trying to talk to termites."

"And then what?" Isaline asked.

"It disappeared. It only lasted a few minutes."

"This must be why they all wear gloves outside of the sub-4th floor," she reasoned.

And then Isaline decided it was time to continue. She tossed the algae into the bowl and told Nahuel to start mixing, as the instructions indicated in the 4th step.

"Something's wrong," he noted after several tries. "I don't see the drops."

"You must turn the striker more quickly and without stopping," she told him, as she answered the questions about the practice assignment.

"Ok."

"I heard the professor say it when she corrected Emma. She also said the most important thing is not to touch the mixture with the striker."

Nahuel rubbed the bowl on the outside as quickly as he could. The mixture in the bowl began turning dark red and began forming tiny droplets around the edges.

A soft and persistent sound started coming from the contact between the striker and the bowl.

"It sounds like the music Mrs. Penington listens to," Isaline said as their classmate's bowls started to join in the same tone.

Nahuel found the sound familiar, it made him think of his grandfather's record collection.

Isaline elbowed him.

The classroom door had opened and Americus came in uninvited. The black faced monkey roamed about the sub-4th floor totally at ease.

Once inside, he made straight for Professor Greenwood. She was writing the instructions for the second phase of the camouflage serum on the board.

"What does Ankona need this time?" she smiled.

Nahuel and Isaline, who were sitting in the front station raised their heads.

Americus gave her a note and waited cautiously.

Nahuel saw how her smile slowly faded as her eyes crossed over the paper. Her cheeks lost color until she was pale as a corpse. When she finished reading, she looked down at Americus for an explanation, but she couldn't communicate with animals.

The note slipped from her hands and landed in the trash can. As she ran to the door, her eyes glazed over, she said, without looking at anyone in particular:

"Carry on everyone."

No one else noticed the sudden departure of their teacher with Americus behind her. The students were busy with the sound of their bowls and their own conversations.

"What was that?" he wondered.

"Surely something very serious. Did you see how her face was changed?"

"Yes."

"And Professor Greenwood doesn't seem like someone who worries much about things," Isaline commented.

"The note," Nahuel said. He looked around to make sure no one was paying attention, "I'll get it."

"Are you sure?" Isaline asked.

But Nahuel was already on his feet.

"Alright. I will make sure no one sees you," she whispered nervously.

Nonchalantly, Nahuel reached down the thrash can and clutched the note in his hand. As soon as he was back at his station he read quietly:

> *The Ignobles have attacked Security Committee agents.*
> *Their helicopter is down. They are looking for survivors.*
> *Klaus is waiting for you in his office.*
> *I'm sorry.*
> *Kudzai Ankona*

"Professor Greenwood's husband works on the Security Committee. Aremi told us." Isaline noted.

"Do you think he was in the accident?"

"No, Nahuel. It wasn't an accident," Isaline said gravely. "It was an attack. Look here," and she pointed at the note. "An attack by the Ignobles."

"But, who are they?" Nahuel asked, scowling.

"I don't know," Isaline said, shrugging. "But they have made the helicopter of the special agents of the Council of Privileges crash."

"Right…"

Isaline folded up the note and put it in her bag so no one else would see it and said: "I'm taking it. No one is going to look for it. The sub-4th floor has greater concerns."

Nahuel and Isaline continued imagining possible explanations for the attack and the attackers until Victoria arrived to oversee the last half hour of class. She gave them the steps for completing the final phase of the camouflage serum and then walked among them, examining everyone's bowls.

"She isn't the teacher. She does not have the authority to criticize the color of our serum," Isaline huffed as soon as Victoria walked away from their station.

"I think it looks just like the book," Nahuel said, comparing the two.

At that moment, a deep whistle was heard followed by a buzz that made the door vibrate.

The class stayed silent.

"What was that?" Damian asked.

"Nothing to worry about," Victoria answered. "There's a search that is being carried out on the sub-4th floor. It must have been the sound of the wind created by the CymMens."

"What are they searching for?" Isaline wanted to know.

"None of your business. It belongs to Sebastian."

Nahuel automatically rotated in his seat to see Tristan.

He lifted up his head and gave Nahuel a defiant look, like saying "dare to say something and you'll see." Nahuel well remembered how, on the orientation day, Tristan kept the ivory pass card that Sebastian had dropped for himself.

At the end of class, Victoria poured some of the drops from Aremi's serum into a test tube. She drank it and then put her hand in the huge fish tank. Then she asked the students to try a dosage of the serum they had each made. If the serum was properly made, when they stuck their hand in the water, it would transform and blend in with the surroundings. Her fingers reflected the red tones of the coral and it looked like even the texture of her skin had changed.

If everything turned out well, like Victoria demonstrated, the sharks would be unable to distinguish their hands from the coral and would not hurt them.

Tristan decided he would be the first to risk it, even though his serum was much lighter in color and thicker than Aremi's. Nahuel noticed that for the few seconds he had his hand in the tank, Tristan didn't even dare to breathe.

Other kids waited in line to try their serum. Damian came second, but his serum was definitely not working. As soon as he had his hand in the tank, two out of three of the sharks turned to him, but Damian was fast enough to take out the hand just in time.

Nahuel decided not to risk it, even though Isaline assured him their serum was perfect and he would be fine. But he figured, if she wasn't going to drink it, why should he?

"So, you are a chicken…" Tristan's voice made him flip out.

He was standing behind his desk observing him from above.

"That's none of your business, *thief*," Nahuel said suddenly.

Tristan gave him half a provocative smile, put his hands in his pockets and walked away.

By the end of the class, only a few students had dared to put their hands in the fish tank in the lab. Most were not confident in their own creations.

It wasn't until the last class that afternoon that Nahuel understood the meaning of that smile. When he opened his backpack to take the Zoology book, he found the ivory pass card that Tristan had stolen. That damned bastard had planted the evidence.

What could he do now? If he returned it, he would be considered a thief, and, if he tried to explain what really had happened, he could be considered a liar or, worse, a tattletale.

He silently pleaded that the search wouldn't include an inspection of the students. He looked both ways and quickly put the card in his back pocket of his khaki pants. He thought it would be easier that they registered their backpacks instead of the students.

Nahuel and Isaline were the first to return to Mrs. Penington's house that day. Fortunately, no one had inspected the students.

They ran into Benjamin in the living room.

"Hey," Nahuel greeted him as he got closer.

Benjamin raised his hand, asking for silence and didn't even turn to look at them.

He was sitting just inches from the television, and he grabbed his head with his hands.

The news reporter was standing at the site of a helicopter crash.

Nahuel looked at Isaline, who instinctively clutched her bag, with the note of the Ignoble's attack hidden inside.

CHAPTER 13

Four hours earlier.

The helicopter was waiting for them on an improvised platform.

The fifteen agents fastened their seat belts and put on their headphones. They wore gloves and green vests with black trim. The NAGAS were an elite team dedicated to preventing threats to global security. It was a team comprised of the most seasoned agents, a mixed group of researchers, scientists, and soldiers, who lived a tough life of secrets, espionage and complex missions.

The motor whirred above their heads and the blades started to spin until they made a silver blur. The hum turned into a growl and the helicopter lifted into the air.

The pilot turned to them and shouted:

"I've been told you'll tell me your destination once we've taken off."

Agent Greenwood gave the pilot a microchip with coordinates in the Red Sea. They would fly a few miles above the Suez Canal and then land on a covert aircraft carrier.

The pilot put the microchip in his navigation system. The route that would take them directly there was quickly established. The pilot increased their speed, the helicopter leaned forward and veered East.

The blades turned at an impressive speed, and cut through the air like knives, making that deafening sound typical of helicopters. This helicopter carried the seal of the United Nations and was one of the fastest in the world.

Even though he knew the risk of even attempting to contact his boss, agent Greenwood reached for the telephone. The call wouldn't be encrypted, so he would have to be very careful with what he said.

"This line isn't secure," a female voice said on the other end.

"I know, but I have to tell you that we have finally found it," the agent responded. The wind beat against his face. "It's vital you be ready to receive it."

The map he had with him featured illustrations hand-painted on leather. A great deal of the world hadn't been explored or mapped when it had been made, more than five hundred years before.

"Very well. Proceed to the drop-off site immediately. It's still the same. I will inform the dissuasion team of your arrival and tell them to be ready for the next phase of the mission," the voice replied.

"We're already in the air," the agent notified her.

The woman on the other end of the line ended the call.

The sun was sinking and threw long shadows on the narrow and noisy streets of Cairo, the capital of Egypt.

From the air, the giant silhouettes of the thousand-year-old constructions were even more impressive. The three pyramids of Giza could be seen on the horizon and the immortal Sphinx. Agent Greenwood happily knew the origin of the plans and the construction of these marvels of the ancient world. The reasons for the building of the Sphinx were not a mystery to any of them. The monumental sculpture with the face of a man and the body of a lion had been planned by a CymAnis ancestor who had risen to a position of power in the area. The body and face had been painted red and the noble headdress had been painted with yellow and blue stripes, clearly in honor of the three privileges.

The shadow of the helicopter sped over the sand.

The pilot sat up taller in his seat, studying his radar screen. The system had emitted a "beep", indicating that an unexpected vessel was within a perimeter of ten miles, within the reach of the radar system.

The pilot changed their path slightly, checking to see if the movement registered on the radar was random. The dot on the screen remained in the same position, but soon, another one appeared and within a few more seconds, there were four blips on the screen.

This time, when the pilot veered suddenly to the right, the four points on the screen veered with them, coming toward them.

"What the hell?" the pilot said.

"What's happening?" agent Greenwood asked through his headset.

"Something's wrong," the pilot replied.

The agent took off his safety belt and moved forward.

The pilot pointed at the radar screen. The four points slowly merged into one and headed straight for them.

Agent Greenwood pressed the radio and warned his team: "We've got company. Forty-five seconds to possible impact."

The mirages thrown up by the heat hid them at first. But soon, the point on the screen was visible, in front of the agents. It was a large group, about a hundred black birds, with fierce beaks who were headed directly for them.

"Begin defense tactic silica," Greenwood ordered.

The CymMens agents stood up.

The grains of sand on the horizon began shaking. The particles rose in the air, higher and higher. In seconds, the CymMens had created a giant wall of sand, a threatening desert wave. The horizon turned orange, contrasting with the pale blue sky.

Even though Greenwood was used to his fellow agents' skills, he was still impressed when he saw them in action. That wave was as magnificent as it was terrifying.

The wave was soon taller than the great pyramid Keops, ready to stop the attack. The wall of sand hung in the air, separating the helicopter from the birds. But they didn't slow down. Their manipulators wouldn't allow it.

Soon, the impact came.

The CymMens agents felt the quake. The first row of birds fell like lead as they hit the wave, but not before poking a few holes in it.

The enemy regrouped. Some birds flew in a spiral formation, breaking through the holes left by the first birds. Others flew vertically straight up the wall, seeking to fly over it. They flew so fast, that they out flew the rising wall.

Soon, many of the birds were close to the helicopter.

For a few seconds, they flew in circles around the agents, like a hunter studying its prey. Their movements were symmetrical and organized. They looked like a twister made of feathers. The agents in the chopper appeared strangely calm. Greenwood knew his partners had more tricks inside their vests.

The CymMens weren't finished.

This time they created shots of sand which rose from the ground into the sky.

Greenwood and the rest of the agents put on protective goggles, the sand bit their skin. The shots were like bursts of water spouting up from an enormous fountain of sand.

The eruptions were constant and precise, happening all around the helicopter. They shot down the birds, knocking bunches of them out of the sky. The shots hit them from below and as they fell, the sand seemed to swallow them whole.

In a few moments, the NAGAS, the elite team of the Council of Privileges had regained control of the situation. Greenwood was satisfied, but some voice inside him told him the attack wasn't over.

The radar system emitted another beep, a longer one.

The screen showed a black stain which extended beyond the 10-mile scope of the screen and was coming up behind them.

The sky turned black, like during a solar eclipse. Images of biblical plagues in Egypt, thousands of years ago, leaped to Greenwood's mind.

"Mayday! Mayday!" shouted the pilot into the radio, on a frequency that only the Council of Privileges could hear.

It wasn't long before they saw them. Tens of thousands of birds had come to finish what their relatives had started. The first bunch had just been to distract them.

With the birds, another image flew into agent Greenwood's mind like a lightning bolt. There had been one attack like this before. Starlings had flown into the turbines of a commercial jet that crashed in the Alps.

"Prepare the net," he said.

Now it was CymTers' turn.

Some agents carried roots wound around their bodies and they didn't hesitate to make them grow. They executed their order instantaneously.

The roots began to spread out the sides of the helicopter. They wove themselves together until they had knit a compact and sturdy web. They encased the helicopter like a cocoon, leaving only the front window and the helixes uncovered.

Inside the chopper, it was like night. The cabin lights came on.

This mesh didn't allow the birds in through the windows or sides of the helicopter, giving the CymAnis time and space to spring into action.

The CymAnis agents tried to control them, but it was an arduous task. The birds were being controlled by a number of enemies and they were just four, making it truly difficult to reverse their orders.

And then, without warning, the helicopter started shaking. The birds were attacking them.

They threw themselves against the Council's helicopter, engulfing it in a giant cloud of black feathers. From the ground, no one would have believed there was a helicopter flying within the birds.

They poked at the net with their beaks and pulled at it with their claws. Many of them threw themselves at the blades in a deadly flight. The steel was splattered with blood each time the birds lashed out.

Agent Greenwood wasn't sure how much longer their cocoon could withstand the attack.

"Findlay, proceed with the operation you had planned to do on the aircraft carrier," he requested.

A petite woman held out her hand to take the map he handed her. She placed it on her lap and took a briefcase from under her seat. Even though she opened it with extreme caution, she couldn't prevent a test tube from falling on the floor, shattering to pieces. Luckily, it wasn't the one she needed.

"It won't' be as effective with these amounts," she said.

"Doesn't matter. Do the best you can," Greenwood replied.

She nodded. She took out a paint brush and spread a brown liquid over the map. She strained to keep her hand steady as she painted the map. The birds continued crashing into them. The serum would harden the leather and seal the drawings, protecting them from the birds pecking beaks.

"It will work for now," Findlay said handing the map back to Greenwood, who put it in his vest.

The CymAnis agents had merged their energy, Greenwood joining them. They soon managed to gain control of a hundred birds. They had no choice but to force them to battle against the other birds controlled by the enemy. They wanted to take the fight yards away, distancing the helicopter in its cocoon from the birds. But it wasn't enough.

They were simply outnumbered.

Although some birds were distracted by the fight, the majority kept on throwing themselves at the cocoon. They destroyed the base of the roots, so that the CymTers couldn't regrow the mesh.

They could already see some beaks poking through the roots. Agent Findlay smashed her briefcase against them. Through the hole now exposed, she could see the chaos on the outside, a mess of feathers, blood, roots. It took her breath away.

Some birds tried to enter through the holes in the cocoon. Their sharp beaks and fierce claws were ripping through it.

Soon, all the birds were breaking through the protective mesh created by the CymTers.

A chunk of roots slipped through the air and fell onto the desert floor.

The CymMens made wind to push the flock out of the helicopter, but the gusts of wind couldn't be too strong, as they ran the risk of upsetting the chopper.

A thunder of rotors exploded over their heads as the helicopter veered. The pilot tried one last evasive tactic. The noise gave way to a blood curdling hiss as the machine shot to the side and tried to change direction and escape.

But this was a perverse and exaggerated attack.

In moments, the helicopter blades began turning more slowly, the birds' bodies sticking in them. Agent Greenwood felt nauseous. Only a cruel and ruthless enemy would kill so many innocent animals like that.

The mesh was gone, and the CymTers couldn't see the enemy, still invisible in their binoculars. The few CymAnis agents couldn't control the thousands of birds attacking them. The blades turned slower and slower and the helicopter shuddered in mid-air.

The agents knew that they had no way to defend themselves. They had never experienced an attack of such a disproportionate magnitude.

They put on their parachutes. They were specially made from feathers from a Tanzanian bird, the marabou stork. They were both fire and water proof. They responded to wind and provided a safe and precise flight.

The helicopter had been completely destabilized and started to fall. One by one, the agents jumped, with their parachutes on their backs.

Flocks of birds surrounded each agent in the air. Their eyes were possessed, their pupils dilated. They tried to peck them. The agents' suits were resistant, but before long, they started to break though. The CymAnis could feel the pleasure of the birds' controllers as they ripped into their skin.

Agent Greenwood waited until the last agent was out of the chopper before jumping himself. The pilot on the other hand, committed to his principles, had decided not to abandon ship.

It was his turn, when Greenwood saw it for the first time. The moment that Findlay jumped, dozens of birds surrounded her. As they flew around the woman, they began to swell, their controllers commanding them to swallow air until they looked like balloons.

Greenwood had no way of predicting it. The birds' eyes popped out of their head and their stomachs expanded to the point of no return. Then it happened. All the birds surrounding Findlay exploded, covering her in a purple liquid. The venom they harbored in their bodies burned the agent. Her skin turned red, cracked and filled with sores. She seemed to be making a great effort to breathe, as she fought against the swelling of her own throat.

Findlay's flame took its time to burn out. She faded slowly, the light from her eyes dimming with resistance, an imploring look.

At that moment, Greenwood heard the terrible and inhuman cries of all his team, above the sound of the beating wings and humming engines.

A paralyzing stupor seized him. Desperation itself threatened to kill him, before anyone else could. Greenwood realized everything was lost. The birds exploded, bathing whoever was nearby with the burning poison they carried within. Their attackers would not let them get out of there alive.

Greenwood summoned Dolano. He hoped deep inside it could be avoided. The eagle was his inseparable custodian. His eyes guarded over him from far away, keeping watch and ready to intervene if necessary.

The agent looked at his wedding ring and his heart froze as his insides melted. He grabbed his parachute. He owed it to her to at least try. He would face the end with dignity.

He jumped.

He was immediately surrounded.

He was still protecting the map with his body. The mission was never over, not even if it was his end.

The eagle flew at a great elevation and only descended in a dead fall when he saw Greenwood. He forged a path through the birds surrounded the agent, pecking out their eyes and pushing them away with his talons. Greenwood gave him the map. Maybe his protector would be able to make it out of there and the mission wouldn't be a total loss. There was too much at stake.

Dolano gripped the map in his talons and the bird of prey flew away toward the horizon.

Agent Greenwood followed the bird with his gaze and dove into its mind. He joined with him and guided his flight, measuring with precision the distance between him and the enemy. Greenwood had two goals: save Dolano and end the mission.

The eagle was strong and powerful. His two focal points showed him the same thing, a swarm of birds plaguing Cairo.

Dolano was pulling ahead of them, winding through the air. The birds made maneuvering difficult, he barely dodged them. Greenwood placed all of his attention on his flight. He and Dolano were one.

Until the agent felt the burning and the pain. Bullets of poison tore at his body. His skin burned from the liquid of the exploding birds all around him.

He was weak and the connection was fragile. This diminished Dolano's strength. He decided it would be better for the eagle and the mission if he let Dolano go with the order to escape. In this state, he couldn't help him, so he severed their connection.

He followed him with his eyes, blurred by pain.

The eagle was faster than the birds, but they were more. Greenwood watched, his heart full of frustration as many were sent to crash against Dolano, blocking his path and forcing him to slow down. Others grabbed onto his wings, using their talons like hooks. Dolano couldn't shake them all off. His wings were heavy and he flew lower.

They had him in their grip.

The birds hanging on the eagle's wings began to swell.

Greenwood realized that all the moments of panic he had felt in his life were crystallizing in one final and terrifying reality. He would die, his team had died and the eagle would meet the same fate.

The mission had failed. The Ignobles had taken possession of the map.

Then, the last body fell to the ground and the world of the agents disappeared in silence and darkness.

Agent Igaki arrived at the site of the accident. She was the head of the elite army that worked in the shadows, the NAGAS, an underground network of special agents whose only goal was to maintain stability in the world.

The scene she came upon was visceral, palpable and unforgettable.

The poisoned bodies had a violet tinge that could be seen through the blood and broken arms and legs.

"What have I done?" she asked herself.

The guilt she felt was overwhelming and sickening. Even if the agents knew what their mission entailed and the risks it involved, she was the one who had sent them to their death.

She slowly took in this new reality.

It was too late to save them.

She gave the order to search for the map, even though she knew the objective of the attack had been to steal it.

She spied the helicopter on the ground. With shaking fingers, she took the phone and as it rang, she remained silent, putting her thoughts in order.

"May God have mercy on their souls."

Someone picked up on the other end and waited. She said only: "They have escaped and have the object in their possession."

An old pickup truck came toward her quickly. The passenger hopped out and took a large camera out of the back. He put it on his shoulder and ran toward the crash.

"Stop there," he was stopped by one of the men with agent Igaki. He showed the man a badge and said, "This accident is under investigation."

The reporter probably knew he would be in trouble if he insisted. He turned around, cursed under his breath and sat on the hood of his truck until they would give him permission to film.

The Council of Privileges maintained heavy control over all the major media outlets worldwide. The organization had a far-reaching influence on the police, the consulates and the embassies. No one dared threaten them or challenge them, except for their one persistent and slippery enemy.

It only took agent Igaki a second to make the decision. She reached for the phone again.

After only three calls, the head of the NAGAS had coordinated a series of emergency meetings to take place in Istanbul within a few hours. Specialists from several committees of the Council of Privileges were already on their way, and she herself would be on a flight shortly, to inform them of the situation, deal with the crisis and develop a plan of action.

CHAPTER 14

Nahuel's life settled into a routine as quickly as the fall colors settled into the New York trees, and before he even realized, the leaves were giving way to winter.

The one thing that kept him connected to the life he lived before was chess. At first, they played by phone at 8pm every night, after dinner. Even though Nahuel had a few hours to consider his move, his grandfather was a tough adversary. Later on, when homework started piling up, and his assignments in Animal Communication became more difficult, Nahuel needed every evening for his studies. Chess was moved to the weekends, after lunch.

The days were getting cooler and cloudier. The leaves of the Norwegian maples which lined the streets of the residence were turning yellow and orange and then slowly dropping to the ground.

The days fell into a routine despite the fact that no day was like the one before or after it. Mrs. Penington's residence became Nahuel's home and the sub-4th floor his reality.

The tunnels were an extra plus of belonging to this secret society. Nahuel enjoyed their practicality every day. He rolled out of bed, ate some breakfast, and in less than ten minutes he was in the sub-4th floor of the Council of Privileges. He didn't have to get up too early, pray for an empty seat on a bus or subway, and he never got cold or wet on his way to school.

Everyone who moved through the tunnels had to go through the room with the hanging chairs, but no one except their teachers seemed to take any notice of the constant presence of twenty-four young students at the Council.

The faces moving through the sub-4th floor changed constantly. The Council of Privileges' agents came one after another. Some came every day for work, while others came and stayed on until certain projects were finished. The sub-4th floor wasn't where they all worked daily, or where they carried out their duties on different Committees.

Nahuel spent a lot of his time trying to quiet his mind. It took him a whole month and many painful headaches to silence all the invertebrates he had learned to hear. Once a CymAnis was able to open the portal of communication with the animal world, he had to learn how to close it as well. And though it seemed crazy, controlling the flow of sound waves was a much harder job than opening the portal.

It was no easy task to keep his energy levels up either. Nahuel soon learned that every privileged person lost energy when they used their privilege, as if their body was a huge battery. Just like after doing strenuous exercise, they had to rest to regain their energy, but there were also other more efficient ways to regain energy, depending on what your privilege was.

Nahuel had to pet an animal to get energy from it. Ankona had let them try with Americus, who, since he was a monkey, had almost as much energy as a human. The CymTers had to eat mushrooms and root vegetables - each type delivered a different amount of energy. And much to Isaline's dismay, the CymMens gathered energy from bacteria, particularly those concentrated in old and dirty places. CymMens could regain energy quicker than the others, but they also got worn out faster.

Nahuel's favorite class was Animal Communication and Behaviour and he hated it when Ankona was absent and left them with the Zoology teacher, Hector Reyes as a substitute. Professor Reyes was a small man, with a curved spine and big belly and he stuttered so much when he spoke, it was hard to understand him.

Nahuel imagined Ankona was in some exotic place, and he spent the classes imagining the tracking missions his professor must be on. He wished Ankona would tell them about the missions.

The second Monday in December, Mrs. Sparling announced that their first Hazna, a type of evaluation, was approaching.

"It will be all-encompassing and the same for each privilege," she said. "You will receive more detailed instructions the day of the event, but make sure you bring all your materials."

Nahuel felt a tremor of heat run through his body. Exam time had come. Uncertainty was a fearsome enemy and Mrs. Sparling was never generous with her explanations. All-encompassing evaluation was the only information available.

The only thing the professor added about the evaluation, even though Isaline had forced Emre to try to find out more about the Hazna, was that there would be two of them in the year and these marks would be added to a theoretical assignment in order to obtain the final grade of each students. These marks would allow the students to continue studying in the Educational Program in the coming year.

"You have to take the Haznas very seriously if you want to become distinguished members of the privileged society," Mrs. Sparling said. "The privileged can go up a level when they get good results in the Haznas. If you move up a level, you are given a different a-bula - a stronger one - which represents the level you are at.

"You must take into account that each level is more than one Hazna and the Haznas become increasingly more difficult in time. The first three a-bulas, in order of importance are steel, bronze and copper."

Nahuel looked at his a-bula, it was dark gray and steel. He wanted to know how many Haznas Mrs. Sparling had to pass to get a golden a-bula. And what about Ankona's? He had a platinum a-bula. Nahuel assumed it represented the highest level if Ankona and Klaus had them. For now, he would focus on getting the bronze one.

"Professor, what does it mean that there are stronger a-bulas?" Tristan asked.

"It means that larger talesmas can be used with them, capable of channeling more energy and therefore manipulate more frequencies. Above all you should know that the amount of energy you can recover changes with each a-bula. The stronger your a-bula is, the more energy you can take and the more quickly you can take it."

Nahuel couldn't imagine how the hours of study and practice could be made even longer. Mrs. Penington had finally unlocked the room on the third floor. It was a room set up with everything they needed to practice their privileges.

The first time he entered, Nahuel thought it was a type of game room for people with privileges. He liked it better than the library. Here, he could try out his skills.

The room was divided into three sections, one for each privilege and in the middle there was a common space with low tables and bean bag chairs made out of flower petals. A large corner space was for the CymTers and Nahuel imagined it must be a true to life recreation of the hanging gardens of Babylon. They could practice with all kinds of seeds, dirt, bonsai trees and anything else they might need.

The CymMens section looked like it had been brought directly from Tibet. There was part of a Buddhist Temple with a backdrop showing the Himalayas and their snow-covered peaks. Isaline had told him that there were small jars which held concentrations of microorganisms for them to practice with and when you got close to them, you could feel a cool mountain breeze blowing on your face.

Nahuel thought the section for the CymAnis was the best. It was like stepping onto the African savannah. The smells, which were even stronger for the CymAnis, transported them directly to another place. It smelled like manure, mud and animal skin. Just like in a field, small insects flew in swarms and bothered whoever came near. The flys were the most annoying. The CymAnis who entered this area had to continually concentrate to manipulate the bugs so they would leave them alone and let them work. Just like in the tunnels, these bugs seemed to be held in a force field which kept them from flying into other parts of the practice room.

They only had one day left before the unnerving evaluation.

Nahuel found Isaline inside her sector. She had been up since dawn, probably even awake before Mrs. Penington. She was sitting on a deep yellow carpet with a straight back, her eyes closed, her legs crossed. If it weren't for the way she continuously moved one foot and opened one eye to spy on a jar, Nahuel would have thought she was deep in meditation. Soon, he understood what she was up to. She was actually trying to manipulate the microorganisms inside one jar to make them pop the lid off the jar.

Nahuel plopped down in one of the bean bag chairs while he waited for Isaline to finish her task. He wanted to convince her that they should study the two subjects they had in common together. Emre had told him Isaline's notes were amazing and if they used them, there was no way they could fail.

"I hate that Victoria is the substitute professor of Serums," she blurted out as she sat down next to Nahuel. "They could have got someone more competent by now. There must be millions of better candidates."

"I think they said Greenwood will be back next week," Nahuel said.

"From Toronto, I know, after the funeral she took some time off," Isaline replied. "Can you lend me your notes from Zoology and Animal Communication and Behaviour?"

"Here you go," Nahuel said, handing her the folder from his backpack. "What do you want them for?"

"To study them of course," Isaline responded. "Mrs. Sparling said the evaluation was all-encompassing and would entail all the privileges and all the subjects. Do you think you could teach me to communicate with the insects in there?" she said, pointing to the savannah. "Or at least give them basic orders like come, go away, bring me that…"

"Bring me that tiny leaf, that crumb...that would be really useful," he interrupted sarcastically. "Isaline, you are CymMens, remember?"

Isaline was beginning to make him lose his patience. Nahuel was already at his wits end just keeping his own anxiety in check.

"Oh, yes it's true. But why is that? I mean, why do we have different privileges and not all the same? I always wanted to have a tiger for a pet. They are so beautiful, right?" she rambled.

"And dangerous," Nahuel concluded for her. "Why don't we study the formula for the inhibiting serums instead? I'm having trouble with the taste inhibitor," he said as he took out his book, *Serums and Essences from Around the World*. "What chapter were we on?"

They spent the rest of the morning studying the longest subjects they had in common, Serums and Limits.

Thousands of natural catastrophes were caused by the irresponsible use of the privileges, which is why the class Limits was so important.

"Each and every one of the privileges can be used as a weapon," their professor Salim Swarup had warned in their first lesson. "This is why you must know the consequences of your actions as well as those of the other privileges."

The problem was that even the smallest actions could generate terrible outcomes.

"If you order 25% of worker bees to leave their hive, you can collapse the entire hive," Isaline said, as she memorized the information out loud. "But if you use only 15% of female bees, this too can destroy the colony."

"And any example about the CymTers," Nahuel asked, rubbing his eyes.

"The professor said that if they accelerate the growth of wheat to achieve more than five harvests a year, it will result in desertification due to loss of fertility in the soil."

"You have written thirty pages of examples of Limits. THIRTY," Nahuel noticed as he paged through his friend's notes and continued to fight off the urge to take a nap. "If we have to remember all of this, maybe it's better to not even use our privileges at all."

Isaline simply looked at him like he had lost his mind.

By the afternoon, the practice room was full and the level of desperation within was running high. By nightfall, Nahuel was fed up and went down into the garden to be alone. The fresh air, even though it was freezing, felt wonderful.

"Hi Nahuel," Aremi, sitting on the ground by the vegetable garden, waved at him.

Clouds heavy with snow, hung over their heads. If it weren't for Mrs. Penington's CymTers privilege, the garden would have been completely lifeless by this time of year.

"Everyone is so tense in there, it's like you could cut the air with a knife. I prefer the cold," Aremi admitted, even though her teeth were chattering.

"Me too."

Nahuel sat down facing her, a wall of tomatoes behind him. He hadn't expected anyone else to be in the garden. Aremi's nose was red with cold and the tips of her blonde hair were frozen. He thought she looked funny, wearing a wool hat with koala ears. He wanted to know if she was really as calm about the test as she seemed to be. But instead he asked, "What are you doing?"

"I'm trying to make this cauliflower ripen until it's as white as that one," Aremi said, pointing with her chin toward a cauliflower to her right.

Both Nahuel and Aremi were wearing the gloves from *The Bowl Path*, which hid the marks from using their privilege and protected them from the cold temperatures.

A worm poked through the snow and slowly others like it appeared. Their bodies contracted and elongated, until they pulled to the surface. Nahuel tried hard to make them follow his order, and once they were out of the snow it became easier. He made them zig-zag around the lettuce plants for a while and then circle around Aremi, without touching her.

The kitchen window which looked onto the garden opened all of a sudden and a cloud of smoke blew through.

At that moment, a flock of black pigeons took flight from the roof and started to circle over the kids.

"Oh, wow, is that you, Nahuel? Are you the one who is making them fly that way?" Aremi asked looking at the pigeons with admiration.

"Mm, no, I still cannot connect with birds."

"If it isn't you, then their behavior is really weird, don't you think?"

"But…they always do that. Well, it's true that they only fly in circles when we stop, but they always join us."

"What are you talking about, Nahuel?" Aremi wanted to know.

"Haven't you noticed that before? That flock of black pigeons follow us every time we get out of the residency."

"I've never seen them following me."

That's weird, Nahuel thought. The first time he went to the Hedge Garden with Isaline, a flock just like this one had followed them all the way. At that moment, he thought it was really extraordinary, but then he noticed that every time he left the residency and didn't use the tunnels, the pigeons appeared. Maybe Aremi hadn't simply noticed them.

"I think they follow us for our safety," Nahuel said, as he had thought about it.

"Mm…Maybe it is to be sure no one gets lost in the city," Aremi suggested.

"I don't think so, it must be for our safety."

Nahuel made her swear she wouldn't tell anyone and told her about the note he and Isaline had found in the Serums class. The note that talked about the attack of the Ignobles to the helicopter of the Council. Nahuel's instinct told him that he could trust Aremi; when he was around her, he felt he could be himself.

"The first time I heard about an attack was when Professor Greenwood went absent, but it just seemed like a rumor…" Aremi murmured, scooting over a bit to look Nahuel square in the face. "It's so scary to think that you can lose someone you love so unfairly."

"Death is seldom fair," Nahuel heard his grandfather's words ringing in his head. "Though, I hope the Ignobles get what they deserve."

"What do you think they want?"

"That's what I would like to find out" Nahuel answered.

That night Nahuel couldn't sleep. It wasn't just the Hazna awaiting him in the morning, but the Ignobles lurking in the shadows.

Even though he had been awake almost all night, dawn seemed to come too soon.

Benjamin and Victoria were waiting for them at the entrance of the tunnel. As soon as Kana, the Japanese girl, managed to make it down the narrow flight of stairs and the 24 students were lined up in front of the glass carts, Benjamin told them where they would be going.

"But, aren't we going to the sub-4th floor," Emma asked, confused.

"The Council of Privileges of the United Nations has different establishments throughout New York. The sub-4th floor is simply the headquarters," Victoria explained.

"As you can see, you still have a lot to learn," Benjamin said slyly. "And one thing is for certain. If you want to obtain an a-bula as cool as mine," he showed them the reddish copper necklace he wore, "you must surpass all expectations today."

Levels, of course, thought Nahuel remembering Mrs. Sparling's explanation.

"Time to go," Benjamin said, motioning for them to get into the carts. "Pay attention to the code you enter on your screens. Don't get lost. I don't want to have to rescue anyone today," and with a fleeting smile he winked at Isaline.

She blushed slightly and looked at the ground, letting her hair fall over her face.

The first part of the route was the same one they took every day. They ducked down when the roof of the tunnel got closer and they turned toward left as normal. Then they entered the second split in the path, the one they usually went past.

Within moments, the hum of the fireflies couldn't be heard. Yet the tunnel still glowed.

Now, the light came from below, from the ground.

"They're jellyfish," Nahuel noted.

He had leaned over the side of the cart and pointed at the large gelatinous bodies.

"This is a giant fish tank," Isaline added.

The bottom of the tunnel was full of water and thousands of jellyfish slid around in it. They were protected by a hard glass cover which separated them from the carts and the people passing over them. Their bell-shaped bodies exuded a faint light. The only sound that broke the silence was their tentacles splashing lightly in the water.

"It seems like we are leaving the city," Isaline commented, once she was over the shock of the jelly fish. "We have already been in this cart for more than 30 minutes. I will go over my notes from Cultural History to take advantage of this time," she decided, opening her beige bag. Soon she was repeating out loud the similarities and differences of the three privileges with the theory of three souls by Plato.

"Watch out they don't blow away," Nahuel said. The carts were moving faster and faster, but the route was easy. After that first turn, it seemed to be an endless straight line.

At the end of that long stretch of tunnel, a slippery marble staircase was waiting for them. The students gripped the wooden hand railing as they climbed up.

As soon as Nahuel reached the top of the stairs, he saw he had to go through a small hatch to get outside. Benjamin was already standing up on the outside of the tunnel, lending a hand to the girls in case they slipped on the last step.

It took Nahuel a few seconds to get used to the light outside. The sun shone brightly in a clear sky. The air smelled like wet grass and there were only a few patches of the snow that had covered New York just a day before.

The first thing Nahuel saw was a sign carved in stone that said, *Ardemir*.

"The Daconte family had built Ardemir three centuries ago and named it in honor of the ancient god of the hunt of the privileged society," Victoria explained.

Ardemir was a large mansion, two stories high with stone walls. An impressive pine forest rose up behind its Gothic columns. The trees were nearly four times taller than the house, and formed an impressive green wall.

"Giant Sequoias in New York!" Emma exclaimed, pointing at the enormous trees. She added, "I thought they only grew in California, where I'm from."

"This is only a sample of the things that grow in this place," Benjamin said. "Follow us."

They walked carefully over the wet grass following Benjamin and Victoria around the side of the Estate. Ankona passed by followed by two men and entered the mansion, he was back from his last mission.

A few steps further, dwarfed by the giant wall of trees which rose up behind them, stood the professors. Mrs. Sparling, wearing a sharp suit, was standing next to Sebastian and a glass tray hovered in the air in front of them.

"Welcome," Sebastian greeted them. The part in his dark hair was perfectly straight this morning. "This land has belonged to the Custodians of the privileged society for as long as anyone can remember. We use it assiduously as it grants us a certain freedom since no one else visits it. Not the government nor private sector are authorized to enter the grounds or to fly over them," he explained puffing up with pride.

Mrs. Sparling, who hated introductions and such niceties, interrupted him. "You must form groups of three students for today's hunt."

"Hunt?" Damian asked.

"The Haznas recall the hunts of yesteryear," Mrs. Sparling answered shortly.

Nahuel thought that everything he had studied with Isaline would not be useful at all in a hunt. Memorizing the formulas for serums and the great Greek philosophers had been a total waste of time.

"Each privilege must be present in each group. This way you will experience the dynamic of how the three privileges work together," Sebastian clarified, trying to regain control of the speech. Upon seeing Kana's terrified face, he added, "Consider this situation a chance to adapt to your new skills."

Sebastian stopped speaking, giving the students a chance to organize in three groups. Isaline started searching among their classmates for someone to represent the CymTers in her group. Nahuel invited Aremi to join them, Isaline bit her lip and accepted. Whether Isaline liked it or not, Aremi was more skilled than her when it came to using her privilege.

"Now then," Mrs. Sparling said, "Send one member of each group to take an envelope from this tray," it was round and crystal and hung in the air between the professors and the students. "Each envelope contains your instructions."

Nahuel went to the tray, took one of the white envelopes and walked back to join Isaline and Aremi.

"Each student will be assessed on their individual work, but above all, we will assess how the group works as a whole," Sebastian added as Damian took the last envelope from the tray. "You should apply what you have learned from each subject and encourage the equal participation of each member of the group to achieve your objective. You may use all the supplies you were given the first day. And don't forget to bring back the prize."

"You are not allowed to consult among different groups, and we will not answer any questions," Mrs. Sparling explained, speaking for the teachers. "You have until 3 pm to make it back to this point."

"We wish you good luck," Sebastian added.

The professors, followed by Victoria and Benjamin walked toward the grand house, leaving them alone.

The silence of the forest and the immensity of the unknown engulfed them.

Isaline took the envelope from Nahuel, the three were anxious to see what was inside.

CHAPTER 15

Forever here to serve the Custodians and the Guardians.
Behind the veil of what can be seen, lies its essence. This essence lies with it alone and is manifest in its form.
It will remind you of many things, among them green and brown.
Its home lies at the peak of Titans.
Its weakness is none other than its sustenance. When the wind blows, the umbrellas carry the fruit.
Hidden deep in the woods, you will find the creature. You will arrive here and go no further.

"So…It's a riddle," Isaline said.

Nahuel took the envelope. Aremi leaned in and read it again out loud.

"Remind you of anything?" Nahuel asked, looking up as Aremi finished reading.

"Not really, no," she admitted.

"Let's start by going into the forest," Isaline suggested.

The three teens crossed into the forest, beyond the edge of giant sequoias.

Their lungs were filled with fresh air and life itself as they stepped into the forest. Nahuel loved the irresistible smell of pine trees and let it wash over him. He felt at home.

The air was dry and cool. His senses were becoming more and more heightened as he developed his privilege. He focused on the smells, sights and sounds of birds, squirrels and insects.

The groups started dispersing into the immense forest. Nahuel saw Emre, Damian and Kana disappeared behind a giant log, a sequoia that had fallen long ago. His own group set out in a diagonal line from the Estate and before long couldn't even hear their classmates.

Nahuel was glad the setting for the Hazna was a forest. He was used to this type of habitat and felt comfortable. He had spent his last years venturing into the Patagonian woods. When he was little, his grandfather had taught him to appreciate the power of the serenity that Nature provided.

As they moved on in silence, shadow took over the forest. When Nahuel looked up toward the sun, he noticed that the enormous evergreen trees extended to the sky like majestic towers. He knew the sun was shining brightly up there, but the branches wouldn't let him see it.

He turned around. Already couldn't find where they had entered the forest.

"We'll get lost," he warned his partners. Even though Nahuel usually had no problem finding his way out of places, this was a magic forest.

"You're right," Isaline agreed. She had also turned around to look for the Estate.

"We need to mark our trail to find our way out," Aremi confirmed.

"We need Ariadna's thread! This is like a labyrinth…" Isaline added.

"What?" Nahuel asked.

"In the legend of the Minotaur," Isaline replied. "Theseus uses the thread the princess gives him to find the way out of the labyrinth after he kills the beast. But we don't have any spool of thread."

"If you had mentioned Hansel and Gretel's bread crumbs, we would have understood you faster," Nahuel grimaced.

"It is the same. We have to mark our path in some way."

Isaline opened her bag in search of something they could use. She took out each object one by one and spread them on the ground. Besides her school supplies, she had a wallet, a first aid kit, a hand mirror decorated with glitter, a keychain shaped like an elephant and even a hairbrush. What good would a hairbrush do her in a hunt, Nahuel wondered. Once the bag was empty, Isaline turned it over and shook it, hoping the solution would fall magically from it.

"I could try to make a trail of ants, but I don't know if I could hold it steady from far away," Nahuel wondered.

"Any ideas, Aremi?" Isaline asked. She turned in a full circle, "*Aremi?*"

Aremi was a few feet away, crouching down in a thick spread of wild ferns.

"Look what I found," she told them, pointing at something with a muddy hand.

"What is it?" Nahuel asked.

"It's a type of yellow moss I could make it grow behind us as we walk," Aremi said, smiling.

"Ok, now we must focus on what we have to find in the forest," Isaline declared. "Getting out of here with our hands empty would be worse than not getting out at all."

Aremi straightened up, looked down and concentrated a few seconds on the ground. Under her feet, small yellow hairs started poking through until a circular patch of moss had formed.

They walked on a way, in no particular direction, in silence. Behind them, the yellow moss followed Aremi like a shadow.

They walked by pools of stagnant water, and by a tree whose branches were dripping with triangular, woody pinecones.

Nahuel fixed his gaze on the ground, as if he were hypnotized by the steady growth of moss under Aremi's feet.

"Its shape reminds us of many things…" Isaline recited. She had walked over to a rock and looked for a flat place to sit down.

"What are you talking about?" Nahuel asked, leaning against the trunk of a sequoia.

"About the creature," Isaline sighed in exasperation. "What are you thinking about? Focus on the riddle."

Once she was comfortable, she put her bag on the ground and hunched over the clue, reading it again.

"Maybe it means that it can change its shape," Isaline pondered.

"Or that it looks like something else," Aremi suggested. She had settled onto a pile of moss she had created for herself.

"Something green and brown," Isaline added, citing the riddle.

"Like everything in this forest," Nahuel pointed out, taking a look around.

"True," Isaline accepted, somewhat disappointed. "How will we find it if it is hiding among the leaves and branches? We can't even see up into the very tall parts."

Nahuel looked up. This place was incredible and the trees were truly enormous.

"Let me see it for a second," Aremi asked, reaching for the envelope.

They were all quiet and concentrated on the riddle. An almost disturbing stillness had settled in on them. Aside from their own breathing, the only thing Nahuel could hear in the distance was the sound of insects.

A branch cracked to his right, drawing his attention that way. He tried not to breath, as he listened carefully. He wondered what type of creatures lived here.

Aremi mumbled something and then was quiet. Then she said, "The answer is in the last verse."

"Read it," Isaline asked.

"*Its weakness is none other than its sustenance. When the wind blows, the umbrellas carry the fruit.*"

"Of course!" Isaline shouted, jumping up. "If we find its food, we will find the creature."

CRUNCH

A loud sound interrupted them. It sounded like someone had broken a piece of wood with their foot.

"What was that?" Isaline asked cautiously. "Who's out there?!"

Her voice bounced like an echo off the tree trunks. No one answered her question. Nahuel took the silence as a bad sign, he felt a shiver down his spine.

"It came from over there," Aremi pointed carefully.

Without thinking about it twice, Nahuel walked toward the sound. He pushed aside shrubs until he saw a smaller tree that hadn't grown as tall as its brothers.

"Something's moving," he whispered.

"What are you doing? STOP!" Isaline shouted.

But it was too late, Nahuel had instinctively stretched out his arm, grabbed a branch and pulled it to the side.

Then two things happened at the same time: an old owl, who had been resting in the tree, flew heavily into the air and Nahuel began to feel unbearable pain.

Nahuel blew on the hand that had pulled back the branch. It felt like his skin was on fire.

He knew the owl hadn't made that noise, had it been one of his classmates? That didn't matter now, the pain was overwhelming. Blisters filled with green pus started popping up on his hand, and spread to his wrist. His hand looked horrific. One blister burst and oozed yellow liquid that smelled like vomit.

"The Letharia Vulposa is a poisonous mushroom," Isaline explained. "It lives in young evergreens whose growth has been accelerated by CymTers privilege. This is what happens when you don't take into account the presence of the Bistranti Owl, which it would seem, also lives in this forest."

"How do you know all this?!" Nahuel asked, louder than necessary. He was trying to quiet his pain by yelling.

"We learned it in the fifth class of Limits," she replied. "Professor Salim Swarup taught us that the excrement of these animals has a corrosive effect on the bark of manipulated trees, the perfect habitat for this kind of mushrooms."

"Just tell me what I have to do now," Nahuel asked desperately. He was hoping Isaline had also listened to what you should do if disgusting growths appeared on your skin.

"If I remember correctly, you must get pitch from the trunk of a young, manipulated tree that is not infected with the mushrooms," Isaline replied. "But I don't see any around here."

"Aremi, can't you make one grow?" Nahuel begged. "From a pinecone, from the roots, whatever it takes."

Aremi picked up a pinecone, took a seed from it, and buried it under her feet. She made an effort, turned red, and sweat broke out on her brow, but it wasn't enough. Unlike the moss, she couldn't get anything to grow from that seed.

"I'm sorry, Nahuel. That's too advanced for me," she said.

Nahuel nodded. The burning sensation was driving him crazy. He looked at Isaline imploringly.

"Let me see it."

Isaline opened her bag, took out some gauze, covered it with a dark orange liquid and handed it to him.

"It will help a little, but not as much as the pitch," she explained as Nahuel spread it on his arm. "I don't have any more left, so I hope it works…and we don't need more."

"Is that any better, Nahuel?" Aremi asked.

"Yeah, a little." The pain remained, but at least the blisters were not expanding so quickly.

"Well, I have some good news and some bad news for you guys. Which do you want to hear first?" Aremi asked them in a soft and lilting voice.

"The good," Nahuel said.

"The bad," Isaline said at the same time.

"The good news is that I think I know what the creature eats."

"Wonderful! What is it?" Isaline asked.

"Dandelions. They are flowers that when they have seeds look like white pom-poms and the seeds travel in the air like little umbrellas or helicopters. I thought of it when I saw you blow on your hand. When I was little, I used to blow on the dandelion seed pom-poms," Aremi explained.

"And what is the bad news," Isaline wanted to know.

"I don't have any seeds left. They were the first ones we used in Botanicals."

They continued to walk deeper into the woods. They were looking for a dandelion, and on Nahuel's behalf, for a tree not infected with mushrooms that would help ease his pain. The wounds on his hand throbbed incessantly. He looked at the wounds closely. The eruption of blisters was worse. Even the tips of his fingers and his forearm were swollen and blistered.

"Emma has been here. She is the only one who would wear such a horrible lipstick."

Isaline pointed at the trunk of a giant tree smeared with bright pink lipstick. Emma and her group were using the lipstick to mark their way through the forest.

They went deeper and deeper into the woods. It was a thousand-year-old forest that stood as if untouched by time. The sequoias made Nahuel imagine a time when dinosaurs had roamed the earth. The trees looked strong enough to withstand freezing, drought and even fires.

Aremi's hands also seemed to be stronger than they could have imagined. They were overcome with circular marks, like tattoos that were not fading away, due to the effort she was making to keep the moss growing. Nahuel's hands on the other hand looked defeated. He was holding the gauze on them, that Isaline had given him.

He had ripped the sleeve off his shirt. The fabric rubbing on the blisters was very painful and the fabric was sticking to his skin.

"I think we should go back," Aremi said suddenly. She looked at Nahuel, worried and added, "There's no dandelion around here and by the time we find one we don't know if the blisters will get worse."

"If we go back now, we will fail the Hazna... But, of course, if you are really dying of pain, maybe we should go back," Isaline said, looking at Nahuel.

"Let's keep going," he said. The truth was that it hurt like hell, but he could deal with it; he was more interested in completing the Hazna and moving up a level in the privileged society.

They kept going. With each step they took, Nahuel asked himself how they would pass the exam. His mind started racing, the clock was ticking. Where would they find a goddamned dandelion?

Aremi stopped a moment and ate some small bell-shaped mushrooms to recover some of the energy she had lost. They kept walking and stopped seeing traces of their classmates. Nahuel felt they were going too far.

"Something touched my hat!" Isaline screamed.

Nahuel turned around. The bits of snow left on the trees were starting to slip and fall.

"It's just some snow."

Their footsteps got louder and louder. The silence this deep in the forest was deafening. A layer of branches and leaves crunched under their feet.

Nahuel took the lead, going around the right of one of the huge trunks, jumping over a rock and waiting for his friends to follow the same way. Before going on, he checked on all sides, saw nothing strange, took a step forward and then stopped in his tracks.

More than he could see it, he could intuit it. There was something in front of them. He squinted, searching for something in the thick vegetation.

But there was nothing there.

"Over here, guys," Aremi said.

Nahuel turned and saw that the girl had gone away to one of the sides. Aremi was crouching down while digging the soil.

"Finally, our stroke of luck," she said when her friends came close.

Nahuel saw a single yellow flower waiting for them among the roots of a sequoia. But something else caught his attention.

A tingling sensation travelled all over Nahuel's backbone. He had spent enough time in the woods to trust his instincts.

"These footsteps aren't ours," he said pointing at the footprints on the ground.

"Luckily, they hadn't stepped on the flower. Could you make more Dandelions grow now that we have found this one?" Isaline asked Aremi, unable to mask her anxiety.

"I'll try to," Aremi promised.

First, a short stalk appeared, then a yellow flower emerged, followed by long green leaves. Next to it a longer stalk grew, and on its tip a soft, round, white pom-pom formed.

Slowly, more and more flowers bloomed, spreading along the ground until all the empty ground among the trees was covered with them. Even though he had seen it before, Nahuel was amazed by all that Aremi could do.

Nahuel, Isaline and Aremi were surrounded by white and yellow.

"There are enough here," Aremi said, satisfied.

Isaline picked one of the fluffy white pom-poms, raised it to her mouth and blew, as she had done as a little girl. The hairs of the seeds floated through the air. Altogether, the thousands of white fluffy seeds lifted into the air, floating higher than a simple breeze could lift them. They rested all along the branches of the trees around the group.

"It's beautiful," Aremi smiled.

The scene was captivating, they were enveloped in a swirl of white fluff.

They waited a few moments in total silence, anxious for the creature to reveal itself. Nevertheless, only a curious squirrel snuck toward them.

"No, it's not you, shoosh," Isaline scared it away. "The riddle says it lives in the top of titans, so it must be high up in the trees," she said looking at the treetops. "We need the serum for eagle vision. It's not fair that they haven't taught it yet."

"Actually, the magnifying glass might be enough," Aremi figured, raising the glass to her green eyes.

Among other things, these special lenses allowed them to see far into the distance with total clarity.

Nahuel didn't need his. His sight had improved with his CymAnis practice.

"I think I see it," he announced.

"Where!?" Isaline shouted and ran over to him.

The shape of her steps was left imprinted in the carpet of dandelions. They were so thick it was impossible not to step on them.

"There," he pointed.

Isaline looked to where he was pointing.

"That is definitely the creature we are looking for," she stated in triumph. Her magnifying glass showed a strange dark blue creature.

"It's a stick bug," Nahuel said. "It's a perfect example of insects that camouflage themselves among branches. They have long stick-like bodies and are usually brown, but this one is changing color like a chameleon."

The forest was a magic realm, full of wonder and danger.

Nahuel searched for the frequency the bug was on. He was leaning slightly back, the talesma inside his a-bula was the winged beetle, the one for communicating with insects.

He stopped for a second.

The hairs on the back of his neck stood up and he got the feeling they were being watched, even though the forest seemed deserted.

He looked around. The spot they were in now seemed hostile and rough.

Nahuel concentrated again, he felt the urge to get out of there. He sharpened his gaze and channeled the energy from his talesma to the stick bug's frequency.

He just needed one precise order. Then, the stick bug let a small bronze plaque fall from the tree. Nahuel caught it in the air. On it was inscribed *First Hazna.*

"Awesome," Aremi said.

"We got it!" Isaline added, raising her arms in success.

But Nahuel didn't have time to rejoice.

Now he was sure there was someone behind them. He could feel a hostile presence. He turned around quickly and then continued looking in circles, searching in the darkness of the forest. He held his breath, his instincts proved to be right.

The gravel cracked near where they were. And a man emerged from the shadows.

The stranger wore a dark, plain wool overcoat. His white skin shone against it. He carried a quiver full of red arrows on his back, but no bow. He looked like a ghost. His hair was white as chalk and the long coat hung below his feet, making it look like he was floating.

Nahuel felt a sudden chill run through his entire body. Aremi's green eyes filled with fear as her gaze met his.

"Nahuel," the stranger said in a ghastly voice. The word lit a fire of adrenaline within the boy.

Then, another man appeared. He came out of thin air, from behind the tree Isaline was standing next to. He was wearing a hood, but they could see his bloodshot eyes and the wild look on his face. He stood next to the first man, in front of the three friends. They looked straight at Nahuel, unflinching, like predators who can't take their eyes off their prey.

Then a woman appeared. She walked over to the others, her long strange white hair spreading out behind her like a long cape. She had a snake wrapped around her neck. It was a black mamba, the most deadly African weapon Nahuel had ever seen in his life.

It took him a few seconds to make sense of what was standing before him. He blinked, trying to get a good look at them. Two more men appeared, there were now five strangers standing in front of them. All had matching white hair.

His insides were gripped with tension. The beautiful forest, now a scene of terror.

The strangers came near them, slowly and silently, their eyes fixed on

Nahuel as they walked, closer and closer. Their black clothes dragging on the ground and their white hair unifying them.

The three friends drew close together, as if they could protect themselves better. Nahuel clenched his fists at his side. He felt a stab, but the pain of the blisters had been relegated to the background.

"Who are you?" He asked, facing them.

Nahuel had an idea of who they were, and it made things worse. The last time he had heard about them, there hadn't been any survivors. But what did they want now?

"It was too easy to alienate you from your classmates," the man with the quiver said. "Now, be a good boy, Nahuel, and come with us."

Nahuel tried to swallow, his throat tight with fear. The immensity and darkness of the forest only made the situation more terrifying.

The strangers circled around them, just steps away.

Nahuel didn't take his eyes off the man with the quiver. He moved the fingers on one hand like he was playing the piano. He had no fingernails. It looked like he had ripped them out himself. His fleshy rotten fingers were revolting.

Nahuel had to think what to do now. How to get out of there with his friends. A surge of adrenaline rushed up his spine. Before he could decide whether to try running away or to face these strangers unarmed, he sensed a movement far off. At first it sounded like a buzzing inside his head, but then it became recognizable. It was the sound of a stampede across the forest floor.

The snake twisted around the woman's neck and hissed the way only poisonous snakes do. They had heard it too. The woman gave an almost imperceptible signal to her group and then they all faded back into the forest as quickly as they could.

"Where are they going?" Isaline murmured, her voice shaking.

The strangers ran, pushing through an area full of branches. They mixed in among the trees and disappeared. They seemed to fade into thin air as easily as ghosts.

"Do you hear that?" Nahuel asked.

"What?" Isaline asked.

It was a monotonous and wild sound full of claws, paws and hooves hitting the ground. He could feel the ground shake as it drew closer. It made Nahuel's heart beat like a drum.

Between the sound of the stampede, the crunch of leaves and sticks and the buzz of insects in the forest, it was hard to tell where the sound was coming from.

Nahuel pushed the girls under the protective shade of a huge tree. He climbed the trunk quickly, almost supernaturally with feline agility, without paying attention to the pain of the blisters. He felt a branch slap him in the face. He pushed it aside and saw furry red animals moving through the trees, with antlers poking through the branches. There were few images that could amaze him like this one.

Soon, the sounds changed into dry, strong thuds that were quickly drawing near.

The stampede was getting closer.

A herd of deer came tearing through the thick forest at full speed, jumping over any obstacle in their way.

Nahuel was flooded with relief. He could see Ankona, striding quickly along and dodging obstacles with surprising agility. His beaded necklace shook against his tough skin.

Nahuel climbed quickly and easily down from the tree and once on the ground, he told the girls what he had seen.

Isaline and Aremi came out from their hiding spot. Nahuel waited impatiently, trying to control the fire raging through his nervous system. He raised his hand to his forehead and wiped away the sweat.

"Here you are," Ankona said in his deep voice. He was slightly out of breath and his face was unusually tense, he looked worried. Other footsteps came to rest on the carpet of flowers all around them. Their professor wasn't alone, he was with a herd of deer and a few more men.

"It seems they took the path north," one of the men said, examining tracks in the dirt like a professional hunter.

"You keep following them," Ankona ordered. The men with Ankona took off quickly down the path. The herd of deer split in two, half going with the men.

"Is anyone hurt?" the professor asked, looking closely at Nahuel.

"No. What's going on, Professor?" He asked.

As soon as Nahuel looked him in the eyes he knew what would happen. *He won't tell us the truth*, he thought.

"Go back to the Estate. Sleipnir will take you," Ankona said.

A majestic deer, the one with the largest antlers, took a step forward.

Ankona turned to them, sternly he said: "You shouldn't have gone so far."

They were about to object but Ankona and the others turned away leaving the students to follow Sleipnir to the fastest way out of the forest.

Nahuel wanted to communicate with Sleipnir. He wanted to confirm who the strangers were, how they had invaded the peaceful forest, but he hadn't learned how to communicate with mammals yet, let alone such complex ones.

He couldn't help but stare at the deer. He was amazed by his presence, by the perfection of him. He was elegant and calm, and his step was firm, like he was the guardian of the entire forest. He was the one Ankona had chosen to take care of them, which made Nahuel trust him immediately.

They walked on a while, zigzagging through the underbrush. The deer walked on firmly and seemed to be hearing all the sounds of the forest the students couldn't.

Soon, they could see the columns of the Estate through the trees. Safety close at hand. So no one was prepared for what happened next.

It happened so fast, there was nothing Nahuel could have done to stop it.

A single arrow flew through the sequoias, making its way through the dense forest straight to Sleipnir's heart. The deer fell instantly. The crash of his antlers against the ground echoed through the forest.

The stranger with the quiver appeared out of nowhere, like he was levitating among the branches. He was a very skilled CymMens.

"Nahuel," he said again in that raspy and unnerving voice.

A bright red flame crossed his body, anger or terror, or his wild instinct, Nahuel didn't know.

The man leaped down from ridiculously high and landed practically on top of him. Nahuel was exposed, with Sleipnir wounded and his partners unarmed, he was an easy target.

But he wouldn't give up without striving. His instincts emerged almost immediately and a primitive power roared inside trying to get out.

With a precise leap, Nahuel placed himself between his friends and the man with the quiver. If necessary, he would use his brute force.

But just then, from the right, Council agents appeared, running at full speed from the Estate. The stranger had no choice but to run away, chased by his enemies. Nahuel watched again as he scampered away with supernatural stealth.

Nahuel kneeled down next to the deer and felt the pain he could see expressed in the animal's eyes.

His heart beat in his chest with terrifying ferocity. With an uncontrollable urge, he threw his head back and let out a scream of rage. In the same wave of energy, he grabbed the arrow and pulled it from Sleipnir's chest then threw it upward, aiming at the spot where the attacker had been. The arrow stuck firmly in the tree.

Aremi's lips were pale and Isaline stumbled aimlessly, looking for something to steady herself against.

Nahuel crouched down close to Sleipnir.

The blood pouring from his wound stained his fur. Nahuel covered the spot with his hand and pressed hard. At that moment, Sleipnir started to shake, his limbs grew tense, his gaze faltered, and thick saliva hung around his snout.

Nahuel hugged him tight. With one hand he covered the wound and with the other he gripped his back. The boy's eyes burned with fear and rage. Why hadn't he learned yet how to share his energy with animals? The professors had only explained to them how to borrow energy.

Sleipnir's body temperature raised, as if he were burning up on the inside. Between the spasms, his eyes filled with shadows.

Aremi let out a stifled cry.

"It's poisoned." She was on tip-toe with her magnifying glass studying the arrow stuck in the tree. She knew exactly what had happened. "In the desert they use them to kill the foxes when they start hunting the sheep. I can tell by the purple tip."

Bastards, Nahuel thought.

"What do we do? What do we do?!" Isaline was about to have a nervous breakdown. She ran over to Aremi and Nahuel and tried not to look at Sleipnir, who had stopped convulsing, but still had a vacant stare, like he was possessed.

After a few moments, the deer regained consciousness. He was upset, like something inconceivable had happened. And he looked tired, worn out, exhausted… In this state, he was unable to communicate with Ankona from this far away.

Nahuel looked into his eyes. They were large, dark, almond-shaped, and outlined with white fur, which gave him a kind air.

Sleipnir knew what he needed in order to save himself. There was something on his face that led Nahuel to understand that much. He instantly realized that the survival of this animal depended on one crucial thing. He had to help him.

He experienced a desperation wave. And, suddenly, the space lost all its meaning; there was no up or down, just the force, the pressure, and the acceleration that immersed him into a cold and raging nothingness.

He felt like he was underwater. He couldn't understand why his mind was trying to make its way through a dark and sticky world. His senses of hearing and smell were extremely heightened. The coppery smell of the blood filled his nasal cavities. For a moment his mind swam through a murky world.

Nahuel jumped backwards. Then he turned suddenly, looking for something. He had heard sounds and a voice all mixed up in his head, like a lunatic in the middle of a breakdown.

"What's happening?" Aremi asked him.

Nahuel knew what they had to do, with the type of clarity that only his privilege could give to him. A shot of adrenaline brought him to his feet.

"Satiam, at the Estate," he said, releasing the air he had been holding in his lungs, "RUN!"

The girls looked at each other, scared and clearly shaken by his request. Nahuel's hands were dripping with Sleipnir's blood.

"Who is Satiam?" Isaline asked.

"He has the antidote. Find him. Sleipnir only has a few minutes left," Nahuel told them.

"And how do you know?" Isaline asked him.

But Aremi had already taken off running, so Isaline followed her.

There was nothing more Nahuel could do, except wait.

CHAPTER 16

The girls came rushing back with Satiam, riding a wave of hope.

He was a Health specialist and had the antidote with him.

Satiam had a shaved head and sincere eyes. He took the antidote from his bag and injected it into Sleipnir's veins.

The deer's mind began to clear and his eyes started to focus.

"Will he survive?" Nahuel asked.

Aremi held her breath.

"Yes, he will, we are lucky."

Two months earlier the Serums Commission of the Council of Privileges had taken samples of the poison used against the NAGAS agents at the attack of the helicopter in Egypt, and just three days ago they had been able to produce a successful antidote using baobab root.

"Are you ok?" Satiam asked, turning to Nahuel, while he put the syringe in his briefcase.

The boy was pale, he swayed for a moment and took a step back so as not to fall. His legs were not responding, he felt dizzy, as if his energy had been sucked. His vision was blurred and he saw everything dark for a second.

"You are weak and I don't like those blisters", Satiam said.

"They appeared due to Letharia Vulposa," Isaline explained.

"That explains the greenish color; we'll have to treat them with…"

"Pitch from the trunk of a young, manipulated tree that is not infected with the mushrooms," Isaline completed.

"Exactly. Follow me now, we'll go to the infirmary," he said and grabbed Nahuel from underneath his arm to help him walk to the Estate.

The kids together with Satiam made their way back to the Estate. They were forty minutes late after the Hazna's time limit, but they didn't care about that anymore. They had saved Sleipnir.

Nahuel was directly taken to the infirmary; he had lost too much energy and the blisters had already covered his hand, his arm, his shoulder and part of the neck.

As soon as he felt a squashy mattress underneath his body, he gave himself entirely to the blackness that had been stalking him since the attack to Sleipnir.

When he opened his eyes, it was already dark, he could see the moon through the window next to his bed. It took some time before he understood where he was. The Ardemir infirmary was small, the walls were covered in light wood, and it had room for three beds. He was on the one in the middle.

And he wasn't alone. There was a grey ball of hair over his legs, a cat, that's what it was. It was peacefully sleeping in a curled-up position. He had to take another second to understand what that cat was doing there. It must have been part of the healing. In the classes, they had explained that when a CymAnis lost energy, being in contact with an animal could help them recover it.

Nahuel quickly examined his body to assess the damage. He had bandages around his arm and his neck smeared with sap. Besides that, he was fine. Sleeping, and probably the cat, had made him feel better, he felt strength again.

He looked at the watch that his grandfather had given him and it stroke 2 a.m. It seemed that he would spend all night at Ardemir.

At that moment, the door opened. Ankona heard the change in Nahuel's breath and knew he had awakened.

"The energy you used to connect with Sleipnir that way was too much for you."

Nahuel sat on his bed all of a sudden. The abrupt movement made the cat on his feet to awake and frowned upon him.

"Generally, a CymAnis needs at least one copper a-bula to achieve something similar to what you have done with Sleipnir," Ankona continued while standing by the window.

"Who were they?" Nahuel wanted to know. Both knew who he was asking about.

"If you don't learn to recognize your limits, your privilege could kill you," Ankona seriously pointed out.

"Were they caught?" Nahuel insisted, as he didn't want to be lectured at that moment.

"They managed to escape," Ankona answered. He looked away without being able to hide his disgust.

Nahuel took off the bed sheets, pulling at them with excessive force. "Will you track them down?"

"I have done so till the evening, and some of my best trackers are still at it," Ankona answered.

"They said that they have drawn us away from the group intentionally, but, why? What did they want from us?"

"They evaded our defenses. They camouflaged their smells and sneaked in our security lines," Ankona said, his lips had turned into a fine line. "But, be calm, this won't happen again."

"Everyone had white hair, but they looked young," Nahuel added while he stretched his arm to pet the cat that seemed upset with too much chat and was digging its claws in revenge.

"Black clothes and white hair, those are their distinctive features."

"Were they Ignobles?" Nahuel said. That idea had been rolling around in his mind since they appeared in the forest glade.

"How do you know about them?" Ankona looked with curiosity.

Nahuel simply held his gaze. He wasn't going reveal that he had read the note that Ankona had sent to professor Greenwood about the attack to the helicopter. Instead, with boldness he asked:

"Why did they know my name?". He couldn't take his mind off that horrible feeling of listening his name in the mouth of the man with the quiver,

"I don't know, they shouldn't know who you are."

"Why were they here?" Nahuel asked again.

"I think you already know."

"They were looking for me…but I cannot find the reason why." What did those people wanted? A few ideas beat inside his head, trying to take it all in and what it might mean, but he couldn't make sense of it.

"It's not for me to explain that to you. But I can warn you about the danger. The Ignobles are opposite forces of the Council. They have been present since the beginning of our history, but, recently, they have gained more power and followers."

"But, why did they want me to go with them?" Nahuel insisted.

"It's important for you to be careful," Ankona said. "Just use the tunnels to move around the city and let me know if you find something out of the ordinary."

Ankona approached the desk at the other side of the room and turned his back for a while. Then, he came close and left him a food tray over the table next to his bed. "Eat," he said.

And he left.

This wasn't the world Nahuel thought he knew, but some other, full of dangers and threats which had apparently been lurking there for all time.

Christmas break came and went in the blink of an eye.

The aroma of the delicacies Mrs. Penington was treating them to the following day could already be smelled through the entire residency. That morning, as the first rays of light appeared at dawn, she had shut herself in the kitchen to begin preparing what she announced would be "the best lunch of their lives."

The days after the Hazna, Nahuel and Isaline started spending more and more time with Aremi.

The forest had brought them together. The traumatic attack and the experience of almost seeing Sleipnir die had united them in a way they couldn't share with their classmates. Nahuel had made a point of inquiring about the deer's health before winter break. Ankona had told him he was strong and making a quick recovery.

Nahuel had told the girls about the conversation que had had with Ankona at the infirmary, even though he had intentionally omitted the question he did to the professor about why the Ignobles knew his name. The fact that those people knew his name couldn't be something good. The girls hadn't mentioned that either. Maybe with the shock they hadn't listened well.

In turn, they did ask him, more than once, how he had managed to connect with Sleipnir. Isaline claimed that a CymAnis needed many years of study to connect with such a complex animal. That is why she wanted to have all the details of what Nahuel had done and felt to achieve it. Meanwhile, Aremi couldn't stop mentioning how extraordinary Nahuel was for having saved Sleipnir.

Nahuel, Aremi and Isaline were in the living room, enjoying some free time. They had received the results of the Hazna that day. Nahuel's stomach knotted as he took his envelope. His grade for the evaluation was inside and it would tell him whether or not he had any hope of gaining a level this year.

He took his time opening the envelope. Then he read:

FIRST HAZNA.
EVALUATION OF NAHUEL BLEST.
Highest Mark: 10. Passing Mark: 4. Lowest Mark: 1.

—Individual Mark: 6.
CymAnis Performance: 10.
Solving of the Riddle: 4.
Willingness to work as part of a group: 8.
Application of all knowledge acquired: 3.

—Group Mark: 9.
Performance of all three privileges: 10.
Solving of the Riddle: 9.
Willingness to work as a group: 9.
Application of all knowledge acquired: 8.
Meeting all conditions and requirements of the exercise, including punctuality: 7.

Bit by bit, his breathing steadied. The possibility of obtaining a more powerful a-bula was still intact.

"You got the 3 because you hurt your hand," Isaline said, reading his letter over his shoulder. "You didn't read my notes from Limits very carefully."

Nahuel grimaced in agreement, remembering the burning sensation. Isaline had got a 10 on that part.

Aremi had also received a 10 on solving the riddle and another 10 on performance of her privilege.

"It's not fair that our grade was lowered for being late, haven't they noticed that we were saving the world?" complained Isaline and scowled at the mark.

"Oh, *Mon Dieu!*" Nahuel teased her, trying to imitate her distinctive french accent.

There was another page, after the grades that provided further information. For example, explaining that the Kamaflaz Phasmatodea, commonly known as the Stick Bug, was known and greatly appreciated by the privileged as one of their most respected spies. The bugs cooperated on several missions, providing valuable information. The Stick Bug is one of the few animals able to understand what any privileged person says, not only those who are CymAnis.

There was also a historical summary of the Hazna, explaining it was a millennia old practice, going back to the golden age of the privileged society. At that time, it had been an aggressive and dangerous competition among privileged ones. In order not to repeat the errors of their ancestors, the rules had been changed. The goal now was for all three privileges to interact in a real environment, recognizing the strengths of each privilege.

There was wood crackling in the fireplace and the living room was the coziest spot in the residency.

Now that they knew the results of their Hazna, the friends were more relaxed and at ease. Aremi was hanging red and golden glass balls on the Christmas tree Mrs. Penington had made grow in the living room. The circles that had covered her soft hands the entire week after the hunt were beginning to fade. While the ones from Nahuel could be distinguished from afar.

The tree was twice Aremi's height and everyone who saw it through the large bay window was stunned by its beauty.

For the privileged society, Christmas was just one more celebration and not as meaningful and relevant to them as other celebrations they had inherited from their ancestors. All the same, Mrs. Penington, put great effort into making each celebration special, so the students wouldn't miss their homes and how they were used to celebrating.

Isaline was sitting on a fluffy cushion and, with a rainbow-colored pencil she had borrowed from Aremi, was making a list of gifts and cards to send to her family.

From France, her mother had already reminded her that her father expected a gift from her. Isaline was dying to buy him a precision serum. They sold it at a shop called *Sports in your Hands* in the Hedge Garden. The clerk had assured her that with just three drops of that serum, you could throw any object with absolute precision during three hours. Isaline knew that would improve her father's golf game. But after rethinking it, she realized there was no way she could explain where the gift had come from, so she chose instead to send him some simple leather gloves.

"Isaline, can you move the newspaper off the table for me?" Nahuel asked, balancing his chess board in his hands.

She glanced up from her notebook and slid the newspaper over with her mind.

Nahuel set the board down on the cleared space and accidently knocked a pawn onto the floor. It rolled under the Christmas tree.

"Isaline…"

She looked up at him.

"Can you get me that piece, please?" he asked, pointing at it.

It flew through the air until it landed in his hand. After putting it back in place, he sat on the floor and tried to think of his next move. Now it was his bishop's turn to take down his grandfather's king.

"Isaline," he called a third time.

"What now?"

"Would you be so kind as to pass me that green pillow?" he asked in his politest voice. He couldn't concentrate if he was uncomfortable.

"No," she replied curtly and looked back at her notebook.

"I've already sat down and it's right next to you," he insisted.

"Then it is only 6 feet away from you," she retorted.

"Please…."

"Stop looking at me with orphan baby deer eyes. You remind me of Bambi. I will do it this time, but I am not going to keep enabling your laziness," she scolded him, trying hard to look indignant. In the meantime, the cushion rose in the air, and landed gently on Nahuel's lap.

"I need a chess partner who is at least in the same hemisphere as me," Nahuel declared once he was comfortable. "When do you want me to teach you to play?"

"Mmm, someday…", Aremi replied reluctantly.

"Someday a long time from now," Isaline clarified.

Aremi stifled a giggled and turned her head away.

Nahuel gave them a disgusted look and at the same time a small moth flew over his shoulder and headed at full speed for Isaline's hair. She tried to swat it away with her pencil, until she had no other choice but to get up and move over to the window, where Aremi continued to hang up the Christmas decorations, selecting the prettiest ones.

The moth didn't give up though. It followed her to the window and this time began bothering both girls.

Isaline shook her hair obsessively, trying to get the little bug out and Nahuel, who had been containing himself exploded in laughter.

"You did it!" Isaline cried.

"You don't need to attack us with your privilege Nahuel. We'll learn to play chess...someday," Aremi commented slyly.

Nahuel gave up, smiling and shrugged his shoulders. The moth buzzed by Aremi's eyes one last time and then escaped toward the kitchen.

Christmas morning, Nahuel woke up feeling pleased to find himself thousands of miles away from Ushuaia.

It had been a long time since he had a good Christmas. On that day, his mother used to get out of the house early and came back after her son was asleep. Nahuel thought she did that in order not to have to pretend to be happy.

That date was special for her, as, apart from being Christmas, it was her birthday and, before moving to Ushuaia, those festive days were her favorite.

Nahuel had them instilled in his memory. He still remembered how his mother used to completely decorate their childhood home. She would put a huge Santa Claus next to the front door, garlands on the window frames, colorful centerpieces, and a Christmas tree, that it may not have been as impressive as Mrs. Penington's tree, but Nahuel remember it as being extraordinary. Besides, those days his father was always at home, as he never allowed his trips to intervene between him and spending Christmas with the family.

The most anxiously awaited moment for everyone was when opening the presents. He would have the tree full of small, medium, and big presents. His father gave his mother a painting created by him which would portray the best moments as a couple and as a family. Besides, she would receive a bouquet of flowers with the number of flowers representing her age. Nahuel had no idea what his mother had done with the paintings after moving to Ushuaia.

Sometimes, Nahuel thought he had imagined those happy moments. Since his father disappeared, his mother's attitude had completely changed. She was not only sad all day, but she seemed to be angry at him. There were even some moments in which she seemed to blame him for her misery. Didn't she realize that he had also lost his father? And, with that, his mother as well.

"Merry Christmas!" Aremi greeted him as she sat down next to him at breakfast.

It was lunchtime and Mrs. Penington had extended the dining room table. As she served freshly baked bread, Nahuel thought that the Christmas apron she wore every day finally made sense.

Emma, who had been trying to hide an acne outbreak since the Hazna, was full of tears as she read and reread a letter from her family. Kana had a Manga comic at the table. Damian, who loved comics, was trying to look at the illustrations over her shoulder, but he couldn't make sense of the writing in Japanese.

Emre shook the white pom-pom on his Christmas hat in circles. He did it incessantly until it finally broke off and flew onto Layla's plate, splattering her veil with mashed sweet potatoes.

Isaline and Aremi chatted lively about the world globe Aremi had just bought for their room. From what Nahuel could gather, the globe showed the changing seasons throughout the year, around the world. With each passing month, the continents changed color according to the season. That winter day, the northern hemisphere was covered with white snow and frozen rivers.

"Is this seat taken?" a male voice asked.

Isaline sat up straighter. Nahuel turned around. Benjamin was standing behind them. He took off a wool cap spotted with snowflakes and shook out his golden hair.

"No," Isaline replied.

Benjamin sat down next to her and casually placed a box of chocolates on the table. It had a large red bow and brushed against his plate and Isaline's.

"For a minute there I thought you all would be the best," Benjamin said provocatively.

"What are you talking about?" Nahuel asked.

"About the Hazna grades. You came in second place by only a few decimals but were well behind Rebecca's group, which came in first," he explained, with a taunting smile.

"Those results are confidential," Isaline said.

"Not when you've got the right contacts," he shot back at her playfully, winking.

Isaline stiffened in her chair.

"All right, love, don't get mad. I understand you had a few inconveniences."

"Let's just say they were more than inconveniences," Nahuel replied, suddenly interested in the turn the conversation had taken. "And what do you and your contacts know about the *inconveniences*?"

"A bit…"

"Come on, don't make us beg," Nahuel insisted, leaning across his plate to get a better view of Benjamin.

"Only that they caught one of them," Benjamin said, lowering his voice. "But they couldn't get much information out of him."

"Why not?" Isaline asked.

"He killed himself the first chance he got," Benjamin replied, shrugging.

Nahuel was shocked; committing suicide seemed to be a decision that only a fanatic would take, or maybe someone who actually had a big secret to hide.

Just then, the kitchen door opened and Victoria and Mrs. Penington came in carrying a stuffed turkey on a large tray. Benjamin stood up with the box of chocolates in his hands and went toward the two women.

"Merry Christmas, Ophelia. This is just a tiny symbol of your immense sweetness," he said handing her the box of chocolates.

"Oh, Benjamin, you're always so lovely," Mrs. Penington exclaimed, blushing a bit.

Nahuel saw Isaline hiding a smile.

That afternoon, Nahuel called his grandfather.

"Hello?" As soon as he heard his grandfather's gruff voice on the phone, he immediately wished he was there with him.

"Merry Christmas grandpa," he greeted.

"It's been so long since I heard your voice, my boy," the old man said.

"I'm sorry. I couldn't call for the past two weeks," Nahuel apologized, although, all things considered, he didn't think fifteen days were too much time, at least the time had slipped by rather quickly for him.

"Don't worry. How are things going up there?" his question carried a concern in his voice that Nahuel couldn't help noticing.

"Everything is...fine." He didn't want to hide from him what had happened in the Hazna with the Ignobles, but he was pretty sure that it was part of the secret of the Council of Privileges and, therefore, he couldn't share it with anybody. Besides, he didn't want to worry his grandfather who, by the way, already sounded concerned.

"I still ask myself how I could have let them take you," the old man sighed.

"You said it was a great opportunity, that I couldn't turn it down," Nahuel reminded him.

"And I was right. It's just that, I wish you weren't so far away," his grandfather confessed.

"I'll be back in just a little more than six months," Nahuel said.

"Speaking of which, I've been thinking about coming to visit you sooner. I just have one thing to finish here and we'll soon be together, face to face, in New York."

"That would be great, grandpa!" Nahuel eagerly said. "So, it's only a little time before we meet again!" he added, trying to cheer him up.

"I know. Don't pay any attention to me. It's old people problems."

"You're not old, grandpa."

"You're kind, my boy, but I can feel the years, my strength is not the same as before."

Nahuel didn't know what to say.

"You just take care of yourself," his grandfather insisted.

"I will," Nahuel promised him.

"Now, tell me all about New York. I remember it was impressive in my days, so I can only imagine what it must be like now," the old man went on, in a more relaxed tone.

Nahuel couldn't shake a bittersweet feeling the rest of the day.

The first day of classes, after winter break, had come to an end. The entrance to the tunnels was jammed full with people. Professor Ankona's lesson had flown by. Vertebrates promised to be harder, but more challenging.

Nahuel had planned to meet with his friends to take a cart back to the residency together. He spotted them at the top of the stairs, crammed in a corner. Aremi was wearing a purple and yellow blouse, which peaked out from her black vest and wide legged trousers, hiding her petite figure. Nahuel smiled. Aremi was always challenging the rules of fashion.

The girls let the men and women in a hurry pass them. They all wore identical black vests with green trim and a golden symbol was embroidered on the chest: *Security Committee.*

The atmosphere was unusually tense. Nahuel didn't recognize any of the faces in the crowd, but he could tell they were brimming with nervousness.

"What's going on around here?" he asked his friends as soon as he got within earshot.

They turned to look at him.

"I don't know, but it doesn't look good," Aremi suspected.

"I don't remember ever running into so many people here," Nahuel noted.

"It is because there have never been so many here," Isaline told him. "I have already counted twenty-eight agents from the same committee and we have never before seen more than ten together."

"Something's definitely going on," Nahuel figured. "I wonder what…"

"We heard something," Aremi said in a low voice.

"They are going to an emergency meeting," Isaline explained. "We heard a man say they had been summoned with urgency."

"Let's figure out why," Nahuel said, elbowed his friends and hurried to blend in with the rest of the agents. Luckily their own vests, also black, helped them to blend in.

They followed the agents, without standing out, acting like they belonged with the group. It didn't hurt that the agents were so absorbed in their own worries that they didn't pay any attention to who was around them.

A man rushed past them, until he reached a woman wearing her hair in a sloppy bun, and he grabbed her by the arm.

"Cristina."

Nahuel told the girls to speed up their pace to come closer and put his finger to his lips slowly, to signal they should all be quiet and pay attention.

The woman turned around.

"You of all people must know why we are here," the man said in a low voice. "It's the canals, isn't it?"

"No," the woman replied, shaking her head.

"Tell me the truth, the Ignobles found what they are looking for?" the man insisted.

"No. Julian will share us the complete report as soon as we reach the Control Room," the woman explained, without elaborating.

"Today was my day off and I had plans with my girlfriend," he complained.

The woman looked at him severely.

"This is no time for useless comments. What has happened might be irreversible," she warned and firmly stepped away from the man.

The three friends walked by the classrooms and continued down a wide hallway. Nahuel didn't think he had ever been down this part of the labyrinth that was the sub-4th floor of the United Nations. If Ankona wasn't going to give him more information, he would have to find out more about the Ignobles on his own.

They stopped in their tracks when they heard Sebastian's voice coming toward them from behind. They automatically stepped to the side and hid behind a large clock next to the wall. It was a giant hourglass time piece, taller than Nahuel and all three of them squeezed in behind it so they wouldn't be seen. They held their breath until Sebastian's wide shoulders were out of sight and the echo of the agents' footsteps had faded away.

They came out of their hiding spot and noticed the Control Room just a few feet away. The agents were coming in, but the kids were not able to get even closer without being seen.

The last agent entered the room and the door swung shut.

The Control Room was used to solve all sorts of emergency situations. A high-definition screen filled an entire wall. There was also a team of technicians, analysts and project managers who were in constant contact with the various international headquarters of the Council of Privileges.

"Sir, our delegates are not responding," an analyst announced.

Julian began the meeting. His face was drawn, he was standing, tense, and breathing heavily as if he were dealing with the pressure of an enormous wave.

"I'm afraid that the damage they have done this time is of a different nature. Their interest was not purely tactical. Granted, this doesn't make it any less pernicious.

"Our source at Sigma Information has notified us that the Ignobles have moved. We now know that they have headed…*toward the end of the world.*"

CHAPTER 17

The dogs' tracks led away from the house, down the street. The two Siberians had left the backyard just in time. They had been sent to the edge of the city, where they would be safe.

The sun was just beginning to set, behind the snow-covered mountains. The few rays of light streaming in through the window lit the room. The old man waited, calmly, prepared to face his unavoidable destiny.

He was sitting in the living room, completely defenseless. His lips curved in an almost imperceptible smile of resignation.

Two bodies lie in the front yard, the marks on them revealing their last battle. Even though he tried, he blamed himself for not being able to get his protectors to leave him alone, to fend for himself.

The door opened quietly, and the couple entered the room. Their faces were hidden in the shadows, but the old man didn't need to see them to know who they were. Their white hair gave them away.

"Don't you recognize your house guests, Blest?" asked a cold, male voice.

"I don't think house guests is the right word. What is true is that it's a surprise to find you here, but not a very nice one," the elder replied. "You can have a seat if you like," inviting them with a sweep of his arm to sit on the couch in front of him.

"Your hospitality won't save you, old man," the woman hissed.

"I wasn't counting on it," he replied calmly.

For a split second, he thought of escaping, but dying while running away was not the end he wanted for himself.

"It's been a long time since we wanted to reach out to you," the man said. "Only rats are able to hide this well, and you've done it wonderfully."

"I had my reasons," said drily the old man. He didn't want to show how much it bothered to him that they had finally found him, although he knew that he had taken that risk since the moment he let Nahuel go.

The couple stepped further into the room. The door slammed shut. The woman sat down with exaggerated poise and spread her long black overcoat out behind her. The man went and stood next to the impressive fireplace, behind the sofa. When he turned to look at the record player next to him, the scar digging across his skull came into view.

He moved the needle toward the record, trying to make the old thing work. But nothing happened.

"You have to give it a few seconds to get going. It's an antique," the old man explained.

The man turned and shot the elder a menacing look over his shoulder. He never liked being told how to do things.

The turntable started moving and the sound of singing bowls filled the room. The old man thought that after all these years of listening to that sharp and penetrating melody, it had never sounded so sinister.

"You're after me," the old man said, meeting and holding the gaze of the woman seated across from him. "You didn't need to kill those young men."

"Your bodyguards were truly annoying," the woman retorted. "You have no one but yourself to blame. You shouldn't have let two inexperienced boys play babysitter to an old man. It was ridiculously easy to kill them," the woman concluded, flashing him her best smile.

The old man's eyes studied the man slowly.

"I must say I'm not that surprised that you've been seduced by the empty promises of grandeur of this woman," he mused. "But there were people who expected more from you, Marco Pozzan," he reprimanded.

Marco's eyes filled with a deep hatred. It had been a very long time since someone had called him by his last name. The man with the scar across the back of his head would not let the ghosts of his past into the room in that moment. It had been years since he had turned his back on that identity. He no longer acknowledged his family surname as his own.

"She showed me the path of redemption and liberation," he replied with conviction. "You, on the other hand, are fooled by the official speech, by those who believe they have the monopoly on truth."

"You know you'll never convince me with that preaching," the elder stated. "You yourself know the reasons behind our stance."

"You're all so faithful to the Pact," the man confirmed with disgust. He sat down next to his lover and continued, "A virtue you've been bragging about since the beginning of time."

"I don't understand how you aren't bored by it," she scoffed. "It's obsolete, just like you, old man."

The sun sank behind the mountains and shadows fell in the house. The woman didn't hesitate to light the lamp next to her, with her mind. The couple sat under a pool of dim light. Their white hair looked like a terrifying silver in the glow.

The old man's expression was inscrutable as he faced his guests. The wrinkles on his face conveyed no emotion. The last decades of his life had prepared him for this moment. He hadn't yet reached his seventieth birthday.

"Where is your a-bula," Marco asked.

"It's not here," the old man replied. "You can look for it if you like. I have all the time in the world."

Marco pursed his lips. He believed the elder. He would take care of that later.

"Can you imagine what's coming next?" the woman's eyes shone with eagerness.

"I have been ready to face my death for years. I'm not afraid," he challenged her.

"That may be," she said. "But we still have several hours before anyone will find you. No one will hear you scream."

It was a relief to the elder to be alone. If anyone else had been there, they would have the same fate as his bodyguards.

"Only Moira will have fun with you today," the man mumbled. "We don't want to leave any traces of violence on you."

This wouldn't be the first time he was tortured. Experience had taught him that if he didn't scream, the psychopath didn't enjoy it and the pain ended sooner. All the same, the woman's sick face made him wonder whether or not there was any limit to her cruelty.

Moira remained seated on the sofa. The only movement she made was to raise her gloveless hand and smile, as if warning him she was starting. The old man's body went rigid immediately. It started like a slight tickle and bit by bit increased in intensity. He was overcome by uncontrollable convulsions. Suddenly, all the muscles in his body contracted, as if he had received hundreds of electrical shocks on every inch of his body.

The woman looked at him with ruthless eyes. She enjoyed seeing her victim's pain, like any serial killer would. The palm of her hand was awash with circular tattoos.

The old man gritted his teeth and breathed through his nose, trying to remain as quiet as possible.

After a few eternal seconds, the pain ceased. The woman looked at him, frustrated.

"You know I won't beg," the old man murmured from his chair, raising his head to look her in the eyes.

"Always so arrogant," Marco said.

The old man did not reply. He knew he would die by this man's hand, just like so many before him. He wouldn't give him the satisfaction of begging for his life.

The pain returned, this time more intense. He didn't know if it was coming from the inside or the outside. It felt like his arms and legs were being stretched. He was suspended in the air, face down, as if his extremities were being pulled in four different directions, by four wild beasts.

It felt like his body was tearing apart. The pain made him sweat. His forehead was dripping and he was afraid his spine would snap.

He remained silent. Not a single sound of pain escaped from his throat.

The woman was red with anger. He could see a halo of dark energy seeping from her a-bula.

Just as he thought he was going to be torn to pieces by the invisible beasts, the pain ceased and he fell roughly on the tile floor.

"He's not even defending himself!" The woman turned at her lover. She could sense that he was not resisting her torture in any way.

"Have you forgotten your combat techniques? If I remember correctly it's *Roar or Die*," the man questioned him with a calm and evil voice.

The old man knew he was going against his fighter instinct, but he didn't have the energy he once had. With dignity, and the help of the chair, he managed to stand on his feet.

"I don't find it very useful in this circumstance," he replied. "I can feel the presence of your followers, surrounding the house."

They stood ready, around the house, awaiting orders. There were a dozen white haired people, with wild dogs, ready to back up their leaders.

"Everything they say about you seems to be true," the old man mustered the words. He looked solely at her. "You have been well trained and your privilege is strong, very strong. If you would only use it for good…" he lamented.

"Good is overrated," she growled coldly.

The old man's eyes opened wide as saucers. He couldn't breathe. He gulped for air, trying to get oxygen into his lungs. But it was no use. His throat was sealed shut. He could almost feel the millions of bacteria that lived in his body gathering at the back of his throat. He was suffocating. It felt like metal bars were squeezing around his chest.

Moira laughed and watched him with a maniacal fascination. He fell over the chair, and just as he was about to lose consciousness, oxygen rushed into his body.

Marco had raised his hand slightly, asking his lover to stop for a moment.

"You think that causing me pain confirms your power over me," the elder said. "But fear is not what shows the strength of one man over another."

Moira looked at the old man like he was out of his mind. Pain and fear were the only things she understood.

"You know what we want from you, for this to end," the man stated, meaning the torture.

"You will never convince me to influence him," the old man spoke with difficulty. "You'll have to kill me."

"In the end, we will. You can count on that. Your rejection of our offer just confirms your stupidity," the woman responded.

He had always considered it highly likely, but now his death was an imminent reality.

"But before we kill you, I want you to know that we are going after your grandson," the man threatened.

"You'll never get his consent, and you will need it," the old man stated, still calm.

"We never would have got yours," the man replied, "But we won't rest until we get the boy's. As soon as we tell him the truth about what you've done, he will join us."

The old man's mouth was dry, and it was hard to swallow. He looked at the man dismally.

"He won't be any good to you without the instructions," he said.

"Don't worry about that, you rotten old man. We're closer than anyone ever before to finding them," Moira spat.

"Your torture will be to die knowing that your grandson will be ours," the man declared.

The old man straightened up and looked at him defiantly, in the eyes. His soul was fortified against defeat, but to hear his grandson threatened was something he wasn't prepared for.

At that moment, Moira let out a bloodcurdling scream and grabbed her head with her hands. She shook herself frenetically. She knew what was happening and it increased her suffering. Her tick had just released an excess of toxin.

The old man's lips curved upwards. The order he had given the tick had been a good use of his last ounces of energy.

A lock of her white hair turned black. She was furious, knowing very well that she would never be able to lighten it again.

"Damn you!" Moira shouted.

"You will pay for what you've done even after you're dead," Marco cursed.

The old man felt a scratching at the hem of his pants. He looked at his feet. A black scorpion was climbing up his leg. He used his threatening pinchers to climb the fabric.

"You'll leave your unique mark on me," he warned, looking Marco in the eyes. "Of course, I have left my mark on your lover, so I will receive yours with honor," he added with irony.

"It's a gift your friends at the Council of Privileges won't discover," and his eyes shone in the dark eager to take vengeance.

The mark that the scorpion would leave would be almost imperceptible and the poison of its tail was altered with snake's poison. All this was done to keep Marco's identity secret.

The scorpion moved slowly across the old man's chest. It moved up his shoulder and then made its way down his arm, resting on his wrist. It felt like a nail was puncturing his skin. When the animal removed his stinger, a few drops of blood appeared on the inside of his wrist and fell, hot and wet, to the floor.

He had only a few seconds to live.

He was consoled by the thought that at least his death wouldn't leave his grandson an orphan.

He felt his hand and then his arm go numb. As the poison ran through his veins, burning intensely, he thought the only regret in his life was not having told his grandson the history of their family and not being able to prepare him for the inevitable destiny awaiting him.

The old man dropped to his knees on the tile floor and fell heavily to one side. The music of the singing bowls, that he enjoyed so much, enveloped him in his final moments. His last hopes were for the happiness of his grandson. Lying on the floor, his face hardened and little by little he plunged into darkness.

The man with the scar on his skull gave the old man one last look of disgust before leaving the room. The lovers walked into the cold night air, satisfied.

The corpses of the bodyguards still lay on the grass. One of them showed the bloody signs of an attack by the wild dogs. The body of the other young man, whose face was covered with freckles, was still intact. He had died strangled by a cord around his neck. Neither of them was even thirty years old.

"Get rid of them," Marco ordered.

The next morning, a woman would come face to face with death's finality. The old man's cold body was waiting for her in the living room. The autopsy would say he had died due to cardio-respiratory failure. An imperceptible circle burned onto the inside of his wrist was the sign left by the Ignobles attack.

A thousand miles away, the wrist watch Nahuel had inherited stopped, frozen in time forever at 7:20pm.

The students were back in the residency. Nahuel, Isaline and Aremi had been the last to arrive for dinner. Mrs. Pennington had been worried by their delay. Time had flown by as they had snuck around trying to eavesdrop on the Security Committee agents.

"At least now we know they are looking for something," Nahuel said. "If we find out what it is, maybe we will understand what they are planning to do with it."

"The Ignobles are going to great pains to get it. It must be very important," Aremi deduced.

"Ssh," Isaline shushed them. Some of their other classmates were still at the table and Mrs. Penington was coming and going from the kitchen. "We must say the *Ign*..." she explained to them in an inaudible whisper.

"What?" Aremi asked, putting her ear by Isaline's mouth.

"The *Igno*..." she whispered. But almost no sound came from her mouth.

"What is she saying?" Nahuel asked, looking at Aremi.

"The *Ignobles*," Isaline said again, barely letting any sound out of her mouth as she said the word, so only her friends could hear her.

"The problem is, if we say it like that, we will never know what we are talking about," Aremi observed, teasing.

"Sh...e is right. I coul...dn't hear...anything," Nahuel agreed, his mouth full of broccoli.

"The point is that now we know, thanks to that big guy, that they are looking for something inside the canals," Isaline replied, picking up on Nahuel's original comment.

"There are hundreds of thousands of canals all over the world," Aremi blurted out. "I wonder which ones are they talking about?"

Nahuel remembered something that now seemed to have happened ages ago.

"The first day we went down to the sub-4th floor, the orientation day, Mrs. Sparling stopped at the News Room and..." Nahuel stopped for a moment while thinking, "and, while she was there, all screens synchronized a scene of a flood where we saw a broken canal, do you remember?"

"Now that you mention it, I do. Mrs. Sparling entered and gave orders to everybody in there," Isaline remembered.

"What I don't know is where that canal was from," Nahuel doubted.

"The newscast was in French, and the canal was from Belgium" Isaline firmly confirmed.

"So, the European canals," Aremi determined.

"Now we can guess that the Ignobles are looking for *something* in the European canals, but that still leaves unexplained what they were doing in the woods during the Hazna," Isaline said.

Nahuel had a lump in his throat. He knew the Ignobles were looking for him in the Hazna...but, why? All he could do was wonder.

CHAPTER 18

The next day, the air at dusk tasted strangely bitter.

As soon as he pushed open the door from the basement, he found Mrs. Penington waiting for him. She looked grief-stricken and her eyes were red.

"It's for you, Nahuel," she said, handing him the phone.

He looked at her in surprise. His grandfather never called during the weekdays.

"Hi, grandpa," he greeted, as he rushed up the stairs to his room.

"It's your mother, Nahuel," an apathetic voice replied.

"Mom?"

It was the first time she had called him since he had left Ushuaia four months ago. The unexpectedness of the call couldn't bring any good news.

"Yes, it's me. I have some bad news to give you," she said without pretext.

Nahuel waited silently. His stomach turned and without even realizing it, he sank onto his bed.

"Walter is dead," she said simply.

"Grandpa?" he asked, confused.

"Yes, I found him last night," she explained.

Nahuel's mother had come home and found her father in law stiff on the floor of the living room. She had gone toward the body, to check whether or not he was breathing. She had found the phone and reported the death of the elderly man she had been living with for more than eight years. Without crying. Without grief. Her husband's disappearance had consumed all of her pain and there was simply none left. She was condemned to a life of not feeling.

"He's *dead*?" Nahuel asked again. It came out more like a plea than a question.

"Yes, his life has come to an end," she repeated the definition. She told him about the death of the only paternal figure in his life as if she was telling him it was getting cold outside.

Nahuel tried to say something, but no sound would come out of his mouth.

His mother told him what had happened since she had found his grandfather's body.

"The doctors said he died of cardio-respiratory failure," she paused. "From what they said it would seem he didn't suffer."

Nahuel repeated the words to himself, sifting through them, trying to find the sense in them.

"This is no reason for you to end your studies in New York. The funeral is already over," she stated. "If your dogs come back, don't worry I will feed them. Have a good day," and she hung up.

Nahuel glanced over at his desk, as he held the phone, now silent, to his ear. The chessboard was there, next to a half-eaten bag of Emre's candy. The pieces were waiting for the next move. A move that would never be made.

He couldn't believe his grandfather would abandon him. He didn't want to believe it, couldn't think about it.

He couldn't remember even saying goodbye. His grandfather would never have left without saying goodbye. If he had done it, it would have been inexcusable, and therefore, impossible. His eyes gazed at nothing.

He slipped into a lethargy that would not let him think and he held onto that state of numbness. He would rather ignore that which he could not cope with.

He was deep in a place on the edge of time. Two centuries passed. The nighttime stories, the walks in the forest, the chess lessons, the passionate debates on current affairs, the pats on the back, the wise words and all the other uncountable moments shared with his grandfather bombarded his mind.

Days rushed by, the world turned cartwheels and then turned into nothing. But only minutes had passed.

He felt a bitter wave going up his chest, he knew that feeling, he had experienced it before … as a child. The difference with that time was that now he knew what it was. It was distress, a profound distress that was burning inside. First it was his father, and now…his grandfather.

Reality began to take shape in his mind and then pierced him like lightning. Everything was over. He would never see those deep eyes again; never be able to seek their guidance. The overwhelming awareness that he was alone, alone in the world, hit him hard.

He opened his hand and the phone slipped from it, thudding to the ground.

The world opened up under his feet, everything crumbled around him.

Anguish swirled inside him, choking him. The knot in his throat made breathing hard. His hands went numb and his body grew stiff.

His cheeks burned. Without being able to control it, his whole body began shaking. Something horrible was stuck in his chest like a dagger. His soul was hurting.

He stood up, prisoner of an animalistic rage.

That power was striving to get out; it was an ancient and powerful force. And Nahuel, this time, had no energy to control it.

He felt how it was taking hold of him, how it travelled all around his body and pumped in his blood. Nahuel was pure instinct and now the instinct was governing him, exactly the opposite to what his grandfather had taught him for years.

In no time, his room went dark. And, with a dangerous crash, the window of the room exploded.

The black pigeons, which used to watch him, had hit the glass and now, some of them were dying and were covered with blood on the floor.

When the light and the cold air entered through the hole that was left on the glass, Nahuel swiped at the pieces of the chessboard with his arm, sending them flying in all directions. He grabbed the board and banged it against a chair. He kept beating it furiously, unleashing the rage he felt, splintering it, until there was nothing left to break. His eyes were dangerous and alive.

Then, he couldn't keep it inside anymore and he let out a guttural moan. He threw himself on his bed, buried his head in the blanket and cried. He cried hot tears for the first time he could ever remember.

Nahuel didn't go down for dinner that night. Darkness closed over him. His bedroom walls separated him from a reality that would continue its course no matter how hard he wanted to stop it.

He was too young to realize that life is short, there's no time to waste lying down.

He didn't realize that Benjamin, upon Mrs. Penington's request, had cleaned his room and fixed the glass. At some place in his mind, Nahuel felt ashamed of it and especially for the pigeons, but his sadness overshadowed any other feeling.

That night his slumber was deep and black, the sleep of the desperate.

He was awoken by his own sadness and a ray of unwanted light that pierced his eyelids. It was morning. It didn't take long to remember why he felt so bad. He didn't know it yet, but this wound would never heal.

His body was stiff. The pins and needles in his legs were uncomfortable. He tried moving them, to wake them up. He looked at his wrist, to check the time and noticed his watch had stopped working. But he didn't take it off.

He went down to the dining room, but he wasn't hungry.

"Hi Nahuel," Aremi greeted him and took her bag off the chair next to her, to make room for him. But he just walked by, his head down.

"This afternoon we are going to see a show of acrobatics. This is the last week it will be in the city. You are coming, right?" Isaline said loudly, so he could hear her. "Mrs. Penington told us it can't be missed. One of her cousin's sons is performing. He has his own solo with rings. Of course, he is a CymMens," she explained.

Nahuel came back from the kitchen with a glass of ice cold water. He didn't bother answering the girls or even looking at them. They couldn't see that his eyes were swollen and had dark circles. Nahuel kept going toward the stairs, back to his room.

"What is his problem?" Isaline asked.

"Maybe we did something to annoy him," Aremi suggested.

"I doubt it," Isaline disagreed, adding out loud, so he could hear her, "He's just become rude for no reason."

Nahuel's bottom lip shook and his anger threatened to erupt. He had more than enough reasons. Why didn't Isaline mind her own business and leave him alone for once? He knew that if he tried to answer her, the only thing that would come out of his mouth would be angry screams, all aimed at his best friend.

He didn't sleep the whole night through for another two weeks.

He was still expecting his grandfather to call and prove his mother wrong. That was the problem with not attending the funeral. They had denied him the chance of seeing his grandfather one last time, and of convincing himself that he was truly gone.

Apollo and Atila had abandoned him too? His mother had said that his dogs had left. It only made things worse.

It wasn't long before Nahuel stopped being the serene person he had been. Now he was irritable, aggressive, and the slightest thing put him on edge. He was often upset and he didn't try to act like everything was ok. This way, people left him alone and he didn't have to explain anything.

He forgot about his 14th birthday, or else simply thought there was no reason to celebrate.

His behaviour upset Aremi and exasperated Isaline. They had tried on more than one occasion to try to understand what was bothering him. They could tell something had happened to him, but Nahuel remained stubbornly quiet and when he met their eyes seeking his, he tried to get away quickly.

At first, he had to hang behind intentionally, because the girls waited for him to share a cart to the sub-4th floor. However, after a few days of this, they stopped waiting for him, realizing he was avoiding them.

During class, he sat at the back, even in Mrs. Sparling's class, which meant running the risk that she would single him out with questions. He would rather take that risk than be hounded by the uncomfortable looks of Aremi and Isaline.

Emre avoided being alone with him in the room. He was grumpy, didn't laugh at Emre's jokes and only spoke in monosyllables. Tristan harassed him about his first failing marks. Only Mrs. Penington offered him a brief and affectionate smile every once in a while.

It wasn't hard to get used to being alone. He'd had fifteen years of practice. But this time he had chosen his isolation, immersing himself in a dark world where solitude was his single, stinging companion.

One winter morning, three weeks after his mother's phone call, the girls managed to drag him to the living room in the residency. If they had been able to predict that Nahuel was going to change into a grumpy ogre, they never would have made him part of their study group at the beginning of the year. Every subject in school had a group project which represented the most important grade of all and the classes that were shared by all three kinds of privileges required that they form groups comprised of one member from each privilege which they had to keep during their entire study program.

Isaline had reminded them countless times that there were only twelve days left before they had to hand in the Hardening Serum, and she clearly didn't think it was enough time.

Nahuel had reluctantly joined them in the living room, but all he did was tear at the cover of his textbook, *Serums and Essences from Around the World*. He did it slowly, methodically, silently, as if it were an incredibly important job.

"Enough, Nahuel!" Isaline exploded. "You have been in this catatonic state longer than I can bear."

Nahuel looked up, toward Isaline, but he didn't seem to see her. He turned his eyes back toward his book and returned to his task, like a robot.

"We will not do all the work for you," Isaline announced. "You must do your part. We have even given you the easiest part. All you have to do is write down the adverse side effects on the skin that can result from an overdose."

"I've noticed you're not playing chess anymore, Nahuel," Aremi said quietly.

Nahuel went tense. *Of course not, my partner died.*

"Tell us what is wrong," Isaline asked, "please."

"Nothing," he said without looking up.

"If you're going to tell a lie, you have to believe it yourself first," Isaline replied.

"I promise you, you will feel better if you tell us," Aremi reassured him.

This time, Nahuel felt compelled to pay attention to them. He looked up and saw his friends' faces, full of worry and concern. He sighed deeply, closed his eyes a moment. When he opened his eyes again, they were a deeper green and glassy.

And then he told them:

"My grandfather…. died," and felt like he was shrugging off the weight of the world.

Isaline felt her heart tighten. "I didn't know," she mumbled as if excusing herself.

"I am so sorry," Aremi said, her voice as soft as a feather.

The girls pushed the books aside and gave him their full attention.

"When did it happen, Nahuel?" Isaline asked cautiously.

"It was three weeks ago. His heart stopped."

Isaline reached out and took Nahuel's hand in hers. She squeezed it tightly. It was the warmest thing he had ever seen her do.

His friends tried to console him, looking for the right words, but there were no words.

"You still have your mother," Aremi said sweetly.

"You don't know her," Nahuel argued. "She's not like most mothers."

Isaline shook her head, filled with grief

Aremi gave him a weak smile and confided in him: "Don't forget, you can always count on us."

"Of course," Isaline agreed, at her side.

It was a promise and for Nahuel it was a relief and something to cling to. He felt the pressure in his chest ease.

The homework took them all morning and Nahuel's relationship with his friends slowly returned to normal.

Once he had started, Nahuel felt it was easy to talk to them and also to remain silent, two equally important attributes in a friend.

As Isaline put the finishing touches on the essay, she turned toward Aremi, who was coming down from their room with a blanket to keep warm, even though she was already wearing three sweaters.

The doorbell rang, the fire was dying and sputtering as the last log flew toward the fireplace.

A few seconds later, Mrs. Penington came into the room. She held in her hands a package wrapped in brown paper.

"Nahuel, the mailman has brought this for you," she said.

Isaline saw a brief smile fall from Nahuel's lips as his mouth set in a fine, firm line.

Aremi watched him with an expression between surprise and worry.

The boy took the package and Mrs. Penington marched toward the kitchen, to give him more privacy. Nahuel put it on the coffee table and the girls leaned in to get a better look at it.

"Who sent it?" Aremi asked.

"It has no return address," Isaline said, as Nahuel turned the package around in his hands.

He didn't need a return address to know who had sent it. He recognized the neat and slanted handwriting his own name and address had been written in. It could only be from one person.

A burst of almost palpable pain crossed his face.

"My grandfather sent it."

CHAPTER 19

"Open it," Isaline said, overcome with curiosity.

Nahuel held the package in his hands. He lifted it up, felt the weight of it. It had the same size and weight of their book, *Serums and Essences from Around the World*, which lay on the ground next to them. He tried to guess what was inside. He shook it and noticed something moved inside.

"What do you think it is?" Isaline asked.

"I don't know..." he replied.

"Open it," she insisted. Nahuel could tell she was making an effort not to tear it out his hands and rip it open herself.

Nahuel's heart beat faster with each scratch he gave the paper. His hands and his mind were trembling.

Once he got the paper off, he looked at it without blinking and swallowed.

He held in his hands a chessboard.

It was an antique wooden base with two drawers, but it was well preserved. The marble surface shined like it had just been polished. A design of animal-like shapes framed the board. Some of the shapes had their faces or limbs rubbed away.

"It's very pretty," Aremi noted.

"I've never seen it before," Nahuel murmured.

"It must be a Christmas present that's arrived late," Aremi said.

"You should see what's in the boxes," Isaline suggested.

Pulling on it harder than necessary, Nahuel opened one of the boxes. Inside were the chess pieces, carved from marble. They were all black, but the unusual thing was that they were all different animals. Instead of pawns, there were oxen, the king was represented by a jaguar, the rook, by a brown bear standing on his hind legs, and the bishop was an eagle, taking flight.

The expression on Nahuel's face hardened. He felt himself moving back in time, to the day he met his grandfather and his father's disappearance had been confirmed. The old man, who at that time was strong and handsome, picked him up in his arms and took him for a walk. In the middle of the hustle and bustle of the city, they entered a building and made their way to an inner courtyard. His grandfather waited there until an eagle descended and gave the man a silver ribbon. Nahuel hid behind his grandfather's legs. He was scared of the eagle's fierce talons. "This will be our first secret, little one." The words rung out from the depths of his mind.

The next day, his mother, together with his grandfather, had told him that they had to move, and that they would go to a special place full of woods and mountains. Nahuel had liked that, as, since he was a child, he felt especially comfortable while being in contact with nature, even though he felt a little bit apprehensive for having to leave with a man he didn't know, even if it was his grandfather.

Now that he saw that moment in perspective, he realized that his mother had given up to that trip, she hadn't fought for staying at home in Buenos Aires and had followed Walter without questioning it.

"Can I see it?" Isaline took advantage of Nahuel's stupor to take the chess out of his hands. The girl inspected it from top to bottom, took the pieces and looked at them in surprise.

"It's a chess set of animals," Nahuel said in a low voice.

"Very unusual, don't you think?" Isaline replied, handing the gift back to him.

"A bit," Nahuel agreed quietly.

His grandfather had given him more than one reason to suspect that he knew about the privileges, and this chess was a set of animals …

Isaline looked into his eyes. She was going to say something, but considered her words carefully and then decided not to speak them.

Nahuel opened the other drawer. The white pieces were inside. He took them out one by one as Aremi, now kneeling on the floor, placed them on the board, as she pleased.

"There's a letter," Nahuel stammered. It was in the back of the second drawer.

He took it out and without warning, began reading it quietly.

Dear Nahuel,
Sacrifice means giving up the things we treasure most of all.
I would have liked to have more time together. There are so many things we should have talked about. I've let valuable opportunities pass us by and for that I apologize. For a long time, I thought silence was the best way to keep you safe. I believe in you. I always have and always will. I know you will choose the correct path.
With love,

Grandpa

P.S. This chess set has been in our family for many, many years. Take care of it. It holds more answers than you can imagine.

He read it over and over again. He couldn't identify which feeling prevailed in him.

Without speaking, he handed it to Isaline.

After studying it closely, she gave it to Aremi and stood up to grab the brown paper the package had been wrapped in.

"Look at the date, Nahuel. January 16th," she noted, pointing out the day the package had been sent.

"That's the day he died," Nahuel admitted.

"This is too much coincidence to be a matter of luck. This letter seems his way of saying goodbye," Isaline said. She was sure it was not a lost Christmas present as Aremi had said. "The letter reminds me of a will and the chess set of an inheritance."

"But if he knew he was sick, that he was going to die, then why didn't he tell me?" Nahuel said with a faltering voice. A pinch of treason passed his throat.

"Maybe he hoped he had more time to talk to you," Aremi suggested.

"In the last call we had, he told me he was planning to visit me," maybe he really thought he had more time.

"He most probably wanted to talk to you about the secrets that he mentions in the letter," Aremi added.

"He owed me a face-to-face conversation", Nahuel said, answering to Aremi and a little bit to himself.

"What do you mean by that?" Isaline wanted to know.

Nahuel told them everything, since the moment his father had disappeared and his grandfather took them to Ushuaia to live. That he was never taken to the doctor when he had his illness episodes and that he then discovered that those were due to the cym enzyme. He told them about the day that the wolves surrounded his house in Ushuaia and the unexpected arrival of Ankona. The way in which his grandfather had reacted and how he convinced him of going to New York by telling him that he had applied on his behalf to the Program, even though Klaus then explained that all of the kids had been found by the trackers.

He also told them he had never asked anything directly to his grandfather out of the fear of the tick and of being kicked out of the Council of Privileges. However, when he implied his suspicions to his grandfather, he promised they would have a conversation in person.

"This is not information that is easy to digest," Isaline said out of words.

The three sat together in silence as the fire in the living room slowly died out.

In spite of the fact that Nahuel had wanted to give his grandfather the benefit of the doubt, now he couldn't continue denying what he had in front of him. His grandfather must have known about the privileges. Was that the only thing he wanted to confess? Or was there anything else he had hidden from him? Now he would take that to the grave forever. And that truth hurt him.

After hesitating a bit, Isaline said, "It doesn't make sense."

"What exactly?" Nahuel grumbled, for him nothing made any sense.

"That your grandfather would take the trouble to send you the chess set if you don't know what to do with it," Isaline explained, rereading the letter. "It says here that it holds more answers than you can imagine. Have you checked the other drawer? There might be something else there."

"I checked."

"OK OK. Let's suppose your grandfather knew about the privileges and that he suspected something was going to happen to him. But the only thing we know for sure is that your grandfather wanted you to have this chess set in your possession," Isaline stated.

Nahuel read the date on the package again, wrinkled the paper up angrily and threw it on the fire.

"Why did he hide it from me?!" he burst out. Now he was angry.

The sadness he had been feeling now turned to irritation upon realizing that his grandfather had known he didn't have much time left, and had decided not to tell Nahuel.

"Just a few words would have been enough. But instead, he sends me this chess set and a useless letter," he spat.

He had lived with the man for the last eight years and he had left him with just three sentences to explain that there were things he needed to know, apparently important things, but that he hadn't been told. The least his grandfather could have done was try to summarize them in that letter. But no. His grandfather had chosen to leave him forever in doubt.

"I don't know what his reasons were," Isaline said, even though she was brimming with hypotheses, she knew that now was not the time to discuss them. "But you will have to accept that there will always be things about your grandfather you won't understand."

"Trust in the love he had for you," Aremi comforted, convinced of her words. "Remember you can only be really mad at someone you truly love."

Nahuel couldn't think about that now. *The world can change in an instant,* he had heard somewhere. A telephone call with irreversible news and a package had turned his world upside down in just a few weeks.

Damn it, he could see the clock hands in Emre's watch striking 2 a.m. and he was still tossing and turning in bed.

Nahuel felt his head was about to explode. Each time he closed his eyes he would have all these memories of his grandfather coming to his mind, and those memories brought him new questions, he had too many questions…

If he was not going to sleep, at least he needed to do something to keep his mind occupied in something else.

Isaline reminded him at the last minute that they had to read the Creation Myth because Mrs. Sparling would ask questions about it on the following day at the Cultural History class.

Nahuel hadn't forgotten about it, but he had just simply decided not to do it. Frankly, he hadn't been in the mood of doing any homework lately. But now… that Myth didn't sound that bad.

He stood up as stealthily as a cat and opened the window of his room. He stood there for a moment, while the fresh air blew all over his face. Then, he approached the desk, where his backpack was, and took the book of *History of the Ancient Thought*.

With a soft hum, a light sphere entered and Nahuel closed the window.

Ten fireflies approached to Nahuel's bed, the boy hid beneath his blankets and opened the book.

CHAPTER 20

In the beginning, the world was ruled by three gods, children of Chaos and Harmony.

Chaos was linked with Anarchy for a long time until they discovered they could never create descendents. One fine day, Harmony, who couldn't find a mate, decided to disguise herself like a fox and seduce Chaos. Chaos, who was tired of Anarchy's rejection, and who was lamenting not being able to reproduce, followed the clues the fox left for him like a bloodhound. Harmony, still disguised, seduced Chaos and gave birth to three gods simultaneously. These three sky gods were given the task of creating the earth, and that was the start of the world.

Chaos realized Harmony's deceit. While she purified herself with Lotus flowers in the waters of heaven, he abandoned his three children to an earthly fate. The three gods grew up equally, shaped by Harmony's principles.

These three Gods possessed the peculiar ability to reproduce without a mate and the first thing they did was populate the world in their likeness. Each God chose to dedicate himself to one ingredient so the world would be complete.

The first God offered heirs who would defend the Terra, and would be responsible for sustenance.

The second God, devout in sacrifice, created the Animalis to protect those who might dare to terrorize his brothers.

The last God, amazed by knowledge, created offspring whose Ments were dedicated to understanding and planning.

For longer than anyone could remember, the siblings and their children lived in accordance with the teaching of their mother, Harmony, and the world was a peaceful and luminous place, governed by the three Gods.

But it was only a matter of time before one of them believed himself superior to the others. Chaos was alone and came back to the world to upset its balance. Corrupted by his father's betrayal, the Ments God believed himself to be the irreplaceable ruler and subjected his siblings, believing them to be replaceable. He planted seeds of subordination and weakness in their minds. Without realizing it, they let themselves be ruled, and in this way, Ments enslaved his siblings.

Time passed and two of the three gods became immobilized; petrified by submission and mediocrity. It was their children who suffered, because the dictator became crueler and took advantage of them.

They had to awaken. The two Gods knew it intuitively, toward the end.

So the war began. Gods against gods. Siblings against siblings. The Terra against the Ments, the Animalis against the Ments. And war corrupted them and the Terra began fighting against the Animalis.

Each God in the end lost their heirs. The world would soon be lifeless and they knew that Chaos would be the only victor.

The God Ments saw a field of hearts, red and beating. They were the hearts of his children and the children of his siblings and it was then, almost near the end that he understood. They were all the same. He called for his siblings and begged for their forgiveness and asked them to remember the values their mother had taught them. Harmony had to be brought back to rule over the world.

The three Gods hid in a cave at the feet of Blue Mountain, far from their own children who they feared could not be redeemed.

They found a solution and when they came out of hiding, their descendents had lost their unique traits. There was no longer anything to distinguish one from another.

——

The door to Cultural History opened punctually at eight o'clock to let the students into the classroom. The chalk floating in the air had already covered three-fourths of the blackboard with writing and was still noting the instructions for the day's lesson.

It bothered Nahuel that Mrs. Sparling started the class before they even entered the room, because he was never able to catch up and copy down everything she wrote on the blackboard.

Only the CymMens students who had mastered their privilege to a certain degree were able to copy everything into their notebooks as quickly as the professor wrote it. Isaline made a great effort to control her pencil, but before long the writing was almost illegible and she gave up and wrote normally, with her hand.

"The privileged society has existed since man has walked the earth," their professor was saying, "It is the mother of all ancient civilizations."

"Even before Egypt?" Emma interrupted, her lips the usual bright pink.

"Before them all and with a presence in them all," the professor replied. "As I expect everyone has read, the Creation Myth explains, by way of fantastic illustration, the creation of the world and the privileged society."

Fantastic is the word...A field of beating hearts, Nahuel remembered a dream he had had the previous night. His grandfather was moving away from him while he passed through a red and throbbing field. Nahuel wanted to come closer, wanted to reach him, but his grandfather begged him to keep far away. Towards the end of the dream, his grandfather had disappeared until he became a small and weak heart, and he had become twice as big.

"For many years, all humans possessed privileges. There was no society but our own and no type of human except the privileged," she went on.

"And they were all the children of hermaphrodite gods," murmured Emre.

"But as the myth clearly shows, the three privileges did not coexist peacefully. There were three distinct castes, each very separate from the other. Discrimination and slavery were very common among them. The CymMens governed and dominated the other privileges. Most of the CymTers were their slaves, while the CymAnis were in charge of keeping everyone in line," Mrs. Sparling explained.

Nahuel turned toward Aremi, who smiled back at him. It was hard for him to imagine a world in which everyone had privileges yet people like Aremi would have been slaves for people who were their equal yet believed themselves to be superior. It meant that to be born with a specific privilege would determine your fate. There would have been no chance to change your luck.

"Thousands of generations passed until the war destroyed the marrow of our civilization," Mrs. Sparling explained. "But you will not see any trace of it, or hear about it. Thousands of people died and most of them lost their privileges."

Nahuel didn't want to believe that could happen. He never considered the possibility of losing his privilege. At that moment, he realized that in just a few months, his privilege had become part of his very identity. To lose it would leave him with a hole in his very being. He thought he should find out more about losing the privileges so that he would be sure not to make any mistakes.

The professor handed each student a card with the name of a character on it.

They were red and a bit larger than playing cards. On one side, they had the symbol of the Council of Privileges and on the other side, a portrait with a caption stating the name, date of birth and date of death of the person.

"These are the noteworthy people from the history of the privileged society. We call them *The Custodians*," Mrs. Sparling explained. "After the war, only a handful of people maintained their privileges and they swore to keep the secret hidden. *The Custodians* have protected the true history of humanity, the secret that the world was once inhabited only by people with privileges and that even now, some of them remain, mixed in among regular people."

Mrs. Sparling assigned one custodian to each group. Nahuel, Isaline and Aremi got Robert Wissing. They had to write an essay detailing everything they could find out about him: his family tree, his biography, his achievements, his strengths, and his mistakes. The assignment was due in the last month of classes.

There were just five minutes left of class when two envelopes appeared suddenly under the door. One of them whizzed under Nahuel's nose as it went flying toward Mrs. Sparling's desk, where it landed abruptly. Mrs. Sparling's lips were set in a thin line. For some unknown reason, those envelopes upset her.

She announced clearly, "This year, the memorial celebration to mark the end of the war between the three privileges will be held by our institution. Each year the heads of the Council of Privileges and the privileged society worldwide gather in a different city to reaffirm our values and this year Ardemir Estate will be hosting the event." She paused and emphasized, "*Il Finale* is the emblematic event of our society."

She raised one hand and the envelopes flew from her desk to her palm. She held them in her grip and said, "I took it upon myself to share with you part of the explanation Mrs. Penington had prepared for you about the celebrations of *Il Finale*, as it seems some of you have been invited to join the official celebration at Ardemir."

A buzz of excitement rushed through the room. Isaline, who was sitting next to Nahuel, straightened up and stiffened like someone was pulling on her head from above, like a marionette.

"It would seem that the latest fashion is to reward those who simply perform their duties," she grumbled. "Which is why the two groups who received the highest score on the first Hazna will be allowed to participate in the official celebrations."

The first envelope flew to Rebecca Hamilton's desk. She picked it up without a trace of surprise on her face. Everyone knew her group had been the best.

The second envelope paused at eye level with Isaline and fell on her notebook. Happiness gushed from every pore of her body, but she repressed the urge to shout out in joy, so as not to contrast with the attitude of superiority Rebecca had displayed just seconds before.

The chalk scrawled across the blackboard in record time, the last instructions for the homework on the heraldic shields of the Middle Ages, and then placed itself back in a box on the desk. Without saying a word, Mrs. Sparling picked up her things and left the room at a brisk pace.

Isaline was sitting by the door and leaned forward to watch Mrs. Sparling walk away. As soon as she was out of sight, Isaline raised her arms in the air victoriously in a moment of pure and uncensored enthusiasm.

Inside the envelope were three blue cards, each labeled with the students' full names across the top.

"This one is for you, Nahuel."

Dear Mr. Nahuel Blest:
The Council of Privileges of the United Nations is delighted to invite you to the
annual celebration of Il Finale.
The event will take place the 7th of March at 6pm at Ardemir Estate.

Formal Attire.
Admission with invitation only.

"Congrats, bro!" Emre said, slapping his roommate on the back. "We would have scored higher if Damian hadn't insisted on using his horrible Boy Scout training."

Nahuel was pretty sure he knew who had wanted to make a campfire halfway through the Hazna to heat up food, and it wasn't Damian.

"Wonder where he got that idea…" Emre muttered as he walked away.

"We must hurry back and talk to Mrs. Penington. At this kind of official event, all the protocols must be respected," Isaline said, walking quickly.

"This is the first time I've been invited to a party with a formal invitation," Aremi said enthusiastically.

Nahuel wasn't sure he was in the mood for a party.

CHAPTER 21

Mrs. Penington was able to answer some of their questions and arranged an appointment for them at *Rubirio and Brothers, Exclusive Clothiers* where they would be able to find the appropriate attire for *Il Finale*. Just as Isaline had anticipated, the event was full of particular etiquettes and protocols to be followed and their clothing had to be carefully chosen.

That same afternoon, the three friends headed toward The Hedge Garden. Mrs. Penington gave them the code they had to use to get there through the tunnels and told them in advance that The Hedge Garden was an amazing place. When Nahuel assured her that they already knew the place, Isaline promptly gave him a good stomp on the foot for opening his big mouth. They weren't supposed to know that place yet.

They decided to take the long way there, avoiding the tunnels, even though Ankona had warned Nahuel to always use them for his safety.   Aremi felt like getting some fresh air and enjoying the sunny day. The girls didn't know about what Ankona had requested Nahuel, and he didn't feel like obeying.

But it wasn't long before Nahuel realized that taking the normal route of subways and streets wasn't a very good idea. The streets were crowded and everyone turned to look at them wherever they went. The residency's flock of pigeons hovered above their heads like a crown.

Every time Nahuel saw them, he felt a knot in his stomach. He remembered the day his grandfather died, when many of them crashed into the window due to his power outburst.

Now, thinking it over, it didn't seem to be such a good idea to ignore Ankona's request. He knew that Ankona would get to know about this because of the pigeons.

This time, the man in charge of the carrousel didn't act very suspicious and let them through without any questioning. When they arrived at the entrance, they took off their gloves and placed their hands on the access panels. Each one was proud when the circle appeared on the back of their hands this time. Now they knew the reason each circle was a different color.

The Hedge Garden was festively decorated. The shapes of the hedges had changed since the last time Nahuel and Isaline were there. There were no longer the shapes of animals in the green, but the outlines of the great custodians who had kept the secret of *Il Finale* safe.

The fountain in the middle was lit up in different colors by luminescent plankton which had been added to the water. Aremi was amazed by what she saw. The sunlight was filtering through the lake water and reddish flashes of light lit up her hair and bounced off her skin.

"It is a pleasure to have you in my humble shop," Mr. Rubirio greeted them with a slight bow.

He was a very well-mannered Italian man. He wore an impeccable purple cashmere vest.

The shop had been completely rearranged since the students had walked by it months earlier. The vests in the window had given way to gowns, tuxedos, tunics, and elegant fabrics, all in the same shade of ivory. The mannequins were dressed for a ball and bowed grandly to everyone who walked past.

"*Certo*! Right this way," the shop owner stated, leading Isaline and Aremi toward the collection of dresses for young ladies, when they explained the reason for their visit. "You, my young friend will find the tuxedos in your size to my left," he explained to Nahuel.

The girls started looking at the dresses Rubirio had on display. Long, short, flowing, tight, low-cut, high-collar, every single style was ivory colored. Mr. Rubirio explained that everyone at the celebration had to wear that shade.

"They are all my own designs," he said, not even trying to hide his pride.

Isaline scanned the selection quickly, took two dresses in her hand and said, "I'll try these two."

"Excellent choice, Miss. They will look so nice with your hair," Rubirio said, complementing Isaline's dark, straight hair that fell neatly to her shoulders. "Allow me," he said, making the dresses fly through the air to the dressing rooms. "Take the second room, please."

Thanks to her father's job with the French Government, Isaline was no stranger to formal dress and she knew what looked good on her. Aremi, on the other hand, was at a loss.

"If you will allow me to suggest something, Miss, your petite and graceful figure would be complemented by a dress like this," Rubirio said, selecting a short dress, with a sweetheart neckline, a ribbon under the bust and a full skirt. He made it levitate in front of Aremi and she took it in her hands, an appreciative smile on her face. "The third dressing room is free."

Next, Mr. Rubirio explained to Nahuel that he should select a bow-tie from the many on display. Nahuel approached them. They were spread on two stands in front of a large mirror where he could see himself as he tried them on. Nahuel was not excited about the bow-ties. He was sure he would look like a doll on top of a wedding cake in any of them.

When he looked in the mirror, he saw something more than his own reflection. He could see the dressing rooms behind him. Aremi hadn't closed the curtain of hers completely and he could see her pulling up her dress. Her back looked so smooth, her skin looked soft... *What am I doing?!* Nahuel blushed and started coughing. He quickly looked down at the bow-ties, grabbed the first one he saw and rushed toward the front of the shop.

It had taken him less than a minute to choose a shirt for his tuxedo. They were all the same color and therefore all the same in his eyes. Isaline was still deciding.

"Now, the next thing you'll need are the capes," Mr. Rubirio said.

He ran to the back of the shop. Nahuel thought it was funny that a man that tall and lean would run with such short steps.

He returned pulling a rack of capes. They were all short, falling at the waist, with large hoods, all ivory colored. They were organized from small to large.

"Not many choices to make here," Mr. Rubirio explained, disappointed. "It's only a matter of size."

As the three tried on their capes, he explained, "The use of capes is purely traditional. Our ancestors used them for protection and each privilege wore a different color. But now, since we are trying to celebrate the equality among all three privileges, all the capes are the same color." Then he added, with a touch of vanity, "I've designed each to complement the other suits."

Finally, Mr. Rubirio handed them special gloves for the celebration. The girls' gloves were long, reaching all the way to their elbows. Nahuel's were short, just until the wrist.

Before finishing the rest of the shopping for the party, Isaline wanted to stop in *Calendula, Ten Thousand-Year Bookstore*. She hadn't forgotten the last time she was there and the terrible way she had been treated, but she was willing to ignore it because she was eager to find a historical novel about the *Il Finale* celebrations.

Nahuel and Aremi looked for *Milevich Jewels*, the next shop they had to go to.

When they found it they returned to get Isaline.

"Did you get what you wanted?" Nahuel asked, implying she was after more than just a book.

"Yes, I think I found the perfect book, a romantic story about two star-crossed privileged lovers situated in the Middle Ages...and I told the shopkeeper that he is a cretin, completely and totally backwards and stuck in the past if he hates CymMens, as if it were a thousand years ago," Isaline replied with complete ease.

"And how did he take that?" Nahuel asked, guessing what her answer would be.

"He has forbidden me from entering his shop again," she said without betraying any sign of surprise.

"If you could only hold your tongue...," Nahuel teased her.

Mrs. Penington had told them it was customary to exchange ornamental pins at the celebration. During *Il Finale*, a type of folk dance was held which concluded with the exchange of pins between dance partners. During the dancing, the partners changed but you only exchanged pins with the person who was your partner when the last note of music hung in the air.

In *Milevich Jewels*, there were hundreds of pins to choose from. Each one symbolized something different about the privileged society history, or about each privilege or the end of the war.

The most common pins were simple, with three circular gemstones. There were also pins in the shape of musical notes, crowns, swords, and coats of arms showing heraldic emblems like the ones studied in Cultural History class.

The owner of the shop, a hunched over elderly man who needed his small round glasses to see anything, explained that the most requested pin for the celebration was a cameo silhouette of the custodian of the privileged society that the buyer most admired.

Finally, the little old man showed them pins shaped like animals. Nahuel didn't know why, but once he laid eyes on a pin shaped like a jaguar, he knew he wanted that one.

They were less than a week away from the celebration. Mrs. Pennington had already gathered all the required ingredients to make the traditional dishes. Delicious smells came wafting from the kitchen, filling the downstairs, but the students were forbidden from trying any of the delicacies until the special day. The festive atmosphere was ten times what they had felt around Christmas time. They were all excited to discover what this new ceremony was going to entail.

Mrs. Penington had forced the six students invited to the celebration to take dance lessons with Benjamin and Victoria. It was the first time they had ever seen her be so strict, and she had explained that it was absolutely necessary that they learn the traditional dance of the privileged society to perfection, as this represented the most serious moment of the celebration.

"Stop stepping on my feet, Nahuel," Isaline grumbled under her breath.

"Look how Victoria does it. You're supposed to turn the other way," he replied loudly enough for everyone to hear. Isaline refused to speak to him for the rest of the day.

The dance began with the men standing in front of the women. They wove calmly and gracefully among the men. The exchange of partners happened after every turn.

"If you would like your charming dance instructor to give you some private lessons, you must first promise me that you will save a dance for me at the celebration," Benjamin whispered to Isaline. He was moving among the boys to correct their turns.

Isaline froze. "I don't need any help," she babbled.

"Of course not love," Benjamin replied, winking at Nahuel. "You just need three more months of practice."

Isaline scowled at him. Nahuel knew she hated it when her weaknesses were revealed.

"I hate this," Eric confessed, even paler than usual. "I would have rather not been invited if I had known it meant I had to learn this dance."

"What are you talking about Eric?" Aremi joked. "We're having a great time. We've even made up a new dance step!"

Aremi was practicing with Eric Schultz at that moment and demonstrated for everyone what she called the "surprise turn". Nahuel thought everything about her was full of light.

Over the next few classes, Isaline got noticeably better. Every night after dinner, she forced Aremi to help her with the steps, which meant she also had to incorporate the "surprise turn" into her dancing.

Emre had become a specialist in the new dance step. Apparently, he was quite a dancer. He joined Aremi and Isaline every night to practice the dance steps for the celebration he hadn't been invited to. Then Benjamin asked him to join the group lessons in order to help the others get ready in time for the big event.

"Feel your feet, my friend," he said as they practiced.

Nahuel was impressed. On one hand, he couldn't understand how his roommate, who was such a klutz at some things, could be so graceful at dancing. On the other hand, he couldn't understand why someone would want to join a dance class if they weren't forced to. He suspected it had something to do with Rebecca. Nahuel had come to learn that Emre had a weakness for smart, hardworking girls.

Nahuel stepped out of his room. He felt ridiculous. He was wearing shoes, pants, a shirt, a vest, a tuxedo jacket and even socks, all in various shades of ivory. He was glad no one from Ushuaia could see him. If they could see him now, his classmates who hadn't even spoken to him before, would surely label him the true "weirdo" of the school.

"We look like extravagant eccentrics, dressed like this, don't we?" Aremi observed, having the time of her life.

Nahuel didn't think Aremi looked strange at all. The short dress she wore looked tailor made for her. It captured her innocence but also added some elegance. She was wearing mascara for the first time and Nahuel couldn't stop looking at her sparkling green eyes.

"Why haven't you put your capes on yet?" Isaline asked, joining them at the head of the staircase. She was wearing her dark hair in an upsweep and her impeccable floor-length gown made her seem more grown up. She looked perfectly comfortable. She liked dressing glamorously.

"That's some bow tie," she commented, tilting her head to one side and staring at it.

Dammit! It really stands out, Nahuel thought. In his rush, he had grabbed what must have been the ugliest of all the bow-ties. It was large and flashy. Why hadn't Mr. Rubirio stopped him?

"What's wrong with it?" he asked Isaline, frowning at her.

"Let's just say it's... nothing. Don't forget your gloves, Nahuel," she added.

"I'll wait till we get there to put them on," he responded without hesitating. He planned to do the same with the cape. "I've got them here," he explained, patting his pocket where he also had his invitation and the pin.

In the residency's living room, the melody of singing bowls was playing. It made Nahuel's hair stand on end, that music reminded him of his grandfather. He wanted to get out of there as soon as possible.

These last few weeks Nahuel had intentionally been busy, so busy he had finished each day completely exhausted and fallen quickly asleep, leaving no time to think about his grandfather. He had put the new chessboard and the postcard of the lighthouse at the very back of his closet.

They met up with the students from the other group in the tunnels and to no one's surprise, they also wore ivory. They took two glass carts directly to the Estate. Isaline took great pains to not dirty her dress or her cape, but before long she realized that Rubirio had used his special skills on the fabric. The dresses didn't wrinkle or get dirty, which was extremely practical, especially when it came to the gloves.

On their way, Isaline set to work braiding Aremi's hair. Both benefitted from the experience. Isaline proved to herself that she could do a hairstyle she had seen in a magazine using her privilege and Aremi looked more polished. Luckily, the ride to the Estate was a long one because it took Isaline a few tries to get it just right.

Ardemir rose up before them majestically as they came out of the hatch door, like something from a fairy tale. It felt like they were entering a magical realm, beautiful, but dreamlike.

Aremi crouched down and when she stood up again, she had a small white flower in her hand. She had recognized it among the grass and made it bloom.

"So handsome," she said, placing it in Nahuel's lapel.

He felt his cheeks begin to burn.

As the sun set among the treetops of the thousand-year-old forest, small luminescent bugs emerged. The six students stood frozen in the middle of the stone path that led to the main entrance.

The deep voice of a man in a hooded cape, urged them on from behind, "Hurry up, the celebration is about to begin."

CHAPTER 22

Nahuel and Isaline paused at the entrance. Aremi was standing on the covered verandah while the other group of students showed their invitations and entered Ardemir.

"What is it?" Isaline asked her.

"Have you seen this?" Aremi replied. "Come look!"

Nahuel stepped aside to let a Middle Eastern man pass. He was wearing a golden a-bula around his neck on a thick chain. Nahuel went and stood next to Aremi.

"Look up there," she said, pointing at the sky from between the columns of the verandah.

Nahuel looked up. The sky was so clear they could see the Milky Way. Shooting stars shone like fireworks, as if the privileged ones had put them in the sky just for the party.

"How is that even possible?" Nahuel wondered out loud.

"It was the CymMens," Isaline said smoothly. "We can clean the atmosphere and clear the sky."

As they entered the main hall, they ran into Rebecca, Eric and Layla. Rebecca was wearing a different pair of glasses. They were more delicate, with ivory colored frames. Layla's black hair was tucked under an embroidered ivory veil, and Eric's bowtie had clearly been more wisely chosen than Nahuel's. It was somber and didn't sparkle, like Nahuel's. None of them stood out from the crowd, they all looked elegant and distinguished.

"Oh, it's crowded!" Eric complained.

"Relax Eric. We are here to dance," Aremi said, patting him on the back.

"There are diplomats here from all over the world," Isaline said, her eyes sparkling with admiration. "I bet there are even members of custodian families, who have kept alive the true history of the privileged society since the very beginning."

"I'm going to get something to drink," Eric said frowning.

"I'll come with you," Nahuel added.

The Estate was dazzling, truly out of this world. Water streamed freely down the vertical columns of the hall, but didn't need glass walls to hold it in place. The drops of water sparkled, lighting up the room. Delicate flowers of all shapes and sizes covered the walls, each sparkling in some special way. The air was sweet and perfumed. Everything gave off a sense of perfect harmony.

The students ran into Mrs. Sparling. She was wearing a simple floor-length tube dress. By her side was a man Nahuel assumed to be her son, except for the lingering kiss he gave her wrinkled cheeks. *Is that her husband?* He thought. *Gross!*

Benjamin was there also, talking to Victoria. She was wearing a flowing silk dress that looked great against her olive skin.

The catering was very unusual. Trays of an enormous variety of food flew among the crowd, offering bites to all the people. Once they were empty, they flew back to a large table made from thick roots that took up an entire side of the room, they refilled themselves and set off again into the crowd. The drinks were served in a similar way, but you had to point to the different pitchers to signal which one you wanted to be poured into your glass.

"Hello Nahuel, hello Eric. *Brotherly Finale* to you."

The boys had run into Sebastian at the table.

"That bowtie sure has a life of its own," Sebastian added fixing his eyes on Nahuel. "Let me present you to Mr. Basir, head of the Egypt station."

Nahuel and Eric shook his hand. It was the same man Nahuel had noticed at the entrance, with the thick gold chain.

"*Brotherly Finale*, for you both," Basir wished them well.

After thanking him, Nahuel chose a strange purple colored juice and Eric asked for water.

"That's right," they heard Sebastian say to Mr. Basir, "my cover at the United Nations is the logistical and intelligence work I do for the peacekeeping missions."

Sebastian took a new appetizer from the tray hovering beside him, unable to circulate among the crowd because their professor reached for a new mouthful after every other word he spoke. He seemed to relish each bite.

"This job allows me to be at the United Nations without anyone suspecting my other position. Furthermore, it also grants me access to all the information the heads of the UN receive," Sebastian went on, pointing out his own importance.

Nahuel stalled close to them, pretending to be undecided on whether he should take his friends glasses of juice or water.

"I see," the Middle Eastern man said. "My *day* job is as mayor of a city in the south of Egypt, but luckily most of the population is privileged."

No matter how hard Nahuel and Eric tried to discern who the CymMens were that were controlling the food and drinks, they couldn't make it out. No one was dressed differently, like a waiter and there wasn't even a single person with a look on their face that would lead them to believe they were commanding all those trays.

Nahuel went back toward his friends with two glasses: tomato juice for Aremi and lemonade with ginger for Isaline.

"My favorite!" Aremi said as he handed her the glass. "I was just telling Isaline that's the woman who brought me here from Australia," she said, pointing to a large woman who seemed trapped in her own mermaid style dress. "She's part of the Committee of Trackers. I'm going to say hello to her and thank her."

Aremi seemed to glide over to the woman on the shimmering marble floor.

"I don't know who my tracker is," Isaline said, disappointed.

Nahuel looked around the crowd until he saw the black eyes of his teacher. Ankona was standing next to one of the glowing columns of water, discussing something with an African man. The contrast of their skin against their tuxedos was striking. Americus was at their feet, frowning at the African man.

Nahuel hadn't forgotten how suspicious he felt when he saw Ankona in his house smelling like wolves, but, as time went by, those feelings were replaced by much stronger ones. Feelings of respect, confidence and admiration, not only for his powerful privilege, but also for his personality.

"We can't take off our gloves," Rebecca told Eric as she saw him tugging at his gloves. "It's an old custom. People wore them so others wouldn't see the marks on their hands and so know who was using their privilege."

"So, even though you don't like it boys, you will have to leave them on," Isaline scolded.

"Ugh."

Aremi came back to the group.

"Alex seems really tired lately," she said. "I think he's had a lot of extra work because of *Il Finale*."

"Who is Alex?" Nahuel asked.

"What do you mean, who is Alex? Mrs. Penington's son, there are photos of him at the residency," Aremi explained. "He's over there, talking to my tracker. From what I heard, taking care of the foreign dignitaries is no easy job. Especially those from the Privileged International Court, who need twice the security."

Alex was about thirty years old, but the dark circles under his eyes at the moment made him look much older. He had blonde hair and plump cheeks, clearly inherited from his mother.

"Alex hasn't stopped complaining about Zuma," Aremi said, lowering her voice a little.

"Who?" Nahuel asked.

"I think it's that man, over there. The one talking to Ankona," Aremi replied, looking toward Ankona.

"Why is he complaining about him?" Isaline wanted to know.

"Apparently, the man is obsessed with the security protocols and affirms that the privileged in New York aren't well protected," Aremi added.

"Is it because of the Ignobles?" Isaline whispered.

"I have no idea. I haven't heard anyone mentioned them, but I think they are holding back because we are here. And they probably don't want to bring up such sad things," Aremi responded.

The bright sound of a musical note called everyone to attention. The *fa* echoed through the room for a few seconds. Nahuel looked around for the origin of the sound. A nightingale was perched on the long stem of one of the many hanging plants suspended in the air all around the room.

Another chord was heard and all the guests gathered in the center of the room. Long, thick roots started to grow from the hanging plants. They spread out among the men and women and turned into seats for each. The guests sat down as a small stage was formed in a similar way in front of them. The students copied what the other guests were doing and sat down in the six root chairs that had formed closest to them.

"I'd like to wish you all a very lovely evening," Klaus greeted everyone from the stage. Nahuel couldn't be sure, but it looked like the Director had dyed his beard off-white for the occasion.

Klaus took a paper from his pocket, but didn't look at it. He decided not to follow the script that had been prepared for him.

"It is truly a pleasure to have you all here. It has been seven years since New York was the host of *Il Finale*. I haven't seen many of you since the last gathering in Istanbul."

Klaus smiled spontaneously at a woman wearing a refined Kimono beneath her short cape.

"I'm so glad you were able to make it on time, Mrs. Igaki," Klaus said, straying from his speech. "I know we've had a few problems lately with transportation coming from the East."

The woman responded to his comments with a slight bow. The Director went on as if he had never interrupted his train of thought.

"Aside from being the perfect excuse for a celebration, *Il Finale* must also be considered as a moment for reflection. This year, more than ever, we must remember the reason why this event is held; to commemorate equality among all three privileges and the very secret of our existence."

Klaus cleared his throat dramatically and continued, "This is the moment we take each year to reaffirm the sacred agreement made by our ancestors, those wise ones," he said, nodding in agreement with his own statements. "This is the day we honor and perpetuate the decision they made - the decision to take the privileges away from the three castes after the war."

"It was a *decision* that everyone lose their privileges?" Nahuel asked, whispering.

"Shh," Isaline warned him.

Klaus rubbed his hand over his bald head.

"Let us remember the reasons that led to the creation of the *Pact*. Don't be embarrassed if you feel as if you are falling into a volcano of emotion," he said, enunciating each word. "Even though some wish to rebel, we must respect the *Pact*, because we believe in it. We are convinced that keeping the privileges a secret is humanity's best chance for survival. In the past, mankind faced extinction, but thanks to the *Pact*, we made it through. It is our responsibility to make sure that near extinction never happens again. Humanity is not mature enough yet to handle the benefits of a life with privileges."

The man sitting next to Nahuel agreed effusively with everything that was said.

Klaus was speaking with a tone of authority he had earned from almost a decade as the head of the Council of Privileges.

"Therefore, I believe we all deserve a moment of celebration. What would man be without a few moments of leisure?" Then, in a smooth voice he said, "These last few months have been very difficult, but together, we have made it through. Some of us have lost loved ones - agents who gave their lives to defend the values of the *Pact* and we must toast to them today."

Professor Greenwood was sitting a few seats away from Nahuel, diagonally and he could see her sigh deeply. She still wore a black ribbon in her hair. The Director raised his glass and said, "For those who have lost their lives fighting, for all of us, and for the *Pact. Brotherly Finale* for all!"

The guests all raised their glasses together and joined Klaus, repeating his last words. The room exploded in applause and Nahuel joined in, enthusiastically.

Everyone stood up and in an amazing act of synchronicity, the roots receded, shrinking back into their pots, leaving the space clear for dancing.

The first nightingale Nahuel had seen was now joined by others, who entered, flying over the guests. They all perched on the floating plants on one side of the room. As they did so, all the guests put on their hoods and prepared for the dance. The women stood in a line and the men stood in front of them, bowing.

"The first change of partners is to the right?" Nahuel asked quickly. He had assumed he would have some time to practice the dance steps after the speech. Unfortunately, he was completely taken by surprise by the order of events.

"Nahuel, it's the women who have to change places. You don't need to worry about that," Aremi answered, smiling at him as she stood in front of him. "Anyways, Isaline is coming after me, she'll be your next partner on the left."

"This is going to be a disaster," Nahuel said desperately.

"You have no way of knowing that. You just have to try first," Aremi responded reasonably, in that special voice she only used to say things that were both fun and smart.

Next to Aremi, Isaline stood in front of Benjamin. The hoods were so large that from the side, you couldn't see the person's face. Isaline's hood suddenly slipped back, as if pushed off her head by some invisible wind. She quickly lifted it back into place. Benjamin was smiling mischievously; his eyes sparkling. He raised his chin slightly and her hood slid off again, falling around her shoulders.

"Stop it," she said, clenching her teeth and putting the hood on again.

"Just having a bit of fun, love," Benjamin explained, but he didn't bother her again.

A sophisticated symphony of euphoria and beauty set the dance in motion. The birds' singing marked the pace. The pairs moved in small, sliding steps, barely lifting their feet off the marble floors. Everyone wore their hood, making it impossible to see who would be your next dance partner until they were right in front of you.

The water falling around the columns gave off shimmering glints of light, which bounced off the ivory capes. The most stylish women turned with their chins lifted high, showing off their splendor. The men suddenly became dashing gentlemen, who seemed to have arrived from a medieval ball or an old-fashioned Venetian carnival.

The dance steps were admirably simple, but it didn't make the dance any less divine. The glorious attitude of all present, the refined music from the birds and couture fashion made the dance exquisite.

When it was all over, Nahuel was relieved that he had made it through without making a fool of himself at all. He did almost get stepped on by Mrs. Sparling's impressive high heeled shoe, but he managed to save himself by a hair, turning at just the right moment. Crashing into his teacher would have been tragic.

When it was time to exchange pins, Nahuel was feeling a little dizzy. His black and gold jaguar was pinned onto Mrs. Igaki's kimono. Her almond eyes studied the pin carefully. After several seconds, she looked up, to find out who had given her the pin. Nahuel felt a bit intimidated as her inquisitive eyes scrutinized him. The woman spoke to him in Japanese. Nahuel couldn't understand what she was saying, but she handed him a simple snail-shaped pin.

On the other side of the room, Aremi was standing in front of a Maasai Leader. The man was wearing the traditional robes of this African tribe, but instead of the usual bright reds and blue that characterized his people, he wore an ivory colored tunic. Aremi looked really excited. The man was fascinating to her. He had given her a pin featuring white and yellow stones just like the ones he wore in his ears.

Isaline had given her sapphire pin, in the shape of the Council of Privileges symbol to an older man. He was meticulously well-groomed. His skin was pale and his face was quickly forgettable. His gray hair was cut close to the scalp and his white moustache was neatly trimmed. He offered her the small cameo he had been wearing on his lapel.

"Robert Wissing?" Isaline read the name engraved in the cameo outloud.

"Yes, an illustrious custodian from the lower middle ages," the man said proudly.

"I know," Isaline made clear. "We have to do a report on him for school."

"You are so lucky you get to study him. He has not received the attention he deserves. Probably that is why he is my favorite," the man admitted. "Not many books tell his true story. *In the end, thunder.*"

"Perhaps you could tell me which books to read," she requested respectfully.

"It would be my pleasure," the man offered. He thought Isaline looked well-mannered and eager to learn more. "I could even lend you my own books. I've already read them hundreds of times."

"That would be very helpful."

"On second thought, I could explain his life to you myself," he proposed. He seemed eager to share his knowledge.

"Even better," Isaline agreed, trying to hide her huge smile. "My name is Isaline Fleury. It is a pleasure to meet you, Mr...."

"Angelo Severino," he provided his name. "The pleasure is mine. This is my card. It has my telephone number. Please call me and we will arrange a date dedicated to Robert Wissing." Then he added, "remember to bring your classmates, so they will also do well on the assignment. *Brotherly Finale* to you."

With no further ado, the man turned on his heels and exited through the crowd, moving with a slight limp. Isaline watched him walk outside without saying goodbye to anyone.

"Who was that man?" Nahuel asked, as he came over to Isaline, with Aremi.

"My last dance partner. A distinguished gentleman from the privileged society," Isaline replied, pleased with herself.

"What does he do?" Nahuel asked.

"He didn't say, but I bet it's something essential," Isaline declared. "More importantly, he has offered to help us with our report on Robert Wissing."

"That's lucky," Aremi said and added, "Why is he leaving so early?"

"I don't know. He probably has to get up very early tomorrow. I'm sure he is a very busy person," Isaline justified.

Rebecca, Layla and Eric came over.

"This is a nightmare," Eric blurted out.

Just then, Nahuel noticed that some of the flying trays had started serving dessert. He followed one and could see it was carrying animal shaped chocolates. It was zigzagging toward the other side of the room. Aremi followed behind him, trying to get away from Eric's bad mood.

"Get me a giraffe," she told him.

The other students stayed behind, arguing with Eric. He wanted to go back to the residency, but no one else wanted to leave. Eric had had enough once the dance was finished. He had only attended the party because he thought it would hurt his grades if he didn't go. The fact that he had been forced to dance was too much to bear. He had done it though, and now, in his mind, it was time to go. Isaline had stayed with the others, trying to persuade Eric that to leave so early would be considered disrespectful.

Nahuel finally got close enough to the tray to get some dessert. He chose a Giraffe shaped chocolate for Aremi and a Lion shaped one for himself. Each sweet was decorated with orange frosting that tasted like caramel.

"Delicious," Aremi commented.

Nahuel quickly grabbed another one for her before the tray went whizzing off in another direction.

Soon, Isaline came over.

"Eric is a pain," she declared.

"Yeah, but you don't like anybody, Isaline," Nahuel reminded her.

"What can I say? I have high standards."

"Good for us we can meet them," Aremi said with a sincere smile.

"Listen", Nahuel said suddenly, holding up his hand for them to be quiet. "Something is going on outside."

"What do you mean by 'something'?" Isaline asked.

"The insects in the forest are…strange. I don't know exactly, they feel upset," Nahuel replied.

"You can hear them from here with all this buzz going on?" Isaline said impressed.

"No doubt about it, you CymAnis are powerful," Aremi stated with a smile.

"Let's see what's going on," Nahuel said, and headed towards the gallery.

It was cold outside. The swarms of fireflies swirled through the arches of the verandah. The few people outside had their hoods up, to protect themselves from the wind that had begun to blow.

"Now I think it would have been smarter to have chosen a long dress," Aremi reflected.

From the verandah they had an amazing view.

"That's new," Isaline said.

At the edge of Ardemir there was a large pond of water, just before the forest. It was the first time they noticed it. The day of the Hazna, they would have walked right by it, making Nahuel think they had created it just for the party, to make the gardens more beautiful.

The water of the pond sparkled with the same flashes of light as the water cascading around the columns inside the Estate. There were lily pads and water lilies floating on the surface. It looked like a Monet painting come to life.

"And those are also new," Aremi added.

Just beyond the pool of water, high in the sequoia trees, some wooden structures hung. They were small cabins that were seamlessly woven into the trees. The agents who had come from abroad were invited to stay at Ardemir and for the occasion, the CymTers had created the tree-top accommodations.

Nahuel focused; the fresh air helped him clear his mind and focus his power that sometimes overflowed. He searched for the frequency of the insects of the forest. There were thousands of them. He had to strive to find the right one in order to know where that discomfort among the insects came from. Then, he could find out the reason for it.

"Over there," said Nahuel pointing behind the pond.

The three walked down the verandah steps and through the gardens, towards the forest. They left the covered porch behind, where some guests were deep in conversation and taking shelter from the cold.

A thin path of stones stretched across the glowing surface of the reflecting pool, which stood between them and the forest.

"We should get closer," Nahuel proposed and without waiting for his friends' reply, he started to cross the pool.

The path was long and wavy. Between each stone, there was water. They had to move carefully so as not to step in the water. Aremi, who was smaller, had to jump between some stones. Nahuel moved quickly, with the agility of a CymAnis.

The three continued into the forest, until the only light to guide them was the dim glow from the pool and the fireflies circling high in the trees.

Nahuel heard some voices in the darkness and said, "there's someone arguing. Keep silent, we are close."

Aremi and Isaline followed him stealthy.

When the three of them could hear the voices, they stopped.

"...The Council of Privileges is not taking the necessary precautions," the unknown voice declared.

Two people were arguing. Their hoods made it impossible to see their faces.

"The Directory must do more, it's their responsibility," the man's voice continued and he grew angrier, saying, "The passivity of the Council's response to the attacks is humiliating."

Nahuel realized the tension of this very conversation was the thing upsetting the insects.

"It's not passivity and you know it," the second voice replied. He kept his voice calm, but it was clear he was irritated.

"The evidence that the Council is not doing enough is overwhelming," the first man said.

"The Ignobles will not overpower us again," the second man stated emphatically.

The three friends exchanged nervous glances.

"Let's get a little closer," Nahuel whispered.

"They will see us," Isaline warned.

"Aremi can hide us behind those bushes, right?" Nahuel asked.

"I can try," she agreed.

Nahuel, Isaline and Aremi found themselves behind one of the gigantic sequoias. They moved cautiously through the brush, trusting the dark to keep them hidden. Aremi slowly began growing a spiky shrub until it was large enough for all three of them to hide behind.

As they were crouched in their hiding place, Nahuel could see that Americus was sitting at the feet of one of the men.

"All of the committees are working to defeat them," the man declared.

Nahuel soon determined that the unshakable voice came from his professor, Ankona, and that was the reason Americus sat beside the man. The animal seemed to be on guard in a way that Nahuel had never seen before.

"Of course, and it's just *impeccable* the way the Council is going about it," the unknown man replied sarcastically. He added, "The *unavoidable* flooding of the canals, the *efficient* control of information. But of course, these are the least of the Council's failures."

Nahuel's attention increased with each word that was spoken.

"From the outside, everything seems simpler," Ankona replied drily.

"Excuses. The Court handles situations that are as urgent and important. Don't forget it," the stranger stated. "They are attacking the privileged society directly. In the attack on the helicopter many good privileged agents were lost."

"I am well aware of that," Ankona replied bitingly.

"And now the greatest loss, the terrible end of Walter Blest".

Isaline pinched Nahuel's arm when she heard his grandfather's name. All Nahuel's senses became alert. He made the effort to breathe slowly and pay attention.

"His death has been a great loss," Ankona admitted.

Nahuel couldn't continue hiding behind his voluntary blindness. Now, it was a fact. His grandfather had had privileges, there were no more doubts about it. But that didn't explain why those men of the privileged society were talking about him.

"Blest was one of the most respectable directors the Council has ever had," the unknown man continued.

The answers came to Nahuel before he was prepared to receive them. Not only had his grandfather had privileges, but he had also formed part of the United Nations.

He suddenly realized he had never really known the man, and now he would never have the chance to do so. His grandfather had taken all his secrets with him, forever.

"I knew him better than you. You don't have to remind me what he was like," said Ankona with a hint of disdain.

"His murder at the hands of the Ignobles is unpardonable," the stranger continued.

Nahuel was in shock. He felt as if someone had slapped his face.

Nothing could have prepared him for the cruel and unforgiving information he had just heard.

"It was a memorable death, just like his life," Ankona said.

"...the Council didn't do enough to protect him," the man reproached.

"We sent help," Ankona argued. "It is our belief Mr. Blest did not defend himself."

"He didn't fight back?"

"No. The house was surrounded and if he had fought them, many innocent people would have been hurt," Ankona replied with disgust.

"And he couldn't escape?"

"Mr. Blest always kept his motives private, but we all know running away was not his style," Ankona said with respect.

The thick fog of confusion started to dissipate, and, in its place, crude reality left Nahuel unprotected and sickened. His grandfather had been murdered.

He couldn't help but feeling a deep pang of betrayal. Ankona had known about his grandfather the whole time.

He kept listening.

"They killed him, and it's all about *The Foundations of the Pact*," the stranger stated, convinced. "The Ignobles will do anything to find *The Foundations* and it's time the Council beats them to the chase. Otherwise, the Court will have to intervene."

"Please, Nahuel, control yourself," Isaline whispered.

Without realizing, he had gripped the spiky shrub so hard, its thorns had pierced his glove and his hand was bleeding. He squeezed harder, not minding the pain.

Ankona didn't say anything, but turned to where the kids were hiding.

Nahuel knew that if he could smell the copper odor of his own blood, Ankona could too. He remembered all too well what Benjamin had told them about how his professor had been transformed into a tracker.

Ankona turned again to the unknown man.

"The Council will beat the Ignobles, and you know very well that it is illegal for the Court to intervene."

162

"You have been warned," said the unknown and headed toward the Estate.

Nahuel felt sick. He was overcome with the grief and shock of someone who has just learned the truth about why he became an orphan. His grandfather hadn't died of natural causes.

He stared into the darkness, his eyes stiff and his arms shaking. He wanted to wake up from this nightmare.

He felt alone and lost.

But something more was driving him from within. A feeling he hadn't known before was beginning to grow. It was insidious and persistent, like a blindfold that wouldn't let him see.

His face was dark and his eyes barely open. His blood was running cold in his body.

The insects in the forest were now buzzing at a dizzying frequency.

Isaline and Aremi looked at him cautiously.

"Nahuel, it's time to go," Aremi said in a whisper.

He couldn't hear them. He just wanted to stay there, sitting in darkness.

CHAPTER 23

The extreme change within him caused by that first wave of grief was intact. The mortal rage he suffered grew and spread through his body like an unstoppable cancer. He was the victim of a grave injustice and like so many before him, his thoughts turned immediately to revenge.

The nooks and crannies of his memory that had been filled with nostalgic memories of his grandfather had been emptied, only to be replaced, bit by bit with a desire for revenge. The inexorable feeling had taken control of him. He was afraid these overwhelming feelings would make him lose his mind.

He was furious with the Ignobles for the murder and furious with the Council of Privileges for not telling him the truth. Nevertheless, he swore to carry out his rage against the true criminals.

At the beginning, he was angry at Ankona. Nahuel had felt a deeper connection with his professor during their conversation at the Ardemir infirmary. But, at the forest, he realized Ankona had withheld important truths. Ankona had known his grandfather well and knew the reason for his death; he knew that the Ignobles had murdered him. For days, he felt the esteem he had once felt for his teacher was gone, perhaps forever.

That feeling stayed for a while, until he realized that thanks to Ankona he knew the truth. His professor was not only a CymAnis, but also a tracker, the head of the Trackers Committee. This means that he had definitely been able to smell them at the forest and, in spite of it, he continued the conversation. Ankona wanted to be heard so Nahuel could know the truth about the death of his grandfather.

After rethinking it several times, he decided to call his mother. Maybe she could give him more information about the circumstances of his grandfather's death.

"I've already told you, Nahuel, but I will repeat it if you insist. That night, I arrived home and I found him lying down on the floor of the hall. I realized he was dead when I touched his body that was cold and stiff."

"But, mom, think, are you sure you didn't see anything else?"

"I don't know why you are playing detective. There wasn't any other trace and the paramedics said he had had a heart attack. This is very common among people of his age."

Just as Nahuel had suspected, the call to his mother had been a complete failure.

That didn't prevent him to keep on being obsessed with his grandfather's death and the Ignobles.

"They've attacked a helicopter and its crew, destroyed canals, flooded cities, murdered my grandfather…" he repeated the list coldly, over and over again. He organized the perverse actions and reasons why the Ignobles had to be punished.

At that moment, the Ignobles became not only the enemies of the Council, but also his own personal enemies.

"So, now what?" Isaline asked one day, tired of constantly hearing his diatribe.

"Now we have to find out their next move and beat them to it," Nahuel stated, reasoning with himself.

"Don't let this feeling define you," Aremi begged him.

For Nahuel, Spring was off to a challenging start.

Life in the Council of Privileges was getting harder. Their professors were becoming more and more demanding. The students could see that they were balancing their teaching duties with their responsibilities on the different committees, which meant they were running low on patience.

After the Il Finale, he only saw Ankona in two opportunities. The first one was in class, but Nahuel wasn't able to talk to him as Ankona had to leave before finishing his lecture. The second one was in the tunnels. In one of the breaks, Nahuel saw him get on one of the crystal cars and go away from the Council of Privileges. At that time, Ankona had delegated most of his classes to the Zoology professor, Hector Reyes.

During the month of April, the sub-4th floor hosted the Privileged Convention on the Control of Unnatural Earthquakes. Salim Swarup, their Limits professor was one of the guest speakers and invited his students to attend his presentation in place of Tuesday's class. Nahuel realized on that day that the CymTers could also be dangerous.

Swarup's presentation was a case-study of an unnatural disaster in the lake region of Cameroon. It was caused by a group of CymTers, who brought about a quake on the lake's shores, shifting Earth and causing lethal gas to seep from deep beneath the lake. The gas wiped out an entire village.

The students were experimenting with new frequencies and vibrations, each more complex than the other. The CymMens were immersed in learning about the vibrations needed to manipulate the particles that caused wind. The

CymTers were focusing on how to heal plants.

Nahuel had learned how to imitate the purring of a cat. It didn't mean he walked around all day purring, but that now he was able to vibrate at that frequency, inaudible to normal human hearing. The purring helped the CymAnis, just as it did cats, to increase their bone density and to heal faster. By May, Nahuel had grown. He was stronger. His muscles were larger.

Nahuel wasn't the only CymAnis benefitting from acquiring animal-like characteristics. Rebecca no longer needed her thick-framed glasses to see and Tristan was getting taller and taller.

The second Hazna had been announced for the second Friday in May. Just like before, it would require they work in teams of three. Conscious of this, Isaline insisted that Nahuel and Aremi make an effort to practice their privileges as much as she did.

But all of Nahuel's energies were focused on one single idea: his grandfather's murder. He was constantly bothered by it, his mind under assault. He couldn't think of anything else.

He wanted to transform into a tracker, in order to find his grandfather's killers and perhaps, maybe by some small chance, he could find his father as well - if he was still alive. He thought he had accepted the fact his father could be dead, but now the possibility of finding him was constantly rolling around in his head.

The students were only five days away from the next evaluation.

"You are obsessed, Nahuel, and this is not the right time to carry on like this," Isaline insisted.

Nahuel shot her a defiant look.

"After the Hazna, we will have time to continue thinking about your grandfather and the Ignobles," she added. "But right now we must use all our time to practice. This second evaluation is just as important as the first."

Aremi only dared to nod her head in agreement with Isaline.

The three students were in the practice room on the third floor of the residency. At that early in the morning, they were the only ones willing to leave the warmth of their beds

Aremi's pointy nose peeked out from behind a plant. The shrub she was practicing on was inside a pot that was taller than she. She controlled the growth of a branch, bringing it right up to the tip of a pointy ear. She had learned to make shrubs grow into specific shapes. She walked around the pot, making adjustments to the shrub here and there as if she was trimming and shaping it with a pair of invisible shears.

"What is that?" Nahuel asked.

"It's a gnome. You'll see when I finish its face."

Aremi couldn't hold back her childlike excitement, and even though Nahuel was deep in his own dark thoughts, her enthusiasm was contagious.

Isaline was sitting on the floor with her legs crossed. Benjamin had taken apart a jigsaw puzzle that filled an entire wall. When put together, it showed the Himalayan Mountains. Now it was up to the new CymMens to put it back together.

Isaline had opened one of the jars containing concentrated amounts of microorganisms and put it near the wooden box containing the remaining pieces of the puzzle. She chose a piece and tried to put it where it fit in one fluid movement. The assignments for *Precision* class were harder than all the others. She squinted her eyes, concentrating to make the piece move through the air until it fit exactly into the snow-covered side of the mountains.

Nahuel stepped into the Savannah and quickly sniffed out the den of some lizards. He was now using a talesma of dehydrated tail. Isaline was right. He had to refine his privilege to the extreme. If he did well on this Hazna, he could increase a level, obtain a more powerful a-bula and be more prepared to face the Ignobles. It had even been his idea to start practicing so early in the morning. Isaline loved the idea and his change of heart, no matter what his motivation might be.

Nahuel, Aremi and Isaline were expected at 9 a.m. at Ardemir. They got into their cart at 8:30 a.m. and moved through the tunnels toward the forest of sequoias. The trip was silent. Each student was immersed in their own world, each world ruled by a distinct privilege.

It was only when they took the second turn and found themselves among the glowing jellyfish that Nahuel noticed there was a cart coming up behind theirs. Inside were Tristan, Emma and an Armenian boy named Samuel Avakian.

The first thing that was different in this Hazna was that the groups had been summoned at different times. But now it seemed like this group was expected at the same time as them.

At the edge of the forest, Sebastian was waiting for them. This time, Sebastian was the only professor there and he seemed to like it. He gave the instructions in an exaggerated way and smiled presumptuously.

"Today's Hazna is a competition," he announced. "The challenge consists in being the first group to locate and unearth the salamander hiding at the foot of the canyon. Only one group can win."

As soon as Nahuel heard this, he immediately decided he was not going to let Tristan beat him.

"Beyond the sequoias you will find the hunting ground which my CymTers colleagues have prepared for you," he explained. "Victoria here will be your referee and will accompany you to the site."

She gave them a reassuring smile, although it was clearly forced.

"You have one hour to pass each test successfully and to obtain your objective. Good luck and remember that Wildo will be watching you. If you truly run into danger, someone will come to help you," Sebastian concluded, pointing at the sky.

Nahuel looked up to where the professor was pointing. He saw an eagle-owl gliding above them, Wildo.

The professor took his leave, walking across the large backyard of the Estate.

"Don't fall behind."

Victoria was already on the move. Isaline followed her closely. Victoria cleared the path, pushing aside branches and sticks that were in the way.

Not really knowing how long they had been walking, Nahuel noticed a clearing up ahead. With each step, the vegetation became more sparse, the giant trees were fewer and farther between and the sun even shone down into the forest.

"Keep your eyes on the prize," a voice said. Nahuel turned around and saw Benjamin. He walked with his chest puffed up, his copper a-bula shining against his vest. Nahuel had been so focused on the clearing that he hadn't even sensed Benjamin's presence. He was walking from the canyon with two groups who had just finished their evaluation.

It was the only thing he said as he walked past them on his way back to the Estate.

Nahuel focused on his classmates who followed behind Benjamin. They looked terrible. They were dirty and messy. Most of them had bruises and burns on their arms and faces. A welt the size of a peach was swelling on Kana's arm and her eyes looked dim.

Perhaps this challenge was more dangerous than the previous one and Wildo really did have his work cut out for him.

The landscape suddenly changed and they left behind the freshness of the green and the fertile soil.

Before their eyes, they faced an arid field. Vegetation was scarce. Only a few cactuses remained in the desert. The other shrubs looked wilted in their pale gray and brown tones.

Even though the terrain was desolate and slightly threatening, Nahuel found it beautiful, in an unsettling way.

"The rules for this Hazna are the following," Victoria began to list them:

"Number one: the first team to find the salamander and bring me its treasure wins. Number two: all the traps must be overcome using your privileges. Number three: all three members of the team must remain together until the end of the Hazna. Number four: you may not harm in any way the members of the other team. Number five: you have one hour to complete the task and return to this point."

This was the first time that day Victoria had announced the rules of the Hazna.

"You should go down this slope to the bottom of the canyon where the salamander lives," she explained. "One team should go to the right and the other to the left."

Nahuel looked out in front of them. There was a rock formation taller than the rest jutting up from the cracked earth, dividing the terrain in two.

"I have a question," Isaline said, raising her hand.

"I cannot answer any questions," Victoria shot back with a peevish smile.

Isaline's face turned red and she narrowed her eyes in disgust.

"Don't even dream about it," Tristan suddenly said just to be heard by Nahuel.

"What's the matter with you?" The boy turned while they were walking to the bifurcation.

"You won't be able to beat me, not even in your dreams," Tristan said with an arrogant smile.

A fit of anger heated Nahuel's body.

"And what do your nightmares say?" he challenged.

He couldn't let Tristan get under his skin. He already had enough with the Ignobles to let Tristan annoy him. And, yet, he felt he only needed a spark for his inner fire to explode.

Nahuel, Isaline and Aremi took the path on the left.

Every part of the canyon looked like the other parts. The sun beat down on the red earth. The students walked on, using the diverse rock formations as guides, their shadows spreading over the emptiness of the canyon.

It was not a friendly environment. Nature seemed to be stalking them.

Nahuel couldn't hear anything except silence. He couldn't feel the presence of any insects or rodents or reptiles. So, he was shocked when he saw an armadillo poking out from his den. Its armor was pale and it had white hairs on its belly. When Nahuel looked the creature in the eyes, it dug into the earth, burying itself completely, as if it had been threatened by a predator.

"Hurry up, Nahuel. We only have an hour," Isaline reminded him.

Nahuel had stayed behind with the armadillo, trying to convince it to come out of its hiding place, but it wouldn't even show its nose.

They kept moving over the dry earth, the path spotted with different rock formations. The path was narrow and full of cracks. They had to zigzag over the rocks and dodge the boulders jutting out from the rock walls.

It takes Mother Nature thousands of years to erode the soil, but the CymTers had done it in just a few weeks.

Nahuel looked up. They were walking underneath what looked like a bridge made from red clay.

Beneath Isaline's feet, a rock shook and broke loose. The girl wobbled, the rock fell down into nothing and, before she fell down with it, Nahuel kept her out of the way with a surprising agility.

However, he felt himself falling alongside the rock. He slipped and tried to grab onto something, but the rock walls were smooth. He kept falling. He scratched his face. He tried to raise his arms, to cover his face with his hands, but the space was too narrow. His skin was scratched and burning.

Just when he thought he would smack against the ground, he stopped. The walls of the crack he had fallen into had become so close together that he was stuck in between the rocks.

"Nahuel!" Aremi exclaimed, looking at him from above. "Are you alright?"

"I guess you could say that," he replied. He was five meters below them.

He couldn't believe how stupid he had been, he was unfocused and distracted. He should have jumped and pushed Isaline at the same time so none of them would fall into that hole.

Wildo had flown down directly when Nahuel fell. Upon seeing that he hadn't suffered any major injuries, he flew high into the sky once more.

"Are you ok? Can you get out of there?" Isaline asked when getting up.

"I think so," he replied.

The crack was narrow and he knew how to rock climb. He tried to get into a climbing position and realized quickly that something was wrong.

His foot was stuck. *Damn it.*

He tried to free it, tugging upward, but he couldn't move it, not even a fraction of an inch.

"The clock is ticking," Isaline murmured.

But Nahuel could hear her anyway.

"I'm stuck," he shouted up.

He tried to reach down. Maybe if he could take off his shoe, he could get his foot out. But the space was so tight, he couldn't even bend at the waist to stretch toward his feet.

He looked up again. Aremi was laying on her stomach, her head in her hands, peering down at him through the crack.

"Isaline says it's too bad we can't go on without you, because of that rule Victoria mentioned, you know? But I think she is just joking."

Nahuel rolled his eyes.

Aremi looked to the side then said,

"I think walking helps her think."

Nahuel tried moving his foot again.

"It's a shame I haven't learned to move earth yet," Aremi said.

"Yeah, that would be a big help right now," Nahuel agreed feeling powerless.

"*Quiet. Quiet.*" they heard Isaline's voice very low.

Aremi looked at Nahuel and put her finger to her lips.

Nahuel didn't say another word.

Then he realized what was happening. The other group was crossing the bridge. They hadn't noticed they were below them and their voices were loud and clear. Nahuel could hear them too, albeit a bit distorted from inside the crevice.

"Keep away from that yellow dirt, I saw one of the guys from the losing team that was with Benjamin that had all his body full of that stuff; there must be a trap around here," they heard Tristan say.

Nahuel tightened his fists vigorously. If Tristan won them because he had fallen into that damn hole, he wouldn't forgive himself.

Step by step, the voices faded away.

"We have to get you out of there quickly," Isaline's head peer into the crevice.

"You could try with the tweezers," Aremi suggested.

"I'm not going to climb in there," she replied, frowning.

"All the tests have to be passed using our privileges," Aremi responded.

"Of course," she recalled. "I will try to make the tweezers fly down and excavate the dirt around Nahuel's foot, from here," she suggested as if the entire idea had been her own.

She took the metal tool from the front pocket of her vest. She floated it down toward Nahuel's right foot.

"A little lower, Isaline," he guided her.

She couldn't see the spot she would have to clear away.

"A toe and a half to the right," Nahuel indicated.

"Big toe or little toe?" Aremi asked.

Isaline shot her a disapproving look.

"There?" she asked.

"A little more... stop... a little to the side... there! Right there."

The tweezers sunk into the dirt again and again, trying to break away the rock, trapping Nahuel's foot. Without meaning to, Isaline stuck the pointy end several times into her friend's foot, but he said nothing.

Once Nahuel was free, they quickened their pace.

Tristan and his group had a slight lead on them. If Nahuel could keep Tristan's group from winning, it would be harder for them to continue to the next level and that would certainly help Nahuel feel better.

Slowly, the boulders and rock formations became fewer and farther between and the terrain flattened. The sun, high overhead, shone down on the flat land, making it seem like a dreamscape.

A spot was quivering on the horizon. It grew as they got closer. Until they could see it with total clarity.

It was a sand storm. And to carry on, they would have to go through it.

Isaline raised her palms in front of her and closed her eyes. The intensity of the sand clear a bit in front of them. Until the grains of sand around them were suspended in the air as if frozen in time.

The three of them started walking through the storm. Isaline in the front and Nahuel in the back. They walked very slowly, feeling their way in the mess.

Where Isaline walked, the sand stopped. They walked under the umbrella of her privilege. She was going to great pains to keep the grains around them still in the air.

Nahuel could hear the storm roaring next to them and feel the wind swirling.

Up ahead they could see that once they could past the sand storm, the landscape resumed the shape of the red canyon, boulders, and rock formations.

Further on, they could see the silhouettes of the other group. They were slowly getting closer to them.

They were just a few feet away to emerge from the sand storm when Tristan turned around and saw them. Then he said something to Emma under his breath.

She turned around and moved her hand like she was slapping the air. As she did so, a gust of wind pushed them back into the storm.

Sand hit them all over their bodies. The storm was so strong that the grains of sand felt like miniature meteorites crashing against their bare skin.

Nahuel felt his blood boiling. Attacking another group was forbidden, but Tristan clearly didn't mind playing dirty.

This time, Nahuel took the lead. He told the girls to cover their faces and their eyes with their vests. He grabbed Aremi's hand and pushed Isaline forward. The strategy was hiding within the sand.

They walked very slowly, feeling their way in the dark. The sand was ruthless. At least their face and eyes were protected by their vests.

When they emerged again from the storm, Nahuel uncovered his face, and adjusted his eyes to the sunlight. They were close to the other group. They seemed to be arguing.

"Find the damn animal!" Tristan was saying.

Aremi nudged Nahuel and pointed out a sign. Stuck into the dirt, the sign said, *It's a bad sign if you carry on from here empty handed. Look under the camel's shadow.*

"Maybe the camel is hidden in a crack or behind a rock," Emma guessed.

"Inside a crack? Really?" Tristan asked.

Isaline opened her eyes wide, tugged on Aremi and signaled for her to get Nahuel's attention. When both Aremi and Nahuel were looking at her, she began pointing at the ground in an exaggerated way.

Tristan could sense their presence and he also turned to look where Isaline was pointing.

On the ground, to their left, one of the rock formations was casting a shadow. It looked like camel with two humps.

Nahuel and Tristan sprang into action at the same moment. They both ran toward the bushes under the camel's shadow.

But just as they were close enough to touch the shrubs, they stopped in their tracks.

A snake was waiting for them, its dim colors blending perfectly with the dry landscape. This was its lair and the obstacle they had to overcome to obtain what was hidden there.

Nahuel realized he would have to communicate with it. He made an effort to hear it, but he couldn't pick up on any echo. Animal Communication's latest classes had been about reptiles and amphibians, so he should have no problem in communicating with the snake.

I've practiced, I'm sure. Goddamn! he thought to himself. He tried to focus on the snake frequency, but he could only connect with his anger.

He was letting his emotions dominate him, even though his grandfather had insisted thousands of times that he had to control his instincts. However, thinking about his grandfather at that moment made him feel even more annoyed.

The snake changed positions, shifting to reveal its rattle. Then it started heading straight for Nahuel, challenging him. It slithered toward him, pushing with his tail and rising up with stealth, attacking elegantly.

Tristan had arrived to the snake first and already given it the order to keep Nahuel away.

Nahuel slowly backed away. The snake followed him, showing his split tongue and rattling his tail. Nahuel tried again to enter the snake's mind, but his feelings were intervening with his privilege. He couldn't overturn the command Tristan had given it.

Tristan wasted no time. He jumped into the space and began rummaging among the shrubs. When he stood up, he held two small jars full of yellow liquid in his hands.

"One of those is ours, Tristan," Aremi told him. But she might as well have been speaking to a rock.

Tristan read the instructions stuck on the side of the jar, called his group over and gave them one of the jars. Emma took a sip, made a face of disgust and handed it to Samuel. He drank the rest and left the jar on the ground. Tristan drank half of the liquid from the second jar and smashed the rest on the ground.

"Only one of us can win today," he said.

Tristan's group then ran off quickly and the snake returned to its den.

Isaline quickly lifted the jar from the ground with her mind and read the instructions.

"It was a serum for rhinoceros skin. It makes your skin tough, like a shield," she explained. "Only the CymMens and CymAnis should drink it. There were two doses per bottle - one serum for each group."

"They cheated," Aremi said, crushed.

Nahuel clenched his teeth and tried hard to control his reaction.

"Let's move," he said and started running the same way the other group had gone.

Soon, the three were next to the large ravine where the salamander was hidden.

They heard voices and footsteps ahead.

The path was narrowing. It seemed like they were entering a funnel with reddish brown walls. The room to walk was getting tighter and tighter. They could see the other group's footprints in the clay.

They came around a bend at full speed and there, at the end of the path were Tristan and his group. A green wall composed entirely of cacti rose up before them. Their stalks were as tall as Tristan and they were covered in thorns and spikes.

Tristan pushed Samuel into the cactus forest, turned to throw Nahuel a murderous smile and then slipped into the cactus forest himself.

"This is what the serum was for," Isaline said when they reached the cactus wall themselves.

"Looking for another path isn't a choice," Nahuel warned, in case they were thinking about it. "They will get there first if we take a detour."

"I think I can help," Aremi said, peering closely at a cactus. I could make the thorns go back into the stalk."

"Sounds good. Do it," Nahuel said, already walking into the spiky forest.

Isaline took a step forward, looked at the thorns cautiously, but was determined to continue.

"You'll have to go in one at a time," Aremi warned as she quickly changed the talesma inside her a-bula.

"It will only work if I try a bit at a time."

"We'll have to risk it," Nahuel decided. "The other group must be halfway there."

"Alright," Isaline agreed.

"Now, Aremi," Nahuel urged her.

She nodded. She decided to concentrate on the thorns that were around their heads. She thought it would be important to protect her friends' faces, since she couldn't do the entire body. Their vests would protect their torsos from the threatening spikes, but only the serum could have protected their exposed arms and legs.

Nahuel and Isaline hurried forward even though the environment was not very encouraging.

Aremi crouched down and took advantage of her petite size, crawling along the ground.

The thorns scratched their skin. Isaline whimpered against her will. When she looked down, she could see blood running along her shins. There was the sound of fabric ripping and suddenly a shred of Nahuel's shirt was hanging from a cactus.

But they carried on. They had to continue or fail.

It was driving Nahuel crazy to move so slowly. Aremi was doing her best, but forcing the thorns into the stalk was no easy task and she was trying to do it for all three of them. Her skin was red, she was sweating and she was covered in scratches. You could see she was in pain. She was focusing more on the thorns that could scratch her friends than on those that were hurting her.

Nahuel couldn't hold back any longer and without a second thought, he took off running. He figured that way Aremi would have less work to do, focusing solely on Isaline and herself. He tried to run sideways, but soon tripped and fell face-first to the ground.

"Wait, Nahuel. I can't reach you if you move that fast," Aremi told him, raising her voice.

But Nahuel didn't want to stop. He stood up and started running again. He knew he was getting close to the other group. He could smell the sweat. He breathed in dust and hot air. His arms were wet and sticky with blood.

He refused to give in to the pain, even though the thorns were merciless. Just a few more feet and the ordeal would be over.

A thorn tore across his cheek, but he carried on, with only a groan.

They emerged from the cactus forest as from a battle. When they finally made it out, they were hurt, their wounds throbbing, and they were exhausted.

Tristan savored the moment. He showed them the salamander medallion in his hands. It was like he was rubbing salt in their wounds.

Nahuel felt responsible of a failed mission.

CHAPTER 24

"What's done is done," Isaline stated in resignation.

Isaline had formally requested the presence of Nahuel and Aremi in the library after dinner. Nahuel and Aremi sat at Isaline's favorite desk. She stood in front of them, like a teacher giving a lecture.

"It is no use to continue lamenting and beating ourselves up over what happened at the Hazna."

It had taken Isaline a good long while to accept this mature position she was now preaching.

"We have fallen behind, it is a fact," she went on, shuddering as she announced the cruel truth. "Nevertheless, we were almost the very best in the first Hazna. This means we have one last chance to remedy our mistake."

Even though he hated to admit it, Nahuel had to agree with her.

"I will only accept brilliance in our final mark essay," she announced.

Her friends nodded in agreement.

"It must be EXCELLENT!" she stated energetically. "Lucky for us, we have this."

Isaline took from her pocket the cameo of Robert Wissing and showed it to her friends.

"This is our salvation."

Nahuel looked at Aremi, puzzled. She shrugged her shoulders in return.

"My last partner at the dance, Angelo Severino, gave it to me," she told them. "We will call him first thing tomorrow to arrange a date to meet as soon as possible. He has promised to help us with the essay. And it would be foolish to waste the opportunity."

Nahuel knew that their abysmal failure in the last Hazna was largely his fault. He would try to dedicate all of his energy to the Robert Wissing essay to make up for it.

They knocked on the door. They had arrived at their meeting with Angelo Severino ten minutes early.

The house was identical to every other house on the block. It was straight and narrow and wedged in between its neighbors. The curtains were drawn across the windows and the brick walls had recently been varnished.

"Come in children. I have been waiting for you."

The old man led them slowly and surely down the dark hallway toward the living room. He leaned on a cane with a silver handle to walk. His left leg was the culprit. It made him sway or stumble when he moved. At the beginning he had detested this aspect of growing old, but with time he had learned to bear it with elegance.

The inside of the house was bare. It felt lonely and empty. There were no pictures, photographs, or decorations. There were only four chairs and one table in the room. On the table, a steaming tea pot waited for them, next to four teacups.

"Have a seat," Severino invited them to sit down, taking his own place at the table.

As soon as the students were seated, the tea pot floated into the air and served a bit of tea into each cup. The tea set was Japanese porcelain, with a scene of a geisha against a background of cherry blossoms painted on it. Something behind Nahuel began to play. The sitar strings began sounding a metallic, high-pitched melody. The musical notes accompanied the pace and rhythm of Mr. Severino's voice.

"We already know the reason for your visit, so let's skip the pleasantries, shall we?" Severino began, instantly grabbing their attention. "Robert Wissing was a remarkable custodian of the Middle Ages, who asked for no recognition for his achievements."

"What achievements do you mean?" Isaline questioned, her pencil poised to note down every word that came from Severino's lips.

"We will get to that. Let's begin at the beginning," he replied calmly. "Robert Wissing was born in 1463, of the unprivileged calendar, in Salisbury, England and died in 1508 in the same city. His childhood was marred by the tragic death of his mother. He studied medicine at the University of Cambridge, as was the family tradition. He was married when he was only eighteen years old..."

The three students already knew all of this. Nahuel himself had been in charge of summarizing the custodian's biography.

"....that is all the information most books will provide," Severino concluded after his lengthy description of Robert Wissing's life.

Nahuel had become hypnotized, watching Aremi's foot keep time with the music.

"Now, the interesting and captivating thing is that Robert Wissing became a Custodian for our society and in a very brief time he was entrusted with the greatest secrets of our history. *In the end, thunder.*"

"How is it that he "became" a custodian?" Isaline asked carefully, hoping her question wouldn't come across as rude.

"From a very young age, Wissing noticed that he had particular qualities which his peers did not possess. He searched high and low for someone with the same peculiar traits. When he met Edgar Lannaud, what had seemed like a figment of his imagination, was confirmed as fact. These peculiar traits had a name, an origin and a history. Lannaud introduced him to the international organization that governed the privileged society at that time, The Order of the Legitimate. Once there, Wissing gained the trust of everyone, rose through the ranks and responsibilities and became a dignified custodian."

The mood of the melody played by the sitar began to unravel. It became hard and sombre, generating a feeling of impatience and suspense in the listener.

"You must remember that the Custodians have been members of, and even originators of international organizations throughout history. The United Nations is just one example of that. The Custodians formed it for the purpose of knowing what was happening worldwide and to therefore be able to hide the secret of our existence in a more practical way."

Nahuel remembered hearing something similar in their Cultural History class.

"The greatest achievement of our custodian, Robert Wissing, is still kept a secret," Mr. Severino stated provocatively. "I don't know how much more I should explain, although I have promised to help you."

Severino turned to look at them with a penetrating stare, as if he were studying them. Nahuel didn't know why, but he was holding his breath. True to his word, Severino entrusted them with the custodian's secret story.

"Robert Wissing was the one who translated, compiled, and hid *The Foundations of the Pact*. But he never received the acknowledgement he deserved, even though he never expected to be praised for doing it. He knew his work was considered extremely confidential and important. The responsibility they had bestowed on him would be the greatest honor of his life, and to ensure the safety of everyone, he would have to keep it a secret. *In the end, thunder.*"

Severino squinted, as if searching for something in the air, perhaps the very ghost of Wissing, to confirm his story.

"His real identity, as custodian of *The Foundations of the Pact*, was only known to one other person. In my own research I have found and read the letter which states…"

At that moment, Nahuel lost track of the conversation.

He was suddenly taken back to the moment he had overheard everything that had happened the day his grandfather died, and he reheard the voices, like some kind of intriguing torture. He hadn't thought about it recently, but now the words, *They killed him, and it's all about The Foundations of the Pact*, replayed perfectly in his mind. Bewildered by the sheer rage he felt for the Ignobles, he had overlooked something fundamental - their motive for the murder: *The Foundations of the Pact.*

He felt his anger give way suddenly to a whirlwind of confusion. How could he have pushed that aside? How could his memory have lost track of the cause of his great pain? He had become so concerned with WHO had killed his grandfather that he had forgotten WHY they had done it.

"What do *The Foundations* actually consist of?" Isaline's voice brought Nahuel back to the plain room.

"Very few actually know, others speculate," he replied with discretion and mystery. "Legend has it that it's pages hide a marvelous secret."

Nahuel turned his head. He thought he saw a hint of evasion in Severino's eyes. He stretched his back on his chair, and the thought crossed his mind: *I bet he knows.*

"*The Foundations* were created with the *Pact* to end the war among the privileges. That is the only thing we know for certain," Severino clarified. "Of course, none of this should be on your essay."

Nahuel would have liked to have had all his doubts erased in that moment: What secrets did *The Foundations of the Pact* hold? Why were the Ignobles looking for it? How had his grandfather been involved?

It made him shudder to think that *The Foundations of the Pact* might fall into the hands of the Ignobles. He didn't need to know what they contained to fully understand their importance and how dangerous it would be if the wrong side got ahold of them.

"You said that Wissing translated, compiled and hid *The Foundations*. Is it known where they are hidden?" Isaline continued her interrogation.

Nahuel turned his head automatically toward Severino.

"No, it is not known for certain. However, the theories as to their whereabouts are more probable than the other legends. *In the end, thunder*," Severino replied, drumming his fingertips on his empty teacup.

"Are the canals an option?" Nahuel questioned eagerly. He had just had a frightening realization.

"It seems you have been paying attention," Severino replied seriously, a glint of satisfaction in his eyes. "Yes, the canals are the most likely option."

Severino held the group's full attention.

"In the ancient times, the tunnels were created and we continue to use them for transportation. They were made with the utmost care, using Nicca, a stone that can only be broken using the CymTer privilege. During that period and in later years it became customary for people to hide their precious belongings in the tunnels, because as cities rose and fell throughout history, the tunnels remained, intact.

"Nevertheless, in the Middle Ages, the privileged society decided to cover the surfaces above the tunnels with water. They did so to prevent those who did not possess privileges from discovering them and the treasures they held. So, these underwater tunnels became known as the canals.

"As time passed, most of the tunnels fell into disuse. Many of them no longer even appear on our maps."

As if in a trance, Nahuel was able to observe how Severino stood up unsteadily on his uneven feet, handed Isaline the books he had promised her on the custodian and bid them farewell with a handshake at the door. Nahuel had the feeling this old man would be the one to answer many of his questions.

On their way back to the residency, the pieces of the puzzle began to fall into place in his mind.

CHAPTER 25

"The Ignobles are looking for *The Foundations of the Pact*," Nahuel blurted out as soon as the door of his friends' bedroom was shut.

The characteristic smell of jasmine filled his nostrils. The headboard of Aremi's bed was always decorated with a wreath of fresh jasmine. Isaline always declined the offer to have flowers around her bed.

"Yes, and Wissing hid them in the tunnels," Isaline added, organizing her notes on her bed. "Excuse me, Nahuel. Sit over there please," she said, nudging him off the bed and pointing at a pillow she had placed on the floor for him.

"And now we know that the tunnels are beneath the canals," Aremi added.

She was sitting by the window, twirling the globe on her desk with one finger. The last rays of sunset came in through the window and bounced off the blossoms spreading on the northern hemisphere. They were the last blooms, as spring came to an end.

"That explains the destruction of those canals in Europe in recent months," Nahuel stated.

"At least *The Foundations of the Pact* are protected by Nicca stone. I've heard it's the strongest substance on earth. The ancient ones found it inside ice volcanoes, but now those are all gone," Aremi explained.

"Who told you so?" Isaline questioned.

"Professor Folger told us during the first lesson of Geology. I think he wanted to get our attention," Aremi replied.

"What we know for sure is that the Ignobles will do anything to find *The Foundations of the Pact*," Nahuel concluded, not wanting to stray from the topic. Thinking about his grandfather's death had become an insatiable vice.

The uncomfortable silence that had settled upon them was broken by Isaline, who, as she numbered the pages of her notes, stated, "We have been incredibly lucky to meet Severino. Look at all these notes. I am sure our essay will be among the best."

"What a surprising coincidence, the way you met him," Aremi reflected as Isaline placed the cameo pin of the custodian on her desk like a trophy.

"The books he lent us are ancient, but look how well he has taken care of them," Isaline said, standing up to turn on the lights to be able to examine the books better. "I will read them first and then lend them to you."

"As you wish," Aremi agreed in her easygoing way.

"That way I can summarize them as quickly as possible."

"There is something strange about Mr. Severino," Aremi pondered outloud. "The house seems like a waiting room. He needs to invite Mrs. Penington over to make it into a real home."

"He was a perfect host in my opinion. And I don't know if you noticed, but his a-bula is platinum, like Klaus's," Isaline responded with finality. She didn't want anyone judging her hero.

Nahuel was staring at the geometric pattern of the pillow he was sitting on. His body temperature rose and his heart rate increased. The thoughts gathering in his mind were feverish, dark, hard to decipher. One thing was for certain. Once he was able to unwrap it and see it clearly, he spoke, "Whatever happens, the Ignobles must not find *The Foundations of the Pact*."

"The entire Council of Privileges is trying to prevent it," Isaline told him, unimpressed by this very obvious statement from her friend.

"You don't get it," Nahuel replied. "*We* have an obligation to keep them from it. At least *I* have to do something to stop them," he determined.

He wasn't fully revealing his intentions. He didn't dare to admit the real reason motivating him, afraid his friends would think less of him. He wanted revenge and now he knew how to go about it. This certainty provided him with some hope for closure. Through revenge he would be able to heal his wounds. He would do everything in his power to throw a wrench in the Ignoble's plans.

"The best agents in the world are busy with the Ignobles. What could you do?" Isaline reminded him, trying to bring him to his senses.

Nahuel's determination was put to the test in the face of Isaline's challenge, but his mind was made up.

"For starters, I'll find out what *The Foundations of the Pact* are."

It wasn't long before Nahuel realized that getting details about *The Foundations of the Pact* was no easy task.

He began his search in the residency's library. After dinner, he would eagerly steal himself away, seeking any useful information he could find in the books. The worst fears arose when he simply couldn't find anything.

After a few days of this, the girls joined him. They also felt incredibly curious to know what the Ignobles were after and also felt a moral responsibility to keep their friend company.

Once the three were intent on the search they had to change the way they used the library. They had no choice because Mrs. Penington was always coming into the library, surprising them with books that had nothing to do with their studies, and asking them endless questions which they didn't have the answers for. They also didn't want to draw any unwanted attention from their classmates for all their extra library time.

They decided the best thing would be to check the books out very late at night, take them to the girls' room to search for information, and then return them first thing in the morning, so no one would miss them.

But no matter how much they researched the topic, they couldn't find anything about *The Foundations of the Pact*. It was like Mr. Severino had made the whole thing up. If he hadn't heard them mentioned that night in the forest, at the party, Nahuel would have worried he was leading his friends on a wild goose chase.

During class, Nahuel couldn't stand hearing Tristan brag about the Hazna and it took all his willpower to keep him from letting loose all the anger he felt. When the second Hazna finished, they had decided not to accuse Tristan and the other team of cheating, as Nahuel didn't want to be a snitch.

The most annoying thing of all was that every time they got near Tristan they had to listen to him say things like, "This Hazna wasn't for everyone. It was way more complicated and exciting. Salamanders are more dangerous animals and hunting one has been a true challenge, nothing like finding that pathetic stick bug." Tristan was arrogant the way only idiots can be.

Isaline, given the chance, had stepped on Emma's homework, which had fallen off her desk. Aremi spent her time trying to calm her friends down every time the topic of the Hazna came up.

It was no surprise when Mrs. Sparling let them know they had received a horrible grade on the second Hazna. They had fallen into every single trap, taken longer than the allotted time, and failed to find the salamander.

Nahuel wasn't even surprised to learn that his individual grade was the lowest in his group. He hadn't even been able to hear the sound of a tiny insect.

But what improved Nahuel's mood was seeing Tristan's face when he read his evaluation letter. He had been disqualified for not following the rules.

And even better, just as Isaline had foretold, their essay on Robert Wissing was excellent. Nahuel had put just as much effort into it as his friends. He felt he could pardon himself once and for all for the mistakes he had made in the Hazna.

They received the highest mark on the essay thanks to Angelo Severino's extensive knowledge on the subject and the generous way he had shared his books.

Much to their relief, their performance on the first Hazna, and the excellence of their essay on the custodian Robert Wissing meant that Nahuel, Isaline and Aremi still had a chance to pass to the next level next year.

"I'm so happy that Tristan got what he deserved," Isaline confessed as they left Mrs. Sparling's classroom. "I can't say I'm surprised that Kana's group is the worst. Although we all know I wish Tristan's group was at the bottom, we would all be better off without Emma and her stupid giggle. She is so superficial…"

"But it wasn't right, what Mrs. Sparling said to them. Kana turned as red as a tomato," Aremi said.

"What? That she was going to take away their a-bulas and give them to Americus because he knew how to use them better than they did?" Nahuel asked.

"Yes, that."

"Americus would love that. The problem is that they are pretty far from passing to the next level. They still need to pass three Haznas," said Nahuel, worried for his classmates. On his part, he needed to move up the levels quickly, to be ready for a possible standoff with the Ignobles.

"We are in debt to Mr. Severino," Isaline said, changing the subject. "We should all go together to thank him personally and return his books."

"We could take him flowers. His house needs some cheering up," Aremi added.

Nahuel agreed to go too. He wanted to see Angelo Severino again. He was sure he had more mysteries to share with them.

The last class on Wednesday was Serums, with Professor Greenwood. Her class on waterproofing serum, which allowed you to stand under a waterfall and not get a drop of water on you, was long but enjoyable. Nahuel, Isaline and Aremi could follow along while checking the news in the papers from the last few weeks, as they stirred the gazelle oil in their bowls.

They read the news every day, reading between the lines of every international event, no matter how insignificant it seemed, seeking some clue as to the whereabouts of the Ignobles.

The only thing that seemed suspicious, after days of unrewarding searches, was a story about a group of children who claimed to have seen a pack of wild dogs in a town in Northern Italy. Even though one of the children had been attacked and bitted by one of the animals, and the other children were witnesses, no one believed them that the dogs weren't normal strays.

As soon as Professor Greenwood dismissed them, they loaded up the heavy books about Robert Wissing and left the United Nations straight for Mr. Severino's house, the pigeons following them like bodyguards. The last time that Nahuel had infringed Ankona's request, he didn't tell him anything, and he doubted this time would be different, as he knew that his professor was out of New York. Three blocks before arriving, they passed by a flower stand. The flowers were arranged on an old wooden cart and a young man was selling them. Aremi chose a bouquet of tulips and daisies because they were the most colorful.

Even though they hadn't warned Mr. Severino they were coming, he welcomed them inside without batting an eyelash. He was dressed in black from head to toe, as if he had just come from a funeral. The house was still as sterile and tidy as the last time they had been there. The hallway remained dark and the living room was lifeless. The tea was served and waiting on the table.

Four cups. Looks like he was expecting us, Nahuel thought.

"You've brought me a present," Severino noticed, pointing at the flowers. He didn't seem very appreciative, but was not ungrateful either.

The tea cups hovered a bit in the air, allowing the four plates to slide out from underneath them. The teacups placed themselves in front of each person, already seated at the table, and the plates stacked up in the center.

Then suddenly, the plates came apart in the air. The cherry blossoms painted on the porcelain pulled apart until there were thousands of tiny pieces floating before them, as if the plates had shattered against the floor. Each part hung in the air and then shook. One by one, the bits began fusing together until a delicate flower vase stood before them. The multi-colored flower arrangement Isaline had presented Mr. Severino flew through the air and into the vase, taking its place as a centerpiece.

"Transfiguration," Isaline stated. Then she whispered to her friends, "It can only be done when the two objects are made from the same material."

"Can you do it?" Nahuel asked her, clearly impressed.

"Of course not. It's incredibly complicated. In Structure and Transfiguration class we are only studying the theory."

"Once you learn how to deconstruct the object, putting the next one together is much simpler," Severino confided.

"We hope we are not interrupting you with our visit. We wanted to thank you for your help." Isaline said.

"Have you received your grade for the essay?" he asked.

"We did an excellent job," Isaline replied proudly.

"We brought you the books you lent us about Wissing," Nahuel cut in. "I have read them cover to cover but I can't find any mention of *The Foundations of the Pact.*"

"It would be quite difficult to keep them a secret if they were mentioned in any average book, don't you think?" Severino asked. "*In the end, thunder.*"

Good point. Nahuel wanted to ask Severino what that phrase he repeated meant… But unable to contain his anxiety about *The Foundations*, he asked:

"Where can I read about them?"

Severino eyed him slowly. "Why are you so interested in them, Nahuel?"

"I'm just curious," he replied, trying to conceal his real interest.

"Curiosity is not always a characteristic that is well received… But I believe it is the very key to success," Severino confided.

Nahuel said nothing, patiently waiting for Severino to answer his question.

"Very few texts speak about *The Foundations of the Pact*. I can safely assume that not even a single book you have access to even mentions them," Severino went on, adding, "I should never have mentioned them. That is a secret part of history."

Nahuel didn't believe for a second that Severino regretted telling them about the unwritten details of the custodian's life. He didn't seem to be suffering too much when he replied to their questions.

"Help me bring these books to the library, this isn't the place for them," Severino asked Nahuel.

Nahuel followed the man through the dim house. The shutters were hermetically sealed on all the windows. It seemed the man liked to keep the house shut tight. When they entered the library, the old man turned on the lights, chasing away the shadows.

The shelves drilled into the walls were empty. There was even a ladder to reach the books kept up high - books that didn't exist. On the floor, some boxes gathered dust.

"You can leave them inside any of these boxes," Severino indicated. Then he walked out of the room, trying to conceal his limp.

Nahuel placed the books on the nearest shelf. He knelt down and opened one of the boxes, bursting with books, he quickly read the titles, which seemed to be chemistry books. When he opened another box, the dust settling around his feet, he discovered that it was also nearly full. The third and final box had room for a few more books. This must be the box Severino had taken them from in the first place.

Nahuel stood up, took the books off the stand and tried to fit them inside the third box. But they didn't fit inside easily. There was an old photograph frame in the way. He took it out, in case the weight of the books might break it, and placed it gently on the ground. He put the books away and lifted up the photograph frame, to put it back in the box.

He could see that inside the frame was a photograph of four young men. One face grabbed his attention. It was Angelo Severino himself, but with a head full of dark hair and thirty years younger. By his side was a young Klaus, without wrinkles and a bright red beard.

Nahuel's mouth went dry.

Next to Klaus was a smiling man who looked very familiar to him. He gripped the frame and brought it close to his face, until it almost touched his nose. He blinked and looked again.

He recognized those gray eyes and intense gaze.

He tried to swallow, but had no saliva.

He was sure, without a doubt, that the man in the photograph was his grandfather. He was upset and confused. This sudden encounter with a young version of his grandfather made him shudder. He stared at the photograph, trying to make sense of their faces. The four men wore dress slacks and vests. They were outside. The hair of Severino and the fourth unknown man was blowing in the wind. Nahuel looked at the unknown man closely, he had a black scorpion on his shoulder, like some kind of pet.

He pondered the image of his grandfather. Mr. Blest had been a strong and sinewy man. The photograph displayed his grandfather in a past life, one unknown to Nahuel.

The image of his grandfather in the photograph disturbed him. What was he doing there? What was he doing with Severino and Klaus? Who was the fourth man? The four of them had known each other. That much was captured in the irrefutable image.

Nahuel was certain of three things.

His grandfather had been a privileged one, he had been the Director of the Council of Privileges, and he had left it all behind to take care of Nahuel when his father had disappeared. Nevertheless, none of this explained why they went into hiding in Ushuaia.

"The girls are wondering where you are," Severino spoke, looking at him. He looked just like his younger, messy-haired self, except for the deep lines of age on his face.

"You knew my grandfather," Nahuel blurted out, his tongue sticking in his mouth. He held up the photograph, pointing to the smiling man. He couldn't bring himself to say his grandfather's name out loud.

"A twist of fate."

"How did you know him?" Nahuel wanted to know. He had to ask, because despite the interrogation his eyes had given the photograph, he couldn't answer that question on his own.

Severino's eyes looked into the past, his gaze softening, as he saw images from memories that were almost forgotten.

"We worked together. But that was a long, long time ago."

CHAPTER 26

During the following days, Nahuel's obsession with locating *The Foundations of the Pact*, grew. His stubborn plan to ruin the Ignoble's plans was still forefront in his mind, but now it was emboldened by the melancholy look in those eyes. His happy memories of time shared with his grandfather hadn't faded, but rather, because of the photograph, they had been brought back to life.

His desire for revenge was like an invisible cloud that spread over his body, soaking him through. He was chained to *The Foundations of the Pact*. They were the only clue that he could follow in order to one day solve his grandfather's murder. If the Ignobles were looking for *The Foundations*, he had to get to them first.

"This library doesn't have anything we're looking for," Nahuel said, slamming shut a book.

It was late at night and Nahuel was still in his friend's room.

"Severino warned us that the books we had access to wouldn't say anything about *The Foundations of the Pact*," Aremi reminded him. Her eyes red with fatigue but she kept flipping through a thin volume that had lost its dust jacket.

"It's true. Every minute we spend on these books is a minute we lose," Nahuel grumbled angrily. "We have to look for information somewhere else."

"But where?" Isaline asked. She sat at her desk re-reading the day's paper closely.

"In the sub-4th floor there is a library," Aremi mentioned, rubbing her eyes.

"I've never seen it," Nahuel said, sitting up.

"Of course you have. We walked past it the first time we went down to the sub-4th floor with Mrs. Sparling," Aremi replied.

"Are you talking about Klaus's library?" Isaline asked, turning to look at

Aremi.

"Yes, that one," Aremi replied innocently.

Isaline opened her eyes wide, trying to signal to Aremi to keep quiet. She knew that if Nahuel found out about that library, he wouldn't stop until he got inside it and the thought of breaking into the sub-4th floor struck her as highly unlikely.

"I walk by it…" Aremi kept talking despite Isaline sitting behind Nahuel, shaking her head vehemently to get her friend to stop talking. "…What is it, Isaline?"

"Will there ever come a day you understand my signals?"

"What signals?" Nahuel asked, turning around to look at her.

"Nothing, it's nothing," she replied nonchalantly. "We cannot go inside that library. It would be too risky. Klaus's office is right next door."

"Of course we are going inside," Nahuel declared. Then after a few seconds of reflection he offered, "Well, I'll go." It was a risk he would take on his own. There was no reason to get them involved.

"I can go with you," Aremi offered.

"Stop!" Isaline blurted out. "We are forgetting about *Calendula*. We should look there."

"You're not banned from there," Nahuel reminded her, trying to cut her plan short.

"But you two are not. And if necessary, I will wear a costume. That man is so obtuse he won't even realize it's me."

"It's a good idea. *Calendula* probably has everything," Aremi said, trying to mediate between both plans.

Even though Nahuel was imagining a million arguments against going to *Calendula*, he knew none of them were that strong.

"Ok," he accepted reluctantly. "But we're going first thing tomorrow morning."

The Hedge Garden was in full bloom, but that day clouds hung low in the sky and were reflected in the pool. Nahuel had taken his summer khakis pants out of his closet once again. They headed straight to *Calendula, Ten-Thousand Year Book Store*.

"You look ridiculous," Nahuel said to Isaline, still harboring a grudge for her reluctance to try the library in the sub-4th floor first.

Isaline was wearing a white scarf with red flowers around her head like a 1950's movie star. She wore large, square sunglasses, which covered half her face.

"I stole them out of Emma's room," Isaline offered as a sort of explanation.

"Let's just go in and please try to behave," Nahuel begged her bluntly.

"I always behave," she replied in a hurt voice.

Nahuel pulled open the door. It smelled like burnt wax. There was no one inside, not even the shopkeeper. The group split up and started searching among the books. They moved fast, but with a focus.

Then, Aremi tripped on the foot of a cage and almost knocked it down as she grabbed onto it to steady herself. The books piled inside slipped to the floor.

"Be quiet," Isaline whispered. "We will be better off if that crazy old man does not come out."

Aremi was more careful after that. It was true, they would be more at ease without the shopkeeper nagging them or hurrying them along. It wasn't long though before he came out from the rear of the shop, with a grumpy face.

"What are you looking for?" he asked.

"Just some light reading, to pass the time," Isaline burst forth, cutting in front of Nahuel, afraid he might say something to give them away. They needed to keep the shopkeeper away from the historical books they were looking for.

"How can you even see with those grotesque, dark glasses on?" the man asked, slowly looking her up and down. He was staring at her right hand, and could see the blue circle that marked her as a CymMens.

"Actually, we are just here keeping her company," Isaline said, avoiding his question. "Aremi, come here please. This man wants to help you choose a book."

"I think the question should be how can I see in the middle of this mess?" Isaline whispered to Aremi as she passed by her side.

Aremi made her way over to the man, who was only an inch taller than she was, a smile on her face. Isaline had repeated several times that her role was to distract the man long enough for Isaline and Nahuel to find information on *The Foundations of the Pact*. They got the feeling, according to what Severino told them, that they wouldn't be allowed to openly ask about the topic anywhere, which is why even in *Calendula* they had to hide their true intentions.

Isaline had also told Aremi several times that the word "Riddle" was the codeword to use in case the man was very close to them and they needed to move. And "Puzzle" was the code word that meant it was time to leave the shop.

"Hello, Sir. What happened to your flowers?" Aremi greeted him, noticing the wilted calendula flowers on the counter. "With your permission, I could revive them. I promise to leave them glowing and fragrant."

Nahuel and Isaline continued to search methodically through every book. Nahuel had no intention of leaving the place empty handed. He settled into the History section of the book shop. Meanwhile, Isaline explored the books that weren't on the shelves. The disorder of the shop made their search difficult. Books were never put back where they belonged, but just left in the nearest spot at the time, whether this was on the ground, a chair, or the cage.

Isaline dragged herself along the floor like a worm, searching under shelves for books. When she stood up, her scarf had fallen off and the glasses were at the end of her nose.

"Tch, tch, tch," Isaline clicked her tongue at Nahuel to get his attention.

"What did you find?"

"Lost Memories from the War," she read after shaking a thick layer of dust off the book. "It looks like a forgotten book."

"Let's check it quickly to see if it says anything."

Isaline ran her finger down the table of contents. A chapter entitled, "The Bravest Custodians" caught her eye.

She quickly turned to page 54 and began scanning the chapter meticulously.

"Puzzle."

"Puzzle," Aremi's worried voice interrupted them.

"What are you two doing back there?" the shopkeeper asked in disgust. "That section is not for young students."

"Nothing," Nahuel and Isaline replied in unison. She had fixed her scarf and glasses instantly, using her privilege.

"Well, if you're not going to buy anything, be on your way," he muttered, pointing to the door.

"Have a nice afternoon, Sir," Aremi said as they left, still smiling, "See you later."

Nahuel, Isaline and Aremi hurried out of the shop. Once outside, they took in deep breaths of fresh air from The Hedge Garden.

"I can't believe it," Nahuel complained, frustrated. "We were getting close to finding something."

Isaline beamed at him.

"I wouldn't be so sad if I were you," she said mysteriously.

"Tell us," Aremi asked, happy her acting hadn't been in vain. "What did you find?"

"I have this," she replied, showing them a page with a drawing on it. "I had no choice but to tear out the page."

"What does it say?" Nahuel asked.

"Actually, it doesn't say much," she replied.

It was an oil painting of a young man wearing the formal uniform of a King's Lieutenant. The man was sitting behind a desk, with a large roll of papyrus before him, lending an air of distinction to his high shiny forehead and bland smile. The painting was dark and clearly worn in places, but the deep red of his coat was visually interesting. Under the portrait they could read, "Portrait of Robert Wissing, Milan 1489."

"That doesn't help us," Nahuel stated, disappointed.

"Of course it does. If you look closely, you can see that on the scroll it says

Pactum," Isaline argued impatiently, and gave him the page. "This proves that what Severino has told us is true."

"What good is that? We still don't know what they are!" Nahuel said raising his voice, overcome by sudden anger.

Isaline and Aremi exchanged worried looks. Nahuel's reactions were getting extreme and he often took it out on them. He seemed to be aware of it this time and slowly, his breathing returned to normal and he calmed down.

He stood there, silently. He knew at that moment he didn't have many options. He had to decide what to do next. He wouldn't give up, he just couldn't.

He folded up the picture of the stupid custodian that looked up at him, full of calm and prestige and put it in the back pocket of his khaki pants.

The girls noticed a strange gleam in Nahuel's eyes.

"I'm going down tonight," he stated.

"But..." Isaline started to argue

"But nothing. You don't have to come. But I'm going. It's the only choice I have. I have to find out why they killed my grandfather," Nahuel declared. "I even have a key that will let me inside."

Like it was a sign from destiny, he took Sebastian's ivory colored card from his pocket.

"That isn't yours," Isaline confirmed. She knew well enough what it was. "Where did you get that?" she asked.

"Tristan found it when Sebastian dropped it on orientation day, and, when they did the search during the first days on the sub-4th floor, that coward put it to me."

"And why haven't you returned it?" Isaline asked.

"Now, I'm not sorry I didn't return it," he said defiantly.

"How about we decide what we are going to do instead of arguing?" Aremi interrupted them.

"It's decided. I will go down while everyone is asleep," Nahuel stated. "I don't want to wait anymore. You don't need to come." Nahuel had a passkey of the sub-4th floor and, with it, he had an actual possibility to go down in search for answers, and all that...thanks to Tristan?

Aremi went forward and stood next to Nahuel, taking sides.

Isaline stared at them, considering all the possible angles.

"You know we will come with you," she said to Nahuel.

She couldn't let her friend put himself in such a dangerous situation alone. Nahuel wasn't thinking straight, he was blinded by his own strong emotions. Isaline was afraid he would do something risky and that it would cost him his scholarship at the United Nations. Also, she couldn't let an adventure like this pass her by. She wouldn't let it become a story Nahuel and Aremi told her about later.

"Now we just have to draw a map of the sub-4th floor, those hallways are a tangled web," Nahuel went on, hiding how relieved he was, as if Isaline's decision hadn't impressed him.

If he tried hard enough, he would be able to remember how to get to the library. It wouldn't be easy though, he had only gone that way once, many months ago. If he was lucky, his sense of smell and the odors there would make it easier.

"I always visit Katya during the break between Botanicals and International Security," Aremi commented. "She works in the same hallway the library is in," she told them. "It's easy to get there, you just have to know where to turn."

Isaline rolled her eyes.

"And *you* know where to turn" she pointed out.

CHAPTER 27

The clocks struck midnight. Nahuel poked his head out his bedroom window. The moon was shining brightly. Emre was in the other bed, muttering incomprehensible words in his sleep. Nahuel dressed quickly, put Sebastian's card in his pocket and snuck quietly down to the basement, where he would meet the girls.

"Are you ready?" he asked them.

He scrutinized their faces, looking for any signs of hesitation or regret, but the only thing he could see was drowsiness in their eyes.

"Of course, we are," Aremi replied enthusiastically. "I'm glad Mrs. Penington trusts us so much. This door wasn't even locked."

At that moment Nahuel realized that it was truly good luck that the door was open. He had the passkey to enter the entire sub-4th floor, but he had never paused to consider that it was up to Mrs. Penington whether or not they could even get out of the residency.

"I've got everything we'll need right here," Isaline added, her leather bag loaded to the brim. "Are you sure no one saw you?"

"I'm sure. Emre sleeps like a log. Here's the card," Nahuel answered her.

"Ok, then let's move," Isaline said, opening the door that led down to the tunnels.

The trip by glass cart seemed longer and more silent than any time before in the many months they had been riding in them. Nahuel knew there was no turning back and that certainty pleased him.

They rushed up the steep staircase that led to the entrance of the sub-4th floor floor of the United Nations. It was the first time they saw the door shut. Nahuel took out Sebastian's card, which turned red as soon as it touched his skin. No one was surprised when they touched the door with the card and it slid open effortlessly.

The ivory pass card didn't work like normal modern technology, it couldn't be deactivated and it couldn't be used by non-privileged people.

The room with the floating chairs was immersed in shadows, barely lit by the dull glow of a few fireflies. Nahuel had brought some of the fireflies from the tunnels with them, and they followed above the group, like a glowing ball of light.

"Good idea, Nahuel. If we turn on the lights down here we might draw attention to ourselves," Isaline said. "In fact, we should put on our gloves and not leave any fingerprints."

This seemed a bit over the top to Nahuel, but he didn't want to argue with her, so he took his gloves from his pocket and put them on. In the end, he was grateful they had decided to come with him. In an instant, the gloves molded to his hands and it felt like he wasn't wearing them at all.

"Can you lead the way, Aremi?" Nahuel asked her.

"This way," she pointed.

They turned away from the hall that led to their classrooms. They made their way down a narrow corridor. The fireflies bumped against the diamond encrusted ceiling and it was like they were looking into a tiny bit of space itself.

The corridor led to a small room with three identical openings.

With small and quick steps, Aremi went through the middle one. They walked by the *Committee for Uncovering Mysteries*, but didn't stop.

"If we don't find anything in the library, let's come back here," Nahuel told them.

Isaline bit her lip but said nothing. She was hoping the library would answer all their questions.

They passed underneath two marble archways and passed the cherub statue. Nahuel looked behind him and saw that the darkness was impenetrable. They walked past the laboratory and research area until they came to the round room with the mosaic floors.

"This is the perfect place for the *Il Finale* ball, don't you think?" Aremi commented, and began dancing gracefully under the large chandeliers of sparkling silk. She offered them a quick show of her "surprise turn".

Nahuel couldn't help but smile. He also thought the room looked like a ballroom from the middle ages, but he also knew the only person bold enough to dance in there was Aremi.

A few moments later, they came to the end of the labyrinth-like walk. Nahuel used his card again and the lock separating them from the main hallway creaked open with a tomb-like echo.

Nahuel stepped forward boldly.

"Wait," Isaline stopped him. "We have no idea if there is an alarm system in this section."

"And we have no way of knowing now," Nahuel shot back.

He walked forward, pushed on by his stubborn audacity.

No lights went off, no alarms sounded, no sign of danger could be heard. Isaline and Aremi stepped in behind him. Isaline turned on the lights and the thin shiny covering that spread along the hallway walls dazzled them.

Aremi led them to the end of the hallway, where they would find the library. The shadows of Nahuel and Isaline bounced off the ceiling behind her.

"Now that Katya isn't here, the climbing plant is sleeping," Aremi whispered as they walked past it. "It's too bad. I love it when it blooms yellow."

The conference room which was home to the library was shut with something more than a single lock.

Nahuel tried to open the door using the pass card but there was no where to place it. The glass room seemed to be hermetically sealed. The door didn't even have a doorknob. Beyond the glass wall, they could see the outline of a large black table. The walls were covered with wooden shelves where the books rested, safe and sound.

"How do you open the door?" Isaline asked.

"I don't know. I've never seen anyone go inside," Aremi replied, feeling insecure for the first time.

"There must be a way," Nahuel said.

He started poking at the door, trying to push it open, but it didn't budge. Aremi went over to the reception desk, where Katya worked to see if she could find anything useful. Meanwhile, Isaline searched through her bag for something that might be useful.

"Nothing over here," Aremi said loudly. "Just some lemon cookies. Does anyone want one?"

"Put those down! They will discover us!" Isaline shouted in a whisper.

"I'm wearing gloves... no fingerprints!" Aremi laughed, holding up her hands.

"Here's something," Nahuel said suddenly.

At eye level, something was etched into the glass, in tiny letters.

"It says something."

"What does it say?" Isaline asked, picking her things up off the floor and putting them back in her bag.

"I don't know, I can't make it out."

Nahuel ran his fingers over the letters, but nothing happened. Instinctively, he took off his glove, to feel the glass and texture of the letters under his own skin. They were rough and bumpy. As he slid his index finger over them, the words got big enough to read. He read outloud,

"Di les crietsreu qui hi canacida sala tris mi hen impecteda".

Suddenly, Nahuel felt the overwhelming urge to cry.

"What did you say, Nahuel?" Aremi asked, swallowing her lemon cookie.

"Of all the creatures I have known, only three have made an impression on me," he

replied.

It wasn't the first time he had heard that language. He knew exactly what the words said. He also knew what they meant. He had known since he was a small child.

"You have to complete it," he murmured, his voice shaky and breaking, "It's a singing poem."

"What?" Isaline asked. She had stood up and come over to read the lines carved in the glass.

Like the man was standing by his side, Nahuel heard the gruff voice say, *Remember Nahuel, strength lies in these three virtues.*

Then he recited, out loud:

"Di les crietsreu qui hi canacida sala tris mi hen impecteda.
Le primire par us campesian.
Le sigsnde par us velintie.
Le tircire par us uinsetiz."

Automatically, the door to the library swung open, inviting them inside.

"Your grandfather taught it to you, right?" Isaline asked.

"Yes. He used to repeat it when times were tough," Nahuel replied.

"What does it mean?" she asked.

"Of all the creatures I have known, only three have made an impression on me
The first for its compassion.
The second for its bravery.
The third for its sharp mind."

Here was another mystery his grandfather had left behind, without explaining it to him. He used to recite it to Nahuel when he was sick and now it was the key that opened the door for Nahuel who, years later was trying to solve the man's murder. Could this have been his plan all along?

The library was the sanctuary of the directors.

Nahuel stepped inside, his legs shaking. He couldn't tell if it was in anticipation of what he would find or fear he would find nothing at all.

The room looked just as it did from the other side of the glass, but now Nahuel could smell the fragrance of old wood, leather bound books and paper. The room was paneled with wood, soundproof and had no windows. Every single inch of the walls was covered with books. There was only one disarranged chair, and on the table, a notepad, a ruler, some pencils and a cup of cherry tea, now cold. On the floor were balled up pieces of paper that hadn't made it into the trash basket.

"Looks like Klaus was up late reading," Aremi commented, walking around the table.

Nahuel, Isaline, and Aremi split the library into three sections and each one started looking in their part.

Nahuel took the largest section, the back wall and began reading the titles of the books one by one, hoping something would grab his attention. He had to calm down. He had known that his grandfather was part of the privileged society, but the shock of the words to access the library kept running through his head.

Most of the books were leather bound and cracked with age. The titles were etched in gold and decorated with fancy details against either dark brown, black, blue or red leather.

Aremi stood on the chair to be able to read more easily the titles of the books on the highest shelf. Isaline had already placed all three volumes of *Biography of a Modern Knight* on the table and continued scrutinizing the rest of the books in her section. She brought the books close to her face, using her mind and read their titles. If she felt they weren't what they were looking for, she put them back in place. This method meant she was three shelves ahead of her friends in the search.

"This place is a gold mine!" she said excitedly. "If I was the director, I would sleep in here! Wow... *Tibetan Techniques for Advanced Transfiguration*," she read. She had already taken it off the shelf and held it in her hands, ready to browse through it.

"Keep your eyes on the prize," Nahuel reminded her. "*The Foundations of the Pact*," he added, wishing he didn't have to remind her what they were looking for.

He felt a little dizzy, the letters mingling on the pages. But the clue they were looking for had to be there, among these controversial and incomparable books. He had to stay sharp. If any book held the answers they sought, it was most probably in that room. But all the books looked alike; old and complicated.

After an hour of silent and uncomfortable searching, a book finally caught his eye. It didn't have a title, and seemed as old as time.

He took it and sat on the ground with his legs folded. It was a hardcover, leather bound book, with no writing on the outside. When he opened it, he could see it wasn't exactly a book, but rather a type of notebook with thick paper bound together with a braided string. Inside, it held almost translucent pieces of parchment held in place with corner frames and protected with silken paper.

Nahuel began turning the pages of the album, looking at the head of each page, until he stopped. The header of the second to last parchment read:

Manuscript by Robert Wissing, written days before his death, August 14499.

"I found something," Nahuel announced.

Isaline and Aremi came over and sat on the ground by his side.

Nahuel looked at the words written in the custodian's handwriting, more than five hundred years before. His handwriting was angled, perfect, the script showed confidence and instinct.

But he couldn't understand what it said. It was written in that language that he only knew bits and pieces of.

Nahuel glanced at the page and turned it quickly. There was nothing on the next page. He felt his soul plummet to his feet. It was possible the answers were in his hands, but he was still miles away from them.

"We are right where we hoped to be," Aremi said positively. "Now we just have to translate it."

"That's right and I'm sure I saw a dictionary on the second corner shelf," Isaline said, standing up.

"How strange no one has translated it yet," Aremi pondered.

"Not that strange," Nahuel said quietly. "All the directors must know this language."

Once Isaline found the bilingual Priveco dictionary, the translation was slow and tedious and took them a long while.

Nahuel was annoyingly impatient, he paced around the table like a caged animal. At one point he even had the wonderful idea of ripping pages from Klaus's notepad that was lying on the table and throwing balls of paper at the girls. He carried on like this until Isaline started yelling at him angrily, reminding him they couldn't replace the pages in the notepad and their presence in the library would not go unnoticed.

Aremi decided to use a technique she often used with her baby brother. She found Nahuel a book full of images of extinct feline species and this kept him quiet for a while. Meanwhile, she oversaw the translation job quietly.

"Finally," Isaline sighed, placing the last period on the paper.

"Give it to me," Nahuel begged, stretching out his hand.

Isaline handed it to him with clenched teeth. In the end, she had done all the work and thought she deserved to be the one to read it out loud for the first time.

"Do the honors, Nahuel," Aremi piped up.

He read out loud, for his friends:

About The Foundations of the Pact, I can only warn you.
I won't die without shedding light on the dangers they contain.
They hold the formula for reversing what was decided the day our fate was
sealed, the day the privileges were taken away from the rest of the world.
This formula will allow, whoever possesses it, to awaken the privileges of the
chosen, betraying the will of its creators.
It is my understanding that every mortal being possesses a dormant privilege.

"That's all it says," Nahuel blurted out. The message from the manuscript was too brief. He stood up and went to growl at the other end of the table.

Isaline and Aremi sat for a moment, quietly, taking in the seriousness of the situation. What they had just read was beyond anything they could have guessed or imagined.

"Does this mean what I think it means?" Aremi asked.

"Yes." Isaline replied without taking her eyes off the page.

"But how is it possible?" Aremi asked again.

"It's not possible," Isaline replied even though she was staring at the proof that it was possible.

She reread Wissing's words once more, wanting to be sure she understood them.

"This means that everyone in the world actually has a privilege," Isaline said, struggling to be as clear as possible. She was a little letdown. She had liked the idea of being special.

"But they are dormant in most people," Aremi added.

"Yes," Isaline accepted. "Humans didn't lose their privileges naturally, but the founders of the *Pact* took them away from them when the war ended. To avoid more tragedy," she said making an excuse for their actions. "The war among the three castes almost led to the extinction of humans."

"We already knew that!" Nahuel shouted, throwing up his arms on the other side of the room.

"I know, I also remember what Klaus said at *Il Finale*. But look at what Wissing says. This part is new: the founders left a way to return the privileges to humans," Isaline explained, "*The Foundations of the Pact* can awaken the dormant privileges, when it doesn't manifest on its own, of course."

"Like it did in us," Aremi completed Isaline's thought.

"This still doesn't explain why they killed my grandfather! Why *him*?" Nahuel said, and *why are they looking for me?* he thought to himself.

"Maybe he knew where *The Foundations* are hidden," Aremi suggested, wanting to answer his question.

"No," Isaline shook her head. "From what it looks like, Wissing took the location of the hiding place to his grave. What's more, if your grandfather knew it and didn't tell them, which I don't believe he would do, they wouldn't have killed him. They would have tortured him, or tortured you, Nahuel, to force him to reveal the location," Isaline speculated. "There has to be another reason."

But what other reason could there be?

Nahuel could tell he was on the edge of a major disappointment.

He hated to realize that he had placed all his hopes on *The Foundations of the Pact*. He had thought that if he could find out what they contained, he would be able to solve the mystery of his grandfather's death. He couldn't have been more wrong. It wasn't enough. Knowing there was a formula to awaken the privileges didn't clear up anything. On the contrary, it added another level of questions. He had to find *The Foundations* and read them for himself to get the answers he sought. He couldn't imagine any other way.

One thing he was certain about was that the Ignobles must not have the satisfaction of finding them first. His grandfather, he was sure of it, had tried to stop them, and he was convinced he must do the same.

"We have to find them," Nahuel said sternly. He was starting to understand how someone could die protecting them. "The Ignobles must not get a hold of them."

"Of course not," Isaline agreed emphatically. "They are more dangerous than we thought."

"The Ignobles could form an army of privileges, giving privileges to whoever they wanted," Nahuel stated.

"And the privileges are a powerful weapon. Imagine if tsunamis and earthquakes happened every day…" Isaline said.

"Not to mention plagues," Aremi added, shuddering.

Nahuel thought about it for a moment. A dark world, where the forces of nature are used against man and against nature itself. Famine and suffering. Animals eating one another. He didn't want to think about it for long.

"There's something else that worries me," Aremi said suddenly. "If *The Foundations* explain how to give back the privileges, wouldn't they also explain how to take them away?" she wondered.

"If that is the case, the problem is even more serious," Isaline admitted. "The Ignobles would be able to take the privileges away from the Council members if they wanted to. If they got a hold of this formula, they would be able to dominate us all, according to their own interests. And then everything would be lost."

The three friends sat in meditative silence, analyzing the complexity of a world that could abruptly and drastically change. They had a lot to think about, possibilities they had never before considered.

"I have to find them," Nahuel declared again. He needed to know what they said.

"We know," Aremi said painfully.

"They are buried out there, somewhere," Nahuel went on.

"Wissing must have left some clues," Aremi said, convinced of it.

"Let me look through the books I separated. They might help us," Isaline added.

She got off the ground and sat in the heavy wooden chair at the table. She pushed aside the cup, pencils and ruler, but only after she had carefully checked where they were in order to put them back in exactly the same spot when she was done. She took the smallest of the books, the one she had floated down from the highest shelf and began scanning it.

"This is useless," she sighed in resignation after a while. She had examined every book she had placed on the table and found nothing they didn't already know.

In less than two minutes, the room was returned to how it had been before they entered, except for the notepad. Each book was back in place and the cup, pencils and ruler and chair in exactly the same messy place as before. Isaline ordered Nahuel to pick up all the balls of paper he had made and take them with him.

They left the library reluctantly, each with a different reason for wanting to stay a bit longer in that precious space.

At the last minute, Isaline had to force Aremi off one of the chairs, where she was standing trying to take out the book *Aquatic Plants for Mermaid Nutrition*, trying to convince the others that no one would notice it was gone.

Even though all their questions hadn't been answered on this mission, at least they knew what *The Foundations of the Pact* entailed.

"Now, what do we do about it?" Isaline asked once they were back in the glass cart.

"Stop them from finding them," Nahuel responded.

"Stop the unstoppable."

CHAPTER 28

The whale's song spread through the water. It was a high frequency sound which carried an important message. The whale had been entrusted with the signal just minutes before, but it had already traveled thousands of miles across the dark oceanic waters.

A sperm whale picked up the message and its sophisticated ears helped it identify immediately the origin of the sound. It came from the Mediterranean coasts of Europe. Now it was his turn to pass it on; the sperm whale emitted whistles and soundless vibrations which went bouncing along the Atlantic Ocean until they reached the next receiver.

It was a communication chain which had been in place for many many years. To avoid attention and leave no trace, it was necessary to avoid technology. The oceans and the echolocation of the whales made this type of communication possible. Sound disperses in the air, but in the water it is concentrated and transmitted more effectively. This was a safe and fast way to share information.

The sound navigated the deep ocean waters until it arrived to the ears of a blue whale. The majestic mammal amplified the vibrations effortlessly, sending the message along. She knew it wouldn't take long to arrive at its destination. After pausing to send the message, the whale resumed her trip south. She had been traveling for months. Mating season would begin soon.

Before long, the message arrived intact to the shores of North America.

A hummingbird shot from its nest, flew under a small waterfall and zoomed toward the horizon. It was green and blue and its beak as sharp as a needle.

It buzzed over fields, where the shrubs spread for miles and miles. The air that morning was warm and stirring, but it wouldn't affect the bird's marathon race. It flew past a hanging bridge, zigzagging through the steel cables toward the center of Manhattan. It merged with the New York traffic, dodging vehicles. It moved so fast that everything seemed to move in slow motion next to it. It flew high and could see its reflection in the glasses of the tallest buildings.

Its heart beat as fast as its wings, which looked transparent to the untrained eye. Before taking flight, it had bathed in a stimulation serum, giving it a supernatural speed.

From the heights, it located the East River and began its descent. It skimmed the surface of the water. It had its eyes on its prize. Even though it was getting closer and closer, it was worried it would run out of energy before reaching its goal.

The hummingbird shook its tail and emitted a high-pitched sound, like something from a melody of classical music. Other hummingbirds appeared and flew alongside it. They flew like a blue and green cloud toward the United Nations headquarters. The flock sped into a secret passage inside a tree that led straight to the tunnels.

They were very close.

The hummingbirds were faster than the glass carts and dominated the air like no other bird. In seconds they were inside the sub-4th floor of the Council of Privileges.

That morning, the sub-4th floor was as it normally was. It was the clear, bright, bustling version the students were used to. The hummingbirds spread out once they reached the room with the hanging chairs. They flew toward each Committee, laboratory and room within the Council.

The CymAnis would receive the entire message. The other privileges would understand they were in the face of an emergency upon seeing the hummingbirds.

The first hummingbird stopped mid-flight, changed direction and flew back where it had come from. It knocked on a door with its beak. All the other birds had flown past the closed door.

Nahuel heard the tapping at the door and the sound of wings beating on the other side. Rebecca stood up and opened the door. The hummingbird sped in and flew straight toward their professor.

Ankona held still as the hummingbird hung in the air at eye level. Its extraordinary beauty hypnotized the students. Nahuel could see the hummingbirds' chest shaking frenetically with strain. Their professor listened attentively, acknowledging everything with a slight nod of his head.

And then the hummingbird simply fell from the air to the ground. Its wings stopped and its heart gave out.

One of the students cried out in surprise.

The marathon had cost the bird its life, but it had completed its mission.

Nahuel looked at the stiff hummingbird on the ground and had to fight against the sense of fatality that flooded him. Something really terrible had happened. He knew it in his guts.

"Stay here everyone," Ankona told them and he left the room.

Rebecca went to the hummingbird and lifted it in her hand. It was smaller than her palm. She placed it gently on Ankona's desk and started stroking it gently but methodically. The circles appeared on her hand as she passed it energy. The other girls came over to watch her closely, but there was nothing Rebecca could do for the hummingbird.

Nahuel walked straight to the door. He wanted to know what was going on. When he stuck his head out, he could see all the members of the Council leaving their offices and moving in the hallway. Some agents headed straight for the tunnels, while others took the hall toward the Control Room of the sub-4th floor.

Ankona didn't return to the classroom. This was the first lecture they had with Ankona in months, and it didn't last long. But this time, no substitute appeared to replace him. The students had no idea what to do and simply waited in the classroom until the time the class would have finished.

Nahuel met up with Isaline and Aremi in the hanging chairs. Benjamin was waiting for them, so they had no time to share thoughts on the hummingbirds.

"Ladies and Gentlemen, Mrs. Sparling's class has been cancelled, so you may return to the residency," Benjamin announced once all the students were gathered together.

"What's the meaning of those hummingbirds?" Nahuel wanted to know. They were just about to start to use the arrowhead talesma to communicate with birds, so he hadn't been able to understand the message the hummingbird had given Ankona.

"They are an alarm system the Council uses," Benjamin explained.

"And why has an alarm gone off?" Nahuel asked.

"There's been an emergency, but nothing you have to worry about," Benjamin replied. "It didn't happen in New York, so you can return to the residency without hassle."

"So where has the emergency happened?" Isaline asked.

"I don't know yet. As soon as you leave the sub-4th floor, I can go find out. So, let's go, let's go," Benjamin said, herding them along with his arms.

The students slung their backpacks over their shoulders and walked toward the exit to take the glass carts that would take them back to the surface world.

Neither Nahuel or Isaline or Aremi moved an inch.

"Reluctant to leave?" Benjamin asked, standing in front of them.

"Yeah, no… In a minute…" Nahuel stalled.

"I'm in a bit of a hurry, you know," Benjamin said impatiently.

"Umh, it's just that I forgot my talesma case in Ankona's room," Nahuel replied flatly.

"I see. I'll go with you," Benjamin stated.

"No, you don't need to," Nahuel replied, standing up and signaling for his friends to come with him.

"I have orders not to leave you alone. Someone used the tunnels last night after hours and they're holding me responsible for it. Unbelievable..." Benjamin said, rolling his eyes.

"Someone must have felt like a midnight joyride," Aremi said smiling.

"Well, I certainly hope they invite me next time," Benjamin retorted.

The three students followed Benjamin toward Ankona's classroom. They walked slowly, trying to stall for time, to think of another, more convincing excuse.

Nahuel entered the room of *Animal Behaviour and Communication*. He pretended to look for the case on his desk, under his desk, but of course he hadn't left it there. He looked on the ground and near the birdcage, kept looking around his classmate's desks, until it was more than clear the case was not there.

"Oh, what a fool I am. I just remembered I lent it to Damian."

Acting was not one of Nahuel's talents.

"Let's go then. I'll take you to the tunnels," Benjamin said, sighing.

They made their way to the exit, with no other options at the moment.

"Victoria told me to keep a close eye on you three," Benjamin said as they walked. "We have been talking about you, you know? I've been told that you like to wander around the residency ... *at night.*"

Isaline came unglued, if they associated when they went out during the night around the residency with the time they went out the night before through the tunnels, they would be in trouble. She tried to sound calm, but her voice came out thin and strained.

"You're very good at gossiping."

Benjamin looked at her with peevish enjoyment.

"Beautiful and angry. What an explosive combination," he said smoothly, not batting an eyelash.

They had arrived at the top of the stairs that led down to the tunnels. The three friends walked down as Benjamin supervised them from above.

"We can't leave," Nahuel said as soon as they were out of Benjamin's earshot. "Whatever has happened, it must have something to do with the Ignobles."

"I've got an idea," Aremi said suddenly. "This is what we should do...."

It ended up being a very good plan. The three got into a cart and Aremi turned around to wave goodbye to Benjamin. They put the cart in motion and at the same time a firefly flew down Benjamin's shirt, especially sent by Nahuel to distract him. When he looked down and shook his clothes to get it out, the three friends jumped out of the cart and hid behind a rock. Isaline did her part too, pushing their cart with her privilege at full speed down the tracks, out of sight.

They hid until Benjamin walked away. When they lost track of his golden locks down the hallway, they felt it was safe to come out.

"I don't think he trusts us much," Aremi noted.

"Who cares," Isaline said shortly. "Now we have to find out why the alarm went off."

"It can only mean one thing," Nahuel said seriously. He had been forming his own hypothesis since the hummingbird had appeared.

"What is that?" Isaline asked.

"They know. The Ignobles know where *The Foundations of the Pact* are."

Nahuel, Isaline and Aremi took the same path they had the night before. They moved toward the main hallway of the sub-4th floor, where the Director's office and library were located. They hoped that Klaus would have gone with Sparling and Ankona and that he might have left behind some useful information. The walk took them longer than it had the night before, they had to check at every turn to be sure no one could see them and turn them in later.

They kept away from the Control Room, suspecting that the agents still on the sub-4th floor floor must be gathered there. After passing the Serum Laboratory, they crossed paths with a man wearing a purple-ribbed vest who confirmed this for them.

"The hanger has been cleared. I'm on my way to the Control Room," he said into a radio. The Council members tended to use these radios to communicate with each other inside the sub-4th floor. "Yes, you've heard correctly. That is the enemy's main objective... I'm going to need diagrams of all the entrances, on the surface and in the tunnels. Isolation and containment procedures are already being carried out," he added, picking up his pace and shooting them an uninterested glance as he walked by.

It was crystal clear that the answers to all their questions were in the Control Room, but they couldn't go there. They would not be welcome.

"If the Council members have left some trace of where the emergency happened, it won't just be lying around," Nahuel ventured.

"They must be careful," Isaline added.

"Right, but I don't think they suspect that some students have Sebastian's missing key, or that they know the secret passwords of the directors," Aremi replied mischievously.

That buoyed their spirits.

They paused near the Sound Frequency Lab.

"Where do we look?" Isaline asked.

"What are we looking for?" Aremi asked back.

"Something that will tell us what the emergency was and where it happened," Nahuel replied. Then he added. "The most likely place to find something will be Klaus's office."

"We can't go in there," Isaline interrupted him. "We already took a huge risk last night, breaking into his private library. We should be grateful that after today's emergency, what we did last night doesn't matter to anyone."

"Do you have a better idea?" he grumbled.

"*Any* idea is better."

His conscience wasn't bothering him enough to stop him from breaking into the Director's office. He needed to know if his frightening hunch about the Ignobles was right, more than he needed to be morally spotless.

Nahuel explained his plan quickly. It was simple and safe. Isaline and he would hide behind the cherub statue which flanked the entrance to the main hallway. Aremi, meanwhile, would go toward the main hallway and tell Katya that she was wanted in the Control Room - that a man named Julian was waiting for her and that she had to be sure to take her phone book. Then Aremi would follow her down the hallway, hurrying her along and halfway back she would spill her bag on the floor, and then proceed to pick it up *very* slowly, making the secretary nervous, who would eventually leave Aremi there, on her own, and continue to the Control Room.

The plan was a complete success.

Nahuel, Isaline and Aremi stood in front of Klaus's office.

Nahuel used the password he had inherited from his grandfather for the second time in less than twenty-four hours and the door of the Director's office opened.

He paused at the door and then entered with small cautious steps, like those of a stealthy feline on the hunt. Aremi followed close behind. Isaline, on the other hand, hung around the door frame, unwilling to cross the threshold.

The office had an eccentric air, just like its owner. It was filled with unique and one of a kind objects, among them the first ever created sculpture of Osiris, the Egyptian god.

"Look at this treasure!" Aremi exclaimed.

She couldn't contain herself and held a crystal ball, filled with water, in her hands. Inside the ball a translucent seahorse slept peacefully. She had never seen anything like it in her life.

Filled to the brim with objects, Klaus's office was like a miniature museum. There was an astrolabe and other navigational tools. Nahuel felt like he was traveling within Klaus's intimacy, like an invader in a foreign land.

"I hope we don't have to search too much," he said.

"Where should we start?" Aremi asked.

"You try the files and I will look on these shelves," Nahuel replied, moving toward an object that had caught his eye. When he was next to it, he could see it was a Chinese compass. A floating spoon served as its needle.

"Isaline?"

From outside, she fidgeted. She looked left and right, making sure there was no one else around.

"Oh, fine," she gave in.

She went straight to the seahorse, to confirm whether or not it was alive. Then, she began examining the large oak desk, with curving legs. She avoided the chair she assumed Klaus sat in and took the one across from it.

On the desk, were leaves of transparent paper. When she looked closely, she could see that most were maps hand drawn by Klaus. None stood out from the rest because they all showed different parts of the world, though mostly in Europe. She recognized several cities where they knew the Ignobles had attacked, but no map showed with certainty which place was the site of the Council's concerns this time.

"The files are all locked up," Aremi told them, standing next to a tiny Ficus in a pot. "Have you ever wondered what are the algaes Klaus eat for?"

Nahuel had to admit he had wondered that himself, but this wasn't the time to think about it. He hadn't found anything useful on the shelves either.

"I think I found something," Aremi said, staring closely at the Ficus.

A glimmer of hope shone in Nahuel's eyes. In the blink of an eye he was standing next to Aremi, staring at the plant, without knowing what he was looking for.

"What did you find?" he asked.

"There's dirt on the floor," she replied, crouching down to take a closer look at the pot. "And it's been moved around recently."

"Maybe Katya just watered it. Let's keep looking on the shelves," Nahuel disregarded Aremi's observation and walked away.

But Aremi wasn't ready to give up on her idea.

"The Ficus has been manipulated by a privilege," she added.

"That's no surprise, Klaus is CymTers," Isaline replied.

"Hand me my bag," Aremi asked her.

As soon as she had it in her hands, she took out her talesma case. She took a tiny grain of sand from the Gobi Desert and placed it in her a-bula.

"What are you doing?" Isaline asked her, raising one eyebrow. "This is the Director's office."

Aremi had started moving dirt around in the pot and Isaline knew she would make a mess.

"There is something under here."

Nahuel went back toward Aremi.

The Ficus trunk grew and the roots started to poke out of the soil.

Nahuel's breath quickened.

There was something in there.

Soon, they could see the roots clearly. They formed a small box. It was the Director's safe. It had been hidden in the dirt, at the bottom of the pot.

Nahuel glued his eyes on the Ficus, in between the roots that formed the box, they could see some papers.

"You are a genius," Nahuel told Aremi.

"Let's see if this is what we are looking for," Isaline said.

Aremi placed her hands on the box shape and concentrated. Nahuel held his breath, but the roots barely moved. Nahuel tried to get his fingers inside to grab the papers, but it was no use. Then he grabbed the roots and started to pull, as if he would tear them apart, but Isaline stopped him, shouting that he was out of his mind, and pushing him aside.

Then, using her privilege, she rolled the papers up into a tight tube, small enough to fit through the space between the roots.

Nahuel pulled the rolled up bit of paper out of the box.

"Read it, quickly!" Isaline pressured him.

Please tell me something, he thought.

United Nations	P/op/1218

Council of Privileges NY.

June 1, 15008

Underground Roots (Op.RS.)

Operation XXVII. June 1st, 15008

Authorized by the Council of Privileges with the participation of the head of the Directorate.

It is Observed that the actions of the group known as the Ignobles presents a threat to the foremost interests of the Privileged Society, and let them be acknowledged, the multiple attacks carried out this morning, the first of June.

It is Decided to set into motion the operation Underground Roots, (Op.RS), head committee in Salisbury (England) and supporting committees in Milan (Italy), Annecy (France), Aveiro (Portugal) and Geneva (Switzerland).

It is Requested in Resolution 2558; an indefinite period of action until goals are met.

It is Determined to obstruct any further action on part of the Ignobles and endeavor to obtain that known as *The Foundations of the Pact.*

After seeing Klaus's signature at the bottom of the page, Nahuel quickly flipped it over.

Head Committee

Details:

Members: General Director; NAGAS agents; agent collaborators (Ankona, Kudzai; Kendrick, Sebastian; Sparling, Martha); **overseas delegates** (Avila, Ximena; Waldenstrom, Markus; Wood, Olivia; Zac, Marcel).

Location: Salisbury Cathedral, England

Meeting Time: 0100 local time.

Departure from New York: 1400

Nahuel pushed up Aremi's sleeve to see the time.

"The plane is about to take off."

"Yes, but look. There is more in the folder," Isaline pointed out.

The three put their heads together to read the other documents they had taken from the Ficus. Behind the initial memo were a pile of similar documents.

Nahuel flipped to the second page. The following pages were annexes that provided more detailed information: flight information, a map of Salisbury, blueprints for the Cathedral, profiles of each member of the operation, among other things. Then a more detailed breakdown of the information was provided for each secondary committee which would be spread out among the European cities.

At the back, were photographs of the attacks. The last photograph was a horrific photo of five decapitated swans floating in water that was dyed ruby red with their blood.

"*The Foundations* can't be in all those places at the same time, can they?" Aremi asked. "Why have they attacked so many different places at the same time?"

"To divert and split up the Council agents, to confuse them," Nahuel explained.

"Very smart," Aremi said.

"Salisbury seems to be the the city where *The Foundations* really are, as the head committee of the Council is going there," Nahuel continued.

"Go back to the previous page please," Aremi requested.

On the page, there were two images. The first showed the face of a woman with white Ignoble hair and severe features. She looked intense. The second photograph was of a man's silhouette, but his face was hard to make out.

"Her name is Moira," Isaline said reading the captions on the photo. "And she has white hair and black clothes, the same as the Ignobles that attacked us in the first Hazna."

"Ignoble hair," Nahuel said.

"The name of the man is unknown, as well as what he looks like. They are the leaders of the Ignobles," Isaline added, pointing to the heading above the photographs.

"The murderers of my grandfather," Nahuel finished. He felt an electric pulse race through his veins.

"The Council of Privileges is going after them, Nahuel," Aremi said. "They won't let them get *The Foundations*."

After putting the box back inside the Ficus and cleaning the dirt around the pot, the friends left the office. They finally knew where *The Foundations* might be buried. There were several options, but the main one seemed to be Salisbury, where the prime mission took place. The Council had sent secondary missions where the Ignobles had attacked. They had also learned what one of the leaders of the Ignobles looked like, but no one, not even the Council, knew who the other leader was.

As Nahuel closed the door shut behind him, he thought he saw a branch of the Ficus move at a supernatural speed.

They raced through the corridors and passed through the rooms of the sub-4th floor without pausing.

Nahuel, taking the lead, stopped unexpectedly in front of the News Room.

Behind the glass wall that separated the office from the corridor, it could be seen that it was more crowded than usual. Dozens of agents of the Council were working at full speed. Nahuel imagined that with simultaneous attacks in different cities, the job of controlling the information and keeping the privileges hidden had become much harder.

The screens streamed news programs from around Europe in real time. Nahuel turned his head frenetically from screen to screen, showing the multiple attacks carried out by the Ignobles.

Nahuel walked towards the glass wall, he wasn't afraid of standing out, as the agents were too occupied trying to control the disaster in the media.

"Watch this," he said, pointing to one of the screens.

A breaking news story spread out and held still. Red letters announced the closure of all access to the main plaza of a city. A water pipe had burst, causing a domino effect in all water and gas lines throughout the city center.

"Is this one of their attacks?" Aremi asked.

"It would seem so," Isaline replied. After looking closely at the image, which showed an impressive church made of pink marble, she said: "This isn't the cathedral of Salisbury, but it is somewhere in Italy…Milan to be precise."

"They sent a group of agents there, a supporting committee." Aremi said.

"That's right," Nahuel said. "But look at this man. I'm sure I've seen him somewhere."

The frozen image from the Milanese news channel showed the cathedral surrounded by police and curious bystanders. A man with white Ignoble hair and black clothes could be seen in the midst of the chaos, as if exiting the scene.

"Who is he?" Aremi asked.

"I saw him in the photograph I found at Severino's house. The photograph that shows my grandfather, Klaus and Severino when they were young. This is the fourth man in the photograph," Nahuel explained.

"That's impossible," Isaline remarked. "That photograph must be more than thirty years old, and the man in Milan looks like he's in his forties."

"Maybe it's not him, but his son," Aremi suggested.

"That could be, he has a black scorpion on his shoulder, the same as the man in the photograph. The big difference is that this man has *Ignoble* white hair," Nahuel said, noting that it was no minor detail.

"So are you trying to tell us that the son of an agent for the Council of Privileges is an Ignoble?" Isaline asked, frowning.

"That's right," Nahuel replied.

The three friends stood there in silence, considering the implications of the idea.

It was not new that there were Ignobles in Milan, that is why the News Room agents were not surprised; there was a secondary mission heading over there.

But what called the kids attention was the scorpion man; if he was who he seemed to be, that would change everything.

"It's safe to say *The Foundations* are in Salisbury, right?" Aremi guessed.

"I wouldn't bet on it," Isaline replied, with a hint of suspense.

"What do you mean?" Aremi asked.

"I've always suspected that Wissing hid *The Foundations* in Milan," Isaline explained. "The image we found in the book in *Calendula* convinces me."

"The portrait of Wissing?" Aremi asked.

"Yes, it was a painting from 1489, done in Milan. It turns out that Wissing established a friendship with a famous Italian painter. This man, in addition to the artistic services he provided for the Sforza family, was also in charge of organizing all the aristocratic social life of the family. He orchestrated all the large parties held in the Castle and suggested who should be invited."

"Can you get to the point?" Nahuel asked, impatiently.

"Yes," Isaline agreed, even though she didn't like condensed versions of history. "Wissing was always on the guest list and always in attendance and, from what I can tell, he met the love of his life at one of these parties."

"What?! *Love?*!" Nahuel blurted out, unable to hide his sarcasm.

"Yes, Nahuel. In that day and age, love was everything. Wissing traveled to Milan every year, most likely to see her, but he always lied about the destination of his trips."

"You have read much more of Wissing's history than us," Aremi said. She was convinced of Isaline's theory.

"Yes, I read the books Severino lent us more closely than you two. Besides, it turns out the book I bought in *Calendula* about the *Il finale* in the Middle Ages tells the same story, with the names changed, of course."

"That may be," Nahuel said, not very convinced of the love story. "However, if this white-haired man, with a scorpion on his shoulder, is in Milan, it can't just be a coincidence."

His instincts told him this was another clue his grandfather had left behind for him. To have seen that man, or rather the man's father, in the photograph with his own grandfather and to see him now, in Milan, was something he couldn't ignore. As soon as he saw the man on the screen, he was overcome with a terrible thought: *What if this white-haired man is the other leader of the Ignobles?* He was surprised by how likely this possibility seemed.

"What does all this mean?" Aremi asked, hoping her friends weren't thinking what she herself was suspecting.

"It means the head committee of the Council is headed to the wrong place," Nahuel said.

"We must warn them," Isaline stated.

"They have done their own analyses and they think it's most probable *The Foundations* are in Salisbury," Nahuel said, but he thought they were in Milan and he would follow his gut.

"But...we must say something," Isaline insisted.

"They won't believe us, they won't change their plans because of us, and *The Foundations* will end up in the hands of the Ignobles," Nahuel spit back.

"Then what are you suggesting?" Isaline asked. She was standing in front of her friend and questioning him with a fixed and intimidating stare.

"I'm going to Milan," he replied, following his impulse.

Everything was connected...*The Foundations*, his grandfather, the scorpion man, the attack at the first Hazna...None of this was a coincidence, it couldn't be. The Ignobles had attacked his family, they had even looked for him...Maybe this was his chance to get *The Foundations* and finally get the answers he sought.

And *The Foundations*...*The Foundations* protected a great secret that would endanger all the privileges, in fact, all the world. He felt that maybe he could make a difference.

"Are you aware of what you are saying?"

"Totally," he replied. "I can't let them get *The Foundations*."

"We'll never get there on time," Aremi said.

"That would be true if Nahuel was really suggesting we go there, which we are not doing," Isaline said.

"This time I cannot ask you to join me." It wasn't the same entering Klaus' library without authorization than going to Milan and facing the Ignobles.

"When will you learn, Nahuel?" Isaline sighed.

"We are a team," Aremi said with a gleam in her eyes.

Nahuel hid the satisfaction he felt with those words, and said:

"The supporting mission of the Council in Milan will deal with the Ignobles and buy us time. To take any action, the Ignobles have to wait until the plaza of the city is cleared. With all those people around, they won't be able to investigate the tunnels until well after dark."

"And if they don't wait?" Isaline argued.

"In that case, let's hope the Ignobles don't find *The Foundations* until we get there."

CHAPTER 29

Aremi and Isaline saw so much determination and decisiveness in Nahuel's eyes that they didn't dare stop him. In fact, they decided to go with him.

"This will be dangerous," Isaline said.

It would only be a matter of hours before they realized how true those words really were.

They didn't have the slightest idea what they would do once they reached Milan. It was an immense and important city in Northern Italy. They might run into the Ignobles in any part of it and be ruthlessly attacked.

Nahuel knew the agents of the Council of Privileges were pursuing a fake clue. The Ignoble with the scorpion he had seen in the news footage from Milan had a connection with his grandfather and he had to find out what it was.

Nahuel knew he was just like his grandfather, and like him, he was prepared to do whatever it took to keep the Ignobles from obtaining *The Foundations*. He wanted to honor his grandfather's memory. He couldn't let him down. He also couldn't bring himself to tell anyone about what he knew. He wouldn't let them stop him. He felt that the trip to Milan would answer the questions he had about his own past, his legacy and the life and death of his grandfather. These questions never stopped haunting him.

Flight AA 757 with destination to the city of Milan is ready for boarding.

A female voice ringing out over the loudspeaker brought him out of his reverie. They were sitting on the floor at JFK and Nahuel just remembered how much he hated to fly.

They had snuck out of the residency shortly after returning from the sub-4th floor. They had each packed only the essentials in their backpacks, which they now wore. Luckily, Isaline had remembered at the last minute that they had to take the authorizations that allowed them to travel alone as minors.

Before leaving, they had made sure that Mrs. Penington was in the garden, growing the sweet potatoes for that night's dinner, before scrambling out the front door. Aremi had refused to leave the house unless they left Mrs. Penington a brief note, explaining only that she needn't worry about them.

"Ophelia is always so kind to us, we can't cause her a heart attack," had been her justification.

They had arrived at the airport just in time to take a flight that placed them only three hours behind the Council agents. Nahuel had changed his return ticket to Ushuaia for one to Milan. He would figure out how to explain it to his mother later, although she probably wouldn't care. *The Foundations* were out there, only a world away.

The plane took off smoothly and began digging into the air, as Nahuel felt that horrible sensation in his stomach and his ears.

"These turbines are not going to let me sleep," Aremi complained, when the motors kicked in.

"How can you think of sleeping?" Isaline asked, in disbelief.

"I need to. We went to bed really late last night."

As they flew toward their enemies, Nahuel realized they had crossed the point of no return.

Nahuel, Isaline and Aremi walked off the plane and stepped onto European soil. The sky was still dark and the airport lit up with artificial lights. Nahuel, Isaline and Aremi walked quickly by the luggage carousels. They needed a map that would show them which transportation would take them downtown. They were lucky Isaline had decided to join them. As usual she was prepared and had a travel guide with her.

As everyone slept, Isaline had got up to go to the bathroom. She walked by a seat, where she spied a travel guide on the lap of a man deeply asleep. She had doubted for a few seconds whether or not to take it, but in the end, she swiped it. She needed to buy time. She couldn't wait to get to the airport to buy her own guide. Before taking it, she had made sure the stewardess was distracted and had justified the theft in her own mind with the argument that her actions were for the greater good and more important than those of a single tourist.

"The only clue we have is the image we saw in the News Room," Nahuel said.

"Yes, the one which showed the Ignoble in front of the big cathedral," Aremi remembered.

"We should head there first," Nahuel proposed.

"This train will take us directly to the heart of the city," Isaline added, pointing at a sign hanging from the ceiling. "I have Euros, so we don't have to worry about that."

They hurried to catch the next train, leaving in five minutes. They arrived just in time to slide into the last car.

They were so close to the Ignobles. They had left New York, taken a plane, crossed the ocean and were now only a few kilometres from *The Foundations of the Pact.*

The moment had arrived.

Sitting in a seat at the very back of the train, Aremi became obsessed with tying knots in a shoelace she had taken out of her sneakers. She tied the knots until there was no more room for anymore and then began untying them to repeat the process. Every once in a while, she looked out into the night through the train's window and scratched her neck, her head, or her shoulders. Isaline, on the other hand, held perfectly still. Nahuel could see though that her hands were shaking and her right eye twitched with a nervous tic. He desperately wanted to seem calm, but his fear was easy to see. He wasn't succeeding at putting his friends at ease. He focused instead on trying to elaborate some plan with the help of the travel guide.

"Look mommy, look at the pretty necklaces," said a little girl, pointing at Aremi's a-bula. She couldn't have been more than four and was traveling with her mother. The two were, like them, foreigners.

"What strange fashion," the woman commented to herself as she turned back. She had been looking at the steel a-bula hanging around Nahuel's neck.

"And guess what? I have a bull's tail inside here," the boy laughed at his own comment. His nervousness made everything seem funnier than it really was.

"It's impossible!" Isaline shouted, out of control.

"No, it's not. I'll open it up and show you," Nahuel told her.

"It's not that!" she said desperately. "I left my a-bula in New York!"

No tragedy could be worse than this.

"I took it off to clean it and change the talesma. I got nervous when I heard Victoria walking down the hallway. I got up to close the door, so she wouldn't see us packing, and left my a-bula on the nightstand, and didn't put it back on," Isaline now remembered, almost crying. "My a-bula is my life. How could this have happened to me?"

"Don't worry," Aremi said.

"*Don't worry?*" Isaline asked, shaking. "I can't do anything without it. Without the ostrich feather I can't even make a pin move through the air."

"Remember what the professors said in our first classes," Aremi told her.

"They said that only people with their privilege *very developed* don't need talesmas. Do you think I'm one of them or something?" she asked while taking off her gloves with rage.

"Yes, but they also explained that sometimes when a person is in an emergency they don't need their talesma to activate the skill they need," Aremi added, trying to console her. "Don't worry, Isaline. I'm sure your skills are advanced enough to make objects levitate."

Isaline wished she could have the confidence and steadfastness Aremi had, just once.

Nahuel, Isaline and Aremi hid behind a blue and white patrol car.

The disastrous sight of Duomo Plaza, in the heart of Milan spread out before them. It was crowded with police and the red flashing lights from their cars. The tile floors around the grandiose Gothic cathedral, the Duomo, were cracked and tall streams of water spewed from beneath them. As they entered the mist created by the streaming water, Nahuel had the terrible feeling that he was crossing the threshold into the world his grandfather had protected him from.

As he got closer, he could see the area was roped off with police tape and that the statue that used to sit on the highest point of the church was now lying on the ground. The copper Madonnina had fallen off its pedestal. Through the mist, he saw that the other marble sculptures that decorated the front of the cathedral were still intact. They had survived the disaster.

"I bet you all the cops in Milan are here," Aremi noted.

Everywhere they looked they saw heads wearing the distinctive white cap of the Milanese police. During a weekday and at that late hour, locals and tourists were peacefully resting in their bedrooms.

The three friends crept forward, crouching low, until they reached the police tape surrounding the cathedral. In the distance between them and the entrance to the church, they saw a crack in the ground that tore across the plaza from one end to the other, like the stamp of an earthquake that had impacted only that area.

"What happened here?" Isaline wanted to know.

"It's a Schism," Aremi explained. "It's a topographic manipulation done by CymTers. It's being able to shake the earth and produce an earthquake, among other things. But the intensity of this one means it took many people to make it."

Nahuel wanted to sneak closer, to see inside the crack. He moved under the police barrier, but didn't get far.

"*Ragazzo!*" a deep voice yelled at him.

A policeman came from the other side of the patrol car and started asking in rapid fire Italian, "*¿Cosa fai qui? É molto tarde, dovrebbe essere nel letto a quest'ora.*"

"Excuse us, we were just passing by this way," Isaline offered their apologies, coming up beside Nahuel. Even though she couldn't understand a word the man said, she was convinced that it was important to be polite and remain calm. "We haven't done anything wrong. We are tourists," she added, flashing her most innocent smile.

"*Prego, prego. Andate via, a casa.* Home, go home" the policeman ordered, pointing toward the street leading away from the plaza.

It was not a suggestion. The man was ordering them to leave. Aremi joined them and the three headed for the side street.

"It doesn't matter that we have to leave. The Ignobles have already left the scene," Isaline spoke with certainty.

Organized chaos, Nahuel thought.

"Please tell me the Ignobles left empty handed," Aremi begged.

"I'm sure of it," Nahuel replied, convinced. "They made the earthquake to get the police attention. Look around. There is no sign of them anywhere and I was able to see that the crack wasn't even very deep. They haven't opened any tunnel here."

"Yes, it is possible that they wanted to buy time to look for them under other canals," Isaline agreed.

"But, where are the tunnels?" Aremi asked.

"All over the city the canals disappear into the ground. In 1900 they began building on top of them," Isaline explained.

"So many of the ancient travel routes are buried under streets and buildings?" Aremi estimated, seeming disappointed.

"Exactly."

"Where do you think we should start looking?" Nahuel asked.

"The Navigli area is shown in the guide as the only place that still has canals to this day. It's not far."

"Then, let's start there for now." Nahuel agreed.

In that moment, he had the feeling he would need something more than good luck to find *The Foundations*.

Two hundred meters before getting to the canals area, Nahuel could feel the metal, sweat and decay smell.

He felt the hair on the back of his neck stand on end.

For a split second he thought he was entering hell. The Navigli area, which had canals running through it and was surrounded by small picturesque bars, was totally destroyed. But the scene was dead, still and silent, like the calm of a battlefield after combat.

He felt a tingle down his spine. His shoes were wet and as they walked on, the water reached his knees. Traces of red blood ran by them, staining their clothes.

Aremi and Isaline trembled beside him. He was sure it was more from the shock of the violence around them, than from the wet water lapping at their feet.

The canals had disappeared and the water now flooded the streets. Signs and flower pots that had decorated the shops were ruined, broken, stained. The windows of the bars and taverns were broken and water beat against their doors. A typical restaurant boat, which had floated among the restaurants in the area, had been pushed onto the street and its roof torn violently off. Furniture and dishes lay shattered all around, as if they had been used as weapons in the fight.

It was hard to even walk around the site.

Dawn was approaching like a whisper on the horizon. The first light of day was beginning to shine. The lightening sky cleared away the frightening darkness surrounding them.

A smooth current of ice-cold water was headed toward them. Nahuel interpreted the flash of panic that crossed Isaline's face. He had just enough time to cover her mouth with his hand to stifle her scream that would have rung out through the silence. The stirred-up water turned black. The current carried with it a colony of drowned bats. A few feet away, the intestines spilled from a partially eaten cat.

Aremi crouched down. Nahuel watched as she placed two small fingers in the dirty water. They had left their vests in New York, so as not to attract attention. When she stood up, she had an insignia in her hand.

"The secondary committee has been here," she said.

It was true. The insignia she had picked up off the ground was the characteristic symbol of the Council of Privileges of the United Nations.

"Do you think they won the fight?" Aremi asked in a whisper.

"I don't know," Isaline sighed. "They might have been outnumbered. The Council's main mission went to England."

The three continued deeper into the Navigli area. With each step they took, it became clearer that the area had been attacked using privileges. The stones which lined the canals had been shattered to bits, causing the flooding. Only the Nicca stone which protected the tunnel was intact, untouched, perfect, unbreakable.

Nahuel still couldn't see them, but he could smell them.

The three of them turned right, leaving behind the alley they had been walking down, and took the street that would have run alongside the canal. The water was ice cold. Aremi gritted her teeth and trudged on. The ground was slippery because of the broken stones. They had to move slowly and very carefully.

And then Nahuel saw them.

For a second, he thought the laws of physics must have stopped working, then he remembered the privileges.

The dead man hung in the air.

He was about fifty years old. He was hanging upside down as if an invisible rope were tied around his feet. His skin had turned bluish gray. The look of the corpse was twisted and grotesque.

The whole scene made Nahuel sick to his stomach. A cold sweat broke out across his brow and he felt the coffee and snacks he had gulped down in the plane threaten to creep up his throat.

"Don't move," Nahuel ordered. "We're not alone."

A woman with white Ignoble hair was toying with the body. She wore black knee-high boots, a black skirt and a black jacket. When the woman turned around, Nahuel could see that the man had at least taken out her left eye before dying.

A gasp of shock escaped Aremi's lips.

A moment later, he realized something else that made him freeze in fear. The woman was not the only member of the Ignobles there. Two men joined her. It was clear that white hair and black clothes were the trademark of this group of criminals.

"Let's get closer to hear them," he suggested. "In absolute silence."

The three started moving toward the Ignobles. They walked slowly, crouching down, their arms getting wet, the water up to their waists. They moved behind the destroyed cars that had been parked on what had once been a street. They hid behind some trees that had fallen over the sidewalk.

The funk of the place was getting stronger. It smelled like old iron, the distinctive metallic smell of blood. It was pungent, a repulsive mix of sulphur and gutters.

The smell of death was everywhere.

"Clarissa, you haven't left a mark on his forearm," the tallest of the two men said. "Were you saving it for me to play with?"

"Get out of here," the woman replied, pushing him away. "I don't share my preys."

"Don't be like that kitty-cat."

"I know that idiot Serena usually gives you everything," she said.

Nahuel, Isaline and Aremi listened, hidden behind a green awning that had fallen down.

Behind them, a vegetarian restaurant sported decorations in the same bright green color.

"What do we do with the prisoners?" the second man, with a white moustached, interrupted their banter.

Nahuel looked around but couldn't see anyone else from the Council.

"Let the Supremes decide," the woman responded.

"Most likely they will join our ranks, whether they want to or not," the first man said.

"It's so exciting to watch them slowly lose all hope," the woman added with a maniacal gleam in her eyes.

"What did this old guy do?" the man with the moustache asked.

"He said I was rude," Clarissa replied with a look of disgust on her face.

The corpse swung like a pendulum over the heads of the Ignobles. The green vest with black edging hung off his side.

"He was paying you a compliment, kitty."

She turned her back on the man and it made Nahuel's stomach turn to see how she smiled in pleasure.

"I'm tired of waiting around here, in the background. The Supremes always leave us to deal with the garbage," the first man complained.

"Do either of you know how much longer we'll have to wait?" the moustached man asked.

"They just left for that Castle," Clarissa answered scowling. "I bet we have a long time still."

"I thought they knew exactly where to find whatever it is they're looking for," the first man stated.

"Careful. Don't let anyone else hear you talking that way. Loyalty comes first," the moustached man warned him.

"It's just really annoying to know that we won't get to see the towers on that old building come crumbling down," the first man stated.

If the ones they call the Supremes, the leaders, are in the Castle, then what the hell are we doing here? Nahuel thought desperately.

"We're wasting time here, let's go," he whispered.

"But...There are prisoners, we can't leave them behind," Aremi whispered back at him.

"They have already sacrificed their freedom to protect *The Foundations*. Let's make sure it's not in vain," Nahuel said firmly.

Isaline was the first one to stand up. She was planning on leaving the place the same way they had entered it. She pressed herself against the wall and scooted along, crouched down low. Her pants were covered in mud. She wasn't the only one.

"Watch out!" Nahuel blurted out. "The sign!"

But Isaline had already run into it.

Even hours later, Nahuel still couldn't understand exactly what had happened in that moment. One thing he would never forget was the expression on his friend's face.

Isaline, who had been just two feet away from him, suddenly flew into the air, backwards, as if she were being pulled skyward by her hair. She had fallen prey to something dreadful.

And then, she was out of sight.

"Look what I found," Clarissa teased.

"I hope you'll share this little toy with me," the first man said.

Nahuel had never known true fear until that moment.

"Let's not get carried away," the moustached man said.

"And you? What group do you belong to?" Clarissa asked Isaline.

"I don't understand… I am tourist," she murmured, playing up her French accent.

Nahuel and Aremi remained frozen behind the awning, holding their breath.

"What a nosy tourist," the first man said.

"Mmmm, I don't believe you," Clarissa spit out. "Let's see what you have…"

Nahuel poked his head up as carefully as he could. If they captured him too, they wouldn't have a chance to rescue Isaline. From behind the awning, he could see how the woman looked closely at Isaline's neck and hands. Her backpack was just a few feet away from him, on the ground. It had fallen suddenly when Isaline was pulled through the air.

"Nothing. No a-bulas, no marks," Clarissa said finally.

"Does anyone know what we are allowed to do with civilians?" the first man asked.

"No…But the Supremes will punish anyone that messes up this mission," the moustached man warned.

"God Damnit!" Clarissa blurted out. "We can't ruin everything for this little morsel."

"The best thing to do would be to put her in with the other prisoners," the moustached man suggested.

Nahuel and Aremi had no choice but to follow them along the edge of what had once been the canal toward their makeshift prison.

The two men shrunk the enormous tree trunk that blocked one of the exits, under the bridge. Clarissa pushed Isaline inside the jail they had made there. It was a cement bridge in the shape of an arch underneath.

The Ignobles had folded down the metal railings usually bordering the sidewalks, so they now turned the arch into a cage. They had sealed up both ends with thick tree trunks they had made grow to the exact size.

This cell was guarded by white haired men, who prevented any chance of escape.

"I've brought you a new prisoner, but this one is civilian."

Clarissa and the two men went back to where they had left the dead man hanging. Isaline was locked inside the bridge.

Nahuel and Aremi had managed to hide inside a narrow alley across from the bridge. It was a dark, tight path between two buildings. They hid behind a large garbage container that was floating in the flooded street. Nahuel grabbed onto it so that the current, although slow, wouldn't wash their cover away.

Nahuel saw Isaline through the bars. She had her back to him, and seemed to be talking to someone. He was a pale, thin man with dark circles under his eyes and his lips barely moved. Two more men stood up to get a closer look at Isaline.

Most of the prisoners were leaning against the walls of the bridge, many were injured and a woman lay on the ground, unconscious. There weren't many prisoners, and their a-bulas had been removed.

"What do we do now?" Nahuel asked in desperation.

"I don't know," Aremi replied, her face stiff with fear.

They looked at each other intensely, trying with all their might to think of a plan. Nahuel's face was partially hidden in the shadows from the building.

"We have to do something," he said in anguish.

"I know."

"But, *what?*"

His mind was running in high speed, analyzing all the options, trying to find a solution, a way out. His mind told him that there was no way to get Isaline without help. His heart told him that he would never forgive himself if they didn't try. And his instincts…his instincts told him that if they acted quickly, they still had a chance to achieve what they have been searching for.

"There's something I could try…" Aremi hesitated.

"Whatever it takes," Nahuel almost begged. When Aremi set her mind to something, she usually achieved it.

Nahuel watched as Aremi began concentrating. Every muscle in her body went tense and she didn't take her eyes off the tree trunk blocking the bridge. The veins in her forehead stood out and her face went red with effort. She was trying to shrink the tree trunk the same way the Ignobles had, before putting Isaline inside the jail.

Across the way, Isaline turned around and looked for her friends, through the bars. She found them, hiding there, sunk in the same pool of desperation she was.

She met Nahuel's gaze, resignation starting to show in her eyes. He looked back at her, beside himself. Guilt churned inside him. He hugged Isaline's backpack as if her life depended on it.

Then Isaline's attention turned to Aremi. Small and fragile, her arms extended outward, palms out, and covered with marks. Her a-bula glowed from the overload of energy. Neither Aremi nor her a-bula were prepared for the task. Instinctively, Isaline began to shake her head, as if to tell Aremi to stop. She knew the effort Aremi was making to help her escape would harm her.

Nahuel could also tell she was getting weak. Aremi rarely failed when she tried something with her privilege, but that tree trunk was too tall and too thick for a girl with only ten months of practice. It had taken two Ignobles to shrink it, it was without a doubt too much for her

Suddenly, Isaline opened her mouth, in a sign of terror. She went to the bars and gripped them, without taking her eyes off her friends. A piece of crumpled up paper flew from the bridge over toward her friends. Isaline couldn't believe it, but somehow, she had taken the map from her pocket and sent it over to her friends without using her a-bula.

The moment Nahuel jumped up to grab the map, Isaline shouted, "RUN," her voice unrecognizable with fear.

Nahuel turned. They had been discovered.

From one of the sides, the Ignobles were getting closer at full-speed. They sorted quickly through the garbage spread out on the water.

"You!" one of the men called out to the jail. "You brought your little friends here!"

Nahuel felt that the adrenaline rush was going to kill him. His body was crying out that he should run together with Aremi, but that meant leaving Isaline behind.

While he saw how the men were getting closer, he pushed Aremi so she would run, but the girl was standing still, horrified.

"You think we're stupid?! Now that we know you have privileges, just watch what we do!" one of the Ignobles screamed out threateningly.

"RUN!" Isaline shouted again.

The Ignobles were getting closer to catching them. They were just two trattorias away.

Nahuel grabbed Aremi's arm and forced her to move. They didn't have much time and he wouldn't be able to stand it if she ended up imprisoned too, and it was his fault.

Sometimes, circumstances present us with decisions which are impossible to make, he heard his grandfather's voice ringing in his head, almost too loudly.

"WE'LL COME BACK FOR YOU ISALINE," Nahuel promised.

"I know," Isaline said firmly to herself. Her strength was that she believed it wholeheartedly.

Nahuel and Aremi raced off, to put distance between themselves and the Navigli area. Out of the corner of his eye, Nahuel could see two white heads chasing them.

"What do you think they will do to Isaline?" Aremi asked, panting as they ran.

The question hung in the air like an arrow frozen in mid-flight.

A terrible scream of pain slashed through the silence of dawn.

CHAPTER 30

Nahuel and Aremi ran over long stretches of manicured grass. They were entering the Castle grounds through the rear gardens. They went under the Peace Arch located at the end of Sempione Park, looked up and saw the Castle drawing near through trees and greenery. They just had to run a bit more. It was the only way to escape the men chasing them.

At one point, Nahuel thought they had lost them for good. They had run aimlessly, not caring which way they went, just as long as it put distance between them and the Ignobles. As they raced through the main streets of western Milan, they had a chance to catch their breath. They took advantage of the pause to check the map, but it cost them the lead they had gained on their stalkers.

The ghost-like white hair Ignoble popped up from behind an orange trolley, full of people who were going about their morning business without a care in the world.

The last 30 yards before Sempione Park were critical. They had to sprint at full speed to gain an advantage on the Ignobles.

The sun was coming out, slowly warming the enormous garden surrounding the Sforza Castle. Delicate white flowers, sprinkled through the grass glowed eerily in the pale light of dawn.

"Don't stop, Aremi," Nahuel begged her. He couldn't lose her too. He couldn't even think that he had left Isaline behind.

Aremi had indeed stopped in her tracks. Her head hang down, her hands on her knees, her chest heaving, her heart beating so hard it was hurting.

Nahuel knew it wasn't only the running that was wearing her out, but also the heroic effort she had made trying to free Isaline. Her energies were almost completely depleted.

Nahuel stopped and quickly ran over to where Aremi was, trying to muster some energy.

"Come on. I know you can do it. Do you see that tree over there? We'll hide behind it," he said.

Aremi looked where Nahuel was pointing, a huge elm tree next to a statue of Napoleon III. Then she looked at Nahuel, imploringly. She was too exhausted to keep up this pace, even if it was just for a few more minutes.

But there was no time to lose. Nahuel had to take action, immediately. He could see the bloodshot eyes of the Ignobles, pushing him on. Fear fueled his legs and he shot forward, putting his arm around Aremi's waist and dragging her along with him.

The two men were gaining on them. Nahuel and Aremi sought refuge in the thickest part of the park's vegetation. They wove among the trees that towered over the path and crossed a small foot bridge over a pond. Nahuel glanced back and could see one of the Ignobles closing on them. He looked like an enormous bear, his entire being exhaling brutality and fierceness.

"Are they close, Nahuel?" Aremi asked, not wanting to waste any time even looking backwards.

"Not so much," he lied to her. "Just keep running!"

But then the ground started shaking underneath their feet. A red mound of dirt rose up in front of them like a small step. Aremi was caught off guard and fell roughly to the ground. Unable to break the fall with her hands, she scraped the right side of her face.

Nahuel tripped too, stumbled, but stayed on his feet. The Ignoble was almost on top of his friend.

He had to think of something and act quickly.

The other Ignoble was also drawing near; but luckily his gait was more like that of a sloth than a bear.

He would have to make this quick. He couldn't take them both together.

He looked to the side, for something that could help him. Nothing. A simple ant wasn't going to be very useful. The big one was about to grab Aremi by the ankle. She looked at him from the ground, unable to move.

Nahuel looked to the sky. At first, he saw nothing. Then some leaves on the trees moved and he could make something out. Black and yellow spots were flying up there. He sharpened his ears. A beehive was nearby. He concentrated and called out to them.

In a fraction of a second, dozens of bees flew directly at Aremi's attacker. They stung him everywhere. They flew into his ears, down his shirt, stung his arms and legs. The bees were influenced by Nahuel's anger and attacked with spite.

The man writhed on the ground. His head shook from side to side, he tried to protect himself with his arms. If anyone else had been in the park, they would have come running over immediately to find out what was causing all the screaming.

"Stop, Nahuel!" Aremi tried to scream, but she was short of breath.

But he gave them one last order and the Ignobles eyes swelled shut with toxins from the bee stings.

Then, he stopped the bees, repressing the urge he had to finish the man off, once and for all.

"What have you idiots done? You will pay for this!" the second Ignoble swore at them as he came over the footbridge in two long strides.

As the second man stepped over his partner, still writhing on the ground, they felt a sudden, strong breeze. The ducks that had been resting serenely on the pond were lifted into the air and readied for an attack against Nahuel and Aremi.

But Nahuel couldn't move. His mind was adrift between feelings of guilt and justice. If Aremi hadn't shouted at him, he might not have stopped and now there would be a dead body lying on the ground. He couldn't stop looking at each and every sting burning on the Ignoble's body.

"I had no choice," he said in a strange way, as if his voice was coming from far away. "I didn't mean to…"

"You reacted instinctively. He was going to catch me," Aremi replied. "Here they come!" she warned, jumping up.

The ducks came hurtling toward them, from the sky, at full speed.

Without thinking, Aremi threw herself on top of Nahuel, tackling him to the ground to avoid the dive-bombing ducks.

They hit the ground hard. Nahuel hurt his shoulder, crashing against a rock. Aremi's pants ripped open around her knees.

The birds failed their first attempt. But they came around again. Their beaks poked them furiously.

Aremi kept her cool, saw her opportunity and took it. As the Ignoble concentrated on attacking Nahuel with the ducks, she leaped into action.

The roots of a nearby cypress tree began spreading along the ground like slender serpents. They slipped around the Ignoble's ankles smoothly, until they were completely wrapped around his legs.

When he wanted to take a step forward, he discovered he couldn't move and fell on his face, his legs immobilized. He lost his control over the ducks and they calmly returned to the pond and their normal behaviour once his spell over them was broken.

Aremi took advantage of the man's confusion and quickly wrapped roots around his arms as well. The Ignoble was completely trapped, tied to the ground, looking skyward.

Nahuel and Aremi kept going toward the monumental building, which seemed to increase in size with every step they took toward it.

"We know they're in the Castle," he blurted out as soon as they got out of the park. "But *where?*"

"Let me see what Isaline sent us," Aremi stretched out her arm.

A terrible and unshakable feeling, which was haunting Nahuel's subconscious suddenly burst into his conscious mind. The image of his friend, in jail, and the blood-curdling scream they had heard was stalking him worse than any Ignoble ever could. If something happened to Isaline, the remorse would consume him, killing him from inside.

His friends were in Milan because he had decided to come. Even though he hadn't asked them to join him, he hadn't stopped them either. The trip was motivated by his need for answers about his family, and also, he must admit it, by a need for personal vengeance. And now his friends were putting themselves at risk for him, so he wouldn't be alone. It was all his fault.

He hated knowing that the fate of his friends would depend on the choices he had made.

They still hadn't found *The Foundations*, Isaline had been taken prisoner, and Aremi would suffer the same fate if he wasn't careful.

"It shows the layout of the inside of the Castle," Nahuel mumbled, handing the map to her.

They were just a few feet from the back entrance, hiding in the shadows of one of large stone walls. The Sforza Castle was an impressive structure built from red brick, bordered by towers and battlements, and protected by a moat all around.

"There's a spot marked on it," Aremi said.

"Let me see," Nahuel said, taking the paper and looking at it closely. Then he handed it back to Aremi. "I can't understand anything. Everything is underlined and labeled, typical Isaline," as soon as he said it, he felt sadness pierce him.

"I know, but she must have done it for a good reason," Aremi said. Her hair was a mess, her face scratched, her clothes were filthy and torn, but her smile was still radiant.

"She always draws notes on all her maps," Nahuel added.

"I'm sure this is a clue. When the Ignobles said the Supremes were going to the Castle, Isaline must have made some connection, because she started marking this map."

"A connection with what?" Nahuel wanted to know. "She was the only one who knew the story of Wissing's life inside and out."

"That's right," Aremi agreed. "Isaline was obsessed with the love story between Wissing and Bianca...That's it!" Aremi jumped with joy.

"What?!" Nahuel asked, getting more desperate. He couldn't follow Aremi's train of thought.

"Bianca, Wissing's lover, lived in the Castle," Aremi said as if that would be enough to explain everything to him. She saw though that Nahuel was still lost, and added, "Isaline must have thought that Wissing hid *The Foundations* under the Castle, under the home of his beloved."

"Yeah, I can see how Isaline would think that, but..."

"Think about it, Nahuel. Wissing traveled constantly to Milan to see her. I don't think it's strange that he would have hidden his most valuable object where the most important person in his life lived."

"Hmmm…" Nahuel responded, trying to imagine it.

He was thinking about what Aremi had said, and was sure Isaline would have said the same thing. He had to acknowledge that at the moment, it was the best option they had, and also the only option they had.

"Look here," Aremi said, pointing to the map and reading some notes scribbled in Isaline's handwriting, "*Her chambers.*"

Nahuel was quiet, thinking deeply.

"Isaline told us that centuries ago, canals ran through the entire city of Milan. It's not unlikely that a tunnel ran under the Castle. Isaline must be trying to tell us that *The Foundations* are under Bianca's chambers."

"Ok then, let's get moving," Nahuel agreed.

He owed at least that much to Isaline, to follow her clues without doubting her. She had been right the last time, the Ignobles were definitely pursuing *The Foundations* in Milan.

The two friends rushed past the wall toward the inner courtyards of the Castle. The iron gate was open. They went inside, leaving behind the expansive gardens and deep moat surrounding the fortress.

The covered walkways around the back courtyard were desolate. No one was watching them from above either. Nahuel thought of the guards, centuries before, who would have been walking on the Castle walls, ready to sacrifice their lives in defense of the Castle.

"Come with me."

Aremi grabbed Nahuel's hand and led him through the courtyard. They moved past orange and yellow flower beds that bordered a large, crystal clear reflecting pool. Aremi, using the map to find her way, led him under some pointed arches which preceded the entrance.

This door was open as well.

The inside of Sforza Castle was filled with shadows and looked more like a museum than a living space. Dim rays of the first light of morning peaked through the windows. The room was like an obstacle course due to the collection of medieval armor on display. Each set of armor, stored safely in its own glass case.

They walked stealthily, trying not to make a sound.

Nahuel sharpened his senses. Nothing moved, all was quiet as a tomb.

Aremi pointed at the door behind Nahuel and they both went through it. Massive columns held up a dome shaped ceiling. Nahuel studied it for several seconds. A painting of green vines entwined with gold ribbon covered the entire ceiling.

The echo of their footsteps boomed across the room.

"Careful," Nahuel whispered.

Aremi stopped in her tracks and hid with Nahuel behind one of the columns. They looked at each other in alarm. With extreme caution, Aremi peaked around the column.

"There's no one there, Nahuel. It's just the shadow of a statue," she smiled.

She was right. It was only an impeccable sculpture in white marble of a man standing, staring into space, with chiseled features. Nahuel felt a little embarrassed, he had been scared by a shadow. In his urgency to protect Aremi, he was even keeping her safe from inanimate objects.

The next room they went through had no furniture, but the ceiling was remarkable. It was completely covered with relief paintings of animals and mythological beasts.

"It should be here," Aremi announced as they left the room.

They had finally arrived to the room Isaline had marked on the map as *her chambers*.

The room was smaller than the others, cold like an abbey and smelled like old incense. A cold, dry wind blew in through the keyhole. There were tiles on the walls and mirrors with golden frames. The tiles featured medieval coats of arms, displaying the distinctive animals and flowers of each family.

"There's no way to go underground," Nahuel said, glancing sideways.

"There must be."

"Why are you so sure?"

"Because it's about time we had some good luck," she replied.

Nahuel smiled. Aremi was like that. She always managed to catch him off guard with her comebacks.

They didn't know where to start looking, but they suspected there must be some secret passage hidden in the room. Nahuel regretted now that he had never paid much attention to mystery movies. They might have taught him something about where to find hidden doors and secret tunnels.

Aremi studied the walls. He took care of the floor. There wasn't much in the room besides the coats of arms. And Isaline was missing. She was the one who paid the most attention in Cultural History class and who would have been able to tell them the family history of each crest.

"Are you making your escape up the chimney, like Santa?" she teased him, trying to ease the mood. "I hope you're not thinking of leaving me here alone."

Nahuel was on the other side of the room. Only his legs were visible. The rest of his body was inside the fireplace. Aremi had her back turned to him, but could see his reflection in a pretty mirror hanging on the wall.

"I couldn't even do it if I wanted to. The chimney has been sealed."

"Well, that is a relief," she replied with a smile.

Nahuel rummaged around inside Isaline's backpack. He found what he was looking for. She had packed her small and fail proof flashlight.

"The coat of arms," Nahuel announced a few moments later. He was still crouched down, shining the flashlight in the fireplace.

"Which one?" Aremi asked, scanning the variety of crests on the tiles placed around the walls.

"Wissing's coat of arms. It's here."

"Let me see…. Excuse me. Move over," Aremi said, squeezing into the chimney space.

Nahuel and Aremi were leaning forward, staring at the rear of the fireplace.

"This is Nicca stone. It matches the description in the book, *Basic Geology*." Aremi stated, touching the wall inside the fireplace.

It was a smooth stone, like marble, but much cooler to the touch. It was bluish gray like ice and when you hit it, it echoed.

"This must be the place," Nahuel declared.

He started pushing on the wall with all his strength. It didn't budge. He tried hitting it with the back of the flashlight, and then he started pushing it again with his hands.

"You're going to break your hands, Nahuel. Remember that Nicca stone is indestructible."

Nahuel stopped and turned away from his friend, so she couldn't see his face. He felt incredibly embarrassed. Of course he knew Nicca stone was indestructible, so why had he forgotten the moment he was face to face with it?

"Any ideas on how to open this?" Nahuel asked her.

"Hmmm... Let me take a look at the crest. There's something strange about it," Aremi said.

She crouched around Nahuel, moving herself into the place he had been standing.

A small oval was stuck to one corner of the stone. The symbol for the Wissing family was an Alpine violet.

"Something about the petals," Aremi murmured to herself. "They're backwards!"

"Maybe they can be turned around," Nahuel hopped.

Aremi placed her index finger on the indentation on the crest that formed a flower petal. One by one she began turning them. The petals moved easily until they were in the correct position.

When the flower was in its original shape, they both held their breath.

Slowly and silently, the block of stone moved to one side, revealing the inside of the mystery.

Nahuel swore to never doubt Isaline's powers of deduction ever again.

Beyond the stone it was like a small cave, as if the chimney were a portal to another world.

A staircase led down into darkness. Nahuel crept forward and tripped down the first step. He gripped the railing and started slowly making his way down, scared the steps would crumble beneath him if he stepped too hard.

The staircase that led down to the underground tunnel was not carved into stone, but rather fashioned out of wood. This had been Wissing and Bianca's personal staircase.

There could be no life down there. The entrance to the tunnel had been hermetically sealed. Oxygen rushed in with Nahuel and Aremi.

Nahuel went first. He couldn't see anything. He held the flashlight up and a small burst of light tried to pierce the darkness. With each step he took, he felt more confident that they were finally on the right track.

Suddenly, he stumbled. He had hit a step rotten with age and slipped, but he managed to keep his balance. The fall would have been more than just painful. The staircase stretched down into the darkness, and they still couldn't see the end of it.

"There must be mysteries down here no one has ever even imagined," Aremi commented in awe.

Nahuel said nothing. He wanted only to find and solve one of those mysteries.

Once they reached the end of the staircase and entered the tunnel, Nahuel felt like he was breaking into history. The tunnel was an ancient secret, but perfectly functional.

"Which way should we go?" Aremi asked.

"You choose."

"To the right," she replied, randomly choosing.

The tunnel was silent. The thick walls of Nicca stone blocked out any signs of the world outside. Nahuel could only hear his and Aremi's rapid breathing.

He began moving through the tunnel with false confidence, trying to assuage any fear Aremi might be feeling.

"Are you afraid?" he asked her.

"No."

Nahuel smiled at her.

"Well, maybe a little," Aremi admitted.

They were both well aware of the danger of being trapped down there.

"How will we recognize *The Foundations?*" Aremi asked, trying to get her mind to think of something else.

No one could say for certain what was buried down there. It could be a scroll, a book, a parchment, a carving, or anything.

"I don't know. But if he hid them here, we will find them."

The place had been shrouded in secret for centuries.

With each step he took, Nahuel came closer to stopping the Ignobles. He wanted to ruin their plans, save *The Foundations* and hopefully then understand why they had killed his grandfather. He could hear the whispers of his ancestors asking him to defend the honor of his family.

The tunnel was like a long sarcophagus of Nicca stone. The walls, floor, and ceiling were all composed of the bluish gray stone.

They hadn't walked long when the halo of light shone on the end of the tunnel.

"This wall isn't Nicca stone, as every old canal is made of," Aremi noted, touching the wall. "It looks like marble, so they must have placed it after its construction."

"They must have wanted to keep people out of this part of the tunnel," Nahuel guessed.

"That's a good sign," she agreed.

He agreed. That part of the tunnel had been sealed off on purpose... *The Foundations must be somewhere near.*

Nahuel shone the light on the ground next to the wall. His vision, sharp as the one of a predator, allowed him to see a shadow at the end of the wall.

They approached.

"Is that a trunk?" Aremi asked him.

"Two trunks."

The trunks were identical, made from wood and forged iron. They chose the first one closest to them.

"See, it was our turn for good luck, Nahuel! It's open!"

Aremi searched inside the trunk and Nahuel crossed his fingers, his nervousness pinching his heart.

"Love letters," she said after a while. "I'll take Isaline one as a keepsake. She'll love it."

Nahuel agreed.

"Try the other one," he asked. "You're the lucky one."

Aremi crouched over the second trunk, grabbed the lid and pulled.

The trunk didn't open.

Aremi pulled with all her might.

"It's shut tight," she said.

"We need a key," Nahuel guessed.

"But there's no lock," Aremi told him.

A stew of frustration and fear brewed in his stomach. They hadn't come this far to leave empty-handed. If they couldn't open it, he would carry the trunk all the way. But, before...

"Open up! God damn you!" he said, hitting the trunk with his fist.

The sound of the punch echoed through the cavern, but that wasn't what made them jump.

The wood of the trunk had seemed to turn red for a split second.

"What was that?" Aremi asked.

Nahuel didn't answer, but he was smiling on the inside.

This time he placed his hands on the wooden lid of the trunk. As he tried to pull it open, he felt a tickling sensation.

He didn't even have to force it. The wood turned blood red and the lid came easily off.

And there it was.

There was only one thing inside the chest. Hundreds of pages, compiled into a single book explaining *The Foundations of the Original Pact*. The pages were hand sewn into the book by a single custodian, who had been unable to delegate even this task to another person.

"Is that really it?" Aremi asked with a thin voice.

"It is."

"We found *The Foundations of the Pact*…Incredible," Aremi said, awestruck.

Nahuel took a moment. He began to realize they held an enormous responsibility in their hands. Now that they had *The Foundations* in their hands, they had to take care of the book, protect it, ensure the Ignobles couldn't take it from them.

"Let's get out of here," Nahuel urged. "You take this with you, directly to the airport. I will stay here to free Isaline."

"You know you'll need my help with that."

"We'll argue about that later," Nahuel said firmly.

They stood up and began retracing their steps toward the tiny staircase that led up to what had once been Bianca's bedroom.

A loud boom resounded from somewhere, from everywhere, and the cavern shook a few seconds and then all was quiet.

Nahuel dragged Aremi behind the wooden staircase and turned off the flashlight. This time he hadn't imagined it. The danger was real.

They were quiet and waited.

Another loud noise echoed through the tunnel.

The second explosion was closer. They heard deep, male voices.

"We have to hurry," Nahuel whispered.

Suddenly, an unexpected presence appeared at the other end of the tunnel. Nahuel grabbed Aremi by the shoulder and pushed her up the stairs, so she would go up first.

They climbed up as quickly as they could. They couldn't see anything. Nahuel kept the flashlight off, in the hopes those below wouldn't see them. The decrepit state of the stairs meant they had to move carefully.

Once they climbed out of the fireplace, back in Bianca's room, Aremi quickly turned the petals on the Alpine violet, to seal the entrance to the tunnel.

"Were they Ignobles? Did they see us?" she asked, her voice shaking.

"I saw white hair. But I don't think they noticed us," Nahuel replied. "There must be other ways into the tunnel, and they've had to blow up the marble wall that separated *The Foundations* from the rest of the tunnels."

"We got there right before them, by chance," Aremi said.

They had no time to catch their breath. They began running away again, this time from the inside of the Castle to the outside. Nahuel knew that they had to benefit from that time advantage. Soon, the Ignobles would realize that they had arrived earlier. They left through a side door, trying to take the shortest route out of the place.

They ran through the archeological displays in the Castle. Nahuel crashed against the bust of a pharaoh in the Egyptian section, but didn't stop to see if it had broken or not when it fell. He hadn't even had time to put *The Foundations* in his backpack, so he clutched them to his chest as they ran.

They were past the prehistoric section and the portrait gallery. The main courtyard was the last hurdle. It was the only thing separating them from the city outside the Castle.

Nahuel grabbed the door handle, turned it and pushed it open.

Fresh air slapped him in the face and he had to blink to get his eyes used to the bright early morning daylight. The main courtyard was impressive.

But it wasn't empty. Someone was already there, waiting for them.

CHAPTER 31

Nahuel's chest tightened. The air seemed to rush out of the Castle.

There was a woman. He recognized her instantly. It was Moira and she was scrutinizing him with her fixed and piercing gaze.

She was not alone.

By her side stood the other leader of the Ignobles, the other Supreme. He was the mystery man the Council of Privileges was seeking. The son of the man in the photograph with his grandfather. Nahuel could see the black scorpion on his shoulder.

Around them, a pack of wild African dogs crouched, a peculiar breed of wolf and hyena.

High up, on the ramparts, the entourage of Ignobles rose around them threateningly, their white matching hair gleaming in contrast with their jet black attire. They seemed eager for events to begin unfolding.

In one sweeping glance, Nahuel took them all in, and then focused his gaze on the enemy standing in front of him.

"I didn't expect to see you here, Nahuel," the leader of the Ignobles said. "My name is Marco, and I'm very pleased to meet you."

"How do you know my name?" Nahuel asked.

"Your family and mine have been close since long before you were born," the Supreme one replied, a deeper shadow crossing his already dark expression.

"Don't insult my family," Nahuel shot back.

But Nahuel was just learning how little he actually knew about his own family. He wanted to reject everything that man might say to him, but there was a good chance that what he was revealing was the truth.

"You don't know my family. If you did, you would like us. We've always been so perfect and loyal," the man replied repugnantly.

"So how come you ended up like this?" Nahuel replied, looking the man over from head to toe, his white hair and black clothes.

Nahuel couldn't help but notice how the Ignoble's muscles contracted like one solid block. Automatically, the hair on the dogs' backs stood on end, revealing their perfect synchronization with their master. Aremi trembled by Nahuel's side, a sudden shiver running through her entire body.

"And what would you do if I told you that everything you think you know about yourself is a lie?" The Ignoble challenged him, regaining control of his temper. "You have been lied to your entire life, Nahuel. And when you learn the truth, even you will begin to doubt."

Nahuel shuddered. *What is he talking about?* Everything the man said could be true. He wanted to ask him more, but at the same time was scared about what he might find out.

"I see," Moira jumped in, a lock of black hair stood out between her white hair. "You only know part of the story, little foolish boy. They only tell the version that makes us look bad. Our cause is just"

"Killing innocents and forcing others to do things they don't want, doesn't sound just to me at all," Nahuel replied fiercely.

"*Innocents?*" the woman said. "That is what that Council of old decrepits wants you to believe."

Nahuel could tell Moira was a much more irritable and frightening character than the man. She was a woman who shouldn't be crossed, but Nahuel couldn't avoid arguing with her.

"No one makes me believe anything," he challenged.

"Everything we do is so that in the future the simple humans, the weak, can have a fuller life - a life complete with privileges," he explained in his deep voice. "Power depends on privileges, Nahuel," he went on in a condescending way.

"And I suppose you would decide who would get privileges and who wouldn't," Nahuel ventured.

"Everything will be different now that we have *The Foundations*," Moira's eyes sparkled brightly for an instant.

"Not if I can help it," Nahuel blurted out in a heroic rapture.

At that exact moment, a flock of pigeons took flight. They crossed the sky from the park, flying over the Castle, over Nahuel, Aremi and the Ignobles.

The minions on the ramparts were taken by surprise. One of them believed it was an attack. Without thinking, he took an arrow from the quiver on his shoulder, aimed it at his target and without the help of any bow, launched the arrow across the courtyard, straight at Nahuel's forehead.

He had been distracted by the flock of birds and hadn't even noticed the arrow coming at him from the ramparts.

When he saw it, it was already too late. Even though the arrow that would take his life was only inches from him, he refused to believe this was the end. He couldn't accept the irony of surpassing numerous challenges and finally obtaining *The Foundations* only to be killed by a miserable arrow.

But then it stopped, just in time, just before spearing him. A trickle of blood ran between his eyes. The arrow had just broken the skin.

Moira had stopped it at the last second.

"Who did this?!" Moira screamed.

Nahuel couldn't move, the arrow hung suspended between his eyebrows.

"Who?!" she screamed again, her anger growing. "I need him alive!"

The arrow moved backwards a few inches, and Nahuel found he could breathe again. *Why do they need me alive?* Then the arrow moved through the air until it landed in Moira's hand. She turned her furious and vindictive gaze on her disciples waiting on the ramparts.

"Bring down the guilty one," the Supreme one ordered.

He had turned his back to Nahuel and Aremi, and they could see the impressive scar tearing across his skull. Even with his back turned, he continued watching them, his wild dogs perceiving every single movement they made.

Nahuel saw a man appear at the base of one of the towers. He remembered him. He was the Ignoble from the forest, who had wounded Sleipnir during the first Hazna. His white hair was shaved on the sides, framing a pointed mohawk.

He walked forward, full of himself, with slow steps, swinging his arms in an exaggerated way. When he stood before his leaders, he grinned defiantly, ignoring what he knew was coming next.

"We need the boy," Moira spit out, signaling with her hand for her lover to take charge.

Almost all of the wild dogs who had been guarding Nahuel and Aremi turned on the Ignoble with the arrows. Only the Alpha kept his senses focused on the two friends. The other dogs moved slowly toward their prey, dragging their paws along the ground, licking their chops in anticipation.

The moment they had the man cornered, his face took on a demented expression, his mouth twisted in terror, the grin completely disappearing. His shoulders hunched forward and he exhaled in defeat.

Nahuel expected the man to apologize to the Supremes. The dogs continued closing in on the man, sniffing him hungrily. Yet the Ignoble remained silent. Nahuel couldn't understand how he could stay there, saying nothing, not apologizing, not begging for his life, nothing.

"Jeremy...Jeremy..." Moira repeated disapprovingly, clicking her tongue like in disappointment.

The man looked at her, his pupils fully dilated.

"I will not tolerate insubordination," she boasted.

Nahuel started to think that the man must have been waiting for this moment to speak. What he didn't know was that in the Ignobles there was no place for disobedience and even less for forgiveness.

The wild dogs bared their sharp fangs. Sticky drops of saliva dripped to the ground. The beasts could already taste the morsel they were about to enjoy.

Nahuel then became witness to the most horrifying thing he had ever seen in his life.

The Alpha gave the order and the dogs attacked. In one unexpected leap, their quick, agile bodies pounced on their prey, ecstatic to release their killer instinct. They immobilized him with their claws and sunk their rancorous teeth into the Ignoble's body. The piercing fangs ripped into the man's defenseless skin.

Nahuel had to close his eyes and then open them again, such was his disbelief. He mutely watched as blood spilled from Jeremy's body and the dogs lapped up the puddle forming on the stone floor.

A scream of pain was stuck in the victim's throat. He couldn't release it. No sound at all could come from his mouth. Moira, using one of her favorite tricks, had sealed his trachea so he wouldn't disturb the quietness of the Castle.

Horror burst through Nahuel's guts.

The dogs frenetically worked their jaws. They ripped the body apart, randomly, chaotically. They tore off chunks of fresh flesh and swallowed without chewing. They looked like possessed demons, their snouts dripping with blood.

Nahuel turned toward Aremi. His friend was standing by his side, her eyes fixed on the cruel and traumatic scene. For the first time ever, he saw her cry. It was heartbreaking. She was disillusioned, let down by life, by humans, by this atrocity. She had never believed some humans could be innately evil.

Tears streamed down her face, but she didn't take her eyes off the victim's remains.

Unseen by anyone, Nahuel took Aremi's face in his hands and gently turned her towards him.

"Don't be afraid. I won't let anything happen to you," he told her.

The wild dogs devoured their victim just as any predator would with their prey. They fought over the food as if they were still on the African Savannah. They were just as determined to annihilate the man as a mother lion was to defend her cubs.

"Just like you, they never leave scraps," Moira teased her lover.

The dogs lapped up the last traces of the Ignoble.

"I think it is clear that we don't want anyone to attack the boy," the Supreme one stated.

"But we could have fun with the girl," Moira smiled.

A wave of desperation came over Nahuel. He knew exactly what these people thought was *fun*.

"Leave her alone," he shouted.

"Forget about her and come with us," Moira shot back. She looked at him provocatively, sizing up his confidence and strength.

Adrenaline pumped through his body. There was no way he would leave Aremi.

"I won't hold back," Nahuel spit.

"Ha! You have already held back, silly boy."

Moira walked away from her lover a few steps, moving toward Nahuel and Aremi. It was a tactic she used to intimidate. The only sound was her long black overcoat dragging along the ground.

"If you touch her, I'll kill you," Nahuel threatened, his mouth dry.

His heartbeat was racing to the point of incessant pounding in his chest. He was afraid, but he sensed it would be best to hide his fear. If he could act like he was on the same level as his attackers, he might be able to negotiate.

Aremi didn't even dare to breathe, hoping to stay alive by remaining absolutely still.

"Your soul isn't dark enough to do it," Moira stated.

"There's only one way to find out," Nahuel challenged her, betting high.

"Ha ha ha!" Moira laughed, enjoying the game. "What's the darkest thing you've ever done?"

The awful image of the Ignoble on the ground, injured by his bee attack just hours before, blurred his vision. But surely that action, which tormented him, wouldn't even be considered 'dark' in this bloodthirsty woman's playbook.

"I won't let you hurt her," Nahuel said, resuming his initial concern.

"And tell me... How will you defend her?"

"I'll worry about that," Nahuel muttered, losing conviction.

If need be, he would use *The Foundations* to stop them. Involuntarily, he hugged the book tighter to his chest.

The Supreme one's eyes flashed darkly, like black oil.

"Give it to me," the man ordered, breaking the silence he had kept while Moira toyed with Nahuel.

"No," he refused.

"You have no choice. Look around you, boy. You are surrounded," the man observed.

"I can take them with me. I've made it this far," Nahuel pointed out.

"An arrogant idea," Marco scoffed. "You remind me of someone..."

Nahuel could read between the lines. That *someone* the Ignoble was referring to was his grandfather. His stomach filled with knots, as he imagined how his grandfather must have died at the hands of this group of maniacs.

"You have to give up in the face of the inevitable," the Supreme one added.

"Give us *The Foundations*. Now!" Moira fumed, beginning to get bored.

"Let Aremi go," Nahuel demanded.

There wasn't a single animal nearby that could help him, and even if there was, he knew he was surrounded and outnumbered. He wished he was stronger, older, a hero.

"Oh, you, miserable child," Moira said. "I will decide what we will do with your little friend. It makes no sense to keep arguing about it." The woman's eyes revealed her impatience.

Nahuel couldn't hear anything except his heart pounding like a hammer.

"You could join us," the Supreme one suggested. "That way we can discover the secrets inside *The Foundations* together. And if you join us, you will get to know the truth about your family."

"I…No, I don't trust you," he replied.

Moira shot him a look of pure cruelty.

"Little brat," she snorted.

"To join our elite group is an honor some have given their lives for," Marco boasted.

"I'll consider myself warned. I'll stay well away from you."

"Luckily, everything can change," the man said with a presumptuous smile.

"Now give me *The Foundation*s" Moira demanded.

The arrow she held in her hand lifted into the air and flew toward them at the speed of a bullet, sticking in the ground next to Aremi's foot.

A scorching heat travelled all over Nahuel's body, and the primitive power all over his bones, and, his blood, raised in response.

"I can't take the book from him. What is going on?!"

Nahuel saw that Moira's fine chiseled face was disfigured with rage. Her wild eyes were glued to the book he held in his arms and the effort she was making to tear it away from him was palpable. Nahuel had no idea why her privilege wasn't working.

His time was running out. He made an effort to concentrate, his mind racing. *A quiet spirit masters its instincts. Remember*, his grandfather's voice sounded loud and clear in his mind, *you aren't the horse, you are the king. Analyze the situation, don't let your instincts govern you.* He had to save energy for when the right moment came.

Moira was stiff with rage and she sputtered in anger, "Do something, Marco. You have already made me wait too long."

"Yes," he agreed, trying to humor his lover. He turned toward the teens and said, "The time has come Nahuel. Hand me *The Foundations of the Pact.*"

Nahuel tried not to show that he was looking at the ramparts, at the dozens of Ignobles watching him closely, following every word of the conversation.

"There's no way out," Marco said again, stating the obvious. "Think about your friend."

Aremi came out of her shock, moved closer to Nahuel and whispered, "Don't hand them over. They won't let me go either way."

Nahuel felt fear running thickly through his veins. He tried to push the horrific image of Aremi in the same state as Jeremy, from his mind. He was filled with terror when he realized how much Aremi's death would hurt him, to the point that he felt his head would explode.

Suddenly the silence of the Castle seemed thunderous to him. It wouldn't let him think, wouldn't let him find a way out of there. He couldn't come up with a plan which didn't end with Aremi disappearing, *The Foundations of the Pact* falling into the hands of the Ignobles and Isaline imprisoned forever. The remorse that Nahuel felt was haunting him.

His plan, or rather lack of a plan, had been to get *The Foundations* out of there and get away from the Ignobles once and for all. He just had no idea how to do that.

There was no real choice to make.

He would save Aremi.

"As you wish," the Supreme one announced, disturbing the false peace. "We'll do it the hard way. Your friend will suffer the agony of a slow and painful death."

"Wait! I'll give it to you!"

Nahuel held out his arm, gesturing that he would sacrifice the book. The Supreme one stepped away from the pack of dogs and toward the two friends, to take *The Foundations*.

"A round of applause!" roared Moira, as she clapped her hands. "The boy has made the right decision. Now, we'll keep your friend as our little prisoner."

"No!" Nahuel exclaimed, having never agreed to that. He snatched the book back to his chest. The only deal he would make would be to hand over the book if Aremi could escape unharmed.

Moving quickly and spontaneously, Nahuel stepped in front of Aremi, shielding her with his body. If they wanted to get to her, they would have to go through him and *The Foundations* first.

"I'm getting tired of this," Marco declared.

The dogs moved forward, next to their leaders. They dodged Moira carefully, not even daring to brush against her overcoat. When the Alpha came alongside The Supreme one, he rubbed his head against his master's leg.

They were getting closer.

Nahuel's ears were ringing. His vision was blurring, the dogs' faces were getting fuzzy, like red blotches on a developing photograph. He felt that power pressing in against his chest, while something else pushed outward.

It was all his grief, his loss. My grandfather, Isaline, *The Foundations*, and now Aremi.

At his side, Aremi was so scared her heart was beating a thousand miles an hour.

The animals stalked them confidently, like the greatest hunters in the world. They moved as one, keeping the practice of hunting in a pack to take down larger prey. Close up, the dogs were even more intimidating - the mixture of wolf and hyena.

Even though he was holding still, Nahuel felt like the Castle's patio was spinning like a whirlpool.

The wild dogs let out a bloodcurdling howl, like the sharp call of a hundred birds. Nahuel grabbed Aremi's cold hand, stiff with fear and slipped his fingers around hers.

A current of desperation slid through Nahuel's veins like hot lava.

The dogs flattened their round ears and bared their stained and soiled teeth. They raised their white tails like curved swords. They were an army of ferocious beasts, ready to do damage. It was a petrifying portrait, suffocating him.

Nahuel felt himself slipping into a boggy state of consciousness. He thought he must be floating in the steam of soft mud. He was on the edge of consciousness, about to fall into an abyss that threatened to devour him.

The end was near, too near. Aremi would disappear beneath a frenzy of snouts and fangs. And he wouldn't have the stomach or the heart to watch it.

Above the buzzing in his ears, which was getting louder, he could hear the minions, laughing and shaking with excitement.

Nahuel and the Alpha dog came face to face. They looked one another in the eyes with such sinister intensity that Nahuel's pulse raced dangerously.

Suddenly, he felt a flash of heat envelope his body. The ground shook beneath him, or at least he imagined it. His instincts were sharpening, his ears began sensing even the slightest noise. Even though he held still, he could tell he was faster, lighter, more flexible and more agile.

He could sense various smells and substances all around and distinguish each with perfect clarity. He smelled the dry blood on the predators' fur, mixing with their own grease and moisture. But what he smelled most deeply was Aremi's perfume, jasmine and vanilla, a familiar smell he loved.

Nahuel felt he was losing control over his body.

No matter how hard he tried, he couldn't control the spasmodic movements of his body.

And then they did it. The ferocious dogs lunged at them in a savage and acrobatic leap.

He felt vomit in his throat. His heart beat so strongly he could hear the blood pumping in his ears. Nahuel felt his instinct for survival take control of him. He squeezed Aremi's hand tightly and closed his eyes. The storm of emotions swirling in his blood unleashed his power. He felt like a kept animal just let off their chain.

He was immersed in a deadly battle between animal instinct and reason. The danger surrounding him drained away his humanity and channeled it toward the animal.

And without any warning, his consciousness left his body.

The powerful claws of the beasts scratched the ground but didn't harm her. Aremi's smooth skin was untouched. The dogs were still, unmoving. They were caught in the stupor of a new trance. They raised their ears, eager for their new orders.

In the blink of an eye, they turned around, prepared to lash out against their former masters. The about face was completely unexpected.

"Take *The Foundations* and run."

Aremi looked at her friend in amazement, but didn't need to hear his request twice. She grabbed the book firmly and ran through the door behind her, the same one which would take her back inside the Castle

Nahuel now had control of the wild dogs.

Flight or fight. Reason would have him running away alongside Aremi, but his animal instinct demanded he stay and fight. Any logical reasoning had vanished. Nahuel had let himself to be completely overcome by his instincts.

The ten indomitable hearts of the wild dogs now beat to only one command: *attack*, to defend themselves and buy Aremi more time.

All fear was completely gone and in its place the calm of instinct.

Through the superior animal vision, Nahuel could see the concern and fear of the Ignobles.

"Stop them, Marco!" Moira urged him.

"They are no longer mine," the Supreme one responded bitterly.

And Nahuel attacked.

With teeth bared, they threw themselves into battle. The wild dogs ran toward the clash with those who had once been their masters.

The fastest in the pack was struck down by an arrow from the ramparts. The howl of pain tore through Nahuel, more than his ears hurt by the wound. The arrow struck dead center in the animal's back and he fell heavily to the ground, waiting for death curled up in a ball.

Moira broke the neck of the first dog that tried to bite her. The dog had jumped at her throat, straight for the kill. But it didn't even manage to touch her. Its head turned around 360 degrees in the air and Moira took one step back as the dog's body fell at her feet.

The Ignobles in the ramparts attacked with what they could. One of them broke open the ground and a strong root surged forth from the depths of the earth. It managed to wind around the hind legs of one dog and drag it down into the crack.

"Don't hurt the boy," Marco shouted.

The sounds of the fight echoed in Nahuel's head, the howls of the dogs and cries of the Ignobles.

The Supreme one was able to reverse the trance on only one of the dogs, the most rebellious of the pack. He forced this one to fight to the death with any of his brothers who tried to attack him.

"What are you waiting for!?" Moira raged violently. "Get the girl! Go after

The Foundations!"

An Ignoble jumped down from the ramparts, eager to carry out the order so he would be praised later by his leaders. He broke his fall using his CymMens privilege and if Nahuel hadn't known better he would have thought the man was flying. One of the dogs grabbed the man as soon as he touched the ground. The animal bit him ferociously, ripping open his pants, revealing a bloody leg. Nahuel got the feeling the man was used to feeling pain.

Nahuel's hands started to burn, as if he had placed them face down on a hot grill. The circular marks were working their way up his forearms. It looked like a fresh tattoo and hurt as if needles were truly piercing his skin.

He would withstand any torture if it meant giving Aremi enough time to get away from this nightmare.

The order Nahuel had given the dogs had simply been, *hurt.* However, he hadn't been able to repress the savage temptation to cross that line with the Supremes. For them, the command *wound until dead* would be better. A world without them would be a better world. But the animals sent forth with that order set out on a suicide mission. Not one survived against Moira and Marco.

Only five dogs remained.

Nahuel could sense them before he could see them. Repulsive rodents had joined the Ignobles. They were filthy and fierce rats who spread quickly like a black shadow, casting darkness.

They went straight after one of the dogs. Through the animal's eyes, Nahuel could see the thick skin and long, hairless tails. They surrounded the dog mercilessly and bit at his sinewy legs, tearing at muscle, ripping off skin.

The air was filled with shrieks and howls. The rats took comfort in pain.

But the wild dog wouldn't go down without a fight. His sharp fangs tore them off his fur and threw them to the ground.

The dead rats were piling up, but the wild dog had begun drooling and foaming at the mouth, already sick with the illnesses the rats carried.

Nahuel was exhausted and dripping with sweat. His a-bula vibrated against his chest. He felt his body weakening, his energies dissipating.

"Look at you," Marco taunted him. "The effort is too much for you. Just give up."

But Nahuel couldn't. Aremi was escaping with *The Foundations* and the effort he was making was the only thing that would get her out of the city alive.

He started to feel ill, dizzy, nauseous. He couldn't falter. His cheeks were as white as the Ignobles' hair. His knees shook uncontrollably. He wanted to stay strong, but his spirit weakened with every blow the dogs received. Every second rushing at him was getting harder to withstand.

And now there were only three dogs left. Moira had just pitilessly decapitated the last female.

Nahuel was still alive only because they refused to kill him. He didn't know how much longer he could tempt fate.

His energy was being drained at an accelerated rate. He had crossed a threshold. But Aremi was worth it. He kept fighting, he couldn't stop now, he would never forgive himself.

But his spirit and his will abandoned him.

His a-bula shook violently. He knew it hadn't been made to handle so much energy.

Nahuel's heart contracted and his chest seemed to cave in. The inevitable ending overtook him. He knew the consequences of the effort he was making, of the unchecked flow of energy, Ankona had warned him. He was about to lose consciousness and possibly his life. The world would dim and he would most likely die.

Nahuel's a-bula couldn't keep up with him. But he wouldn't stop even if it meant racing towards his end.

And then, in a blast that was as unexpected as it was loud, his a-bula exploded into a thousand tiny pieces.

"They're over here!" Nahuel heard a female voice shout from the battlements.

"We have to leave," Marco pressured what was left of his crew. "Today is not the day we finish them. That will have to wait."

Nahuel couldn't see anymore, his vision clouded over by a gray haze.

"No!!! Not yet!" Moira whined, her voice drifting away. *"The Foundations!"*

"I'll get them for you soon," Marco told her.

Nahuel was losing his control over the dogs. The link with them was quickly fading. His feet didn't move and his arms were unresponsive. Unable to hold himself up any longer, he fell to his knees on the hard stone floor. He barely felt the smaller stones grinding into his pants. His hands felt like they were on fire, like he was being burned alive.

"Hurry up everyone. If you get caught no one will come and rescue you," he heard a voice shout.

The mental space taken up by the external consciousnesses was freed. Nahuel's mind was released from the animal murmurings. He felt only their warm bodies lying by his side. The dogs had not been allowed to rule over their own will like this in a very long time.

"Grab the boy!" Moira shouted.

"If we take him, he will die. He's no use to us dead. He needs urgent help and we don't have anything to give him energy with," a voice replied.

Nahuel heard a confusing shuffle of feet. It was hard to make out where they were coming from or where they were going. Some seemed to move away while others raced toward him.

"Remember, everything changes. Stay alert. We will meet again," a voice promised him before leaving.

Nahuel tried to focus, but the only thing he could see were blurry shapes and blinding lights. He could make out some men hovering over him.

"He's almost dead…"

"Someone help him! Quick!"

"The Health specialists are on their way…"

He wanted to say something, to speak to those unknown voices, but his mouth refused to make any sound. His muscles burned, and the feeling ran through his body and his skin. He had lost all control of his extremities. Tears of exhaustion and pain slid down his face.

The world was growing dim.

"The Ignobles have escaped and entered the Castle."

"If they make it to the tunnels, we've lost them."

"They have a head start."

"God damn it! We were late."

He heard voices, but it was all absurd. Life turned off for moments. Nahuel remembered his friends; he closed his eyes tightly, trying to isolate himself from the outside world. In great pain and in great guilt, he lost consciousness.

CHAPTER 32

"There he is!"

"Where?"

"On the ground, in the middle of those dogs."

"Nahuel!"

"Someone, please help him!"

"A Health specialist over here, please!"

The voices spreading through the air that cool morning were on the verge of hysteria. They rang out clearly above the din of the chaos engulfing the Castle.

As he floated in nothingness, Nahuel wanted to call out to them, but he was completely paralyzed. The crushing weight of fatigue and guilt kept him on the edge of the world. He thought of the betrayal of the human body, which threatened to give up when his spirit was still fighting to stay in the world.

"Come on, Nahuel!"

He felt them, shaking him, but no matter how hard he tried, he couldn't regain consciousness. Darkness was a refuge. It let him hold onto the unreal - he wasn't sure what he would find if he opened his eyes. He tasted the bittersweet conflict of wanting to know, and not wanting to know how things had turned out.

"Move. Hurry."

Through the white fog sucking him away, Nahuel heard new voices and more movement around him.

They sat him up.

"I hope it's not too late."

"This has to bring him back."

He felt an injection in his neck, straight into the jugular. They were giving him a serum of buffalo blood enhanced with charges of caloric energy. The cocktail had a more immediate effect on the nervous system than a shot of adrenaline straight to the heart.

Nahuel instantly felt like his brain was being wrung like a mop. The potent serum hit him like a shot to the head. He blinked. His eyes burned from the same headache he had felt since taking control of the dogs. How much time had passed? He opened his eyes, barely, letting in a slit of light. He was still alive, by some twist of fate.

He slowly became aware of what was happening around him.

Everyone was staring at him, unblinking, as if they didn't want to miss even one second of his reaction.

"He's back."

Even though the drug left him a bit confused, he could make out the different faces watching him. They were dirty, wounded, bruised, scratched, but he could still recognize his friends. An immense and comforting sense of calm wrapped around him like a blanket. They were alive.

He closed his eyes. Exhaustion washed over him. He felt he was slipping once more into the nothingness of unconsciousness, and then someone was grabbing him by the shirt and shaking him.

"Open your eyes, Nahuel. Don't make me nervous," a girl's voice insisted.

This was no time to rest. Isaline was back and in full force.

"The book is safe," Aremi said.

Nahuel tried to ignore the weight pressing down on his brain.

"Where?" he managed to mutter.

"Safe," she repeated.

Nahuel tried to speak more, but sounded like a wounded animal and he realized what her answer meant: *he wouldn't have access to The Foundations*. But he didn't care about that anymore, his friends were safe and sound, and that was all that mattered.

"That's enough of a reunion. We have to get him to the chamber as soon as possible," the medics ordered.

Nahuel could barely remain conscious. Over the next twenty minutes they helped him get up... he tripped…he fell to the ground...he took a few steps...he managed to climb stairs, trembling and weak. The hammer pounding in his head wouldn't stop and his muscles were clumsy and lethargic…

The PG-808 plane had been specially created for the Council of Privileges. Its V-shaped design was inspired by the flight of birds. It was always equipped with everything the CymTers, CymMens, and CymAnis might need on an emergency mission. The plane was the mobile headquarters for the missions carried out from the sub-4th floor.

The plane flew undetected, camouflaged by white clouds. The CymMens made sure a white, ethereal coating of thin clouds hung perpetually around the plane. They flew through the air, blending into the sky no matter where they went.

The interior of the plane was paneled in maple and faux ivory leather. Aremi and Isaline were assigned two seats up front. Nahuel was taken directly to the energy chamber.

It was a clear, wide, comfortable tube, like a capsule. The privileged one placed inside had enough room to lie down or sit up as they chose. A clear glass wall separated the place where the person was placed to receive energy from the compartment below, where the sources of energy were generated.

In the CymAnis chamber, the compartment beneath Nahuel's capsule was packed full of hares. They slept peacefully thanks to a serum they were being given and suffered no pain, claustrophobia or discomfort.

Two men placed Nahuel in the capsule. A Health specialist came over to ensure he was face up and his arms and legs were completely extended and then put a temporary a-bula around his neck. After a few seconds, he felt a mist surround him and move through his body. He stopped shivering. The mist made him stronger, his muscles grew firmer and his mind cleared. He felt he was truly resting. If it were possible, he would ask for one of these capsules to sleep in every night.

The mist with flashes of silver inside the capsule was actually energy. It was transported from the hares to Nahuel in the exact dosage to prevent any harm coming to the animals while allowing the CymAnis to soak in it.

As soon as Nahuel was allowed out of the energy chamber, he joined Aremi to tell Isaline everything that had happened after they escaped from Clarisa and the Ignobles in the Navigli area. They made sure to include every single detail, at Isaline's request.

"You shouldn't be able to communicate with mammals yet," Isaline said as soon as Aremi mentioned the way Nahuel had taken control of the wild dogs.

"I know," he agreed. "I don't know how to explain it."

"I thought I was going to die," Aremi confessed. "And at that very moment, they turned away, forgetting all about me."

"But, how did you manage to turn those beasts against the leader of the Ignoble?" Isaline wanted to know.

"It was amazing," Aremi admitted.

Nahuel had no idea how he had done it. Instinct had overtaken him. He hadn't thought about it or planned it and he was convinced that if he tried to replicate it now he wouldn't be able to.

Reliving the moment meant trying to navigate blindly in a swamp. What had happened and how it had happened was all mixed up. All he could remember was the commotion in his mind.

"That was incredibly risky," Isaline said. "You know that if the connection with the dogs had consumed anymore of your energy, even a tiny bit, you would have died."

"I know," he replied, reaching for his a-bula. He felt naked without it. "But it was worth it."

Aremi reached into her backpack and pulled out the love letter they had taken from Bianca's trunk. Isaline for once was at a loss for words. She took it in her hands delicately. Now she finally had a treasure too.

"Have you read it?"

"Well, no. We were kind of in a hurry," Aremi smiled. "Now, can you tell us what happened when we lost sight of you?"

Isaline took a deep breath and began her story. They had punished her with the branches of the tree sealing up the bridge. Each lashing felt like her soul was shuddering. She only had to take one blow, because another prisoner placed himself between her and the branch, to protect her. He had done it purely out of solidarity, asking nothing in return and offering everything he had.

"The Ignobles like to punish, it doesn't matter to them who is receiving it."

Isaline fought back the tears. There were trails of dried blood on her right shoulder, where the branch had struck.

Nahuel's face was disfigured with regret, but he tried to console himself thinking that the outcome could have been much worse.

Isaline told them how the agonizing scene of watching another suffer in her place had luckily been cut short. An elite team from the Council of Privileges arrived to free them and dole out some justice. With military precision, they neutralized the Ignobles and reclaimed the area.

Isaline told them she saw at least a dozen men in green vests with black edging appear. In a matter of minutes, they had dismantled the makeshift prison and shrunk the trees that kept them trapped inside. Five men overtook Clarissa and two more Ignobles who were in a pharmacy enjoying the goods.

The group that had arrived from England had split into two groups. One group of agents recovered the area of the canals and the other, led by Klaus, hurried toward the Castle.

Finally, Aremi told her friends how, instead of running away with *The Foundations*, as Nahuel had asked her to do, she had hidden in the armory. She had waited inside the Castle, curled up beneath the armor of Sir John Pelling, a.k.a Immortal Knight, until she had heard the Ignobles run away, looking for the tunnels.

It wasn't until she had heard Klaus's voice that she dared to come out of her hiding place and handed him *The Foundations*. She wouldn't have handed them to anyone else but the Director.

Nahuel knew he couldn't be mad at her for doing it. She had done the right thing, but when Aremi gave Klaus *The Foundations*, she took away from Nahuel the chance to read them. Now he would never know why the Ignobles had killed his grandfather.

Having fulfilled her duty to keep *The Foundations* safe, Aremi had run straight back toward Nahuel. To her delight and surprise, she ran into Isaline first, in the main courtyard. She was following the NAGAS agents who had rescued her. Isaline had refused to stay back with the wounded, needing desperately to reunite with her friends.

They found Nahuel together, on the ground, curled up among the wild dogs. Isaline was convinced the dogs had attacked him and it wasn't until Aremi told her otherwise that she relented.

They spent the rest of the flight in the PG-808 in a state of semi consciousness. Every nerve in their body hurt and their brains seemed to press against their skulls. Nahuel sunk down in his seat and surrendered to sleep, worn out, for what seemed like an eternity.

Mrs. Sparling walked by them, straight to the back of the plane. In the rear was a private meeting room where top secret information was discussed. Only the Director and the top agents of the Council were allowed in that evening.

"Have a seat, Mrs. Sparling," Klaus said, offering his seat and finding another chair for himself.

"I suppose some positions on the *Intelligence and Information Committee* will open up after this," Mrs. Sparling said, grimacing.

"There may be some changes," Klaus admitted. "I have to say that this time we came too close to failing in an irreversible way."

"Now that we have them in our possession for the first time ever, we may be able to prevent what some considered inevitable," Sebastian suggested. He was sporting a new beard which was very unlike him.

"How on earth did the entire compilation of *The Foundations* fall into the hands of teenagers?" Mrs. Sparling asked. "We had checkpoints at airports, bridges, train stations. This is unheard of."

"Perhaps someone extremely knowledgeable on the subject helped them," Sebastian offered his opinion. "The discovery these students have made is, frankly, hard to believe."

"That sounds like an accusation," Mrs. Sparling replied.

"What is certain is that anyone is capable of greatness," Klaus stated. "It's not something you are necessarily born with."

"But there's no question that the boy has inherited it," Ankona added, speaking up for the first time. "Knowing his family history…"

"What will happen when he finds out the truth about himself? What he is, who he really is?" Sebastian asked. "I'm afraid he's still not aware of how important he truly is."

"How much longer must we wait before telling him?" Ankona pressed them. "After what happened this morning, it will become increasingly more difficult to hide it from him."

"Nothing good can come from telling him the truth about his identity," Klaus assured them. "We can't burden him with that responsibility. He's too young."

"But we know the Ignobles are after him. They have already discovered who he is," Sebastian added.

"I agree with Kendrick. We should tell him the truth, so he can be prepared," Ankona stated from the corner of the room, where he stood. "What's more, there's always a price to pay for keeping secrets."

Ankona's words hung in the air. Everyone present knew he was right. Nevertheless, no one was prepared to make a final decision that night.

They were silent. Klaus stood and walked around the walnut table separating him from *The Foundations of the Pact*, so newly recovered after hundreds of years in hiding. He placed one hand on the book, but before he could say anything Sebastian asked, "Is it everything we suspected, Director?"

"It truly is," he replied tiredly. "These rules were established hundreds of years ago and there is nothing we can do to change them."

"In that case, there is no choice. The boy will have to make a decision," Ankona stated firmly.

"And the whole world will depend on that decision," Klaus added.

They arrived hours later. The sun was rising. The sky was awash in pink and the feel of New York enveloped them, a gust of fresh air waking them up.

Five boats were waiting for them. They were specially adapted to use sea algae as fuel. They were tied up at the dock just yards away from where the Council plane had landed. There was one landing strip and a single hangar next to a wide, placid river they had to cross to reach the tunnels. Nahuel wondered if they were near Ardemir and if this was a no-fly zone.

As soon as Nahuel got off the plane, Ankona led him to one of the boats. Once aboard the boat, Klaus gestured for Nahuel to sit in the seat opposite him. The boat was made from a light wood and the seats were covered with fluffy cushions.

"Miss Pierwiet and Miss Fleury will also join us," Klaus declared.

Nahuel fidgeted, trying to get comfortable while Ankona went back for his friends. The Director stroked his beard.

Aremi sat down next to Nahuel and pushed him over to make room for Isaline who got in behind her.

Up close he could see that Aremi's freckles were hiding under a green salve that had been spread on her face to help her scratched cheek heal.

Ankona sat down on Klaus's right.

The Director leaned forward and lowering his voice said, "There are some aspects about what happened in Italy that no one completely understands. And there are other things that no one else can know about."

The boat started moving.

"What you have unearthed these last few days is known as *Secpactum* and it is an official secret. It is so confidential that most of us do not possess the proper security clearance to even know it exists. Now that the three of you know about it, we are faced with a dilemma."

"Are you talking about *The Foundations*, Director?" Isaline asked.

"That is exactly what I am talking about. Only a handful of us know what they are capable of doing."

"And we want it to stay that way," Ankona emphasized.

"I won't tell anyone," Nahuel blurted out. "And I think I can speak for Aremi and Isaline too."

They both nodded in agreement next to him.

"Very well, then I think that matter is taken care of," Klaus said. "The next thing I want to discuss is how reckless and dangerous your actions were. I still can't understand what would have caused you to intervene like that, by yourselves, on such a delicate issue."

The girls didn't say a word. They both knew they didn't have the right to speak for Nahuel or reveal the very intimate reason that had led them to know about *The Foundations*.

And Nahuel wasn't prepared to reveal it either. He knew he had a right to know what was happening, to know why the Ignobles had killed his grandfather. At the same time though, he could tell that today would not be a day of further revelations. If they hadn't explained it to him by this point, he doubted they would tell him right now.

And, above all, they had tried to prevent the Ignobles from getting *The Foundations*. The three of them had been the only ones to believe that the main mission of the Council was heading the wrong way and that *The Foundations*, in fact, were hidden in Milan.

"On the other hand," Klaus went on, "we now have *The Foundations* in our possession."

"That's a relief," Aremi interjected.

"Not quite," Klaus replied. "*The Foundations* were safer in their hiding place when no one was looking."

Nahuel stared at him, incredulously.

"What do you mean?"

"If you ask me, I think it would have been better for *The Foundations of the Pact* to stay buried forever. Of course, if someone is going to have possession of them, it is better that it be us," Klaus explained.

Isaline could well imagine the frustration Robert Wissing must have felt, never having been recognized for his accomplishments. Despite their disobedience, they had risked everything to protect *The Foundations* and they had done it successfully.

"Director, who are the Ignobles?" Aremi asked.

"I think you already know that. If you are wondering how they came to be, that is a different question and I can answer it for you," Klaus replied.

It's about time, Nahuel thought, hungry for explanations.

"Their story goes back to the original creation of The *Foundations*, the very day it was agreed to take privileges away from humanity. The creators of the *Pact* seemed to be in agreement that it was the only way to save humanity.

"But their agreement didn't last long. It wasn't long before the CymMens wanted to go back to the way it had been before, when they held power and governed all. So, there was a fracture within the custodians of the privileged society from the very beginning."

The three remained quiet, hoping Klaus would tell them more.

"As the years passed, a sub group formed, living on the margin, growing more and more resentful and it wasn't until the Middle Ages, with the arrival of a certain individual, that they created a sort of political party. Their main goal was to obtain power and rule the privileged society with the intention of returning the privileges to everyone."

"Is that why Wissing hid *The Foundations*?" Isaline asked eagerly.

"Exactly," Klaus responded, staring at the water.

"And then what happened?" Nahuel wanted to know.

"Recently, in the 1970's, the group splintered, led by Moira's father. A violent faction appeared and began waging armed combat against the Council of Privileges. It was around that time that we started referring to them as Ignobles," Klaus said.

"Not noble enough to have privileges," Ankona stated, a hint of ferocity in his voice. He had been completely silent until that moment.

Nahuel tried to understand the strange mixture of passion and detachment the tracker put on display.

"Moira inherited a violent bunch and she's taken it to the extreme," Klaus went on. "Her strategy has been different. She is convinced it would be better to find *The Foundations of the Pact* first and then use them to take power, not the other way around."

The boat reached the other side of the river. Klaus stood up and said, "I trust you will be discreet."

Nahuel nodded yes and the movement sent pain stabbing through his entire skull.

"I was sure they wouldn't expel us from the Educational Program. We have proved to be valuable agents," Isaline told them on the way back to the residency. She had stopped referring to them as students and started using the word agents. "But perhaps it's true that we should work harder to develop our ability to follow orders."

The boats had taken them to Ardemir and from there they had used the tunnels to return to the city. Aside from Isaline's initial comment, the rest of the trip passed by in a quiet way that now felt strange. They sat in silence, reliving mentally everything that had happened in Milan, listing how many moments they had overcome and survived.

It was at that moment that Nahuel realized just how much they had grown and changed during recent months. He thought he had seen everything. He was sure that the time spent living and studying with the Council was the only time in his life he had truly felt like himself. He now understood clearly that unexplainable things had always been and would always be part of his life. The best thing of all was that he had found other people to share them with.

Nahuel went up to his room. Emre's suitcase was by the door. Classes were finished for the year.

He stood in the doorframe. Something was out of place. He knew it as soon as he sniffed the room.

On his bed was the postcard of the lighthouse his grandfather had sent him, the one he kept at the top of his closet. He picked it up. Underneath his grandfather's message, some new words were scribbled:

Your life and the lives of two others are intertwined.
When destiny finds you, the entire world will be changed forever.
We are waiting for you.

Next to the postcard lay a wine-colored leather-bound book.
It was a diary.
He flipped through the pages, feeling adrenaline pump through his veins. He fixed his gaze on a random entry:
We rescued a mockingbird with a broken wing together and I recognized that the privilege instinct starts to appear even before logic and reason.

Nahuel immediately knew who had written it and who the diary belonged to. That moment was one of the rare, crystal clear memories he had of *his father.*

The last entry was dated Christmas day, five years after his disappearance.

ABOUT THE AUTHOR

A.V. Davina is the pseudonym under which Adelina Cortese and Valentina Branca write. They are longtime friends and co-authors of The Three Privileges. The first book in the series The Three Privileges.

For news about the saga please visit:
thethreeprivileges.com

Lightning Source UK Ltd.
Milton Keynes UK
UKHW011301221222
414331UK00001B/42